A VOICE IN THE

WILDERNESS

By

Gwen Lester-Cunningham

ACKNOWLEDGEMENTS

First and foremost, I acknowledge and thank the Lord my God for giving me *A Voice in the Wilderness*. This is my praise piece to you.

I want to give the utmost thanks and appreciation to my children, Tia McGraw and Oscar "Triple Blak" Lester who have always been my biggest cheerleaders and toughest critics. You guys never stopped believing in your mom and I love you for it. Also, my dear husband Larry Cunningham, a strong black man who has stood by me, loved and supported me through all my madness.

And a special thanks to my niece Raquel Johnson who strengthened my faith in ways she may never know. And my dear friend Mabel Burton who was a sounding board and helper when I needed it most.

Thank you all, for making my dream come true.

Published by Tordon Publications

Copyright © 2016

This book is dedicated in loving memory to

Broque Toriano Lester

1992 - 2013

CHAPTER 1

No one saw the angels hovering over him as he pulled his number twenty-nine State Street bus into the bustling CTA terminal at Ninety-Fifth Street and the Dan Ryan Expressway.

"Dan Ryan, end of the line," announced the driver, thirty-year-old Charlie "CJ" Johnson as he pulled the bus up to its designated stop. He turned the switch and the doors flew open. Frantic passengers began pushing and shoving as if there were a prize for being first off the bus.

When CJ stepped off the bus, the humidity smacked him in the face like a wet mop. He removed his shades, revealing light brown eyes highlighted with flecks of gold. Though not movie star handsome, CJ had a rugged appeal that women found attractive. He stood about six feet tall with broad shoulders, a trim, athletic build and a chiseled face that gave him the appearance of being far more serious than he really was.

CJ wiped the sweat from his face with his forearm and stuck his sunglasses in his shirt pocket. He then pulled out a pack of cigarettes, lit one and took a long deep pull. "Ahhh," he sighed, glad the work week was over. After five years of driving the bus, CJ was fed-up to his eyeballs. He had learned to tolerate the broken down buses and inconsiderate passengers, but lately, due to the growing violence on the CTA he had begun to fear for his life. He took another drag off his cigarette and turned at the sound of a familiar voice.

"That's a filthy habit, you know."

"Teddy!" CJ shouted, throwing his cigarette down and rushing toward his friend Teddy Montgomery. A couple of inches taller and a few shades lighter than CJ, Teddy still looked like the high school basketball star he had once been. They greeting each other with the special handshake they'd learned at summer camp some twenty years ago. "When did you get in?" CJ asked.

"This morning," Teddy replied, flashing an infectious grin. "Come on, let's get out of here."

"Let me get my stuff," CJ replied as he jumped onto the bus and grabbed his bag. After turning in his keys and daily report, he and Teddy started toward the employee parking lot. "So how was L.A.?"

"Hey," Teddy replied, throwing his arms out to the side. "What can I say? Beautiful weather, beautiful women. Hey, it was beautiful. However, this sudden change of environment does leave a brother a bit parched," he said in an aristocratic tone, adding a fake cough.

"Perhaps we should drop by Mac Daddy's and partake of a few brewskies," CJ suggested.

"Why that's a splendid idea," Teddy said as if it hadn't already occurred to him. They had to laugh at their own foolishness.

"I just gotta stop by the crib and change my clothes first," CJ said.

"For what? Women love a man in uniform."

2

"Who do you think I am, Ralph Cramden or somebody? I wish I could take this monkey suit off forever. You know some kid shot a driver on the Madison bus the other night because he wouldn't let him ride with a senior citizen's bus pass."

"That's why I quit," Teddy said.

"Nigga, you quit because your daddy died and left you a nice chunk of change," CJ said, looking around for Teddy's old beater. "I'd quit too, if . . ." Realizing that Teddy wasn't beside him, CJ turned to see him standing next to a brand new Cadillac Escalade. Grinning like a Cheshire cat, Teddy clicked the remote on his key fob. The Caddy's headlights flashed and the locks clicked open.

"Get out of town!" CJ shouted in disbelief. "This you?"

"Just a lil' sum'n, sum'n I picked up," Teddy said with mock humility.

CJ ran to the SUV, letting his hands glide along the slick exterior. "Aw, man."

Teddy opened the driver's side door. "You getting in or what?" CJ jumped into the shotgun seat as Teddy slid in behind the wheel.

CJ sank into the soft leather upholstery. "This is slick," he said, sliding his hands reverently over the sophisticated control panel.

"You like?"

"Like?" If this ride was a woman I'd marry her."

"In that case, I'm scared to show you the house he left us."

Nice, huh?"

"Man . . . I'm talking about four bedrooms, a pool and dig this; each bedroom has its own bathroom."

"Stop lying."

"I swear to God. You know one of them rooms got your name on it," Teddy said, then added in a teasing tone, "That is if your mommy will let you come out to visit."

"My mama don't tell me what to do," CJ snapped. "I'm a grown man."

"Whatever," Teddy said with a smirk. He knew he'd hit a sore spot by mentioning CJ's overprotective mother. "So when are you coming out?"

"So, you're serious about moving out there."

"Ain't nothing holding me here. Ain't got no job. Ain't got no woman. Dusty tried to get me to stay when I was out there, but I had to get back and pick up this baby," he said patting the dashboard.

"Hey, man. I'm really happy for you," CJ said, hoping he sounded sincere. He and Teddy had been best friends since the third grade and it had never occurred to him that one day they'd be going their separate ways.

As they cruised down the expressway singing along with Smokey Robinson and the Miracles, Teddy lit a joint and passed it to CJ who took several quick hits. When Teddy tried to hit Smokey's high note, CJ nearly choked to death laughing. Teddy gave him the finger and continued to sing. Their mutual love of classic R&B music (or "dusties" as they called them) was only one of the things that cemented their lifelong friendship.

By the time they reached their exit at Pulaski, they were both singing loud and feeling fine. But when they descended into the urban swamp of abandoned buildings, vacant lots, winos and crack

4

heads Teddy shook his head in disgust. "I don't see how you can live on this whack ass west side, man?"

"West side's the best side," CJ quipped automatically. He didn't know if he really believed that, but having lived on the west side all his life, he felt compelled to defend it when others put it down as they often did.

"Looks like a fuckin' war zone up through here."

"That's 'cuz it is," CJ said, only half joking. "But a nigga's just as likely to get killed on the south side as he is over here."

"True," Teddy agreed. "But at least you'll get shot by a better class of criminal." CJ laughed but this conversation was starting to bring him down.

As James Brown crowed about it being *A Man's World*, CJ wondered what man he was talking about – surely not the black man. He peered out at the filth and decadence surrounding him and it was as if he were seeing it for the first time, even though some of the men hanging out on these corners had been there since he was a kid. Scantily dressed hookers, some barely into their teens brazenly hawked their wares while young boys in baggy jeans and oversized white T-shirts served up dope as casually as they would pass out flyers for a church revival. He leaned his head back against the plush headrest and closed his eyes, unable to look any longer upon the stark depravity of the slum that he called home.

As they turned down CJ's block, the filth and desolation gave way to cleaner streets lined with nice two flats and well-maintained single-family homes, where neighbors socialized on their front porches while watching their children play. When the Escalade pulled up in front of the Johnsons' brick two-story house, a group of teenagers playing music on the porch next door ran over to admire Teddy's new car.

"Aw, Teddy, this is slick," said a gangly boy in unlaced sneakers.

"When you gon' get you a ride, CJ?" teased a flirtatious young girl.

"He already got one," replied a young wisecracker. "Ain't you seen him driving that big red, white and blue limousine?" The kids all fell out laughing.

Even the kids know I'm a loser, CJ thought. But he just laughed and said, "Aw, y'all got jokes, huh?"

As CJ and Teddy stepped into the Johnsons' stylishly furnished home, they heard the loud, angry voices of CJ's parents coming from the kitchen.

"I done told you about drinking in my house, Tony. You know I got the Pastor's Aid Committee coming over tonight," Dee screeched. At forty-five, Dee, a petite caramel colored beauty with a short, curly hairdo, looked more like CJ's sister than she did his mother.

"Your house?" shouted her husband, pouring himself another drink. "I damn near built this house with my own two hands." Tony Johnson, a successful real estate broker, was one of those middle-aged men who seemed to grow more handsome with age. He had caramel-colored skin and naturally wavy hair with just enough gray mixed in to give him a look of prosperity and distinction.

"Don't you raise your voice at me Tony Johnson," Dee warned.

"Ah, I see peace and harmony reigns in the Johnson home as usual," CJ quipped as he strolled into the cozy kitchen. He was used to his parents' fights. He had concluded long ago that this was their way of showing affection – might even be foreplay for all he knew.

Teddy gave Dee a peck on the cheek. "Hey, Mama Dee. What's that stankin' in my nose?" he asked, sniffing toward the pots on the stove.

"Hi Theodore," Dee said through pursed lips.

Standing behind his mother, CJ wrapped his arms around her tiny frame and nuzzled his cheek against hers. "So what's got you so riled up, old lady?"

"Nothing," she said, her fury subsiding. Dee could never stay angry when CJ teased her. "I got some meatloaf over there. Let me fix y'all something to eat."

As Dee piled two plates with meatloaf, mashed potatoes and corn fixed just the way CJ liked it, Tony and Teddy clasped hands. "What's shakin' Pops?" said Teddy as he plopped down at the round butcher-block table.

"Man . . . Ain't nothin' shakin' but the beans in the pot," Tony said. The guys laughed as CJ sat down next to his dad.

"Gimme a coupla glasses, baby," Tony called over his shoulder to Dee. "Y'all come on have a drink with me.

"Naw, Pops. We're just gonna gobble up this grub and run down to Mac Daddy's for a little while."

"Mac Daddy's!" Dee exclaimed, setting the plates before the two young men. "Why you want to hang out at a place like that? Ain't nothing down there but lowlifes and losers."

"I know. But it's not often I find people I can feel superior to," CJ joked.

"You got that right," quipped. Sherman, CJ's younger brother as he strolled into the kitchen looking like Tony's younger, taller twin. He gave his mom a kiss on the cheek and held his hand out to Teddy. "Brother Ted."

"What's up, Sherm?" Teddy replied, grasping his hand.

"Hey pretty lady; you can fix me one of them plates," Sherman said taking his place at the table.

CJ noticed Tony, an avowed clothes horse, giving him the once-over. "What?"

"Is that what you're wearing?"

"Naw, Pops," CJ said in exasperation. He knew that Tony hated the fact that he'd chosen a mundane city job over working with him and Sherman at his real estate office. But, even though CJ detested his job, he found it easier than competing with Sherman at the real estate game. Sherman was one of Johnson & Sons' top salesmen and Tony was extremely proud of him.

"You know the uniform is just one more symbol of the white man's oppression."

"Oh, Lord. Don't get him started," Dee chided, giving Tony a kiss on the top of his head.

"I'm serious. That's one of his psychological ploys to strip you of your individuality."

CJ started to explain that he was about to change clothes and then thought of a better idea. "What about that uniform you wear?" he said with a sly smile.

"What uniform?" Tony demanded, leaping to his feet in indignation.

"The suit!" The brothers said in unison. Everyone fell out laughing – everyone except Tony, that is.

Tony snatched his suit jacket from the coat rack near the back door and held it up for them to see. "You know how much this suit cost? This ain't hardly no damned uniform."

8

"Didn't you tell us that if you want to play the white man's game, you had to wear his uniform, 'the suit' so he doesn't feel threatened?" CJ asked.

Undone by his own words, Tony couldn't help but laugh "Eat your food, nigga." The brothers gave each other a high five. Scoring one on the old man was always a coup for them.

A short time later, alone in his bedroom, CJ relaxed for the first time all day. Several years earlier, Tony had remodeled the attic into two large rooms for him and Sherman, separated by a bathroom which they shared. This was CJ's refuge. Surrounded by his keyboard, his stereo and his books, he was in CJ heaven.

CJ peeled off his sweaty shirt, plopped down on the bed and kicked off his shoes. Relieved of those encumbrances, he slid open the mirrored door to his walk-in closet, revealing a space that looked more like a men's clothing store than a closet. Although Sherman with his reddish creole complexion and brawny build, looked as if his father had spit him out, CJ had inherited Tony's impeccable sense of style.

He searched through the well-organized racks of clothes, choosing a pair of jeans fresh from the cleaners, a crisp white shirt and a tan sports jacket. He then plucked up a pair of leather loafers that matched the jacket. After laying his clothes out on the bed, CJ pulled a chocolate colored silk pocket square from a drawer and stuck it into the jacket's breast pocket. "Yeah," he said, proudly. "Pops gon' like this." With a satisfied smile, he headed for the shower.

CJ sang as the hot water beat down on his tired shoulders and back. As he lathered himself up with the herbal scented body wash that his mother never let run out, an ominous sounding voice cut through the sound of the running water.

"He was despised and rejected by men, a man of sorrows and familiar with suffering."

9

The voice, a man's voice, seemed to be coming from everywhere, but yet from nowhere. CJ turned off the water and listened. Silence. He stepped out of the shower, grabbed a towel from the rack and wrapped it around his middle. "Sherman, man you ain't funny," he said turning the knob on the door leading to Sherman's room. But the door was locked from inside the bathroom. "I know I heard somebody in here," he said.

Puzzled, CJ rushed into the bedroom. He made a quick search of the room and the closet but found no one there. Unable to shake the eerie feeling that had taken hold of him, he stared into the mirror and gave himself a feeble smile, "Better get a grip homeboy. You're letting your imagination run away with you."

CHAPTER 2

"Gon' Charlene! Show him what you workin' with," Teddy yelled from the crowded bar as *It's Your Thang* blasted from the jukebox.

Surrounded by happy chatter and boisterous laughter CJ clowned around on the dance floor, bopping and sliding around Charlene, a regular fixture at Mac Daddy's Lounge as she did her thang. Dressed in a halter top that strained under the weight of her ponderous bosom and a pair of stretch pants that gave new meaning to the word "stretch," Charlene whipped her blonde weaved hair while her colossal rear-end gyrated around the tiny dance floor as if it not only had a mind of its own, but an orbit as well.

CJ liked hanging out at Mac Daddy's, a seedy little neighborhood bar, whose owner thought he could class it up by calling it a "lounge." The customers were cool, about his age and up, mostly regulars. The beer was cheap and they had a lot of dusties on the jukebox.

"Ooo-mother fucking-wee," Charlene, squealed, bumping and grinding as if she were auditioning for a strip club. When the song ended, CJ started off the dance floor only to have Charlene grab him as another song began. "Come on, CJ, this is my jam." "I'm tired girl," CJ said, begging off with a laugh. "You done wore

11

me out. Give Charlene a drink, Skip," he called to the bartender. "Put it on our tab."

"Don't you mean *my* tab?" Teddy said with a laugh. CJ just shrugged and plopped down on the stool next to him as Skip poured Charlene's usual, cognac and cranberry juice and sat it on the bar before her.

"You and Charlene make a beautiful couple," Teddy whispered. "When's the wedding?"

"Don't start none, it won't be none," CJ said, forcing a smile. Determined to put the mysterious voice out of his mind and have a good time, he polished off his beer and yelled to the bartender, "Yo, Skip, can we get a couple more beers over here?"

Suddenly, the unmistakable sound of gunfire rang out. The crowd paused for a moment and hearing no more shots, returned to their revelry undeterred. The sound of gunfire in this neighborhood was as commonplace as the tune played by the ice cream truck. Charlene stood at the bar sipping her drink as the door slowly opened and a bloody hand clamped onto the doorjamb. "This ain't nothin' but juice, Skip. Put a little more cognac in . . ."

"Mama . . ."

At the sound of her son Malik's voice, Charlene whipped around in exasperation, assuming the sixteen-year-old had come yet again to drag her out of the bar. "Boy, I done told you about . . . Malik!" she screamed at the sight of her son stumbling toward her clutching the front of his blood soaked T-shirt, his eyes wide with terror.

Charlene flew to her wounded child "What happened to you, Malik? Who did this to you?"

"Mama," Malik repeated, collapsing into her arms. Unable to hold the lanky teenager up, Charlene started going down with him.

12

CJ raced to help her ease the injured boy down to the filthy barroom floor.

Charlene fell down beside her son, cradling him in her arms, "Oh, Lord. What did they do to my baby?" Malik looked up at his mother and tried to speak, but instead, thick globs of blood spurted out of his mouth. Charlene began howling uncontrollably.

"Call nine-one-one," CJ shouted. Skip whipped out his cell phone and dialed frantically. Charlene clung to her son, wiping the blood from his face with her hand. Suddenly, the whites of his eyes rolled up and his head slumped to the side. CJ stared in amazement as an ethereal puff of white smoke wafted from Malik's chest. Was it just his imagination or had he actually seen the boy's life force leave his body?

"Noooooo!" Charlene wailed, clasping her son's head to her breast. Her heart-wrenching cry was filled with the raw emotion and exquisite pain reserved exclusively for mothers suffering the incomparable sorrow of losing a child. It clenched at CJ's heart, but there was nothing he could do. So he just sat down on the floor next to her and held her in his arms.

Most of the customers had fled by the time detectives Al Brukowski and Carlton Burke strolled into Mac Daddy's and found two uniformed cops and two very frustrated EMTs surrounding Charlene and Malik. "What do we have here?" asked Brukowski, a burly veteran cop in a brown suit and a shirt with a collar so greasy that it looked as if it might slide off his back if not for the sleeves holding it in place.

"Kid got himself shot up. But she won't let the EMTs examine him," said one of the cops with a nod toward Charlene.

Brukowski looked down on the dead boy with contempt and kicked him in the side. Charlene whimpered as though feeling the pain herself and gathered her child closer in her arms. "This hump's dead," Brukowski proclaimed. "Nothing they can do for him now." Turning to Burke, his sharply dressed, high yellow partner he cracked, "Another NHI." CJ glared at the white man, hoping Charlene didn't know that this was cop speak for *No Humans Involved.*

Burke, at 6'5", 220 lbs. just snorted derisively and nodded his head. The sight of the sneering black man made CJ's blood boil. He had seen Burke's kind before and could tell that he hated blacks even more than Brukowski did. He probably even hated himself for being black. Burke turned to CJ and asked, "What do you got to do with this?"

"Nothing," CJ replied. "I'm just trying to help this lady."

"What lady?" Burke scoffed, shooting a scornful look down at Charlene. He then shoved CJ over a table and began searching him. CJ wanted to tell him to get his damned hands off of him, but he was too scared. He knew that a black man had no wind against cop, especially a nigger hating black cop.

"Who are you, the girlfriend?" Brukowski asked Charlene.

"She's his mother," Teddy snapped, shooting up from his barstool.

"Be cool, Teddy," CJ warned.

"Shut up," said Burke, slapping CJ upside his head.

"Get this broad outta here," Brukowski told the uniforms. "You," he said, pointing at Teddy. "Sit your ass down. I'll get to you." Teddy glared at him for a moment, then slid back down onto his stool."

"Who we got here?"

"Charlie Johnson. Age thirty. Works for the CTA," Burke read from CJ's wallet.

"When's the last time you were locked up, Charlie?" Brukowski asked.

"Never," CJ indignantly replied.

Burke grinned. "If you believe that, I've got some swamp land I'd like to sell you."

"So, what happened here, Charlie?" Brukowski asked, propping his arms up on the table across from CJ, mirroring his pose. "You and Mother Posterior here, get into a lovers' quarrel? You smack her around a little bit. The kid don't like it, you and him get into it – Bim boom bam. Shit happens," he said, throwing his hands open in an "Oh, well" gesture.

"No. No, I didn't have anything to do with it," CJ protested.

Meanwhile, the two uniforms were still trying to pry Charlene loose from Malik's body. "No!" she howled, clutching her son's lifeless body even tighter, kissing him, begging for his – and God's forgiveness. "I'm sorry, baby. Mama's so sorry. Forgive me, Lord. Please forgive me."

A look passed between the two detectives and without warning Burke swooped down on Charlene and snatched her up off the corpse kicking and screaming. CJ watched in horror as he body slammed the woman to the floor, jammed his knee in her back and cuffed her. He then leaped to his feet grinning like he'd just roped and tied his calf in record time. "Get this bitch outta . . ." Before Burke could finish, Teddy sprang from his seat and fired on him. Blood spurted out of Burke's nose like a fire hose gone berserk. That's when all hell broke loose.

The two uniforms grabbed Teddy and pinned his arms behind his back. Brukowski reached all the way back to Poland and came up with a punch that sent Teddy's head spinning. Burke whipped out his gun and CJ instinctively kicked it out of his hand. Realizing what he had done, CJ took off running. The enraged cop was hot on his heels. CJ jumped up on tables and threw chairs in a desperate attempt to get away from the blood-drenched detective.

Brukowski plowed a meaty fist into Teddy's stomach. Teddy dropped to his knees and the uniforms began beating him with their nightsticks. CJ grabbed a chair and smashed it over Brukowski's head. He then jumped off the table and ran straight into Burke, whose huge fist slammed into his face like a sledgehammer. CJ's legs turned to jelly. And as he slid down to the floor his only thought was, Wow, you really do see stars. Then, everything went black.

CHAPTER 3

Clamma-lammma, lammma, lammma, lammma, lammma . . .
Waking to the ominous sound of an iron door clanging shut
somewhere in the distance, CJ wondered where he was. But the
interminable noise of men crying, calling for the guards and
demanding lawyers brought him back to reality real quick. He
remembered calling Tony, the last person he wanted to see him in
jail with an eye that looked like a second head. But there was no one
else to call.

He peered down into the bottom bunk and saw Teddy
sleeping peacefully, a bandage wrapped around his head. CJ shook
his head, thinking that Teddy's temper had gotten them into some
deep doo-doo this time. But even though Teddy had started the fight,
CJ didn't feel bad about clobbering those cops. They deserved it. *So
what if Charlene was just a barfly*, he thought. *She was still a
woman and a mother whose child had just died.* He got mad all over
again just thinking about it.

He wished he'd had the nerve to throw the first punch, but he
had never been the hero type. His mother had constantly warned him
not to let anyone provoke him into striking out in anger and he'd
always gone out of his way to avoid confrontation. It had always
been Teddy coming to his rescue, never the other way around. As CJ

17

pondered his predicament, the strange, otherworldly voice he'd heard in the shower once again invaded his consciousness.

"He was pierced for our transgressions, he was crushed for our iniquities and by his wounds we are healed."

CJ leaped out of his bunk like it was on fire. "Who said that?" he demanded, fear crawling up the back of his neck like a menacing spider. He glanced down at Teddy who was still asleep and began pacing the jail cell. "Maybe I've got a concussion. Yeah, that's it. I'm hallucinating," he said, grasping for any logical explanation. "Yeah, I'm having an auditory hallucination, a blow to the head can do that," he rationalized. "But they didn't hit me on the head. Did they?"

"Who are you talking to, man?" Teddy asked, wincing with pain as he sat up.

"You heard it?" CJ asked hopefully.

"Yeah, I heard you," Teddy replied. "Maybe you didn't get hit in the head, but they beat on mine like it was a fucking bongo," he groaned, holding his head with both hands. "When are we getting out of here? I need some aspirin or something."

"I called Pops." CJ said, peering through the bars of the cell so Teddy couldn't see how shaken up he was, "He's on his way."

Later, as they left the jail Teddy said, "Thanks, Pops. I owe you."

"You bet your ass you do – both of you. I ain't no damn bail bondsmen. What were y'all thinking about? They said you jumped on a cop."

"Pops, if you had seen the way they were treating that woman you would have done the same thing," CJ said. "This big, tall detective slammed this woman down on the ground like he was on the WWE or something."

18

"What had she done?"

"She was upset because her son had just been murdered," CJ replied.

"You should have seen your boy, Pops," Teddy said. "I didn't know he had it in him." Even though Teddy loved CJ like a brother, he had always considered him to be somewhat of a coward, weak and sensitive, unable to protect himself.

"Yeah. He can thump if he has to," Tony said as they piled into his Lincoln Town Car. Reluctant to show the pride he felt at his son's courageous act, Tony kept his face blank as the contented purr of his Lincoln kicked in. But CJ could hear it in his voice, which both pleased and surprised him, since he'd always felt like a failure in his dad's eyes. He'd never been the big jock that Sherman was and refused to work at Tony's real estate firm, Johnson & Sons – like Sherman did.

A few minutes later, Tony pulled up next to Teddy's SUV and CJ and Teddy climbed out. CJ leaned into the window, smiling guiltily at Tony, "You ain't gon' say nothing to Moms are you?"

Tony grunted, "You think I'm crazy? She'll figure out some way to make this my fault. You just pay me my money," he said, pulling out so fast that CJ had to jump back to keep from being taken along for the ride.

When Teddy's SUV pulled up in front of CJ's house, Mrs. Wilson, CJ's nosey next-door neighbor eyed them disapprovingly as she swept her front porch. CJ glanced at the clock in the dashboard, "Six-thirty. Moms is probably in the basement doing laundry. Maybe
I can sneak in without her seeing me."

Tempted to make a smart remark, Teddy said instead, "Tell her you were at my house."

"Yeah, we had a sleep-over," CJ cracked. "Did we do each other's nails?"

"Naw, smart ass. Tell her you were helping me make plans for my party."

"What party?"

"My going away party," Teddy said with a grin. "Chi town can kiss my ass, man." He caught the shock on CJ's face and said, "You should come on and go with me?"

"Yeah, right," CJ replied, forcing a smile. After an uncomfortable moment of silence, he opened the passenger door and jumped out. "Peace."

"Hope you don't get no whuppin'." Teddy teased as CJ started toward the back of the house. CJ twirled around and gave him the finger with both hands. Teddy threw his head back and laughed as he drove off.

CJ eased the back door open, poked his head in to see if the coast was clear and stepped gingerly into the kitchen. He closed the door ever so gently and turned around with a sly smile on his face. The smile froze when he saw Dee standing there with a basket of laundry in her arms. "Good morning."

CJ gave her a sheepish grin, angling his head to hide his busted eye. "Hey, Ma. What are you doing up so early?"

"What are you doing out so late?" she replied, placing her basket on the kitchen table.

"I was, uh . . . with Teddy," he said. CJ hated lying, mainly because he was so lousy at it.

"Don't you know you had me worried to death? I didn't know if you were dead or alive. I was about to call the police."

"I'm sorry, Ma. I know I should have called."

"Why you keep turning your head away from me? You've been drinking haven't you?" She walked up to him and took his chin in her hand, turning his head to face her. "Lord Jesus!" she exclaimed. "What happened to you?"

"Nothing, Ma. I just got into a lil' scuffle.

She stared at him, a look of pure dread on her face. "You didn't hurt nobody, did you?" she asked in a near whisper. "Do I look like I won the fight?"

"Not really," she said quietly.

"I need a shower," he said, giving her a peck on the cheek and starting up the stairs to his room.

Dee slumped down into a chair, closed her eyes and shook her head, "Lord, please watch over my child."

A couple of weeks later, as Sherman sat on his bed playing his guitar CJ knocked on the door and poked his head in. "Got a minute?"

"Hey, what's up?" Sherman said as CJ strolled in and struck a GQ pose in his white linen suit and tropical print silk shirt. On his feet were soft as butter Ferragamo slip-ons, blue to match the predominant color in his shirt. Sherman laid the guitar down on the bed and slapped his hands together, "Man! You're sharp as Dick was when Hattie died." They loved tossing around those old time country sayings, most of which made no sense at all.

"Why aren't you dressed?" CJ asked.

"Aw, man," Sherman said, suddenly remembering. 'Tonight's Teddy's going away party. I forgot all about it."

"If you're not going, why don't you let me use your ride, so I can pick Candace up?"

"Candace? I know you're not talking about that lil' fine ass Candace I met at CTA's Christmas party." CJ's smile confirmed it. "When y'all hook up?"

"We've been talking for a while. I was just waiting for the right time to ask her out."

"Yeah, something free." Sherman quipped. CJ's penchant for holding on to a buck was often the topic of relentless teasing.

"Do you know how much money I save riding the bus with a free pass?" CJ argued. "But I can't take a lady like Candace on the bus. She's got too much class."

"I second that emotion. Fine, too. I thought about tapping that myself. But I said, Naw, that's CJ's co-worker and . . ."

CJ smiled. "Shot you down, huh?"

"Like a dog, man," Sherman said, dropping his head in mock shame. "She wouldn't even dance with me, man."

"Maybe she's just not into boys," CJ said, popping his collar in the dresser mirror. He ran his hand over his freshly cut hair and flashed himself a confirming smile, "Evidently, she prefers *men*."

Sherman grabbed the car keys from the nightstand and threw them at CJ, who caught them with both hands.

"You still need a car, nigga."

CHAPTER 4

The fragrance of sizzling pork filled the air as Teddy, dressed in shorts, an apron that read Kiss the Cook and a big Panama straw hat stood over two garbage can grills under the glow of Chinese lanterns and citronella candles. Teddy had turned his backyard into a fantasy wonderland with a dance floor made of cement blocks in the middle of the yard and rows of colored Christmas lights hanging from the back porches of his three-flat apartment building.

Deejay Sonny, Jr. kept the music pumping while Tina, Teddy's sexy little sometimes girlfriend tended the bar. Dancing in place with a bottle of beer in his left hand and a barbecue fork in the right, Teddy looked out on the crowded dance floor and smiled. Dressed in everything from shorts and flip-flops to their finest party gear, his guests were partying like it was going out of style.

Teddy's uncle Jake, an old school player from way back, sat at a card table playing bid whist with his three buddies. Dressed all in green, from his stingy brimmed straw hat, to his gators and silk socks, Jake chewed on an unlit cigar as he refilled everyone's glass from their personal bottle of Hennessey. "Hey, baby girl," Jake called to Tina, "Can we get some more ice over here?"

Tina filled a plastic bowl with ice and strutted out from behind the makeshift bar. "Here you go, Mr. Jake," she said, placing the bowl on the table. "Y'all need anything else."

Jake raised his eyebrows, giving her a wolfish grin. "Now that's a loaded question right there, lil' girl."

"You so crazy, Mr. Jake," she said with a giggle, turning to resume her post.

Jake's Buddy, Al followed Tina with his eyes as she sashayed away. "Good Lawdy, Miss Claudie. I sho' would like to get me some of that."

"What you gon' do with it?" Jake cracked. "You done already had one heart attack." This brought on gales of laughter from everyone at the table.

A good natured, "Fuck you," was Al's only response.

Detecting a sudden shift in the energy around him, Teddy noticed that the men were all gaping and the women glaring as CJ strolled onto the set with a honey colored enchantress on his arm. Blessed with auburn curls and startling green eyes, Candace Bouchet flashed an enticing smile that every man present thought was meant exclusively for him.

When he was finally able to pick his jaw up off the ground, Teddy sauntered toward the newly arrived couple. "Excuse me, Miss," he said to Candace in his most refined manner, "But the Miss America contest is over on the next block."

"You must be Teddy," she said.

Teddy bowed in acquiescence. "At your service."

"CJ said you were a charmer."

"Correction," CJ replied. "I said he was slick as a snake charmer and couldn't help hitting on every pretty woman he saw." They all laughed and CJ said, "Teddy, I'd like you to meet Ms. Candace Bouchet. Candace, Teddy Montgomery."

Teddy took her hand and kissed it. "Welcome to my humble soiree, Ms. Bouchet. May I get you anything? A drink? Some food? A car?"

"A Mercedes would be nice," she said with a flirtatious smile.

CJ politely removed her hand from Teddy's grip. "You have to excuse Teddy. He gets carried away."

"I think he's adorable."

"Ah," Teddy said, "Perceptive as well as beautiful." Then, in a stage whisper, "What are you doing with this bum? You could do so much better."

Candace laughed. "I think I'll have that drink now."

Teddy pointed toward Tina, who was giving him the evil eye. "Go over there and see Tina. She'll hook you up."

"You want anything, CJ?" Candace asked.

"Naw, I'm good," he replied plucking a bottle of beer out of a nearby tub filled with ice.

As CJ twisted the cap off his beer and took a long swig, Teddy watched Candace's gossamer sundress silhouetting her voluptuous curves as she glided across the yard and said, "Damn. She looks just as good going as she do coming."

Caught off guard, CJ laughed causing beer to come shooting out of his nose. He bent over, holding the beer away from him to protect his clothes. "Man, look what you did."

"Where'd you get a hottie like that from?" Teddy asked.

CJ pulled a handkerchief from his pocket and wiped his face. "She's been trying to get me to take her out for a while now," he bragged. "But I've been waiting for . . ."

"Something free."

"That's cold," CJ said, holding his hand to his chest as though wounded.

"Naw," Teddy said, nodding his head toward Candace who appeared to be deep in conversation with Uncle Jake and his lecherous old pals. "Wrong would be if I didn't tell you to go over there and get your woman before Uncle Jake drops that pimp hand down on her."

"What is it with your family? Can't y'all get no women of your own?"

"We can," said Teddy. "But it's so much more fun to let industrious young men like you do the shopping and if we like what you get, we just take it on home."

Later that evening, under the glow of a lovers' moon CJ held Candace close, inhaling the sweet fragrance of her hair as they danced to a slow jam. He was feeling very mellow, very content as they swayed to the music.

"Let's get out of here," Candace whispered in his ear. The warmth of her breath sent shivers down his spine. She didn't have to ask him twice. CJ grabbed her hand and held his other hand up to Teddy as they made their exit. Teddy returned the salute with a "thumbs up."

As CJ and Candace drove toward her house in Sherman's pearl white Infinity, CJ asked, "Did you have a good time tonight?"

Candace dropped her hand onto his thigh and squeezed, sending a warm sensation shooting up his leg. "The night isn't over yet," she said, leaning over to kiss him. CJ saw her glance drift downward and hoped she hadn't noticed the outward manifestation of his growing desire.

When CJ stepped into Candace's second floor apartment, he was impressed at the upscale elegance of the place. Large green plants sat at either end of the silver and black vertical blinds that graced an entire wall of the spacious living room. The furniture looked expensive and fresh flowers sat on a table in a ceramic vase.

Candace kicked off her high-heeled sandals and sighed with relief. "These shoes were not made for dancing," she said as she opened the blinds, revealing a sliding glass door that opened onto a balcony.

"But they sure make your legs look nice," CJ replied.

"Well, aren't you sweet," she said kissing him lightly on the lips. CJ slipped his arms around her and pulled her close. Candace pressed her hands against his chest, allowing them to slide across his rock hard abs. *Mmm, nice,* she thought before gently pushing him away. "I better go change," she said, scooping up her shoes. "Make yourself at home. There's wine in the fridge."

As Candace slipped into the bedroom, CJ strolled over to a glass entertainment system that housed a wide screen television set, a killer sound system and an impressive collection of CDs. A self-confessed music snob, CJ was pleased to see that she didn't have any rap music. Although he loved seeing young brothers making money, the music itself was just too crude for his taste. It also confirmed his theory that the profusion of creativity exhibited in the sixties and seventies had virtually drained the cup of originality.

A big grin spread across his face as he plucked out a Luther Vandross CD. "Lutha, Lutha, Lutha," he said, taking the CD out of its case and slipping it into the stereo. Nobody set the mood like Luther. *Yeah,* he thought. *This girl's got potential.*

27

As Luther's soulful voice filled the air, CJ slipped his jacket off, removed his cigarettes and lighter from the pocket and laid them on the table. Folding the jacket neatly, he laid it across the back of an overstuffed chair that matched the large gray couch.

CJ sang along with *A House Is Not a Home* as he slipped into the combination kitchen/dining area and retrieved the bottle of Sauvignon Blanc from the refrigerator. After a quick glance around the kitchen, he noticed a tray that held two glasses and a corkscrew. "My girl," he said, placing the wine on the tray and opening it. He then carried the tray into the living room, placed it on Candace's marble coffee table and flopped down on the big comfortable sofa. *Now, this is a couch fit for a man*, he thought. He poured wine into both glasses and took a sip of his. "Ah," he said, kicking off his shoes and leaning back on the careless array of gray and red throw pillows.

When Candace sauntered out of the bedroom in a flowing caftan, CJ felt his stomach drop. "I see you like Luther too," she said, sliding onto the couch next to him.

"Yeah. Me and Luther go way back," he said, handing her a glass of wine.

She took a long, appreciative sip. "Mmm," she sighed; resting her bare feet on the coffee table and wiggling her perfectly manicured toes.

CJ noticed the red marks on her feet where her shoes had been. "Want me to massage your little piggies for you?" he asked, taking her feet in his hands and placing them on his lap.

"Oh yes," she replied, positioning her back against the arm of the couch. He took one of her feet between his hands and began massaging it with a firm yet gentle touch.

CJ hadn't met anyone he liked this much in a long time. As his hand strayed farther up her smooth, shapely leg he asked in a voice husky with desire, "You like that?"

"Mmm, hmm," she said, resting her foot flat on his muscular thigh and allowing the soft fabric of her caftan to ride up. "You have magical hands." Her toes curled as he kissed her knee and then proceeded to plant a torturous trail of kisses down her inner thigh. Candace raised her upper body slightly and slipped the intrusive caftan over her head, flinging it to the floor with abandon. CJ felt a trickle of excitement in the pit of his stomach at the sight of her firm, plump breasts. She wore no bra, only a red lace thong which he wanted to rip off with his teeth. But somehow, he managed to maintain his cool.

In one deft move, CJ maneuvered himself between her legs. He gently kissed her lips, taking one of her full, heaving breasts into his hand and massaging it masterfully. She quivered slightly as he ran his thumb over the delicate nipple, which sprang to life at his touch. Candace closed her eyes, her sighs like the purr of a contented kitten.

CJ lowered his head to her breast and took the nipple into his mouth, alternating between gently sucking and lightly biting the sensitive flesh. She stroked his head lovingly. He planted light butterfly kisses on her face and neck before his lips finally found hers. Her hungry tongue met his in a kiss so passionate that she relinquished herself to it completely. CJ explored her luscious body with his hands, letting one of them come to rest between her legs. He could feel the warm moistness of her body through the silky material that stood like a wall between him and the Promised Land.

Suddenly, a familiar voice shook him out of his lustful haze.

"He was oppressed and afflicted, yet he said not a word; he was led like a lamb to the slaughter."

"No!" CJ shouted, leaping to his feet. "No! No!"

"What's the matter? What's the matter?" Candace screamed, jumping around as though she'd seen a mouse. CJ flopped down on the couch holding his head in his hand. "What's wrong with you?" Candace snapped.

29

"Nothing. I'm cool." But CJ was far from cool. He grabbed his cigarettes, lit one with trembling hands and took a deep pull.

"Why are you shaking?"

"I just . . . I just need some water."

CJ detected disgust in her sigh as she rolled her eyes and turned toward the kitchen. His eyes followed her as she walked away, wagging her exquisite backside tantalizingly behind her. He wanted her more than he had ever wanted a woman before. He just hoped he hadn't blown his chance.

Candace returned with a bottle of water and plopped it down on the table in front of CJ. Ignoring the water, he ground his cigarette out in the ashtray and pulled her close, so that she was standing between his legs. Determined to shake this strange feeling and return to the business at hand, he began kissing her taut stomach as he slid the silky thong down her voluptuous hips. "Oh, baby," he whispered, kissing her neatly trimmed bush.

She stepped out of the thong and kicked it aside as he gently laid her down on the couch, covering her body with his own. As their lovemaking reached a fevered pitch, she suddenly froze and her eyes became wide with fear. "Shhh," she whispered as heavy footsteps clomped up the stairs. "Oh, my God!" she said, pushing him off of her and leaping to her feet. "It's Tank. You gotta get out of here."

"Tank? Who's Tank?"

"My boyfriend," she whispered frantically, retrieving her discarded caftan from the floor and throwing it on hastily. "I thought you said you broke up," CJ said, slipping his feet into his shoes and zipping his pants.

"We did," Candace whispered, shoving his jacket into his chest and pushing him toward the balcony. "He wasn't supposed to be out of jail 'til next month."

"Jail!" CJ exclaimed. She shoved him out the door and closed the blinds just as a key turned in the lock.

CJ pulled his jacket on and peeked through the blinds to see Tank step in looking like any coach's dream of a vicious linebacker. Candace threw herself into his arms. "Tank!" she squealed. "Why didn't you tell me you were coming home?"

"Wanted to surprise you," he answered gruffly, his eyes landing on the two wineglasses. "You got company?"

"No," she said, making up her lie as she went along. "This guy gave me a ride home and I figured the least I could do was offer him a glass of wine."

Tank wasn't buying it. CJ's heart stopped when he saw Tank's eyes fix on the red thong crumpled up on the floor. He snatched the thong up and threw it in Candace's face. "You always take your draws off to drink wine?" he snarled, giving her a backhanded slap that sent her sailing.

"He's still here, ain't he?" Candace's mouth opened, but she couldn't think of a plausible lie. Taking her silence as confirmation, Tank began tearing through the apartment like a mad man, looking for the fool who was crazy enough to be up in there with his woman. "Is he hiding out here?" he said, yanking the sliding glass door open. Candace burst into tears, knowing that when Tank found CJ, they'd both be dead.

She held her breath as Tank stomped out onto the balcony. "You better be glad I didn't find that nigga," he said, stepping back into the apartment.

Relieved and confused Candace mumbled, "I told you wasn't nobody here."

CJ's legs dangled in mid-air as he clutched desperately at the ledge of the balcony, fear searing his insides like a white-hot poker. He peered down at the ground which seemed a million miles away.

31

Fighting the urge to scream as first his left hand lost its purchase and then the right, he plummeted down, crashing into a tree before hitting the ground.

CHAPTER 5

CJ dragged himself into his room and locked the door. "Man!" he said collapsing onto his bed. He felt as though every bone, muscle and tendon in his body had been yanked out of place. He removed the shoe and sock from his left foot and gasped at how badly his ankle had already swollen. He tried to stand, but the pain was so severe that he fell back onto the bed.

Holding onto the bed, CJ hobbled over to the mirror on one foot. "Aw, man!" he said, gazing at his scratched up face. Leaves were sticking out of his hair and his beautiful new suit was ruined. With pain accompanying his every move, CJ Peeled off his jacket and shirt, eased down onto the bed and fell into a deep sleep.

A subtle, yet intoxicating fragrance penetrated CJ's slumber. He smiled, thinking in his half-awake state that he'd never had smells in his dreams before. Then, he heard someone calling his name in a soft, singsong whisper. "C . . . J . . ., C . . . J . . ."

CJ opened one eye to see the most beautiful woman he'd ever beheld standing over his bed dressed in a white leather pants suit. Her skin was the color of caramel candy. She had voluptuous red lips and eyes that sparkled like diamonds when she smiled.

When she reached out to touch him, CJ instinctively drew back, scooting to the farthest edge of the bed.

"Don't be scared, CJ." Her soft melodious voice seemed to pierce his very being. *This is one strange dream*, he thought. "No, CJ. You're not dreaming."

CJ peered cautiously at the woman and wondered if he had spoken out loud. He didn't think he had. "Who are you?" he asked in a tentative voice. "How did you get in my room?"

"My name is Ariana," she replied. "I've come to bring you a message."

"A message?" he said warily. "From who?"

"From God."

"God? O-kay." It was at this point that he knew one of them was crazy. "Look, lady, I don't know how you got in here, but you gotta go."

Ariana sighed in exasperation and plopped down on the side of his bed. CJ hurriedly crawled to the foot of the bed. He didn't know if she was a dream, a ghost or what, but he didn't want her anywhere near him. He pulled a chair up to the bed and climbed into it. "Don't be so dramatic, CJ," she said with a dismissive wave of her elegantly manicured hand. "I got something important to tell you," she continued, speaking in a more down to earth tone.

"You ever heard of a telephone? And stop saying my name. You don't know me."

"Oh, I know you," she said with a mysterious smile. "I've known you for a very long time." She then picked up CJ's Bible from the bedside table, tracing her French tipped fingers over the letters on the cover.

He eyed her suspiciously. "Did Teddy put you up to this?"

34

Ariana fixed an unsettling gaze on him and said. "God wants you to know that it's time."

"Time for what?" CJ demanded, his fear turning to anger.

Ariana returned the Bible to the table and rose to face him. "It's time for you to be about your Father's business, CJ."

"I knew it!" CJ exclaimed. "Pops set this up. Well, you can tell him that his trick didn't work. I'm not going into the real estate business and he might as well get that through his head."

"Look, boy," she said impatiently, throwing one hand on her hip and pointing her finger in his face. "I've been trying to be nice, but I guess you're either too stupid or too stubborn to get it. God is fed up with y'all and it's up to you to get your people together."

"Me? What are you talking about?"

"I'm talking about you. God chose *you* to take His word to your people." On CJ's shocked expression, she continued. "He was about to strike y'all from the face of the earth, 'til I convinced Him to give you another chance."

"What!"

"You heard me," she said parking herself on his bed. "See, God gave this country to the black man, just like he gave Palestine to the Jews."

"We were brought here as slaves," CJ protested, thinking that whoever she was, she obviously didn't know her history.

"Oh, I know my history, honey." CJ's eyes bucked as she continued as though she hadn't read his mind. "God left y'all in bondage all those years so that when he finally freed you, you'd be appreciative and use your God-given gifts and talents to make this country great, a monument to his name."

"This country is great," CJ defended. "You don't know what you're talking about."

I know that the black man is the low man on the totem pole in this *great* country," she said, standing up and planting her hands on her hips. "I know that when his body got freed his mind stayed in bondage. And I also I know that he's despised by everybody, including himself."

"Hey, wait a minute now," CJ protested. But she was on a roll.

"That's why he's out there committing genocide on his own race." CJ didn't have a comeback for that. How do you dispute the truth? After a beat, she poked him in the chest with her finger and said, "God wants his people back. He wants y'all to get your act together and worship Him."

"Now, I know you're crazy. Don't nobody worship the Lord more than black folks."

"Nobody goes to church more than black folks," she corrected. That's where you find the biggest liars, hypocrites, backbiters and thieves. Y'all sit up in church shouting hallelujah and praise the Lord, then you go home and start killing each other. That is not what God had in mind. God intends to put these people in check and He's chosen you to do it," she stated emphatically, moving slowly toward him. CJ felt rooted to the spot as she placed her hand gently on his cheek. Her touch was cool and soothing to his bruised skin. Gazing deeply into his eyes she said, "You're the one, CJ."

CJ snapped himself out of whatever kind of trance she seemed to be putting him in and sprang to his feet. "Naw," he said incredulously.

"Yeah," she nodded.

"Why me? I ain't no preacher and I sure ain't no saint."

"You're the one," she repeated.

"Naw. Unh, unh. You got the wrong guy," CJ said turning away from her and shaking his head in denial. "I'm the screw up in the family. You must be looking for my brother, Sherman. He's the salesman. He's the one with the gift of gab. Besides," he said turning back to her, "I wouldn't even know what to . . ." She was gone. CJ ran to the door and found it still locked. "What the . . .?" He stared at the locked door for a moment, his face a mask of fear and confusion.

CJ sat down on the edge of the bed and picked up his Bible from the table. Having always found solace in the Bible, he opened it to a random page. His eyes fell on a verse that read: *For to us a child is born, to us a son is given and the government will be on his shoulders. And he will be called Wonderful Counselor, Mighty God, Everlasting Father, Prince of Peace."*

CHAPTER 6

"Man, that was some dream." CJ said, with a yawn and a stretch. "I must have hit my head when I fell." He rose from the bed and crossed to the mirror to check out the bruising on his face. To his amazement, his face was back to normal. *Maybe I dreamed falling off that balcony too,* he thought. Then, he looked down at his filthy, ripped pants and concluded that he had indeed, fallen. But how could his injuries have healed so quickly? All of a sudden, he realized that he was standing on his injured foot and the body pain he'd experienced last night was gone. He held both arms above his head and twisted his torso from one side to the other several times. Nothing. No pain whatsoever.

"I don't get it," he said staring into the mirror. "What's happening to me?"

"Chuckeee," his mother yelled up the stairs. "Breakfast."

Sunday morning breakfast was a big deal at the Johnson house. It was something they all looked forward to, since their busy schedules didn't allow for very many meals together during the week. But CJ didn't want to face his family until he had figured this thing out. Had it been some weird dream? Of course, it was a dream.

It had to be. Nobody received messages from God through a smart mouthed black woman. But it seemed so real.

When Dee called again, CJ panicked. He knew that if he didn't respond she'd be coming up to get him, so he opened the door and yelled. "Okay, Ma. Be down in a few."

After a quick shower, CJ prayed for God to take away whatever mental problems he was having. *Maybe it's just stress*, he rationalized. His job *had* been getting to him lately. Then there was his dad pressuring him to come and work for him. Not to mention the murder he'd nearly witnessed and his arrest. *Yes, it has to be stress*, he decided as he slipped into a pair of jeans and a T-shirt and started out the door.

As usual, Dee had pulled out all the stops for Sunday breakfast. It was her one chance to spoil her family and she looked forward to it as much as they did. The table was laden with pancakes, fresh fruit, bacon, sausage, grits, eggs, hot biscuits and a big pitcher of orange juice.

Tony and Sherman's eyes were glued to the TV as they ate. "The brutal murder of 9-year-old DeLorean Wilson brings the total number of shootings in Chicago this weekend up to twenty-seven – so far," said the smiling TV anchorwoman. Dee abruptly switched the channel and took her place at the table.

"Hey, I was watching that," Tony said.

"You ain't missing nothing. Just more black folks killing other black folks," she said as her favorite TV preacher, Reverend Thaddeus P. Bradshaw appeared on the screen. Known to one and all as "Rev," Bradshaw, an attractive though somewhat overweight man in his early fifties oozed charisma. Dressed in a gorgeous tailor made suit, he sported a thin mustache and wore his curly hair parted down the middle. The large diamond encrusted cross he always wore completed his look.

Though his bruises were gone, CJ didn't realize how badly he looked until he lumbered into the kitchen. When he dropped Sherman's keys on the table, Sherman glanced up from the stack of pancakes he'd been working on and sat straight up in surprise. "Man! You look like death warmed over. That must have been some party. I'm sorry I missed it now."

"Shut up, Sherman," CJ muttered, giving his brother a warning look.

"Don't y'all start this morning," Dee warned as CJ headed straight to the coffee pot on the counter and poured himself a cup. "I'm trying to listen to Rev." CJ took his seat and Dee noticed his hands shaking as he brought his mug up to his lips. "You all right, Chucky?" she asked, placing a hand on his forehead to check his temperature.

He pulled his head back. "I'm all right."

"You don't look all right," Tony observed. He'd been concerned about CJ ever since the police incident. He had not been himself lately, but Tony hadn't asked him about it. He'd hoped CJ would come to him with his problem as he always had in the past. But he hadn't.

Sherman watched as CJ placed one pancake and a strip of bacon on his plate. Ever since they were kids, they'd always competed to see who could eat the most pancakes. CJ could eat six easily. Sherman was already three ahead of him. "It's called a hangover, Pop," Sherman chuckled around a mouth full of food. "I'm sure you're familiar with the term."

"Shut up, Sherman," Tony snapped. Sherman shrugged and continued eating. As they ate, Dee's eyes stayed fixed on the TV.

"The Lord says that you must give in order to receive," Rev said with all sincerity. "You can't receive nothing with a closed fist." He illustrated by holding out his fist – and then opening it. "But blessings flow easily into an open hand. As you know, God has given me a vision to create The City of Solomon as a monument to his name. I can see it in my head as clearly as if God had painted a picture." Dee smiled serenely as Rev went on to describe his vision. Tony just grunted and rolled his eyes.

"I see beautiful parks and fountains. I see streets paved in gold. I see a lovely village where our seniors can live out their days in comfort and repose. Praise the Lord." He then closed his eyes for a second as though savoring a delicious taste. And then gesturing with his hand as if creating the visualization for them to see, he said softly, "I see a magnificent cathedral." On cue, the choir started to sing softly under his words. "Where my Lord's praises are sung and His glory revealed. Hallelujah!" Dee closed her eyes, caught up in Rev's vision.

"And I see you," Rev Continued, flashing an engaging smile and holding his hand out as in invitation. "I see you being a part of this glorious Christian experience. Pick up your phone and call in your pledge today. Don't miss this marvelous opportunity to be a part of God's glorious plan. It says in Second Corinthians that every man should give in accordance with his prosperity. Not grudgingly or out of necessity, but from his heart. For the Lord loves a cheerful giver." The choir began singing louder and Rev joined in, lifting his arms up toward heaven as contact information scrolled down the screen.

Dee rose from the table with an enchanted smile on her face. As she reached for the cordless phone, Tony's harsh voice snapped her out of her reverie. "I know you ain't finna give that nigga none of my hard earned money."

Dee's hand sprang away from the phone as if slapped. "Don't be like that, Tony. It's for the church. Rev said . . ."

"Rev, my ass," Tony snorted. "Can't we have one Sunday morning breakfast without his beggin' ass at the table? I'd rather give my money to one of them wine heads out there on the corner than that damn pimp in God's clothing."

"Tony!" Dee admonished.

"I just wish we could have one meal without all this fighting," CJ mumbled, picking unenthusiastically at his food.

Eyeing CJ with concern, Dee asked, "Did you have a BM this morning, Chucky?"

"Ma!" Sherman said, screwing up his face. "Don't be asking that man about his bowel movements."

"Why not?" she asked. "I was wiping his butt before he knew he had one. Yours too, for that matter."

"I'm fine." CJ snapped with uncharacteristic harshness. Dee's back straightened and he could see the hurt on her face, but he couldn't help it. The sound of her voice was grating on his last nerve.

"Well, you look like shit," Tony said.

"That's what that wild night life'll do for you," Sherman laughed, refilling his juice glass.

"Why don't y'all just leave me the hell alone!" CJ shouted, causing three pairs of startled eyes to fix on him. "Find something else to talk about and just get off my case." He scooted his chair back with such force that it toppled over as he stormed out of the room.

"What did I do?" Dee asked, fighting back tears.

"You didn't do nothin' baby," replied Tony, throwing his napkin down into his plate. "But I'm damn sure gon' find out what's got his draws in a knot." He sprang up from the table, snatched CJ's overturned chair up from the floor and stalked out of the kitchen.

Tony marched into CJ's room without knocking and found him sitting on the edge of the bed holding his head in his hands. "What in the hell is wrong with you, boy?" Tony demanded.

"I ain't no boy," CJ barked, snapping his head up. "And I wish y'all would stop treating me like one. I'm a grown man."

"Well, act like it. A grown man don't sit around moping and he damn sure don't talk to his mama the way you just did. If you got a problem, spit it out."

CJ wanted to tell him, but couldn't bring himself to admit to his father that he thought he was going crazy. He knew how intolerant Tony was of weakness in men and he was sure to see this as a weakness in his eldest son. "I'm cool, Pop," he said in an apologetic tone, forcing the corners of his mouth up in a smile he didn't feel. "I just got some things on my mind." But Tony could see that CJ was deeply distressed.

"You know you can talk to me about anything, son," Tony said, sitting down on the bed next to him. He then wrapped his arm around his son's shoulders, assuring him that together there was nothing they couldn't fix.

Tony's concern touched CJ, who dreaded the thought of disappointing him. "I'm cool," he said. "I just got some stuff I need to work out."

"You do that," Tony said as he stood. "But if you need to talk I'm here."

"I know, Pop," CJ said, managing to muster up a smile. Tony squeezed his shoulder and left the room without further conversation.

CJ remained in his room until he heard Tony and Sherman's cars drive off. Assuming his mother had left for church, he decided to go downstairs and get something to eat. When he stepped into the kitchen, he was surprised to find Dee seated at the table with a cup of coffee in front of her.

"I thought you'd be at church," he said, attempting to smile as he took a mug from the cabinet and filled it with coffee.

"They can do without me for one day," she said, sipping her coffee.

"Yeah," CJ said, pouring cream into his coffee. "I'll just take this upstairs and leave you alone. Didn't mean to disturb you." He was truly embarrassed over the way he had acted at breakfast and wanted to get away from her as quickly as possible.

"Sit down, Chucky," she said softly.

"Look, Ma. I'm sorry I yelled at you this morning. I'm just not feeling that great. I'm gonna go on back upstairs and lay down for a while." He started toward the stairs and his mother's voice stopped him.

"I said, sit down, Chucky." CJ turned to face her and could see from her expression that it had not been a request. He slid into the chair opposite her. Head down, he sat silently toying with his coffee cup. She watched him for a moment and asked, "What's going on with you, Chucky?"

"Nothing," he said with a shrug. "Just one of those days, I guess."

"Are you going to tell me what's bothering you or not?" she asked. "Because we're not leaving this table until you do."

Afraid that if he spoke he'd break out in tears, CJ just stared at her. Finally, after a long beat he said, "I think I'm losing my mind."

CHAPTER 7

Dee sprang from her chair and cradled her sobbing son's head to her breast. "Why would you say something like that?"

When he was finally able to compose himself, CJ explained to her about the voices, adding, "I tried to play it off, but then last night I had this crazy dream. I dreamed I saw an angel."

"An angel?"

CJ hadn't thought of the woman as an angel before, but now that he'd said it, he realized that must have been what she was. "It had to be," he said. Dee listened attentively as he told her about Ariana and all the things she'd said to him.

"Did she tell you her name?"

"Yeah. She said her name was Alana or Adriana. Something like that."

"Ariana?"

"Yeah, that's it. Ariana. How did you know?" "Because

I saw her too," Dee stated simply.

Her words hit him like a boot to the chest. "What?"

"I saw her too. Ariana. I'll never forget that name."

CJ leaned back in his chair, giving her a peculiar look. "When? Last night?"

"No, baby. Not last night." He watched in confusion as she rose from the table, got her little step ladder from the corner and placed it in front of the kitchen counter. She climbed up on the ladder and opened one of the cabinet doors, standing on her tippy-toes to reach the top shelf.

CJ ran to hold the ladder steady. "What are you doing?" he asked as Dee pulled down an ornately decorated box and handed it to him. CJ placed the box on the table and helped her down. Dee stared down at the box, stroking it reverently before opening it.

When Dee opened the box, CJ saw something wrapped in a sky blue satin cloth. Dee unfolded the cloth to reveal a magnificent white Bible with gold lettering on the cover and the pages edged in gold. She removed the Bible from its bed of satin and handed it to CJ. "Ariana gave me this," she said softly. "She told me to give it to you when the time was right." CJ looked first at the Bible and then at her, a quizzical look on his face. "Remember how I've always told you that you were special?"

"Yeah. All parents tell their kids that," CJ replied.

"But you really were – are," she said, correcting herself. She dropped heavily into her chair, indicating for him to sit as well. "You know I wasn't but fifteen when you were born."

"I know, Ma. What's that got to do with it?"

"When my parents broke up, me and my mother went to live with my grandmother," Dee said. This caught CJ's attention, since Dee had never talked about her family. A deep sadness clouded her eyes as she began to remember a time she hadn't thought of in many years, a harsh and cold childhood devoid of any love, affection or joy.

"You think Mother Fletcher is mean," she chuckled humorlessly, referring to the meanest old lady in their church. Mother Fletcher was so tough that she had once pulled a gun on another sister in the church kitchen simply for, "Overstepping her bounds," a transgression that no one before or since had ever even thought of committing.

"You should have seen my grandmother. Compared to her, Mother Fletcher could be Miss Congeniality. Grandma practically lived in the church, but she was the angriest, most self-righteous, unforgiving Christian I've ever seen in my life." She went on to tell him how her mother, Sharon was afraid Grandma would kick them out, so she never raised a hand to protect Dee from the venomous old woman.

"Grandma never let me go anywhere but school and church," Dee said. "My only friend was a boy named Bobby. She only let him come over because he was the preacher's son. But she still watched us like a hawk. She thought all men were nasty and evil, out to defile any woman they could get their hands on. When I came up pregnant with you, she went ballistic." Dee had to take a deep breath before she could continue, batting her eyes furiously to hold back the tears.

"I understand," CJ said, patting her hand. "Kids make mistakes."

"No," she insisted. "Me and Bobby never even kissed. We were too afraid of my grandmother."

"Well, who . . .?"

"That's what Grandma wanted to know. When I told her that I didn't know, she beat me with an extension cord," she said, rubbing at the "U" shaped scar she still bore on her arm. "She beat me until I passed out, calling me all kinds of liars and sluts and whores. She said I was the spawn of the devil and she was going to beat him out of me. My mother just stood there crying. She didn't say stop or that's enough . . . nothing. To this day I don't know if she was just afraid of Grandma or if she really believed the things Grandma was saying."

Dee recalled that when she continued to deny knowing who had fathered her child, her grandmother assumed it had to be Bobby. So she marched Dee and Sharon over to the pastor's house and announced to him and his wife that Dee was pregnant and that their son was the father. The parents' faces dropped in horror. But no one was more shocked than Bobby.

"I never touched her," he shouted. "Tell 'em Dee. Tell 'em the truth."

"I did," Dee said, bursting into tears.

Bobby's father began to verbally attack him, calling him stupid and telling him how he had humiliated his family, *meaning himself.* Bobby's mother started yelling at her husband in defense of her son and the family ruckus was on. Bobby continued to proclaim his innocence as his mother lit into Dee, calling her a little Jezebel and accusing her of seducing her child.

With Dee reduced to blubbering hysterics and the preacher's family at each other's throats, Grandma rounded up Sharon and Dee and marched out the door content in a job well done.

"When word got around the church that I was pregnant, everybody said I was just trying to pin it on poor Bobby because I didn't know who the real father was. Grandma blamed me because she couldn't go back to that church anymore. Said she was just too ashamed to show her face. My life became a living hell"

"She beat you again?" CJ asked.

"I would have preferred a beating to the hateful looks and spiteful words she was constantly throwing at me. I was so scared and confused that I started thinking maybe I was as bad as she said I was and maybe God *was* punishing me. That's when Ariana came." CJ stared at her in astonishment as she continued.

"I was home alone one night, just standing there looking out the window, crying and watching the snow fall, wondering why this had to happen to me. That's when I started smelling this beautiful perfume. I knew it wasn't my mother's and grandma didn't wear any." CJ wondered if he had mentioned the fragrance to her. He didn't think he had. "Suddenly, I heard somebody behind me calling my name. I turned around and saw this beautiful sister standing there. She had on this gorgeous white dress and a white fur coat and hat. She was sharp. And she had this Bible in her hand," she said, patting the Bible that lay on the table between them.

Tears slipped from Dee's eyes as she told CJ how she had made sure to lock the door when her mother and grandmother left for church, because she had become convinced that someone had sneaked into the house and raped her while she slept. "But, there she was," Dee continued. "She told me her name was Ariana and that she'd been sent by God. I started crying, I thought God had sent her to *get* me. She told me that the child I was carrying – you, was a gift from God and that God meant for you to be the savior of your people."

CJ leaped to his feet in astonishment, "That's the same thing she said to me. I told you that. You're just repeating what I said."

She looked up at him and asked earnestly, "You think I'm lying, Chucky?"

"No," he said. "I don't know. This is crazy, Ma."

49

"Tell me something I don't know," she said, taking a sip of her coffee.

They had long accepted the fact that Dee was a little on the eccentric side, but she wasn't a liar. CJ leaned against the counter, his arms crossed over his chest as she continued.

"When I told Grandma about Ariana and what she had said, she totally lost it. Started talking in tongues and flapping her arms like she was trying to take off. She said I had a demon in me and that she wanted me out of her house. That's the only time I ever remember my mother standing up for me," she said with a hint of a smile.

Dee picked up her mug and walked over to the coffee pot. She freshened her coffee and held the pot out to CJ. He shook his head, anxious for her to get on with the story. "My mother begged Grandma not to throw me out in the snow," she said resuming her seat. She told him that the only reason her grandmother finally relented was because Sharon had told her she would look bad in front of her new church. So she reluctantly agreed that Dee could stay until spring. And true to her word, as soon as the weather broke she kicked her out. By then, Dee was well into her pregnancy, a skinny little girl with a big belly, a ponytail and gym shoes.

"I didn't have anywhere to go. So I sat in the library or the park all day and slept in hallways and the bus station at night. I used to steal fruit and candy from the store to keep from starving. That's how I met Tony. He was a security guard at Jewel's. He caught me stealing, but he didn't turn me in." CJ could see the love in her eyes as she spoke of her husband. "He asked if I'd wait for him to get off work, so we could talk." Blushing, she said, "I didn't have much experience talking to guys and I was a little afraid of them. But I figured I might as well listen to what he had to say. It's not like I had anywhere else to be."

Tony took Dee to an Italian restaurant where she gorged herself on pasta and the most delicious bread she'd ever tasted. As

50

she ate, she explained her situation to him. Tony was appalled. He offered to let her stay at his apartment until she had her baby.

"I stayed at his place and he took care of me like I was his little sister. When it was close to time for you to be born, Tony said we should get married. I never expected that, since he'd never even acted like he thought of me that way. He told me that he loved me. Said he wanted to help me raise my baby and that he wanted us to be a family. That's when I realized that I loved him too," she said. "I don't know if it was romantic love or what, but I did love him. We drove down to Kentucky and got married by a Justice of the Peace and you were born a few weeks later. He saved my life, Chucky." She broke down in a fit of uncontrollable sobs.

CJ wrapped his arms around his mother and tried to comfort her, telling her that everything would be all right. But in his heart, he wondered if anything would ever be all right again.

CHAPTER 8

"I gotta talk to you," CJ said, storming into Tony's glass enclosed office. Tony was sitting behind his big oak desk talking on the phone. He shot CJ an annoyed look, holding his hand up as though holding him back. CJ paced in front of the desk until Tony finally hung up the phone.

"What the hell is wrong with you, busting up in my office like you're crazy?"

"I gotta ask you something, Pop and I need the truth."

"When did I ever tell you anything else? Sit down, you're making me nervous." CJ slumped down in one of the leather armchairs in front of Tony's desk. He rested his elbow on the desk and started rubbing his forehead. "Now, what's got you so upset?" Tony asked.

CJ held his head up and asked point blank, "Are you my real father?"

The question hit Tony in the face like a bag of bricks. He got up from his desk and closed the door. "Of course I am," he answered, facing his son. CJ felt a weight lifting off his heart, but it crashed back down when Tony added softly, "Maybe not biologically, but . . ."

"What!" CJ felt as if a mule had kicked him in the chest. He leaped up from his seat, "Well, who is?" he demanded.

"I don't know," Tony replied calmly. "Does it really matter?"

"Yes, it matters!" CJ shouted. "Didn't y'all think I had a right to know?"

"Know what?" Tony snapped back. "You're my son. You have my name. I was the first one to hold you when you were born and I've been there ever since. What more do you need to know?"

"I need to know who I am. Y'all been lying to me my whole life."

"Ain't nobody lied to you, CJ."

CJ saw the hurt in Tony's eyes and his anger began to dissipate. What was he thinking? This was Pops, the man that had loved him and cared for him all his life. The man that had taught him how to ride a bike, drive a car . . . This was the man that had prevented his overprotective mother from turning him into an emotional cripple. He threw his arms around his father, tears streaming down his face. "I'm sorry, Pops. I didn't mean to go off on you like that. I just didn't want to believe that you weren't my father."

Tony patted his son's back. "It's all right, man. Pull yourself together. People can see you," he said, nodding toward the glass wall of the office. CJ released him and stepped back, glancing out at the dozen or so people pretending to go about their work as they stole quick glances toward the office.

As Tony closed the blinds, CJ snatched a couple of tissues from the box on Tony's desk, blew his nose and wiped his eyes. "I'm sorry, Pop. I didn't mean to break down like that."

"It's all right, man," Tony said, resuming his seat behind his desk. "What provoked your mother to tell you this now, after all these years?"

CJ flopped back down in the chair. He ran his hands through his hair and then over his face, trying to figure out how to tell Tony the bizarre story without sounding too much like a lunatic. "It all started with this dream I had – No. It really started with the voices."

"Voices?" Tony said, giving him a sideways look.

CJ hesitated for a moment and then said, "I've been hearing voices, Pop."

Taken aback, Tony tried to hide his concern by making a joke of it. "Voices? They haven't been telling you to kill anybody or anything like that, have they?"

"Naw, Pop. Nothing like that," CJ chuckled nervously. "Really it's just this one voice and it's like . . . quoting Bible Scriptures. I've heard it a few times, but can't nobody else hear it." Then in a voice that was barely audible, he added, "I think I might be losing my mind, Pops."

"Probably just stress," Tony said. "You know that was a traumatic experience you had, seeing that boy die like that."

CJ knew Tony was just trying to console him, but that's not what he wanted. He wanted straight talk – no matter how hard it was. "Remember that dream I was talking about?" he said. "Well I think it was more than a dream. I think it was like . . ., like a vision or something."

"A vision?" Tony said, raising one eyebrow. "What kind of vision?"

As CJ told him about his dream and about Ariana, Tony stared at him in amazement. For once in his life, the glib salesman had no words to speak. CJ took advantage of his lapse and forged on, telling him everything his mother had said.

"I don't know if I'm crazy or she is. Maybe we both are," CJ admitted.

"You're not crazy," Tony assured him. "But there are some things about yourself you deserve to know."

"Like what?" CJ asked, almost afraid to hear the answer.

"Like why your mother's always been so protective of you." He paused briefly. "Dee told me that same story before we got married. I didn't believe her at first. But when you were just a little boy, I had to admit to myself that there was definitely something different about you."

"Different how?"

"You were just . . . different," Tony said. "You seemed to be smarter than the average two or three-year-old. Know what I'm sayin'?"

"What?" CJ asked. "I learned my ABCs quicker than most kids?"

"I don't even remember us teaching 'em to you," Tony said. "You just picked up a book one day and started reading it to your mother. But mainly you were more aware than other kids were – more in tune. You understood things that no toddler should have. You even knew about things that had happened before you were born, things you had no way of knowing about."

"Like what?"

"Like one day when we were looking at a photo album, you pointed out a picture of my mother and said, 'That's Grandma Coot. Grandma Coot loves me.'"

"What's so strange about that?"

"She died the year before you were born," Tony said.

"You probably showed me the picture before."

"We'd never even showed you the album before. Your mother didn't even know that my mother's nickname was Coot. That's when I started to believe there was something to what Dee had told me. Dee started to obsess over keeping you safe. She acted like she was scared for the wind to blow on you. If you fell on the playground, she'd carry on like you'd fallen out of an airplane. She didn't even want you to go to Head Start. Thought you might get germs from the other kids."

"I remember going to Head Start," CJ corrected.

"I know," Tony said. "I made her let you to go. You were too smart to be sitting up in the house under your mama all the time. She was turning you into a whiny little sissy and I couldn't have it. So I made the mistake of putting you in school."

"Mistake?"

"Yeah, big mistake. One day when I went to pick you up the teacher was looking all crazy, eyes bugged out, hair sticking up." He chuckled. "I thought you little rug rats must have been giving her a run for her money that day. Then she told me how one of the kids had been rushed to the E.R."

"What happened?"

"This little girl named Shana evidently liked you. She was always giving you, "goofy looks" as you called it. The teacher said she thought it was cute, but you didn't like it. Well this day you got mad and told Shana to stop looking at you. She told you that she could look at you anytime she wanted. Then, bam! She went blind."

"Blind? What do you mean, blind?"

56

"Blind, as in couldn't see. The teacher said she started screaming, 'I can't see. I can't see.' They rushed her to the hospital, but the doctors couldn't find anything wrong with her."

Suddenly, the blood seemed to drain out of CJ's face. If he hadn't been so dark, he would have looked pale. Instead, an ashy pallor came over his face as the memory became clear in his mind. "I just wanted her to stop looking at me."

"What?" Tony asked in alarm.

"I remember. She made me mad," he said slowly. "So I wished she couldn't see me."

"Do you remember me and your mother talking to you about it?" CJ shook his head. "We explained to you that you couldn't go around wishing bad things on people when they made you mad. We told you to take the wish back. We didn't know if you could, but hell, we didn't know what was going on. You saw how upset we were and started crying. You said you were sorry you hurt Shana and wished she could see again. The next morning, we called the hospital to see about her and they said she was fine, that her sight had returned just as mysteriously as she'd lost it."

"But, I was just a little kid."

Tony shrugged. "They never outright accused you of anything, but the director of the school suggested we keep you home and just send you back for kindergarten."

"They kicked me out of Head Start?"

"Yep. That's when we decided that your mother should start home schooling you. Now, we were *both* scared to let you out of our sight. We had to admit that you had some kind of power and we were afraid you might hurt someone or make somebody hurt you. You didn't go back to public school until Sherman started kindergarten."

"That's when I met Teddy."

"Yeah. Teddy was a lifesaver. He saw how timid you were and made it his business to look out for you."

"So, what should I do now?"

"You're gonna have to figure that out for yourself. Just remember that whatever cause you put in action you're going to have to deal with the effects. Like a man."

"I know." CJ said, wondering if Tony would have given Sherman the same warning. He doubted that he'd feel the need to remind Sherman to act like a man. He started toward the door and stopped, turning abruptly, a torturous thought tugging at his mind. "What if it's true, Pop? What if I am some kind of Messiah or something?"

"Then you have to deal with that like a man too." After a beat, he said, "You know I've never been the most religious dude in the world."

"To say the least," CJ grinned.

"Yeah," Tony smiled. "But I do read my Bible and I know that it's not unheard of for God to pluck some Joe Blow out of the crowd and send him out to deliver his word. Look at Moses. He took him right out of Pharaoh's house." He placed his hand on CJ's shoulder and looked deeply into his eyes. "You know God really does work in mysterious ways, CJ. I don't claim to know His ways and reasons. Maybe He is trying to use you. If you feel like He is then you just have to go with it. But it's gotta be your decision. I can't make it for you."

CJ had never heard Tony speak of religion with anything other than disdain. But he found this statement profoundly insightful. As if reading CJ's mind, Tony said, "You know there's a big difference between religion and spirituality. I don't mess with organized religion – I've seen too much dirt done in the name of the

58

Lord. But I do believe in God. Times change, but God don't. So, who am I to say H hasn't tapped you on the shoulder?"

"But I ain't no preacher," CJ argued.

"Thank God for small favors," Tony said with a chuckle.

When CJ left Tony's office, he felt better than he had in weeks. But the feeling didn't last. He didn't want to be a preacher and he sure didn't want to be the chosen one, whatever that meant. He just couldn't see himself out there trying to convince those hardheaded niggas to change their evil ways. Them niggers might kill me, he thought. He convinced himself that it probably was stress, just like Tony had said. Maybe if I just relax and put the whole thing out of my mind, I won't have to deal with it at all. But that was easier said than done.

CHAPTER 9

The following week CJ worked as many hours as he could get. He hoped that if he stayed busy he could rid his mind of the confusion and fear of his so-called mission, but it was utterly useless. Ariana's words so dominated his thoughts that he was driving the bus as though on autopilot. By Friday morning, his head was pounding relentlessly and he was shooting past bus stops without even slowing down. Needless to say, this elicited many loud complaints from the irate passengers. But CJ was oblivious to it all.

He was jarred back to reality when he ran a red light and nearly caused a multi-vehicle collision. Assailed by the honking of horns and the screeching of tires, CJ stomped down hard on the brakes and brought the bus to an abrupt stop. His furious passengers, shaken out of their private worlds of I-pads, smart phones, music and books, lit into him with a barrage of oral abuse that threatened to become physical. As if the verbal attacks and the commotion from outside were not enough, the annoyingly familiar voice insinuated itself into his psyche like a snake slithering up the middle of his back.

"For he bore the sin of many and made intercession for the transgressors."

This time the voice didn't stop with just one verse. It bombarded him over and over with one terrifying Bible verse after another. They rained down on him like threats or omens, each one louder than the one before, merging with the angry shouts of the passengers and the blaring horns from the traffic jam to create a torturous cacophony inside his head. CJ clasped his hands over his ears and closed his eyes. His mouth flew open in an anguished, tormented scream that seemed to emanate from the very depths of his soul. He threw open the doors of the bus, leaped out and started running down State Street like all the hounds of hell were on his tail. Some of the enraged passengers jumped off the bus after him, shouting:

"Hey, come back here!"

"Where the hell do you think you're going?"

"You better get back here and drive this bus. I'm going to be late for work."

But their words were hitting his back like pellets of hail in a winter storm. He ran until the voice stopped. Although it was early in the morning, the temperature was nearly eighty degrees and the fresh shirt he'd put on that morning was sticking to him like wet spaghetti. He was totally unaware of the odd looks he earned from pedestrians as he walked briskly down State Street with his hands buried in his pockets and his head hanging down. It wasn't often they saw a sweaty, disheveled bus driver trudging through the early morning foot traffic of the loop.

By the time CJ reached Jackson Boulevard, his head was whirling and his breath was coming in short, labored bursts. He needed to get home. He ducked into the subway, slapped his bus pass against the designated spot and pushed through the turnstile. He heard the train approaching and hurried down the stairs to the platform just as the Red Line train pulled into the station. In his confusion, he'd gone the wrong way; he needed the Blue Line train. He ran down another flight of stairs and into a tunnel that led to his desired train line.

When CJ stepped inside the tunnel, the foul stench of urine and God only knows what else smacked him in the face. His stomach began doing somersaults and the horde of people scurrying in both directions made him feel as though he had stepped into a fast forwarded video. Convinced that if he didn't pass out first, he would surely throw up, CJ started running, pushing people out of his way in a desperate attempt to reach the other end. He thought that if he could just make it to the train platform he could sit down and regroup. But when he reached the crowded platform, the benches were all occupied. He walked back and forth, growing increasingly more frantic as the long seconds ticked by. The chatter and the noise were unbearable and his headache seemed to intensify with every breath he took.

Maybe I can walk it off, he thought, feeling stranger by the second. As he walked farther down the platform, he passed a girl singer doing a not too shabby rendition of Natalie Cole's *Inseparable.* Under ordinary circumstances he would have stopped and listened for a while, but not today. He walked on, passing a saxophone player who had drawn quite a crowd. The wailing of the horn only added to the pandemonium raging in his head.

Finally, the train pulled into the station and CJ pushed and squeezed past several other passengers in his haste to get on board. He plopped down next to a fat woman who glared at him as if to say, *how dare you invade my space* and made no attempt to rearrange her bulk to accommodate him.

CJ perched on the edge of the seat, one leg sitting out in the aisle shaking uncontrollably as he ran his hand over his sweating face. After a few stops, a sudden overpowering impulse hit him and he leaped to his feet shouting, "Repent!" All eyes turned toward him. Hands grasped purses and people pulled back from him as much as they could in such a compressed space.

"God is coming to destroy the black man," CJ announced. Three white college students started cheering and barking, pumping their fists in the air. This, of course set off angry responses from the many black riders who began hurling insults and threats at the three

62

young men. "Repent and be saved!" CJ yelled over the heated shouting match that threatened to turn into a race riot right there on the train. "God sent me to warn you. These are the last days." Some black teens began throwing candy boxes and pencils at him and yelling out insults. The girls were shouting louder than the boys were and hurling profanity so vulgar and crude that many of the older women on the train just dropped their heads in shame. Most of the white adults looked scared, while the black ones looked mad. But one thing was certain. CJ had everyone's attention.

CJ was still spouting Scripture and recriminations when two CTA cops marched on board. One of them, a big redhead looked like he'd been lifting cows all his life, while his partner, a tough little loudmouth couldn't have weighed a hundred and ten pounds soaking wet. Assuming CJ was either drunk or crazy, the cops each grabbed one of his arms. The little one growled, "Come on, buddy. You gotta get off the train."

"I can't!" CJ protested, struggling against them. "I've got to tell these people. I have to warn 'em."

"Yeah, yeah, yeah," said the redhead in a tone that said *I've heard it all before*. The cops dragged him off the train to the amusement and relief of the riders. CJ continued shouting about repentance and the wrath of God as they led him toward the escalator leading up to the exit. "Listen, buddy," said Big Red. "You're gonna have to leave the train station."

"And if we catch you down here making a disturbance again," said the pipsqueak, tightening his grip and yanking CJ's arm, "we're throwing you in the shithouse."

"Get back Satan!" CJ snarled, snatching his arm free and sending the little cop flying backwards. Big Red grabbed CJ, attempting to pin his arms behind his back, but CJ, in his zeal, was too strong for the big cop and quickly broke free.

"Every word of God is pure," CJ shouted, overcome by the power of the Holy Spirit. The cops pounced on him, wrestling him

63

to the ground. Onlookers stared in shock as CJ continued his tirade. "It is the Lord your God you must fear. Fear Him and worship Him!" The cops managed to get the cuffs on him and jerked him up to his feet. "You'll know what righteousness is when God's judgment comes upon the earth!" CJ shouted over his shoulder as they marched him up the escalator and out to the waiting police car.

By the time they got CJ to the police station, he was babbling incoherently. They charged him with being drunk and disorderly and threw him in a cell to *sober up.* CJ didn't know what was happening to him. He began crying and couldn't stop, not just tears falling, but loud, gut wrenching sobs. Lost in utter despair, he prayed that God would stop this torment. He cried and prayed until he finally fell into an exhausted sleep. Everyone in the station was glad when he did.

CHAPTER 10

"Okay, Johnson. You're outta here," said the aging cop as he opened the cell door. When CJ stepped into the lobby of the police station, he was surprised to see Tony and Sherman waiting for him. Sherman looked amused, but Tony was not a happy camper.

CJ Slumped quietly in the backseat of Tony's car as his father let him have it. "I don't know if you're crazy or just plain stupid," Tony said. "What possessed you to pull a boneheaded stunt like that?" After receiving no response, Tony smacked the steering wheel and shouted, "I'm talking to you, boy."

"Yes, sir," CJ said.

"Yes, sir, my ass. Answer my question."

How could he tell him that he'd had absolutely no control over what had transpired? *He'd probably drive me straight to the nut house and kick me out on the lawn,* CJ thought. So, instead, he answered lamely, "You said I should go for it."

Tony's face turned as red as a baboon's butt. He jerked the car over to the curb and turned to look at his oldest son. "I told you to *think,*" he said, tapping his own head. "I told you to think it through and make a decision. Do you think that making an ass out of yourself in public was a wise decision?" "How did you know I was in Jail?" CJ asked.

"Lucky for you, Dave Delgado was on duty.

"Sergeant Delgado?"

Yeah. He called me to come get you. I started to let your ass stay in there and rot."

"At least you didn't have to pay any money this time," CJ said with a dopey grin on his face.

"If you think this is about the money, you're dumber than you look. I'm telling you boy, the next dumb move you make is gon' be on you. I'm through. I've raised you to be the best man I know how. But it comes a time when a parent's got to step back and let a child sink or swim on his own." After a beat, he took a deep breath and said softly. "I know you're dealing with some special issues, CJ. But . . ."

"What kind of issues?" Sherman wanted to know.

Ignoring his younger son, Tony continued. "Like I said, I know you're dealing with some stuff. But you ain't gon' never be able to stand up like a man if I'm always there to pull your fat out of the fire. And I'm not gon' be running down to no damn police station every time you get a crazy notion in your head. I've never had to do it and I damn sure ain't gon' start now. So from now on, you're on your own."

"You're kicking him out?" Sherman asked in astonishment.

"Naw, I'm not kicking him out," Tony said. "I'm just cutting him loose." He turned back to CJ with a tired smile, "Remember that old Willie Dixon song about, *I can't quit you, but I gotta put you down for a while*? Well, that's what I gotta do. Don't call me, 'cuz I ain't coming. If you make your bed rough, that's where you gotta lay. You dig?"

"Yeah, Pops. I dig."

"I don't like doing this, CJ. But sometimes, tough love is the only way. You got anything you wanna say?"

"No, sir," CJ answered. What could he say? He'd disappointed his father again. CJ hated getting reamed out it in front of Sherman, but the truth was the light and he was actually glad that Tony had taken a hard stance. Surprisingly, it gave him a feeling of strength and independence he'd never known before.

The incident on the El had convinced CJ that he was going crazy. At least he hoped he was. *Anything would be better than some mysterious assignment from God,* he thought. He called in sick every day for a week, spending most of his time in his room. He had to figure this thing out. When he did venture out of the house, it was to take long walks in the park. Somehow, being out in nature gave him consolation. Breathing the fresh air, smelling the grass, seeing the beautiful flowers and the stalwart trees that endured the torturous Chicago winters year after year and returned each spring in full bloom seemed to strengthen him.

On Sunday morning, CJ got up and got ready for church. He'd missed the last couple of Sundays and felt that a good dose of that old time religion was just what he needed. Dressed in his blue pinstriped suit, powder blue shirt and a silver and blue striped tie, he arranged a silk pocket square in his breast pocket and checked himself out in the mirror. *Not bad,* he thought, smiling at his reflection. "Not bad at all."

He reached for the Bible he always took to church and hesitated. He then opened the nightstand drawer and took out the Bible his mother had given him. He held the Bible tightly in both hands, closed his eyes and whispered, "Lord God, give me strength."

Dressed all in yellow, from her wide brimmed hat to her silk suit and matching shoes, Dee looked like Sunday morning itself as she and CJ entered Mount Zion Missionary Baptist Church. Since service hadn't started, Dee stopped to chat with a couple of ladies who ooo'd and ah'd over her outfit. CJ took his usual seat at the piano, exchanging pleasantries with the drummer. CJ had been playing the piano at church since he was thirteen and was now the leader of the choir's three-piece band. As the parishioners began filtering into the sanctuary, CJ started playing soft and low.

The guitar player slid into his seat just as the choir started lining up to march in for praise and worship. CJ gave him a nod, wondering if he and Marquita Phillips, the choir director had a thing going on. They always seemed to arrive at the same time. He really didn't care, he just hoped the guitar man wasn't playing fast and loose with her emotions. Marquita was a pretty girl, but she had weight issues that played havoc with her self-esteem. However, as the old folks used to say, that girl could, *"Sho' 'nuf sang."*

Marquita had a range that Mariah Carey could only dream of. When she belted out from the back of the church, *"Walk in the light. Beautiful light,"* CJ's fingers knew instinctively which keys to hit. He loved these old time spirituals. The congregation sang along with the choir as they marched in.

When the entire choir had assembled in the choir stand, Marquita ended the song with a flourish of her hands and grabbed the microphone from its stand, taking center stage or more accurately, center pulpit. "Amen, saints," she called. The church responded with a lukewarm, *Amen.* Unimpressed, Marquita propped her free hand on her ample hip and looked out on the church "I said, *Amen,* saints," she yelled in a louder voice. This time the church responded with a much more exuberant *Amen.* "Stand to your feet and give the Lord some praise," she ordered, waving a large handkerchief trimmed in lace of the same royal blue as the choir's robes.

When they stood, CJ jumped into a familiar fast paced tune that had everyone dancing and praising the Lord with fervor. After a bit, CJ began to play softly and the church settled down as Marquita led them in prayer. She prayed deeply and sincerely, eliciting hand raises, tears and verbal affirmations throughout the church.

As the prayer ended with a collective *Amen,* Marquita gave CJ a nod and he broke into an up-tempo song. The other musicians joined in and Marquita started rocking, clapping one hand against the microphone she held in the other. Her vibrant voice rang out as she led the choir in a rousing spiritual that brought the people right back to their feet, dancing and shouting.

Marquita flitted from one end of the wide pulpit to the other, performing as if she were on stage at the Apollo. When CJ leaned over to the mike and began singing his solo part, the enthusiasm of the crowd shot through the roof. He had a strong, smooth tenor voice that went straight to your soul. When Marquita joined her voice with his, it was like the blending of milk and honey. They sang as if no one was in the place but them and God.

Eventually, Marquita held up her hand ending the praise and worship, "Praise the Lord." When all were seated, she said, "We will now have the reading of the word from brother CJ."

CJ stepped up to the podium, taking a moment to compose himself before he began. "Whew!" he said, raising his hand high in the air. "Praise the Lord!" The church echoed his salutation.

CJ opened his Bible and looked out on the congregation. "I'm reading to you this morning from the book of Isaiah chapter sixty-one, verse one." And he began to read aloud, *"The Spirit of the Lord is on me."* As he read these words, he could feel that same spirit taking hold of him, infusing itself in him. *"He has anointed me to proclaim good news to the poor. He has sent me to heal the brokenhearted; to proclaim freedom for the prisoners and recovery of sight for the blind."*

CJ's heart was like a jackhammer in his chest. He felt overwhelmed, anointed by his own words. His eyes ablaze with the Holy Spirit, he looked out on the congregation and announced, "Today you see that holy prophecy fulfilled, for the one Isaiah is talking about is me. God has sent me to set the oppressed free and proclaim the day of the vengeance of the Lord!"

The stunned audience looked at him as if he was stone cold crazy, amazed at the words coming from his mouth. "Ain't that Sister Johnson's boy?" asked one astonished parishioner.

Seeing their dismay, CJ said, "I can understand if you don't believe me. The Bible says that a prophet is never accepted in his own hometown."

"I know CJ ain't calling hisself no prophet," one of the members remarked loud enough for all to hear.

"It's time to repent!" CJ said his laser-like gaze an indictment on them all.

"Who do you think you are?" shouted one of the deacons as angry muttering drifted throughout the sanctuary.

Reverend Damian Hightower, the pastor of the church didn't know what CJ had been smoking, but he knew he had to diffuse the situation before it got out of hand. Reverend Hightower was a handsome, caramel colored man with a ready smile and relaxed hair that looked like an old school process. He reminded CJ of an aging pimp who'd turned to God when he could no longer make his game. Tony had taught CJ to never trust a man who grinned too much or talked too much – Hightower did both.

The pastor rose from his throne-like seat in the pulpit, clapping his hands. "Amen," he said, strolling over to CJ wearing his most benevolent smile. He placed his hand on CJ's back, indicating that it was time for him to sit down.

"Thank you, Brother CJ. That was an excellent reading."

CJ shook his hand off, determined to continue. He felt the animosity mounting all around him, but he was beyond caring. When he turned back to the audience Dee saw the glazed look in his eyes and bolted toward the pulpit. "God is not pleased with you," he warned. "He wants to wipe you from the face of the earth."

70

Before Dee could reach the pulpit, Reverend Hightower grabbed CJ by the arm, attempting to force him back to his seat. CJ whirled around and pushed the preacher with both hands.

"No!" CJ shouted. "I have to tell them. I have to save them."

Hightower went hurtling back, knocking the drums over with a shattering crash. A collective gasp went up in that holy place and the horrified crowd charged the pulpit. The swarm of outraged humanity knocked Dee to the floor, attacking CJ like a pack of wild dogs, punching and kicking him as if he'd tried to steal their last crust of bread. CJ tried to fight them off, but he was no match for the infuriated Christians. Finally, he managed to break free. Fleeing for his life.

Run, Chucky. Run! Dee shouted. CJ bolted out of the church and flew down the stairs with the holy mob hot on his tail. A police car with sirens blaring and lights flashing pulled up to the curb and two cops jumped out. For once, CJ was glad to see the cops. "Thank God you're here," he said, running to them for protection.

"That's him!" shouted a familiar voice from the top of the stairs. CJ turned to see Mother Fletcher, her bony finger trembling with rage as she pointed at him. Mother Fletcher was a tall, thin, dark skinned old woman whose beady red eyes darted around suspiciously beneath a frowzy gray wig. CJ had once thought that if her hair looked worse than that wig, she was doing everyone a favor by wearing it. She was one of those hardcore, old school Christians, a fearless Bible toting warrior for the Lord who could and did find sin and wrongdoing in everything and everyone. "That's him, right there. That's the heathen who attacked my pastor," she shouted.

"No, no. She got it all wrong," CJ said, moving toward the policemen. One of them whipped out a stun gun and zapped him in the chest. CJ fell to the ground flopping around like a fish on dry land. The cops slapped the cuffs on him and threw him into the police car.

71

The following morning, CJ appeared before the judge and attempted to explain what had happened. But the more he talked the crazier he sounded. So the judge sentenced him to a thirty-day psychiatric observation at the Elgin Mental Health Center.

When the psychiatrist tried to psychoanalyze him, CJ refused to speak. After several frustrating attempts, God hardened the doctor's heart and caused him to give up. *His insurance only pays for thirty days anyway*, the doctor told himself. *I'll just leave him alone and let him cool his heels for a month.*

CJ refused to eat anything or talk to anyone. He just read his Bible and prayed. Although he was as familiar with the Bible as any other kid brought up in the church, he now immersed himself in it wholeheartedly, gaining an in-depth understanding he'd never known before. He prayed for hours on end, asking God for enlightenment, understanding and guidance. He'd often heard the term, "Let go and let God," and that's exactly what he did. He relinquished himself to God with the words, "Show me your will, Father and let it be done."

Each day that passed found him growing in understanding and self-knowledge. He began to comprehend his mission and developed a strong dedication to its completion.

CHAPTER 11

CJ stepped out of the mental hospital and winced as the bright sunlight hit his eyes. After weeks of confinement, the world around him seemed different, everything seemed bigger, brighter, smells were more intense and the noise of the traffic was louder. But it was not the world that had changed – it was him. The CJ that emerged from the Elgin Mental Health Center was a far cry from the man that had entered it only a month before. The suit he'd worn so proudly just a few weeks ago now hung on his frail frame. His hair and beard, left unattended had grown out to give him an older, more unkempt and sinister look. But as much as the outer man had changed, the inner man had been totally transformed.

CJ now had a strange, otherworldly gleam in his whiskey colored eyes. He was a new being, reborn in Christ. He could feel the power of the Lord flowing through him. He felt spiritually strong, but physically weak. He heard his stomach growl and thought it strange that while in the hospital he'd been immune to hunger, but it was now hitting him like a Mike Tyson punch. He checked his wallet and pleased to find his money and credit cards still there, set out in search of food. He knew that if he went home his mother would prepare a feast fit for a king, but he couldn't go home yet. He wondered if he ever would again.

As CJ walked the unfamiliar streets of Elgin clutching his beloved Bible in his hand, he noticed that people were staring at him and stepping off the sidewalk to avoid contact with him. Unaware that he looked like a deranged homeless person, CJ walked on until he happened to glance into the window of an electronics store. The grisly creature he saw reflected there gave him a start. "Man," he chuckled to himself, "No wonder people have been looking at me like I was the missing link."

CJ walked on until he ran across a Kmart store. The first thing he did was buy a taco to ease his gnawing hunger. After wolfing down the taco, he preceded to the men's clothing section where he got a pair of jeans, a couple of shirts and a light jacket, as well as gym shoes, socks and underwear. He also bought a backpack, sunglasses, his favorite herbal scented body wash and whatever other toiletries he might need. After leaving the store with his purchases, he continued walking until he came upon a cheap fleabag hotel with a sign that read, *Hourly Rates*.

The stench of sex, stale alcohol and unwashed bodies assaulted CJ's nose the moment he stepped into the lobby. Disreputable looking men and women loitered around the tiny lobby looking like they'd just as soon cut your heart out as say hello. As he approached the front desk, a morbidly obese white woman eyed him suspiciously from behind the bars that protected her from her unsavory clientele.

"I'd like a room," CJ said.

"For how long?" she asked in a rude, gravelly voice, a cigarette dangling from the corner of her mouth.

"One night."

"Forty bucks." CJ counted out the money and laid it on the desk. The clerk's grimy nailed hand quickly snaked out through the opening under the bars, snatched up the money and stuffed it down the front of her grungy food stained T-shirt. She then slapped a key down on the desk. "Room two seventeen. Elevator's over there," she said indicating with a nod of her head.

"Don't I need to sign something?" CJ asked.

"Don't worry about it," she said, taking a long drag on her cigarette and blowing out a steady stream of smoke. "I trust you."

Once inside the shabby room, CJ shut the door and locked it. A quick survey showed a bed, a dresser with one drawer missing and a small TV bolted down to a stand. Afraid of what might be living on the flowered bedspread, CJ pulled it back before throwing his bags on the surprisingly clean sheet. He then stripped off his clothes and jumped into the shower. He scrubbed his hair and body vigorously with the fragrant body wash, hoping to wash away the institutional smell of the hospital. When he was done, he grabbed a rough towel from the rack and dried himself off. He then slipped into his new boxers, shaved and set about trying to restore some kind of order to his hair.

Feeling amazingly refreshed after his shower, CJ located the phone book and plopped down on the side of the bed. After searching the book, he picked up the phone and ordered a pizza, the taco at Kmart having only served as a teaser. He then found the number to Southwest Airlines and dialed it, making a reservation for the next flight leaving for Los Angeles. He then dialed the hotel operator and placed a person-to-person collect call to Teddy.

Teddy was thrilled to hear CJ's voice. "Hey, man, how you doin'? I called your house and Mama Dee said you were in the hospital. You all right?"

"Yeah, I'm good." CJ said, wasting no time on preliminaries. "You still got that room with my name on it?"

"Hell yeah," Teddy replied excitedly. "When are you coming?" CJ gave him his flight information. "Cool," Teddy said. "I'll be there."

"Cool," CJ said and hung up the phone. He flopped back on the bed, waiting for his pizza to arrive. He had no idea what lay ahead of him; all he knew was that he had to get the heck out of Dodge. Convinced that he was making the right move, he decided not to over analyze the situation, but to just let the Lord lead him. And right now, He was leading him to California.

CHAPTER 12

As CJ stepped off the plane at LAX, he grinned at the sight of Teddy dressed in a pink polo shirt and shorts. He wore low top sneakers with no socks and of course, the mandatory Hollywood sunglasses. The friends shook their special handshake, hugged and slapped each other on the back as if they hadn't seen each other in twenty years. They then stepped back and appraised one another. Teddy was amazed at how thin CJ was. *Damn, he looks bad,* Teddy thought.

"Hollywood, boom, boom, boom," said CJ. "Look at you.

Teddy struck a pose, sticking out one well-muscled leg. "If you got 'em, flaunt 'em," he said with a chuckle. Then, in a more serious tone, "You done lost some weight, homeboy. What was you in the hospital for?"

"Wasn't nothing," CJ said, dismissing the question with a smile.

Teddy could see that there was something different about CJ, something more than just his weight. "Come on," he said, throwing his arm around CJ's shoulders. "Let's get out of here. Where's your luggage?"

"This is it," CJ said, tugging on his backpack. Teddy couldn't hide his shock. CJ was the guy that had brought two suitcases and a duffel bag to summer camp. He decided that once they got back to the house he'd find out what was going on.

As they sped along the 405 Freeway Teddy slipped a CD into the sound system and the legendary voice of Marvin

Gaye sprang to life filling the SUV with the mellow sound of What's Going On. Teddy began singing along with Marvin and glanced at CJ, surprised that he had not joined in. Teddy knew this was one of his favorite songs, but CJ seemed distracted as though he wasn't even aware that the song was playing.

CJ wasn't much of an outdoorsman, but he did appreciate the beauty of nature and the magnificence of the Southern California landscape captivated him. The sky seemed bluer and clearer here. Yeah, he thought, I could get used to this. He turned to Teddy and said, "So, this is L.A. I feel like I'm riding through a picture postcard."

"Yeah," Teddy said. "It's something else, ain't it? Course now, we don't actually live in Los Angeles proper. We live in the valley. It's sorta like a suburb of L.A. Out there where Michael Jackson used to have his mansion." CJ just nodded and smiled, still awed by the incredible beauty of nature. "I didn't tell Dusty you was coming," Teddy continued. "She gon' shit when she sees you. You know she been in love with you since she was five."

"Get out of here, man," CJ said modestly.

"I shit you not. When she was in junior high she used to write your name all over her notebook." CJ laughed. He'd known that Teddy's little sister had a crush on him, but he never thought anything of it. Teddy continued to sing along with the music and CJ joined in. It almost seemed like old times. Almost.

When they pulled into Teddy's driveway CJ let out a low whistle. Gloriously colored flowers and lush shrubbery graced the long walkway leading to an exquisite gray house trimmed in white. A magnificent picture window looked out on a manicured lawn surrounded by a white picket fence. "Man!" CJ said in astonishment. "You ain't seen nothing yet," Teddy said.

CJ looked up and down the street at the expensive homes and impeccable lawns. But what struck him the most was how clean and quiet the street was. There was no music. No children playing. No one sitting out on the front. It looked kind of spooky.

"Where is everybody?"

"It's the middle of the day," Teddy mused. "Everybody's at work."

"What a concept," CJ cracked as Teddy unlocked the door.

As they stepped into the spacious foyer, Teddy flipped on the air conditioner. "It's hotter'n the doorknobs in hell up in here. Let's get some air going up in this piece."

As they entered the stylishly appointed living room, CJ felt his feet sink down into the luxurious carpeting. The carpet and the drapes were the same dusty rose color as the walls, obviously the work of a professional decorator. The centerpiece of the room was an enormous burgundy colored sectional sofa. A large cherry wood coffee table that looked to be hand crafted, sat in front of the couch and on either side of the couch were lamps in the form of African statues. The regal male figure stood tall and the female sat majestically on an end table. Artwork by Faith Ringgold, Annie Lee, and Jacob Lawrence adorned the walls.

CJ walked over to the huge fireplace and leaned back with his elbows resting on the mantle. "This is nice, Teddy," he said, nodding his head in approval. "This is real nice." As he continued to survey the room, Dusty burst in through the front door, calling excitedly.

"Teddy. Teddy. Wait 'til I tell you hear." Dusty, an exuberant cinnamon colored beauty, dressed in a gauzy top and black leggings sprang into the room. She wore long golden braids and earrings that hung to her shoulders. Dusty stopped short at the sight of CJ. "CJ!" she shouted, dropping her oversized shoulder bag to the floor and leaping up around his neck. Her many bangle bracelets jingled musically on her arm as CJ spun her around. When her feet were back on the floor, Dusty slapped at CJ's chest, chastising him. "Why didn't you tell us you were coming?"

CJ shot a quick look over her shoulder at Teddy, who stood there with a silly grin on his face. "Surprise."

"You knew he was coming and you didn't tell me?"

"He just called me last night," Teddy said in his own defense.

"Look at you," CJ said, giving her the once over. You're looking good, girl."

Dusty whipped off her Prada sunglasses and did a little spin, stopping in a perfect model's pose, her dainty feet shod in leather sandals decorated with cowrie shells. "Thank you. You're looking pretty good yourself," she said, being kind. Actually, she thought he looked like he'd just gotten out of rehab. "So how long are you staying?" she asked pulling him over to the couch to sit down.

"I don't know," CJ replied. "Just taking it one day at a time."

"How long do you got off?" Teddy inquired. "A week? Two?"

CJ smiled inscrutably, "Something like that." He didn't even know if he still had a job. He turned the topic back to Dusty. "You sounded like you had some good news when you came in."

"I do," she said, springing to her feet. She stood in front of them as if making an announcement on stage. "Okay, I just got back

80

from this meeting, right? You may have heard of the gentleman I met with. I think his name is uh . . .," she tapped her cheek, pretending to think. "Spielberg. That's it. *Steven Spielberg!*" Just saying the name made her crouch down and squeal, clenching up her fists, face and body, in excitement.

"Get out of here," said CJ, clearly impressed.

"I swear," she said, flipping her braids back from her face. "He just walked up to me on the lot the other day and told me how impressed he was with my work. Then he asked me if I'd be available to meet with him about a project he was doing in Ontario." She clasped her hands to her chest in astonishment. "Am I available? Hellooo. I'd walk through hell with gasoline draws on to work on a Spielberg film. But I was cool," she said proudly. She then slapped Teddy on the knee and assumed a sophisticated air. "I gave him my manager's card and told him to have his office call."

"When did you get a manager?" Teddy asked.

Smiling, she rummaged through her purse and handed them each a business card that read, Benjamin A. Weinstein and Associates, Professional Management.

CJ looked at the address on the card in astonishment and said, "Beverly Hills?"

"It's a mailbox address," she said, offhandedly. "Everybody out here uses them. Call the number, Teddy."

Teddy pulled out his cell phone and dialed the number on the card. Dusty's cell phone rang. She cleared her throat and stood up straight, shaking her hair back before answering in her most professional sounding voice, "Weinstein and Associates." Teddy grinned, making no response as she continued with her imaginary conversation. "Dusty Montgomery? Yes, we represent Ms. Montgomery. Of course. Yes. I'm sure she'd be delighted to take a meeting with Mr. Spielberg. Yes, that sounds fine. Thank you, for calling." She then clicked the phone off, grinning like the cat that ate the canary.

"You lil' witch," Teddy said proudly.

CJ applauded, "You sure you don't want to be an actress? You got the chops for it."

"No way," she replied. "Actresses don't get *any* respect in this town. Besides, you're looking at the *head* hairstylist on Spielberg's next movie," she said, taking a grand bow.

"My girl!" shouted Teddy leaping up and wrapping her in a big bear hug.

"That's great!" CJ said, rising to give her a hug.

After they finished showering her with congratulations, Dusty asked, "Did Teddy show you the pool, CJ?"

"Naw, but I heard about it."

"Hope you brought your swimming trunks," Dusty said, sidling up close to him with a naughty glint in her eye, "Then again, with all those trees in the back yard, a person could go skinny dipping if he was so inclined."

"All right, then," Teddy said, obviously displeased with his sister's brazen flirtation. He placed his hand on her shoulders, turning her away from CJ. "I got a good idea. Why don't you show him the music room?"

"Yeah," CJ cracked. "Otherwise known as the garage."

"I beg your pardon," Dusty said planting her hands on her hips. "Come on." She grabbed CJ's hand and pulled him through the dining room and down a hallway that stopped at a set of impressive wooden doors.

Dusty threw open the doors and CJ stepped into a fantastic media room the likes of which he'd never even imagined. "Whoa!" CJ said with his eyes fixed on the enormous flat screen TV mounted on the wood paneled wall. Another wall was all mirrors. Plush leather sofas and chairs surrounded a huge leather recliner that graced the center of the room.

"Would you care for a drink?" Dusty asked, waving toward a bar that would put many nightclubs to shame.

Teddy plopped down in the luxurious recliner. "This is the Captain's chair," he said, patting the arm of the chair. "This is where I sit to control this mother ship." He picked up a remote control from a table and pointed it at an elaborate sound system ensconced in a wooden entertainment center, complete with double turntables, a microphone and a sea of CDs, 45s and LPs. He clicked a button and music seemed to come from every nook and cranny of the room.

CJ snapped his fingers in time to the beat, nodding his head and grooving with the music. "Man," he said, plucking Marvin Gaye's Trouble Man album from the shelving unit. "Aw, Teddy, this is slick." He marveled at the array of gold and platinum records that graced the walls alongside photos of stars like Whitney Houston, Janet Jackson and Madonna. In every picture, posed with the stars was the same grinning man who looked remarkably like Teddy. CJ rightly assumed this to be the recently deceased father.

As if reading CJ's mind, Teddy said sarcastically, "Yeah that's him. Brian Montgomery. The man himself.

"Ready for the pièce de résistance?" Dusty said, giving Teddy a secret little smile." She led CJ to the other side of the room where stood a spectacular electronic keyboard synthesizer that took his breath away.

CJ slid behind the keyboard like the seat was a magnet and he had a hip pocket full of tokens. "Aw, man! You know how much this thing costs?" he said, running his fingers along the keyboard. He caressed the fine wood lovingly as Teddy clicked off the music and joined them.

"I knew you'd love it," Teddy said. This sucker is more like a mini studio than a piano. You can compose music on here; arrange it, edit it. Everything."

"I know," CJ said, admiring the incredible instrument.

"It's like it's a whole orchestra in there, CJ. It's got a string section, guitars, drums, horns, all at the touch of a button," said Dusty, waving her hand toward the instrument as if doing a car commercial.

"You can even program his bad boy to get that classic Motown sound," said Teddy. "I'm telling you, it can do everything 'cept take out the garbage and wash your dirty draws."

"Oh, well this must be the old model," CJ said, pushing away from the instrument as if appalled. Teddy laughed; glad to see him joking in his old familiar way. CJ had dreamed of an instrument like this, but never in his wildest dreams did he think he'd ever have one at his disposal. "Y'all might not never get rid of me now," he said, running his fingers over the keys and toying with the various buttons and dials.

"Ooooo!" Dusty squealed, plopping herself down next to CJ. She hadn't seen him hit the record button. "Play something for us, CJ," she said, linking her arm with his and resting her head on his shoulder.

"If you insist." CJ said with a put upon sigh, his fingers already tickling the keys. As he sang *If This World Were Mine,* he felt a calmness and completeness with the music that he hadn't felt in a long time. At the end of the song, he gave Dusty a mischievous smile as a series of her recorded "Ooooo" at various levels and intensities concluded the song. "That's me!" she screamed. "You're the bomb, CJ," she said, planting a big kiss on his lips. CJ pulled back, blushing as she gazed lovingly into his eyes.

84

Teddy could feel the steam rising off her from where he stood. "Okay," he said, clapping his hands to break the spell, "How about I show CJ the pool while you go to the store and get something for dinner? I'm starvin' like Marvin and we're looking like Old Mother Hubbard's cupboard up in this piece."

"What do you want, CJ?" Dusty asked, smiling adoringly at him. "Ever had guacamole?"

"I was thinking we might throw a few steaks on the barbey," Teddy said. "We can eat out by the pool. You know, just kick it around a little bit."

"Sounds good to me," CJ said.

"Great," Dusty said. "I'll make a big pitcher of margaritas and my guacamole dip."

"That's all you know how to make," Teddy scoffed.

"Well if you know that, Mr. Smarty Pants, why don't you get married? We need us a wife up in this camp." They all burst out laughing. Dusty was the first to recover. "Okay, I'll run to Ralph's. Be back in a flash," she said. "Anything in particular y'all want?"

"Beer," Teddy ordered.

"I'm good," said CJ.

"Cool," Dusty said. She blew them a kiss and flew back out the double doors.

CJ smiled, shaking his head. "That sister of yours is a ball of fire."

"If you snooze, you lose out here," Teddy said as he walked out of the room and down the hall toward the kitchen with CJ trailing him. The first thing CJ saw when they entered the kitchen was the large island in the middle of the room. Over it hung an array of pots and pans that looked as though fire had never seen their bottoms. The wall housing the sink and marble countertops was made entirely of red brick and the floor of marble tiles. "Whoa!" he said, admiring the built in stainless steel appliances. He opened the giant double door refrigerator and chuckled, finding only an ancient bowl of salad, a few bottles of water and a couple of bottles of Heineken.

"Might as well grab them last two beers," Teddy said. CJ got the beers and followed Teddy through sliding glass doors and out onto the patio where sat a white bamboo patio table with matching chairs and a huge umbrella over it for shade.

CJ looked out over the spacious yard and saw what Dusty had meant by, "So many trees." A forest of trees, many of them bearing lemons, oranges and grapefruit formed an impenetrable wall around the property. CJ stared at the trees in amazement. He'd never seen actual fruit growing on a tree before and it blew his mind. He felt tears welling up in his eyes and shook his head, surprised that something so simple could affect him so strongly. He opened his beer, took a swig and sat down at the table.

"Man!" he said. "This is nice, Teddy. I could sit out here all day."

"How 'bout that pool?" Teddy said. CJ had been so enamored with the trees that he hadn't even noticed the spectacular, kidney shaped pool with its black onyx bottom.

"Aw, man!" CJ said. "You must think you done died and gone to buppy heaven."

"Buppy? Shee-it. I know white men that would die to live like this," Teddy corrected.

"Excuse me, Mr. Modesty."

Teddy smiled contritely, "I'm just saying."

"You know I'm just messing with you, man. You deserve all the good fortune you can get. I'm happy for you, man. You and Dusty both. Y'all deserve this."

Teddy grinned, "Now you sound like the CJ I know."

"Who did I sound like before?" CJ asked.

"I don't know," Teddy said, scratching his head. "When you first got off the plane you were acting kinda weird. I thought something was wrong."

"I'm cool," CJ said with a smile. It touched him to see how in tune his friend was with him. "Maybe it's just culture shock. Anyway, I'm glad I came. It's good to see y'all living so well." He was beginning to feel like his old self again. Being with old friends in this picturesque setting had him feeling incredibly relaxed. He thought about telling Teddy everything that had happened to him, but was afraid he wouldn't believe him. No, he couldn't tell him yet.

"Yeah, the living is good." Teddy said nodding his head. "People make good money and they live well."

"So, what are you planning on doing?" CJ asked. "Just live off your investments and become a beach bum?"

"You know me better than that," Teddy said. "I'm still a hardworking Chicago boy at heart. I'm just not gon' be working for nobody else. I'm thinking about leasing me a couple of limos and going into the limousine business."

"That sounds like a good idea," CJ said.

"Sho' would be nice if I had somebody to help me with the driving, though." CJ gave him a skeptical look. "I'm serious."

CJ smiled. How could he tell his friend that the only thing he had on his mind was figuring out how he was going to bring the word of God to his brothers and sisters, how he was going to get

87

them to change without scaring them with the wrath of God that was
hanging over their heads like the sword of Damocles.

CHAPTER 13

After a scrumptious dinner of steak, baked potatoes and Caesar
salad, Dusty browsed through a magazine as they relaxed on the
patio, drinking margaritas and talking about old times. After a while,
Dusty closed her magazine and stood. She gave herself a good
stretch, flinging her arms out and rolling her neck. "Mmm. This has
been fun, boys, but I gotta go. I need to shower and change before

Chad gets here."

"Who's Chad?" CJ asked. "Your boyfriend?"

"Just a friend. He's taking me to an industry party, so we can
network. You gotta meet people in this business. It's all about who
you know."

Dusty liked going out with Chad. He was fun, he knew
everybody and he was low key. She figured he was gay, because
he'd never hit on her and she didn't know of him having a woman.
But he carried himself like a man – and he always treated her with
the utmost respect. However, no one was really sure of Chad's
sexual preference because he kept his personal business to himself.

Teddy, however, had immediately assumed Chad was gay when he learned that he was a beautician. "Oh, my God," Teddy lisped, affecting an effeminate, limp wristed manner. "Is he bringing Lance? You know Lance is my absolute fave."

"I can't stand your friend," Dusty said to CJ, laughing at her outrageous brother who now sat primly with his knees pressed together, pursing his lips and batting his eyes. Pointing a warning finger at Teddy, she said, "Don't embarrass me in front of my company, Teddy. If he gets here before I get back, just offer him a drink and try not to show how politically incorrect you can be. CJ you'll keep him in check, won't you?"

"Yes, ma'am," CJ said, saluting her. "Officer CJ at your service."

As Dusty opened the sliding glass door to go back inside, Teddy waved at her, still in character. "You hurry back girl, before mother snaps up all that trade," he said, snapping his fingers in a "Z" formation.

Dusty rolled her eyes, shaking her head at his hopelessness, "Help him, Lord," she said, laughing as she stepped inside and shut the door.

"You're a fool. You know that?" CJ laughed.

"She knows I'm just messing with her. Chad's cool. He owns his own beauty shop."

"Sounds like an enterprising young man," CJ said.

"He's not that young," replied Teddy. "He's got to be knocking the hell out of forty. He seems to have taken Dusty under his wing, hooked her up with that TV gig she's got. I have to admit that I feel better with her out there running the streets with him, rather than by herself. It's some dog ass people out here in la-la land."

90

"Couldn't be that bad."

"Shee-it. Don't let the palm trees and movie stars fool you, man. These suckers out here are just as treacherous as they are in Chicago. More so. In Chicago, you know to be on your guard. Out here, these young girls get stars in their eyes and fall into a false sense of security."

"What's that?" CJ asked, looking up at a red light flashing near the sliding glass door.

"The doorbell. It flashes out here, 'cuz you can't hear it with the door closed."

"Now that's slick," CJ said as Teddy rose to answer the door. CJ browsed through Dusty's magazine until Teddy returned with Chad, a tall, light skinned, bald headed man with diamond studs in both ears. Chad strode in looking like he'd just stepped off the cover of GQ magazine in his white slacks, form-fitting shirt and expensive looking sports jacket. One look at him and CJ could tell that this brother spent a lot of time at the gym.

CJ rose from his seat and Teddy introduced them. "CJ this is Chad. Chad this is my homeboy, CJ. He just got here from Chicago." A gold bracelet dangled on Chad's wrist as he gripped CJ's hand in a firm handshake.

"Welcome to the Southland, CJ. Nice to meet you," he said in a deep baritone voice.

"Nice meeting you too," CJ said. "Where are you from?" Teddy had already hipped CJ that this was the first thing anyone asked, seeing that hardly anyone was from Los Angeles.

"I'm from Detroit," Chad said, taking a seat. He crossed his long legs casually and peered into the remains of Dusty's margarita glass. "Looks like you all have been having a party."

"Naw," Teddy said, "Just catching up. You want a margarita?"

"No thanks," he said. "But I'll take a beer if you have one."

"No problem," Teddy said, heading into the house.

"So, you're from Detroit," CJ said, "That makes us practically neighbors."

"Yes," Chad said." The great Midwest. Detroit is a great place to be from – and I got *from* there as soon as I could." They were enjoying a good laugh when Teddy returned with three bottles of Heineken.

Chad opened his beer, turned it up and guzzled several gulps, "Ahhh," he said, placing the beer on the table. "Yeah, I worked on the assembly line at Ford for a while, but I got tired of that real quick. I've been out here about ten years now and I love it. The people are a little flaky," he said, flipping his hand from side to side. "But the weather is great.
I really can't complain. So, how long are you here for, CJ?"

Teddy spoke before CJ could answer, "We're trying to get him to stay."

"You should," Chad encouraged. "I've got friends from Chicago and they love it out here. Are you an actor?"

"Nooo," CJ said, holding up a hand in denial. "I can *act* like a fool, that's about all."

"Too bad," Chad said. "You certainly have the looks for it. Doesn't he, Ted."

"Yes, I think he's absolutely adorable," Teddy said, batting his eyes at CJ.

CJ shot Teddy a warning look. Chad just laughed, waving it off dismissively, "Don't worry about it, CJ. I'm used to Mr. Montgomery's alleged sense of humor."

"So, what do you do, Chad? Are you an actor?" Teddy had already told him that Chad was a beautician, but he just wanted to keep the conversation flowing.

Chad laughed, "Lord, no. I guess you could say I'm an entrepreneur." He pulled a business card from his pocket and handed it to CJ. CJ looked at the card, which read, *Mr. Chadwick's House of Style.*

"Wait a minute," CJ said, picking up the magazine. He flipped through a few pages and stopped. He glanced down at the page and back at Chad. "You're Mr. Chadwick!" he exclaimed.

"Guilty as charged," Chad said with a slight bow of his head.

CJ thrust the magazine under Teddy's nose. "They have a whole write up in here about Mr. Chadwick and his salon. Look at this," he said, pointing to a picture of Chad in the elaborate House of Style. "This is off the chain."

"You never told me you were famous," Teddy said.

"Fame is such an over rated word," said Chad as if he was bored by the whole thing.

"It's good of you to take an interest in Dusty," CJ said.

"I see a lot of potential in that girl. I can see her going places in this business and I'd like to help her get there. You'd be surprised at what kind of low lifes they have out here, just waiting to prey on a naïve young woman like Dusty."

The sliding glass door opened and Dusty stepped out onto the patio in a sleek black dress that draped softly over her curves. She carried a sequined black sweater over her arm and wore her braids pinned up in an exotic style. On her feet were stiletto sling backs. The men all stood. CJ stared in amazement at the transformation of the earth child who had greeted him earlier to the chic woman of sophistication that stood before him now.

"Wow!" said Chad, lifting her hand up over her head and spinning her around. "That dress is fantastic."

"You like?" she asked, looking from one smiling face to another.

"What's not to like?" CJ said. "You look great in that dress. Or should I say the dress looks great on you?"

"You lookin' good, baby girl," Teddy said.

"Why don't you guys come with us," Chad said. "I know you'll enjoy yourselves."

"Yes," Dusty said. "Come with."

"How about a rain check," Teddy said. "CJ's probably tired."

"Maybe another time," CJ added.

"I'll hold you to that," Chad said. "You have my card, CJ. If there's anything I can do for you while you're here, just give me a call."

"Thanks," CJ said, tucking the card into his pocket and extending his hand. "I'll do that."

The men shook hands, and Dusty kissed CJ and Teddy on their cheeks as Chad finished off his beer. He took Dusty's sweater from her arm and gently placed it around her shoulders. "Don't worry, Ted," he said, placing his hand on the small of Dusty's back and guiding her through the door ahead of him. "I'll get your little sister back at a reasonable hour."

"Y'all have fun," CJ said as Chad followed Dusty into the house and shut the door.

"So, now that the children are gone," Teddy said as he cleared the table. "What are we grown folks gon' do?" CJ slid the door open and followed Teddy inside. "Wanna check out the House of Blues?" Teddy asked, dumping the dishes into the sink and the bottles in the trash. "Or we could go to the . . ."

"I thought we might check out Compton or South Central," CJ said.

"For what? Ain't nothin' out there but a bunch of po' ass niggas. You could have stayed on the west side for that."

CJ couldn't explain it, but for some reason he had a burning desire to check out the hood. "Just thought we could check it out."

"CJ." Teddy said with a defeated look on his face. "If you want to travel in rarified circles, you gotta get that ghetto shit out of your head. Ain't nothin' there for you."

"Just humor me. Okay?"

"Forget about it," Teddy said, "I'm not gon' get my ass shot off just because you're feeling homesick for the ghetto. No way, Jose."

CHAPTER 14

As they drove down the streets of South Central L.A., CJ got a look at the underbelly of the City of Angels. Masked with alluring palm trees and Southern California charm by day, South Central lay naked in the darkness of night, crawling with a varied assortment of street vermin; gangbangers, hookers and other predatory types. No glamour here; just the stark reality of a sub-culture enmeshed in poverty and self-inflicted genocide.

After passing a slew of beauty shops, barbecue joints, liquor stores and churches, CJ spotted a small nightclub sitting at the corner of the block between a fried fish joint and an alley. The large neon sign on top read, Shenanigans and featured a neon couple that flickered on and off, making them look as if they were dancing to the hard-core rap music that wafted out of the little club. A group of thugs, players and various other persons of ill repute congregated outside the joint all dressed in their weekend finery, smoking, laughing and talking trash. Something about the place made CJ want to stop. "Pull over," he said.

"You gotta be kidding," Teddy said as he pulled the Escalade over and parked across the street from the club. "This place is a bucket of blood. Somebody gets killed up in there damn near every weekend." They watched as one car after another pulled up to the curb and Antoine, a scrawny twelve-year-old in an oversized white T-shirt, sagging jeans and sneakers that probably cost more than CJ made in a day ran up to the passenger side window and after a brief conversation, exchanged something in his hand for what the passengers had in theirs. After purchasing dope as casually as if they were driving through an In 'N Out burger restaurant, the cars drove off and Antoine returned to his perch on the sidewalk.

"Told you," Teddy said in a bored voice. "Just like home. The ghetto is the ghetto, no matter where you go."

"Yeah, a carnivorous beast that eats it's young."

"So, are we gonna sit here all night, or what?"

"Be cool," CJ said. "I just want to get a lay of the land before we go in."

"Go in? I'm not going up in that hellhole. You must be crazy." When CJ made no further comment, Teddy let out an exasperated sigh and slumped down in his seat. He knew it was no use arguing with CJ once he made up his mind. They watched as several prostitutes strolled the block, jumping in and out of cars as Antoine continued slinging dope with an expertise that said this was not his first night on the block.

A tall, dark chocolate-skinned man with a trim, hard muscled build caught CJ's eye. His complexion had a Caribbean smoothness to it that made one wonder where he was from. Dressed in black pants and a black silk shirt, he stood near the alley apart from the others watching the boy intently. This was Hawk, a notorious dope dealer. Hawk always wore black, thinking that the black clothes on his black skin made him virtually invisible in the night. He wore his naturally wavy hair pulled back into a ponytail that hung to his shoulders and rarely spoke more than was necessary. However, his dark eyes were never still, constantly darting back and forth, suspicious of everyone. Although disturbingly handsome, Hawk wore a perpetual scowl that he had mastered in prison to keep the booty bandits at bay.

97

Antoine ran over to Hawk, grinning proudly, "We makin' some dollars out here, tonight," he said, reaching into his pocket. Hawk gave him a stern look that said you know better and strolled casually toward the alley. The boy followed Hawk into the alley, pulled a wad of bills out of his pocket and handed it to him. Hawk stuffed the money into his pocket and looked around cautiously before taking a rusty old coffee can from a pile of trash and prying it open. He reached into the can and pulled out several small packages of dope which he slipped to Antoine. He then crushed the can with his foot and threw it back on the trash pile as Antoine ran back to his post and continued putting in work.

Carla Cantrell, a withered up looking crack whore with white lips and sores on her gaunt face, stumbled up to the group looking wild eyed and crazy. Dressed in jeans that danced on her bony behind and a shirt that looked like she hadn't washed it since Reagan was in office, Carla struggled to hang onto a good-sized puppy that wiggled and squirmed in her arms. She had her nappy hair pulled back into a ponytail that sat down on her neck with clumps of hair sticking out from beneath the rubber band. "Anybody wanna buy a puppy?" she asked, displaying teeth that looked like someone had hit her in the mouth with a brick.

Some of them laughed, while others simply ignored her. Hawk eyed her with utter contempt. "Whose dog you done stole, Carla?"

Carla trotted over to him, barely hanging on to the discontented canine. "I ain't stole nothin'," she said. "He followed me." This brought such laughter from the crowd that even Hawk had to smile in contemptuous amusement.

"Get your triflin' ass out of here before I call the cops on you myself," Hawk said as Baby Herc, Shenanigans' oversized bartender stepped out to have a smoke. Dressed in shorts and a loose fitting shirt that did little to hide the massive muscles bulging in his chest and arms, Herc was an imposing figure, tall and big with a gentle smile that belied his intimidating appearance.

Carla held the puppy up in front of Hawk's face. "Come on, Hawk, just give me one rock and you can have him. Ain't he cute?"

"Get outta my face," Hawk growled, smooshing her in the face with his big hand. Carla stumbled back and fell to the ground, releasing her grip on the puppy who quickly scampered away. Frantic, Carla rose to her knees, crawling after the dog and trying to stand at the same time. The onlookers screamed with laughter, but CJ was seething with anger. A cruel smile tugged at Hawk's mouth as he rammed his boot into Carla's backside sending her sprawling on her face. "Get your stankin' ass outta here and leave that damn dog alone," Hawk said, yanking her up by the back of her neck. "You crack head bitches make me sick," he said, slapping her hard across the face. That was the straw that broke CJ's back.

"Hey!" CJ yelled, jumping out of the SUV.

"No, CJ!" Teddy shouted. "You ain't got nothing to do with this." But CJ was gone. Teddy jumped out and ran after him. "Come back here, CJ. You gon' get us killed!"

As CJ charged across the street heading straight for Hawk, the veteran criminal recognized him as a would-be do-gooder and his hand went immediately to his gun. Seeing this, Herc stepped forward, intercepting CJ before he reached Hawk. "My man," said Herc, grabbing CJ's hand and shaking it. This threw CJ off, but before he could regroup, the big man threw his arm around his shoulder and started walking him toward the club. Teddy immediately fell in step on the other side of CJ and the two men led him away from Hawk.

"Thanks, man," Teddy said, shaking Herc's hand.

"Thanks for what?" CJ said, burning with rage.

"For saving your ass," Teddy replied.

"No problem," said Herc. I was just saving my job. One more shooting 'round here and they're liable to shut this joint down." He then turned to CJ. "Man, you was about to run up on more hell than you was ready to deal with. Do you know who that is?"

"Yeah," said CJ. "He's a woman beater and a coward."

"He ain't hardly no coward," Herc said. "That's Hawk and he'd just as soon kill a nigga as look at him." CJ glared at Hawk who looked back with an arrogant smirk on his face.

"They call me Baby Herc," said Herc, extending his hand.

CJ shook it, his eyes still fixed on Hawk. "I'm CJ. This is Teddy."

"Why don't y'all come on in and let me buy you a drink," said Herc. CJ was still mad as they followed Herc into the club. They stopped short at the sight of the humongous bouncer looming in the entryway. He was a fearsome looking replica of Herc with a scruffy beard and a bald head. He wore a tank top that displayed his massive tattooed muscles.

"Ten dollars," growled the gatekeeper, holding out a hand the size of a tennis racket.

"They're with me," said Herc, gently moving the bouncer aside. CJ and Teddy eased past the bouncer and followed Herc into the club where lights were flashing, music was pumping and people were partying as if their lives depended on it. They all seemed to be having a great time, but CJ could feel the desperation hidden beneath many of those bright smiles.

The place was twice the size of Mac Daddy's and hosted a younger crowd. Although there were a few old heads sprinkled in here and there as well as the mandatory white girls, you're bound to find wherever black men congregate. Booths lined the walls and small tables filled every space not taken up by the immense bar and generous dance floor. A live deejay kept the music flowing and the distinct odor of marijuana hovered over the scent of sweat and booze.

Weaving their way through the throng of partiers, Herc led CJ and Teddy to a booth off to the side of the bar. "Let me get y'all some drinks," Herc said. "Beer all right?"

"Works for me," Teddy said.

"I'll be right back," said Herc heading toward the bar where the customers were stacked three deep and Cheyenne, the owner's gorgeous young wife was busier than a one-legged man in a butt kicking contest. Cheyenne's pecan colored face shone under the lights of the bar, her dimpled smile and long black ponytail giving her the illusion of being much younger than her thirty-two years.

Cheyenne's paraplegic husband Sammy Rocquemore held court from a table near the other end of the bar. Sammy kept a vigilant eye on everything going on while enthralling several men with the story of the paralyzing injury he received while saving his fellow marines in the war. Some of the old timers knew that the cops had actually shot Sammy in the back, claiming they thought he had a gun. But they went along with the tale, hoping to get a free drink out of the deal.

"Can you hold it down for a few more minutes, Chy? I need to talk to these guys," Herc whispered with a backward nod toward CJ and Teddy. Sammy caught the nod and his suspicious gaze honed in on the pair instinctively.

Confined to a wheelchair for the past ten years, Sammy was an angry and hostile ex-con in his mid-forties who seldom had a good word for anyone. And these two handsome young men hit him the wrong way the moment they walked in. They looked out of place and he figured they must be up to no good. If they're thinking about robbing me they better think again, the paranoid bar owner thought as he adjusted himself in his chair and repositioned the .44 Magnum that sat prominently in his waistband. Sammy always kept his pistol in full view, in case anyone was foolish enough to think they could disrespect him because of his condition. Though his legs were useless, Sammy's arms and upper body were tremendously powerful and his reputation for violence, legendary. And of course, he had Jimbo there, ready to back his play.

Flashing a smile that would melt a polar ice cap, Cheyenne said, "Okay, but make it quick. I'm up to my ass in alligators."

Herc returned to the booth, placed a beer before each man and sat down next to Teddy who asked, "Am I hallucinating or is that your twin out there at the door?"

Herc laughed. "Yeah, that's my brother Derik. I'm Erik. Erik Strong. They call him Big Jimbo. So, where y'all from?"

"Chicago," Teddy said. So, what do you do here?"

"I'm the bartender," said Herc, giving an almost imperceptible nod toward Sammy. "That's Sammy Rocquemore. He owns the joint."

"What's his problem?" Teddy asked, observing the hatred that seemed to emanate from the cripple like a cloud of smoke as he eyed them suspiciously.

Misunderstanding the question, Herc replied, "He got shot up in the war. Been in that wheelchair ever since."

"Who's the hottie behind the bar?" Teddy asked, eyeing Cheyenne hungrily.

"That's Cheyenne, Sammy's wife," Herc said discretely, his elbows resting on the table and his hands covering his mouth. "I would advise you to put your eyeballs back in your head if you wanna keep 'em."

Teddy shot a quick glance at Sammy. "Jealous type, huh?"

"That's putting it mildly," Herc said. "How's your beer, CJ? You want something stronger?"

"No, this is good," CJ murmured. He couldn't understand why he was feeling so anxious and uncomfortable. He'd been in plenty of dives before, but something about this joint had his heart beating a mile a second and the music, laughter and chatter reverberating around him seemed to encase him in an impenetrable wall of sound. It was all he could do to keep from bolting out of there. How was he to know that the events of this night would change his life forever?

Teddy looked around at the despicable cast of characters populating the bar and lied, "This looks like a nice place."

"Yeah, right," Herc snorted. "But, hey, it's a job."

"You been working here long?"

"Couple of years. My brother got me the job. He knew Sammy from jail."

As if on cue, Sammy rolled his motorized wheelchair over to their table and leveled his harsh gaze on Herc. "I need you behind the bar, Herc. Cheyenne got tables to wait on."

"Okay," Herc said. "Be right there."

"Now," Sammy emphasized, his voice tinged with suppressed fury.

Herc rose to his feet with a reluctant sigh. "If y'all need anything else just come on over to the bar," he said, lumbering off to relieve Cheyenne. As soon as Herc took his place behind the bar, Cheyenne grabbed her tray and scurried out to take drink orders.

Sizing up the newcomers, Sammy said, "I'm Sammy. I own this club. I ain't seen y'all in here before. Where you from?"

"The valley," Teddy said, careful not to seem like out-of-towners and possible prey.

"So, where you know Herc from?"

"We've seen him around," Teddy answered.

"What's wrong with your friend?" Sammy asked, nodding toward CJ. "Can't he talk?"

"Yeah, he can talk." Teddy said, eyeing Cheyenne over Sammy's shoulder as she bent over a table serving drinks in her generously packed Apple Bottom jeans. "He's just particular about who he talks to."

"What's that supposed to mean?" Sammy growled as a customer seated behind Cheyenne reached out and squeezed a handful of the bountiful delights she seemed to be offering him.

"You mother fucker!" Cheyenne's voice cut through the loud music as she slammed her metal tray upside the man's head. Sammy quickly spun his wheelchair around and cut a path through the thick crowd. Big Jimbo sailed across the room at amazing speed as the man sprang from his chair sending it crashing to the floor.

"I'm gon' kill you, bitch!" he shouted, lunging toward Cheyenne. Jimbo caught him by the throat.

He grabbed my ass!" Cheyenne shouted, pointing to the culprit. Before CJ realized what was happening, Jimbo hit the man and the man hit the floor. The music stopped. The startled customers scrambled out of the way and Herc waved frantically at CJ and Teddy, signaling them over to the bar.

CHAPTER 15

"Breathe muthafucka and I'll blow your goddamn head off," Sammy said his voice low and deadly as he pressed the barrel of his .44 hard against the man's forehead.

With eyes as big as saucers and blood running from his nose, the suddenly sober man began begging for his life. "Please, Sammy," he cried, tears running unchecked down his cowardly face. "Please, man. Please don't shoot me. I'm sorry, man. I'm sorry."

"Don't apologize to me, muthafucka. Apologize to my wife."

Paralyzed by fear, the man rolled his eyes toward Cheyenne, "I'm sorry, Cheyenne. You know I didn't mean no harm. Tell him to get that gun outta my face."

Sammy stared at him in contempt, his hand trembling with the desire to blow this chump away. The dread of returning to prison was the only thing that stopped him. "Get this piece of shit out of my sight before I bust a cap in his ass, Jimbo," he said, lowering his gun.

Jimbo snatched the man up from the floor like a rag doll. Someone in the crowd shouted, He done pissed on hisself," pointing to the dark stain running down the front of the man's tan slacks. Everyone laughed as Jimbo pushed the piss pot ahead of him and threw him out the door. The music kicked back in and the desensitized crowd resumed their partying.

Sammy wheeled himself over to the bar. "Gimme a drink," he told Herc. Herc poured a double shot of Jack Daniels and sat it on the bar within his reach. Sammy downed the drink and banged his glass on the bar for a refill. Herc quickly obliged. CJ glanced into the mirror behind the bar and locked eyes with Sammy.

"What the fuck you looking at?" Sammy shouted.

"You talking to me?" CJ asked, turning to face him.

"Hell yeah, I'm talking to you, muthafucka. You think I'm some kinda joke or something?"

"Come on, man, let's get out of here," Teddy said, nudging CJ. "Bullshit ain't nothin'."

"I haven't finished my beer yet." CJ said, turning back to the bar, knowing somehow that he couldn't have left if he'd wanted to.

As the night went on, Teddy chatted with Herc and had a few more drinks, while CJ silently nursed his beer, feeling as if he were on the inside looking out at the festivities going on around him. Sammy's eyes kept darting back to the newcomers. Something about them just wasn't right. He concluded that they were either stick-up artists or the police. A stick-up, he could handle. But he wanted no part of the cops. He knew that many of his customers, being bona fide criminals were likely to have any number of illegal substances on them at any given time.

Herc gave Teddy a heads up look as Sammy rolled himself over to CJ. "You Five-O or what?" Sammy asked, boring a hole in CJ's back with his eyes. CJ remained hunched over his beer and said nothing, thus infuriating Sammy even more.

"He ain't no police," Herc assured him. "This is CJ; he's a friend of mine."

"I don't give a fuck who he is. I'm talking to you, nigga," Sammy said, poking CJ in the back with his finger. "Can you hear?" CJ turned to face the man, but said nothing. Sammy pointed to a sign behind the bar. "You see that sign, muthafucka?" The sign read: Anyone attempting to rob this place will be shot. "That ain't there for decoration."

"Look, man," Teddy intervened, "We ain't looking for no trouble. We heard this was a nice place to socialize and we just stopped in for a few drinks, that's all."

"Bullshit!" Sammy snapped. "Ain't nobody told you no shit like that. You must think I'm a goddamn fool."

"Naw, man. Don't nobody think nothing like that," Teddy said. "You got us all wrong,"

"Come on, Sammy," said Herc. "They're cool."

"How the fuck you know? They could have a hundred cops outside just waiting to come bustin' up in this muthafucka, for all you know."

Cheyenne, noticing that Sammy was once again working himself into a frenzy hurried over to him. Standing behind Sammy's chair, she placed her hands gently on his shoulders and leaned over, giving him a kiss on the cheek. "What's up, Babe?"

"These muthafuckas got bullshit on their minds. That's what's up," he said, his eyes never leaving CJ.

"They ain't did nothin', Cheyenne. Sammy got the wrong idea," said Herc.

Flashing a smile, Cheyenne stepped around the wheelchair to shake their hands. "I'm Cheyenne. Welcome to Shenanigans."

"I'm Teddy. This is CJ. We didn't mean to start no trouble."

CJ gave her a nod. "How you doin'?"

"You have to forgive my husband," Cheyenne said. "He gets a little fired up sometime."

"You ain't got to apologize for me," Sammy snapped. "You fuckin' one of these niggas or something?" CJ shook his head and turned back to his warm beer. He wondered how much pain and heartache it had taken to turn Sammy into the snarling demon he had become. He sensed a gentle heart in this man, despite his outward display of hostility.

Ignoring Sammy's preposterous accusation, Cheyenne continued, trying her best to maintain a cordial atmosphere. "Herc, give these guys another drink – on the house."

"Not on my goddamn house you don't," Sammy roared, jabbing a thumb in CJ's direction. "This muthafucka been sitting his ass up in here all night sucking on that same fuckin' beer. Yeah, muthafucka, I been watching your ass. You ain't foolin' no goddamn body."

As Sammy continued his inane ranting, CJ closed his eyes and stilled himself. He could feel the Spirit of the Lord coming on him. Sammy's words blurred in the background of his mind. He no longer seemed threatening, only sad and scared. It was as if a veil had lifted from CJ's eyes. He could see that Sammy's scars went far deeper than his physical body. He was hurting in his soul. Suddenly, CJ knew why he was there. He spun around on his stool unexpectedly, his light colored eyes blazing with the power of God.

When CJ rose to his feet. Teddy noticed a drastic change in his face and demeanor. His eyes gleamed with an intensity that had not been there before, the angles of his face looked more severe and the shoulders that had been slumped at the bar all night now exhibited a strong and determined bearing.

Sammy's eyes widened with fear and he shot his wheelchair backwards. CJ fixed Sammy with an unwavering gaze and said, "Stand up." Although he had not raised his voice, the power in it resonated throughout the room. Everyone looked at CJ as though he had deliberately snatched the lid off of Pandora's Box.

"I got your stand up, muthafucka," Sammy snarled, his hand going automatically to his gun. The music stopped abruptly and the deejay began packing up his gear. CJ started moving toward Sammy and all of the customers, except for those with a perverse bloodlust quickly vacated the premises. They did not want to be there when Sammy killed this fool. Sammy tried to pull his gun, but his hand just laid there like a dead fish and a look of sheer panic invaded his face.

CJ leaned over, clasped his hand over Sammy's face and said in a voice heavy with authority, "In the name of God, I command you to stand up and walk." Sammy's face felt hot and a tingling sensation penetrated every fiber of his being.

When CJ removed his hand from Sammy's face and stepped back, Sammy sat momentarily dazed. Then, after what seemed like an eternity but was really only a few seconds, Sammy placed his hands on the arms of the wheelchair and slowly started pulling himself up.

"Oh, my God!" Cheyenne gasped, clasping her hands over her mouth as Sammy rose unsteadily to his feet. Her words seemed magnified in the face of every person in the place as Sammy slowly released the chair and stood shakily on his own.

You could hear a flea peeing on cotton in that rowdy joint as Sammy took one tentative step and then another. He could feel his legs strengthening with each step. The crowd held their collective breath as tears fell from his eyes and he began to walk faster. Then to their astonishment, a huge grin spread over Sammy's face and he broke into a run, shouting hysterically, "I can walk, Chy! I can walk!"

He grabbed his wife's hands and they danced around like children. "Oh, my God!" Cheyenne repeated with tears of joy streaming down her face. "Look at you." The few customers remaining in the club bolted out of there, terrified by what they'd just witnessed.

Sammy held Cheyenne close, feeling her heart beat next to his. After a long moment, he released her, holding her at arm's length. "I can walk," he repeated in utter amazement. He threw his fists up in the air and shouted, "I can walk! Thank you, God! Thank you." He then grabbed CJ in a grateful embrace, "Thank you, man. Thank you," he said, his voice quivering with emotion.

CJ nodded, giving him a half smile and a pat on the back before flopping down at the nearest table, totally exhausted. His eyes scanned the room that now held only Sammy, Cheyenne, Herc, Jimbo and Teddy. They were all staring at him in wide-eyed amazement. Only Herc dared to speak, "Who . . . Who are you, man?"

CJ felt as weak as a newborn baby, yet exhilarated beyond belief. He looked around at them, his eyes sparkling with an intensity that bordered on insanity. "Me?" he said with an enigmatic smile, "I'm just a voice in the wilderness – Telling you, it's time to repent."

CHAPTER 16

After a long moment of silence, CJ stood and headed for the door. Teddy, as astounded as anyone else in the room gulped the remainder of his drink and started after him.

"Wait," Cheyenne shouted, thinking she couldn't just let them ride off into the sunset. "Why don't y'all come on by the house? I can fix some breakfast."

With a nod from CJ, Teddy shrugged, "Sure. Why not?"

"We'll be out front," Sammy said to Cheyenne, anxious to step out into the night under his own power.

"I'll just be a minute," said Cheyenne, pulling a bank bag from beneath the bar. I just need to empty the cash register. Even at times of high excitement and this was the most exciting thing she had ever seen, Cheyenne made sure to take care of business. She was the brains of the outfit, the practical one. It was due to her savvy business sense and her charm that Shenanigans had become the success it was. "Jimbo. Stay in here with Cheyenne until she's finished," Sammy said as he followed CJ and Teddy outside. Herc trailed close behind as if entranced.

Outside the club, only the hard-core do-or-die hustlers roamed the desolate pre-dawn streets. Chief among them was Hawk, a definite bird of prey and a hardened ex-con who, since the age of twelve was a respected member of the criminal community, stealing, selling dope, pimping whores – Whatever it took to survive.

Hawk leaned against his black Lexus sharing a blunt with a pimp called Poncho. Poncho had witnessed Sammy's miraculous recovery and was giving Hawk the blow by blow. Hawk gave an incredulous snort and shook his head, taking the blunt from Poncho. "You don't need no more of this, man. You done started seeing shit."

"I'm telling you, man. It was bizarre," Poncho said. Just then, Teddy emerged from the club followed by CJ, Sammy and Herc.

"That's him!" Poncho whispered as CJ stepped out.

Hawk gave a sarcastic chuckle and took a hit off his blunt. "That nappy headed ass nigga. Man you must be . . ." But when Sammy walked out Hawk nearly choked on the smoke he was holding in his lungs, breaking into an uncontrollable coughing fit.

"What I say?" Poncho said, patting him on the back.

Hawk couldn't believe his eyes. Sammy had been in a wheelchair ever since he'd known him. He watched as Sammy marched toward a royal blue van with the word Shenanigans emblazoned on the side and climbed in. "This nigga been faking the game all these years," Hawk said, refusing to believe Poncho's incredible tale.

"I'm telling you, man it was that dude," Poncho said fixing his eyes on CJ.

CJ knew they were talking about him. He walked up to Hawk and said, "You. Come with me."

"Who the fuck are you?" Hawk asked, bristling for a fight.

CJ just turned and followed Teddy to the Escalade.

"Who the fuck that nigga think he is?" Hawk said, turning to Poncho. But Poncho was gone. All Hawk saw was Poncho's back as he hightailed it down the street.

Hawk stood rooted to the spot, watching as CJ, Teddy and Herc climbed into the SUV. The dancing neon sign atop the club blinked out as Cheyenne and Jimbo exited the club. After locking the door and the security gate, Cheyenne climbed into the front seat of the van where Sammy sat behind the wheel with a big grin on his face. Jimbo then got into the back seat of the van and it took off with Teddy's Caddy close behind. Seized by an irresistible impulse, Hawk jumped into his ride and followed them off into the night.

Later, as Sammy paced back and forth in their spacious kitchen, CJ and the others sat around the table enjoying a hearty breakfast of grits, sausage and eggs and hot buttered toast. "You need to eat, Sammy. It'll help calm your nerves," Cheyenne said, peering into the refrigerator.

"I ain't nervous," Sammy responded. "I'm happy." Every eye in to room turned to him in surprise. *Happy*?

Cheyenne couldn't remember the last time she'd heard him say that word. She closed the fridge and gave CJ an apologetic look. "We don't have any juice, CJ. I could go to the store.

"Don't even worry about it," CJ said. "Got any pop?"

Teddy laughed, "Soda. They call it soda out here."

CJ smiled. "Oh. Well I'll have some soda then." They all chuckled as Cheyenne grabbed a two-liter bottle of soda and placed it on the table along with several glasses. She filled a glass for CJ and plopped down in the seat beside him. She stared at him for a beat and just burst into tears.

"What's wrong with you?" Sammy asked, rushing to her side.

"I'm just so happy. This is just so, so . . ." She fluttered her hands in the air, trying to find the right word.

Sammy wrapped his arms around. "Aw, babe. Don't cry," he said, fighting back his own tears.

Cheyenne turned to CJ. "I just want to thank you for what you've done for us," she said, placing her hand on top of his. "I don't know how much you charge, but we'll pay it. I don't care if we have to borrow it."

"Yeah, man," said Sammy. "Just tell us what you want." He extended his hand to CJ who stood up and shook it. "I mean it, man. You don't know how much I appreciate what you did for me." With no regard for his macho image, Sammy pulled CJ into yet another hug.

"Don't thank me," CJ said, freeing himself. "Thank God."

Hawk and Jimbo exchanged wary looks; neither of them trusted CJ. If prison had taught them anything, it was that nobody did anything for nothing. They'd never seen Sammy gushing over anyone like this before. Then again, they'd never seen him walk either. Hawk wondered if what Poncho had told him could possibly be true. His logical mind said, "No," but here Sammy was standing before his very eyes. *I gotta figure out what's really going down,* he thought. *Who is this nigga?*

Swiping at the tears that were beginning to gather in his eyes, Sammy sat down across from CJ. He leaned forward and asked in a voice so low that it was nearly a whisper, "How you learn how to do that, man?"

"I ain't done nothin"

"Come on, man. I'm serious."

"Me too," he said truthfully. "That was God. God sent me here to save the black man." The silence in the room was deafening. Finally, CJ said, "But I can't do it by myself. I'm gon' need a few good men."

"Like the Marines," Herc and Jimbo said in unison.

"Exactly," CJ said. "And I know a good man when I see one." He looked first at Sammy and then swept the room with his glance. When his eyes stopped on Hawk, Hawk looked around to see who was standing behind him. *I know he's not talking about me,* he thought. No one had ever accused him of being a good man.

"Yeah, I'm talking about you," CJ said. Hawk's eyes grew wide with alarm.

Realizing he had heard Hawk's thought, CJ was momentarily taken aback. *This is too much,* he thought, rubbing his hand across his forehead. Then he remembered how as a teenager, he had begun hearing people's thoughts and had kept it to himself, thinking he must be some kind of freak. After a while, he learned how to block out the thoughts of others and it had eventually stopped. Now, here it was again.

"You all right?" Teddy asked, rushing to CJ's side.

"I'm cool," CJ said, holding up his hand. *I gotta get a grip,* he thought. He knew that if he were to get these men to help him, he couldn't show any weakness. "God wants me to bring His word to the black man. Get him to change his ways," he said in the most confident voice he could muster. "Good luck," Sammy mumbled.

Hawk wasn't buying it. This dude didn't look like a Jesus freak to him. But he didn't look like a player either. *So, what's his game?* Hawk wondered. All he knew was that he wasn't about to get sucked in by this slick talking nigger.

"Black folks have been living in the dark long enough," CJ said, taking a sip of his soda. "I've come to shed the light, make

115

them realize they're living in the shadow of death. I've come to tell them about grace." He was surprised at how easily the words flowed from his mouth and how comfortable he felt saying them.

"Who's Grace?" asked Jimbo.

"The grace of God," CJ said with a chuckle. "That's when God shows his love to people who don't deserve it."

"What do you want us to do?" Sammy asked.

"Just have my back. Trust me like I trust in God. All I want is your loyalty – Your faithfulness."

"How you mean?" Herc asked.

"I'm talking about making a commitment and following through regardless to whatever complications that might come up," CJ said. "Faithfulness is hanging in there, saying, I won't quit. If you're going to hang with me, you gotta be faithful. God is faithful to you and he expects you to be faithful to him. It tells us right there in Psalms one hundred, '*The Lord is good and His love endures forever; His faithfulness continues through all generations.*'" Heads bobbed in agreement, even though they didn't know if the Scripture he quoted was accurate or not.

"So by being faithful to me, you're being faithful to God."

Now, these were not religious men by any stretch of the imagination. Aside from numerous funerals of murdered friends, the last time any of them had seen the inside of a church was when their mothers and grandmothers had taken them. But there was something about CJ's words . . . Something about the confidence and authority with which he spoke that had them riveted to every word he said.

As the sun outside Sammy's kitchen window began to peek out on the dawning of the new day, CJ told them how the reign of the devil was over and it was time for God's people to claim their rightful place. They took this to mean that he was thinking in

116

revolutionary terms, which spiked their interest even more. To them this was a call to arms. Like many other black men, Sammy and his friends had not given up on the hope of the black man someday rising up to overtake his oppressors. They had just been waiting for the right man to come along and lead the charge. They were beginning to believe that such a man had at last arrived.

Later that day, CJ sat on the patio picking listlessly at his food. He looked as though he hadn't slept a wink – that's because he hadn't. The events of the previous night had so unnerved him that he couldn't get it out of his head.

"So, you ready to tell me what happened?" Teddy asked.

"What?"

"Last night. You didn't want to talk about it when we got home."

CJ sighed. "How long have you been knowing me, man?

"Forever," Teddy replied. "What's that got to do with it?"

"We're boys, right?"

"Yeah, man."

"So, I can count on you to keep what I'm about to tell you on the DL."

"Yeah, man. You know that," Teddy said, annoyed by CJ's procrastination.

CJ took a long swig of his juice and proceeded to tell Teddy the whole story.

After a moment of stunned silence, Teddy asked, "But, how did you *heal* that dude?"

"I don't know," CJ said with a shrug. "It was like my body was moving but my brain wasn't driving. Understand what I'm saying? It's like some kind of power came over me and I wasn't in control. Like it wasn't me, but it was."

"So, you're saying you got some kind of super power. What else can you do?"

CJ shrugged. "I didn't even know I could do that."

After a moment's consideration, Teddy's face broke out in a big grin. He shot up to his feet and he mimed pulling down a slot machine handle. "Cha-ching! We finna get paid, homeboy," he said, slapping his hands together and rubbing them in a miserly fashion.

"No," CJ said, adamantly. "This ain't about the money. This is serious."

"Money ain't serious?"

"Don't you get it, Teddy?" Teddy looked into CJ's eyes and a cold chill raced up his back as CJ said in a low, otherworldly voice, "I'm on a mission from God."

CHAPTER 17

When Sammy and Cheyenne pulled up in front of Shenanigans, they were shocked to see a large crowd assembled outside the club. "What the hell is this?" Sammy asked, looking around at the news trucks and cameramen.

"I have no idea," Cheyenne said as Sammy Parked.

As soon as they stepped out of the van, someone shouted, "There he is! I told you he could walk." Realizing that the crowd was there for him, Sammy waved to them as he and Cheyenne made their way to the front door. As he unlocked the security gate and pulled it back, Meka Maxwell, a tenacious investigative reporter elbowed her way through the crowd until she was standing next to Sammy. Following close behind was Darnell, her tall, lanky cameraman.

"Are you Sammy Rocquemore?" Meka asked.

"Yeah," Sammy said. "What's all this?"

"I'm Meka Maxwell from KBDJ News," she said. "Do you mind if I interview you?" Without waiting for an answer, Meka fluffed out her long, dark curls and gave Darnell the nod to start

119

filming. With an Asian mother and African American father, Meka's exotic good looks boasted the best of both races. Her big, almond shaped eyes sat in an expertly made up face the color of maple fudge. Her generous lips spread into a wide smile as she began, "I'm here in front of Shenanigans bar . . ."

"Nightclub," Sammy corrected, obviously offended. "It's a nightclub, not a bar."

"Correction," Meka continued. "That's Shenanigans nightclub. Right here in the heart of South Central L.A. With me is Sammy Rocquemore the bar, uh, club's owner. Hello Sammy," she said, thrusting the mike under his nose.

"Hey," Sammy said, grinning stupidly into the camera.

"Sammy," Meka continued. "Our phone lines have been jammed with people calling, telling us about your miraculous recovery. Can you tell us what all the excitement is about?"

"Yeah," Sammy said, blushing slightly. "See, I've been in a wheelchair for over ten years. Took a bullet in the back during the Gulf war," he explained.

Meka eyed him up and down. "You look perfectly healthy to me. What happened? Did you have surgery or something?"

"No," he said, shaking his head. "When I came to work yesterday I was in my wheelchair. Well, this dude came up in here last night and he healed me. Now I can walk."

"Incredible," she said. "What kind of a doctor was he?"

"He wasn't no doctor," Sammy said.

"Really," she replied.

The predatory glint in her eye gave Sammy pause and he quickly turned to unlock the door. "Sorry, we gotta open up," he said, opening the door and gesturing for Cheyenne to enter.

"Is this your wife?" Meka purred, reluctant to let him go.

"Yeah," Sammy said. "This my wife, Cheyenne."

Cheyenne gasped in surprise as Meka shoved the mike in front of her face. "What do you have to say about all this, Cheyenne?"

Caught off guard, Cheyenne said the first thing that popped into her mind, "I just want to say thank you, CJ?" Sammy and Cheyenne then zipped inside, closing the door behind them.

"There you have it," Meka said, smiling into the camera. "A controversial healing right here in the Southland. And who is this mysterious CJ Cheyenne spoke about? If anyone has information on this baffling case, give us a call at 1 (800) WE TIP LA. That's 1 (800) 938-4752. I'm Meka Maxwell, live in South Central L.A." She swiped her finger across her neck, signaling for Darnell to cut. He shut off the camera and taking her arm, started back toward their van as the crowd began to disperse. "So, what do you think, Darnell?"
"You never looked better."

"I'm talking about the story," she said, giving him a playful shove. "Do you believe it?"

"Sounds like a publicity stunt to me," he said, opening the door of the van.

"You think he's just trying to get free publicity for his bar?" Meka asked as Darnell climbed into the van and stowed his camera.

"Nightclub," he chuckled, reaching his hand out to help her climb in.

Meka rolled her eyes, "Whatever. He can call it Caesar's Palace if he wants to and it'll still be a dump."

Meanwhile, Teddy clicked off the TV in his music room and turned to CJ, "So much for keeping it quiet."

"Wonder who called the media," CJ said.

"Who didn't?" Teddy replied. "Some of these TV shows pay good money for an exclusive story. Usually it's about some celebrity."

"Well, I'm definitely not no celebrity, so this should die down pretty quick."

"I hope so," Teddy said doubtfully. "That Meka Maxwell is a pit bull. Once she gets her teeth into something, she never lets go. I've seen her make grown men cry."

CJ chuckled, "That little kewpie doll? Gimme a break." He made light of it, but he knew that looks were often deceptive.

Sammy, Cheyenne, Herc, Jimbo and Hawk showed up at Teddy's house every night after the club closed. They prayed together and CJ told them about the nation of God that he had come to prepare the black man for. To them, the nation of God was what CJ was calling the new country he intended to form after taking over the United States. This was their understanding and they never thought to question him on it.

"God never meant for his children to suffer," CJ told them. "He wants you to live in abundance, but first you have to love Him and worship Him with your whole heart and soul." They listened attentively as he told them of the glory of God. Even Jimbo and Hawk found themselves immersed in his words. There was something about the honesty and sincerity with which he spoke that touched these hard-hearted men as nothing ever had before.

Cheyenne, a sporadic churchgoer at best, felt compelled to go to church and thank God for Sammy's healing. After the service, she spoke with Reverend Elijah Thomas, pastor of the New Covenant Church of God. She told him what CJ had done for Sammy and the preacher was amazed. He told her that he would love to meet CJ.

When CJ met the idealistic young preacher, he liked him immediately. He found him to be refreshingly earnest and hungry for the Word. Reverend Thomas had no trouble believing that CJ had healed Sammy through the power of the Lord and was soon a regular member of their nightly sessions. He was in awe of CJ and hung on his every word. Mesmerized by the power of CJ's teaching, the young preacher begged him to preach at his church.

"I ain't no preacher, CJ said."

"All you have to do is talk to the church like you talk to us."

"Naw," CJ said, shaking his head. "Last time I got up in front of a church it didn't end too well."

"What happened?" Thomas asked.

"Let's just say thank God they didn't have a rope. I don't want to go through that again."

"How do you expect to get the word out if you don't talk to nobody but us?" Teddy asked. "You can't hide forever."

"He's got a point, CJ," Reverend Thomas said. "Why don't you just practice on us. Me and Teddy will be your church."

"I don't know," CJ said, rubbing the back of his neck. The thought of standing up in front of a church again terrified him. But, he didn't want to look like a punk. "Okay," he finally said. "Let's rehearse."

Teddy and the reverend pulled their chairs from the patio table and sat them side by side. CJ stood in front of them trying to think of what to say.

"Come on, CJ. Just think of something inspirational," Thomas said.

CJ hesitated a while longer and then burst out with "Father! I want you to open our eyes. Huh! I want you to look down on your helpless children and uh, Father, Oh, Lord . . ." His *church* could barely contain their laughter as he stomped around the patio whooping and hollering like some old time preacher on steroids.

Unable to take it any longer, Teddy burst out laughing and walked toward CJ, giving him the time-out signal with his hands. "Whoa. Stop." CJ stared at him in confusion. "Tell me that's not the theme song from Herb Kent's radio show."

"I figured nobody out here would recognize it," CJ said sheepishly.

"I do," said the preacher, his eyes filling with tears as he tried not to laugh. "I'll tell you what, CJ. Why don't you just pray on it. Ask God to give you the words to say."

"Yeah," said Teddy. "Preferably something that won't get you sued." Unable to hold back any longer, both Teddy and the reverend exploded in raucous laughter. CJ just glared at them, wondering if he'd ever be able to pull of this so-called mission.

CHAPTER 18

Reverend Bradshaw, aka Rev stood in front of the full-length mirror in the study of his New York mega-church primping and preening. "How do I look, Saunders?" he asked, turning to his assistant pastor, Reverend Raymond Saunders, a bespectacled, narrow shouldered lackey. Rev was resplendent in a gray suit; pink shirt, silk tie and maroon alligator shoes. He preferred wearing suits instead of robes for his television show, only donning the robe when he wanted to present an exceptionally saintly image.

"You look great, Rev," Saunders said, brushing an imaginary piece of lint off of Rev's shoulder.

"How's the building fund coming along?"

"Great. The money is rolling in. We still have a few more senior citizen cottages left though. They aren't moving as fast as I thought they would."

"Then we'll up the price."

"What?"

"We'll call 'em VIP cottages. You know how folks like to feel like they've got something better than their neighbors. Give them a larger kitchen and a little more lawn space and they'll go like hotcakes," Rev said, leaning over the blueprints spread out on his desk. "Once The City of Solomon opens I'll be a shoe in for the office of mayor." Rev had been in talks with local politicians who were seriously considering him for their party's mayoral candidate. They knew they could count on him to bring in the black vote. Plus, he had the charm and charisma to attract a lot of white voters who might ordinarily be reluctant to vote for a black mayor. His nomination was all but official and the spectacular tourist attraction was one of Rev's major bargaining chips. It was bound to bring a huge influx of money into the city. "I need you to set a date for the groundbreaking before it gets cold. Make sure you send out press releases to every media outlet in the country. This is going to be huge."

"You got it, Rev," Saunders said, heading toward the door. "You have about ten minutes until air time. I'll send one of the ushers to get you."

"Fine," Rev said. "Oh, by the way, is my godson out there?"

"Yes, sir."

"Good. Good. Tell his mother I'm gonna take him out somewhere after the broadcast."

Saunders gave him a discordant look and rubbed his hand over his balding head.

"What?"

"I, uh . . . I just don't see how you do it," said the accomplished liar. "With all you have on your plate you still find time to spend with those poor unfortunate boys."

"When you're doing the work of the Lord you make time," Rev said, giving him a holier-than-thou smile.

126

CHAPTER 19

The hand printed sign on the front of the little storefront church read, New Covenant Church of God. Inside, the little church was filled to the rafters. "Praise the Lord, Saints," Reverend Thomas called from a pulpit furnished with mismatched chairs acquired from thrift shops and parishioners' homes.

The church answered back with an enthusiastic,

"Praise the Lord."

The congregation, including the choir which consisted of about eight good strong voices, sat on folding chairs and their piano was a donation from the local Salvation Army. Though the décor may have been shabby, they did some serious churching up in that little storefront church.

"I'm not going to take up too much of your time this evening," the young minister said as the door at the back of the church slowly opened. His face lit up at the sight of Carla sliding self-consciously into the church. Even though she wore filthy jeans and had a greasy bandana tied around her head, he smiled at her as if she were wearing the finest Sunday dress that money could buy.

"As you know," the reverend continued. "We have a very special guest speaker with us tonight. But before I introduce him, I would just like to acknowledge Brother Sammy Rocquemore and his lovely wife Cheyenne." Sammy and Cheyenne stood. Cheyenne did a quick Miss America wave and sat back down. Sammy waved and took a bow, thoroughly enjoying the spotlight.

"The Rocquemores have a very special reason to be thankful tonight. As many of you know, Brother Sammy has been bound to a wheelchair for the past ten years. A strapping young man cut down in his prime. How often has that happened in our community?" Over the murmured responses, he went on. "But now through the grace of God," he said looking at Sammy like a proud papa. "Brother Sammy stands before you a whole man, healed by the power of the Lord. "Hallelujah! Let the church say Amen." The church burst into applause, shouting *Amen* and *Praise the Lord* as Sammy waved again before finally sitting down.

Seated in the front row awaiting his introduction, CJ said a silent prayer asking the Lord for strength and guidance. "Now, some of you may have heard about our speaker already," the preacher continued. "So, without any further ado, I give you Brother CJ."

Dressed in jeans and a Lakers Jersey, CJ stepped onto the pulpit to a gracious round of applause. He shook hands with Reverend Thomas and took his place behind the podium. He smiled out at the assemblage, hoping no one could tell how nervous he was. CJ took a deep breath, cleared his throat and as he had done before, began to read from the book of Isaiah. *"The Spirit of the Lord is on me,"* he announced, feeling the Spirit rising within him as he spoke. "He has anointed me to proclaim good news to the poor, the flotsam and jetsam of humanity."

A chuckle rumbled through the crowd when someone quipped, "That's us, all right."

Suddenly consumed by a fire he couldn't contain or explain, CJ said sternly, "And that's all you'll ever be as long as you think of yourself that way."

The church grew silent as he continued. "God says that you are the salt of the earth. But when salt loses its flavor, what is it good for? "We've let other folks use up all our flavor, brothers and sisters and now they want to throw us out like yesterday's newspapers and wipe their feet on us. But we are the children of the Almighty God and nobody tramples on God's kids," he said defiantly. "God has sent me to heal the brokenhearted. To proclaim freedom for the prisoners and recovery of sight for the blind. Amen! I have come to proclaim the day of the *vengeance* of our God. Hallelujah!" The church responded with loud cheers and applause. "I'm here tonight to let you know that you are not forgotten, that God loves you."

Bishop Jerome Hanks, a highly respected member of the Black Christian community and an honored pulpit guest watched CJ with professional scrutiny as he spoke. Hanks had heard about the alleged healing at Shenanigans, but had no idea that the perpetrator was supposed to be a preacher until he got a call from his protégé Elijah Thomas, asking him to attend tonight's service. The Bishop readily accepted the invitation, hoping to expose CJ as a fraud and use it as a learning experience for his gullible young friend.

Hanks, a man of integrity who loved the Lord more than most was a preacher at the top of his field. Not only was he a high-ranking member of the African American Council of Churches (AACC), he was also an author and a renowned Biblical scholar. With a Master's Degree from Harvard and a PhD from Stanford, he taught a graduate course in theology at UCLA and prided himself on knowing the Bible backwards and forwards. Yet when he listened to CJ's teaching it was as though he was hearing the words for the first time. Of course, he was familiar with the text, but had never heard it presented with such conviction and authority.

"The Lord blesses those who hunger and thirst for righteousness," CJ said, his eye falling on Sebastian St. John, a tall, light-skinned man of about his own age. Sebastian, an impeccably dressed public relations expert sat near the rear of the church, ready to make a quick exit in case he found this guy to be too full of it. Sebastian was a born cynic who rarely attended church. To him, religion was just another one of the white man's tactics, a safeguard put in place to keep niggers' minds in bondage long after their bodies were free. Like many fair-skinned brothers, Sebastian was twice as angry and much more radical than the average black man was. When he did go to church, he went to one of the big, prestigious churches like that of Bishop Hanks, where he was likely to meet stars and other influential people. He had only come to tonight's service because he'd heard about Sammy's healing and wanted to see what kind of dog and pony show they were trotting out for the poor dumb niggers this time.

Seeing the skeptical look on Sebastian's handsome face, CJ spoke directly to him. "And if you follow God's word, you too will be blessed." Sebastian blinked uncomfortably, tearing his eyes away from those of the man in the pulpit.

CJ looked around at the faces staring up at him and paused a moment before continuing in a softer tone. "But anyone persecuted for the sake of righteousness is particularly blessed. Because your reward in heaven will be just that much sweeter." At this, Sebastian rolled his eyes and gave a derisive snort. *The old pie in the sky routine,* he thought.

CJ spoke in simple terms, but his message held great power. Bishop Hanks allowed a smile to play on his lips when CJ said, "I know some of y'all ain't gon' like what I have to say. But, so what. I won't be the first preacher ever persecuted for telling the truth in this country. Look what they did to Dr. Martin Luther King, Jr. Look what they did to Malcolm!"

The church erupted in a roar of praise, encouraging him to continue. "You are the light of the world," CJ said. "And it's about time you let your light shine. Let it shine in a way that will glorify your Father who is in heaven." He then broke out in song, "*Ain't gonna let nobody turn me 'round, turn me 'round . . .*"

130

CJ removed the mike from its stand and descended the two steps that led from the pulpit. The pianist picked up the tune and soon the whole church was singing along. Walking the length of the church and back again, CJ sang a while and then preached a while, stopping in front of certain people and directing his words straight to them. The response was incredible. People rose to their feet, shouting, "Gon' Preacher. Tell the truth," and other such encouragements.

He'd touched their hearts deeply, even that of Bishop Hanks. That little ghetto church might as well have been a grand cathedral the way the Holy Ghost reined in it that night.

Carla couldn't take her eyes off him. He seemed to be speaking directly to her – killing her softly. At the conclusion of the sermon, Reverend Thomas joined CJ at the front of the church, bringing along a mike of his own. "Praise the Lord," he said, holding up his right hand. "Amen. You may have your seats in the presence of the Lord," he said with a barely perceptible nod to the piano player who continued to play softly under his words. "Amen. Let's give Reverend CJ a round of applause for that wonderful sermon." CJ couldn't help noticing his sudden promotion from "Brother CJ" to "Reverend CJ." As the church responded with exuberant applause, CJ smiled, bowing his head slightly. He was so filled with the Spirit of God that he felt shaky and wanted to sit down, but he knew Reverend Thomas had other plans.

"As we discussed earlier," Thomas told CJ, "I would like to introduce you to one of the bravest young men I've ever known." He beckoned to Maxine Williams, a slender woman in a brown dress, who hustled up to the front of the church with her blind ten-year-old son in tow. The preacher had mentioned the boy to CJ previously and CJ had explained that he couldn't promise anything. Feeling that he'd had no control over the previous healing he had performed, he explained to Reverend Thomas that he was just a vessel, there for God to use as he saw fit. But this young preacher had faith and he sincerely believed that if God was healing folks He would surely heal this child. As the boy drew closer, CJ felt a peculiar lightness that empowered him. Though there were no windows open in the church, he felt as though a cool breeze was blowing over him.

"This is Terrence Williams and his mother, Sister Maxine," Thomas said, placing his hand on the boy's shoulder. "I'd like y'all to meet Reverend CJ."

"Pleased to meet you, Reverend," Maxine said in a timid voice.

CJ said, "Bless you, sister."

Terrence smiled broadly and stuck out his hand, "How do you do?" he said as CJ shook his hand. "I liked your sermon."

"Thank you, Terrence," CJ said with a smile.

"Terrence has been blind since he was five," Thomas said. "Lead poisoning. He's had several operations and unfortunately none of them have helped."

"The fifth time's the charm," the good-natured kid assured the preacher, unaware that there would be no more operations. The doctors had given him up as a lost cause. Maxine hadn't had the heart to tell him the truth, but had confided the dire prognosis to her pastor.

"Terrence," CJ said, "Do you believe Jesus died for your sins?"

"Everybody knows that," Terrence replied brightly.

"Do you mind if I touch you?" CJ asked.

He saw Terrence tense up and reach for his mother's hand. She had warned him against allowing strangers to touch him, and he suddenly felt threatened. "It's all right, baby," she assured him. "He just wants to pray for you."

"Okay," Terrence said, comforted by her words.

CJ placed one hand over the child's eyes and the other behind his head. A deep silence fell over the church as he began to pray. "Heavenly Father, I just wanna give you all the praise and all the glory. I know that I am nothing on my own, Lord. It's all you. I am weak, Father, but you are strong. I'm asking you to strengthen your servant this evening, Lord." As he said these words he experienced a tingling, like fire in his bones as the power of the Lord surged through him.

"I know all things are possible for you God. So I'm asking you to heal this child. Let him once again see the glory of your world, Lord. I'm asking these things not for myself Father, but for the glory of your holy name. In the mighty name of Jesus Christ, I pray. Amen."

The spirit of the Holy Ghost became almost palpable in the little church as CJ removed his hands from the boy and stepped back. Terrence's body swayed. Reverend Thomas placed his hand on the child's back to steady him.

When Terrence opened his eyes he felt dizzy, disoriented. At first, he only saw the light and then shapes and shadows. The people around him looked like stick figures. The church held its collective breath as he blinked his eyes, trying to focus. As everything around him became clear, they could see the delight shining in his eyes. Terrence turned to his mother with a big Kool-Aid grin on his face and shouted, "I can see, Mommy! I can see!"

"Thank you, Jesus!" screamed Terrence's mother, swooping him into her arms with such enthusiasm that she lifted the boy, who was almost as tall as she was, off the floor.

Maxine showered her child with tearful kisses as Reverend Thomas thrust his fist in the air and shouted, "Look at God!" He then broke into a sanctified dance and the piano player jumped into a fast-paced rhythm that had everyone in the church dancing, shouting and praising the Lord with abandon.

When their exultation finally subsided, CJ, spent but euphoric, faced the awestruck church with his hand on Terrence's shoulder and said, "It is by the name of Jesus Christ of Nazareth, who was crucified but whom God raised from the dead that this child stands before you healed. For there is no other name under heaven by which we can be saved. Hallelujah!"

"Yeah!" Sammy shouted, jumping up and hoisting his fist in the air.

As the people began shouting and praising the Lord again, Reverend Thomas sang out in a strong baritone voice, "*Ain't gonna let nobody turn me 'round.*" The church joined in, singing the familiar spiritual with renewed vigor and intensity. It was the same song they sang before, but the power behind it was at least ten times as strong.

CJ just closed his eyes and said, "Thank you, Father. Thank you, Lord."

CJ healed many people that night in that little storefront church. Bishop Hanks looked on in awe as he healed the sick, the feeble and the lame. He knew without a doubt that this was surely a man of God. Tears streamed down Carla's face as she watched CJ lay hands on one person after another and they walked away healed.

Now, Carla had been around the block and then some. But she'd never seen anything like this. She knew in her heart that this was the real deal. She wanted so badly to go up to CJ and ask for his help. Her disease-ridden body was in constant pain, but she was well aware of what these nice church people thought of her, so she stayed where she was, convinced that if she stepped forward it would ruin the moment for everyone.

People were crying, shouting . . . fainting all around Sebastian, but he remained glued to his seat, his gaze fixed on CJ. Sebastian was educated and he was street smart. To his thinking, it was that winning combination that had earned him the title of public relations guru to the stars. He'd always prided himself on the fact that he was the smartest guy in the room and firmly believed that no one could put anything over on him. So why couldn't he figure out this guy's game? Was he a master magician on a par with David Copperfield? If so, why hadn't he heard of him? Fiddling with the diamond stud in his ear, he told himself that nobody could heal people with just the touch of his hand. *It's impossible*, he thought. – *So, what am I missing?* The more he puzzled over it, the angrier he became. Suddenly, he couldn't take it anymore.

A smile formed on CJ's lips as he watched Sebastian leap from his seat, pushing his way through the frenzied crowd. He brushed against Carla, almost knocking her down in his mad rush to escape. Under ordinary circumstance, he would have walked a country mile to avoid touching a nasty skank like her. But now, it didn't even register. He just had to get out of there.

CHAPTER 20

Later that night Reverend Thomas and Bishop Hanks joined CJ and his crew at Shenanigans. Too keyed up to go home, they sat around rehashing the evening's events. "Man! Was this some kind of night, or what?" said Sammy as he poured three fingers of Jack in a glass and gulped it down.

"Word," agreed Hawk, sitting at the end of the bar with his back to the wall. When Sammy reached for the bottle to pour himself another drink, Hawk said, "Yo, man, why don't you put that bottle out there so somebody else can get a taste."

"Oh, my bad," Sammy said, pouring a drink for Hawk and another for himself. He set the bottle on the bar and said, "Y'all help yourself. Everything's on the house tonight. This is a celebration."

Herc took his place behind the bar and started taking drink orders. "You want a beer or something, CJ?"

CJ shook his head, "Just give me some water." Although everyone else was in high spirits, CJ seemed strangely preoccupied.

"I'll have a beer," said Reverend Thomas.

"I need something stronger than that," Said the bishop. "Let me get a double scotch on the rocks."

"Did my boy get down or what?" Sammy said, holding his fist out to Hawk. Hawk bumped his fist and nodded, never cracking a smile. He was as hyped up as the rest of them were, but he made a point of never showing emotion. "You got down for your crown tonight CJ. You was awesome. Wasn't he, baby?"

Cheyenne fairly glowed, "You were, CJ. You really were. When that little boy said, 'Mommy, I can see' . . .," She placed her hand over her heart, shaking her head to fight back the tears. "Whoo! Umph, umph, umph. Lord, have mercy," she said holding her hand up in a show of praise. "I thought I was gonna lose it right then and there."

"You're the man, CJ," said Herc, shaking his head in awe.

"I'll drink to that," said Bishop Hanks, lifting his glass. Everyone else did likewise.

CJ remained remarkably silent as they showered him with praise. He knew that this night had been a turning point and that nothing would ever be the same again. What he didn't realize was that with each miracle he performed, he would become more deity and less mortal man.

"Excuse me," Sebastian said, venturing into the nearly empty club. "Are you open?" Hawk, from his perch at the bar, eyed the intruder with a hint of recognition in his face.

"This is a private party," said Sammy. "I thought I told you to lock that door, Jimbo."

"I did," said Big Jimbo, scratching his head. He relocked the door and took a seat near it, crossing his arms over his chest. *If anybody else comes up in here, they're gonna have to get through me,* he thought, positive that the door had been locked.

137

"Oh, I'm sorry." Sebastian said. As he turned to go, he spotted CJ. "It's you!" Sebastian said, moving toward CJ with his hand extended. I'm . . ."

"Sebastian St. John," CJ said with an inscrutable smile, standing to shake his hand. "I've been waiting for you." CJ had known that Sebastian would seek him out. From the moment he stared into his eyes in the church, he had known everything about him.

Taken aback, Sebastian stuttered, "Hu, hu, how do you know my name?"

CJ half smiled. "I know all about you," he said. Sebastian stared in amazement as CJ recited his bio to him. "You grew up around here. Attended USC on an athletic scholarship and graduated at the top of your class. You're a logical man who doesn't put much stock in spiritual things. You prefer hard, cold facts. Facts and numbers are something you can deal with. They make sense."

Sebastian's cock sure attitude fell to somewhere in the vicinity of his shoes. He slid down into one of the chairs at a nearby table, his legs no longer capable of holding him up. He stared at CJ in utter amazement, wondering how this stranger knew so much about him. "Who are you?" he asked in a voice that was barely above a whisper. CJ only smiled.

Sebastian told them how he had left the church in a world of confusion and had walked for hours trying to make some sense of what he'd seen. "When I came back for my car I decided to stop in here for a drink before I went home. It was just a lucky coincidence that I stumbled up on this place," he said.

"Was it?" CJ said shooting Teddy a sly look that said it had been no coincidence. From that night forward, Sebastian was a regular member of CJ's growing entourage.

Long after the others had gone, CJ sat talking to Teddy, Sammy, Herc and Sebastian. "My old man is in the real estate business," CJ said with a smile. "He always told me that it was all about prospecting. He says that if you throw enough . . . *stuff* against the wall, some of it's gotta stick. I need to get God's word out to as many people as I possibly can. Some of it's gotta stick. That's what Jesus was talking about when he told them that story about the farmer and the seed."

"What farmer? What seed?" Sammy asked.

CJ leaned back in his seat and crossed one long leg over the other. "See, this farmer went out to plant his seed, right. And as he worked, some of the seed fell along the path and the birds ate it up. Some of it fell on the rocks and withered away as soon as it grew up, because there was no water. And some of it even fell in with the thorns and the thorns choked it out. But some of that seed fell into good soil and grew into a healthy crop. See what I'm saying?"

"No," said Sammy. "Why are you always talking in riddles?"

"I be trying to give y'all something to think about," he said. "But I'm gon' explain this story, because I want you to know the secrets of the nation of God. See, the seed is the word of God. The seeds that fell along the path represent the people who heard the word, but the devil came and took it away from their hearts. This is the listener with the closed mind. You can't teach this brother nothing. He's blind to the things of God, so he won't believe." He spread his hands out like an umpire calling an out. "And he won't be saved," he said.

"The ones on the rocks are the ones who receive the word when they hear it, but they ain't got no root." He shot his thumb backwards, dismissing them too. "They believe for a while, but soon as temptation comes, they fall," he said, slapping his hands down on the table. "I'm talking about the shallow listener now. He means well, but he ain't got no spiritual depth. In the beginning, he's all excited, telling everybody about how saved he is. But after a while, it wears off and his mind wanders on to something else. You've seen the type."

The men all agreed that they had and CJ went on. "Now, the seeds that fell in with the thorns, they're the ones who heard the word but let it get choked out by the everyday responsibilities and pressures of life. I'm talking about that dogfight for riches and success. This is the man so caught up with cares and worries that he can't see what's really important. He's too busy to pray, too preoccupied with other things to study and meditate on God's word. So his fruit just doesn't mature."

He paused momentarily, spreading his hands out wide on the table. "But then, you got your open-minded people. That's the seed that fell on the good soil," he said with a smile. "This person is always willing to listen, willing to learn and grow. That's why he'll be saved. See what I'm saying? I can plant the word, but it won't grow if the conditions ain't right." He then looked from one of them to another, stressing the importance of what he was sharing with them. "God's word has the power to transform us. He gives grace to those who are hungry for His word and have the strength and courage to live according to His will."

Sebastian stared at CJ in absolute awe. He'd heard many professional speakers, but none had ever touched him like this man. He fought to contain his overwhelming emotion. He wanted to cry and didn't know why. But he checked himself, he wasn't about to bust out crying in front of these dudes. "Can I have some water, please?" he croaked, looking around.

"Yeah, sure," Herc said, running to fetch the water.

"You all right?" Teddy asked.

"I'm fine," Sebastian said, flashing a smile he didn't feel. Herc returned with the water and handed it to Sebastian who twisted off the cap and turned the bottle up to his mouth, guzzling the water like a man that had spent the last ten years stranded on a desert.

The following Wednesday night, CJ appeared at Bishop Hanks' church. The enormous sanctuary was filled to capacity and CJ cured all who came forward. Word of his spectacular

140

healings spread through L.A. like wild fire and soon preachers from all over the Southland were clamoring to have him appear at their churches.

CHAPTER 21

"Turn to channel fifty-two," Teddy said, bursting into the music room where CJ and the guys were watching TV.

"What's up?" CJ said.

Teddy snatched the remote out of Sebastian's hand and turned the channel. "Look," he said as Meka Maxwell's lovely face filled the screen.

"Breaking news! I'm sure you remember me reporting on the mysterious man who supposedly cured a paraplegic bar owner in South Central," Meka said.

"It's a nightclub," Sammy mumbled.

"Well. He's baaack," she said with an impish smile. "I have it on good authority that the enigmatic healer known only Reverend CJ has popped up at black churches all over the Southland. And get this; they're saying that he has healed hundreds of supposedly *random* (Here she makes air quotes with her fingers.) people of everything from acne to AIDS. Come on now, people," she said, rolling her eyes incredulously. "Have we reverted back to those old tent-meeting revivals where some faith healer cures the same people of the same ailments every night in a different town? If this is a revival, it's the revival of one of the oldest con games ever known to man." Then, leaning into the camera, her lovely face absent of its trademark smile and looking as if she were delivering a portent of impending doom, she said, "Or is this something much more sinister?"

"That's the dame that interviewed me," said Sammy.

"I'd advise you not to do that again," Sebastian said.

"Do what?" Sammy asked, copping an attitude.

"Talk to Meka Maxwell. That woman is vicious. She'll take whatever you say and spin it around until she has you saying something you don't even recognize."

"She don't look all that vicious to me."

"Don't let those big brown eyes fool you," said Sebastian. "She didn't go from weather girl to investigative reporter by being sweet. She plans on being the next Barbara Walters."

"So she's ambitious," CJ said.

"Try tenacious," said Sebastian, "When that chick gets on your case, she's like a pit bull with the lockjaw."

"Told you," said Teddy.

Meka rushed from the set, barely pausing to snatch the cappuccino from the hand of her assistant, Angie. Shy and pretty, Angie was fresh out of college and anxious to please. She followed Meka into her dressing room where the newscaster was already starting to disrobe. "You were fabulous, Meka." Angie gushed. "I wish I had your poise."

"You will. All you have to remember, is that for those few minutes you're on the air, you are the center of thousands of people's lives." She pulled on her jogging pants and asked, "Did you get that background information on Reverend CJ?"

"Uh, I'm still working on it," Angie said.

"Work harder," said Meka as she tied the laces of her running shoes and threw on a USC sweatshirt. "I want to know everything there is to know about this guy, Angie. Who is he? Where did he come from? I want to know about his family, his schooling. I want to know who the first girl he played stink finger with was. But most of all I want the dirt. People just love dirty laundry. You understand what I'm saying?"

"Yes, Meka. I'm on it."

"I'm going for a run. I'll check back with you before the Evening News." She took a final swig of her cappuccino and started toward the door.

"What's his last name?" Angie asked.

"How should I know?" Meka snapped. "That's what I pay you for." She opened the door and then turned to Angie, emphasizing in a gentler tone, "This story has Pulitzer Prize written all over it, Ange. And that Pulitzer has my name on it. Capiche?"

"Capiche." Angie said with a nod and a smile. When the door closed, Angie's smile collapsed and she slumped down in Meka's make-up chair. Her eyes fell on a newspaper whose headline read, "*Reverend CJ Mobbed by Crowd at Local Popeye's.*" She picked up the paper and stared at the headline. "Who are you, Reverend CJ? Who the hell are you?" She slammed the paper down on the table and ran her hands through her curly mop of brown hair, emitting a low, frustrated growl.

Rev clicked off the wide screen TV in his office and sat staring at the blank screen for several seconds, his massive chest rising and falling with uncontrolled rage. He then snatched up the receiver of his desk phone and hit a number on the speed dial.

When Bishop Hanks saw Rev's name on the caller I.D., he immediately picked up the phone. "Rev, how good to hear from you. How is The City of Solomon coming along?"

"What's going on out there, Hanks?" Rev bellowed. "Who is this Reverend CJ and why did I have to hear about him on CNN?"

Taken aback, Hanks could tell that this would not be the time to sing CJ's praises. "I didn't figure it was worth bothering you about."

"Well, I'm bothered," said Rev. "Who is this guy?"

"He's nobody," Hanks lied. "Just some jack leg preacher got a bunch of folks down in South Central all excited." He didn't tell him that CJ had gotten him so excited that he'd had him speak at his own church.

"What's all this about him healing people?"

"Rev . . . I wouldn't be surprised if he was just some actor, trying to get free publicity. This *is* Hollywood."

"I hope that's all it is. I'm counting on you to keep things under control out there. This is just the kind of thing that could get out of hand and cost me my bid for mayor."

"How so?" Hanks asked.

"He's black, isn't he? And a preacher at that. You know how they like to paint all blacks with the same brush." What Rev was really worried about was that CJ might steal the spotlight from him and The City of Solomon. He'd spent a mint on publicity and he wasn't about to get pushed to the back page by some rogue preacher playing the oldest flimflam game in religious history.

"Yeah, Rev. I know."

"So, I need you to find out what this character is up to and shut him down. Pay him off if you have to, but I better not hear about him preaching in any more churches out there. You hear? I don't know what his deal is, but I'm not going to have his antics affecting my campaign."

"Yes, Rev. I understand."

"I'm expecting you to handle this thing, Hanks."

Rev hung up without saying good-bye. As far as he was concerned, if he'd finished talking the conversation was over. *This is not good*, Hank's thought. After a beat, he dialed Reverend Thomas' number. When Thomas answered, Hanks tried to sound pleasant. "Elijah. It's Jerry Hanks. How's it going?"

"Fine, Bishop. What's up?" Thomas asked, picking up on the tension in his voice.

"I'm calling about Reverend CJ," he said and went on to relay his conversation with Rev.

"I don't understand," said Thomas. "Why is he so upset?"

"Rev is the suspicious type," the bishop said, trying to be diplomatic and not reveal his true feelings about their religious leader "Maybe if we could tell him more about CJ," Hanks said. "Who he is. Where he came from."

"I don't know any more about him than you do," Thomas said.

"He didn't ask you for any money or anything did he?"

"No!" Did he ask you for any?"

"No."

"So, what's the problem?"

"Rev's concerned that CJ might make the church look bad. He doesn't want us letting him preach at our churches anymore."

"Why not?"

"He doesn't trust him. Now, it's up to me to tell CJ. I was hoping you'd go over there with me."

"Sure," Thomas said. I'll call him and let him know we're coming. You know they haven't been answering their door lately. All those reporters and people wanting healing that have been hanging around there. Poor guy's scared to step out on the front porch."

"Yeah, I know," replied the bishop. "Let me know what time and I'll meet you there." He hung up the phone, plopped down in his desk chair and ran his hands through his crop of white hair. "What am I going to do? I can't let Rev shut him down. I just can't."

As Angie sat staring at her computer screen, Meka sauntered into the office they shared wearing a fabulous red suit that hit her just above the knee. "Well, what do you have?" Meka asked.

"I found out that he's from Chicago," Angie said, trying to sound enthusiastic.

Meka gave her a sardonic look, "I could have told you that. What else?"

"I don't know where to start," Angie admitted. "I don't even have a name to work with."

Meka rolled her eyes in exasperation. "Do I have to do everything around here myself?" She parked herself behind her desk and typed a name into Google. "Bingo! Carlton Burke."

"Who's that?" Angie asked.

"This guy I dated in college. He was from Chicago. I heard he became a cop. Looks like he's a detective now. If this guy really is from Chicago, Carlton should be able to find out something about him." She looked up the number for Chicago Police Headquarters and dialed it, asking the operator to connect her with the district mentioned in Burke's profile. She walked around her desk and perched her shapely butt on the edge of it. After a moment, she said with a smile in her voice, "Hello. May I please speak to Detective Carlton Burke?" She held her hand over the mouthpiece of the phone, whispering to Angie, "Listen and learn."

"Carlton," Meka purred. "It's Meka Maxwell. Yes. It has been a long time, hasn't it? How've you been? Oh, I'm great. Yes. I'm working for a TV station in Los Angeles. I see you've done well for yourself. Oh, don't be so modest." After a bit more chitchat, she said, "Listen, Carlton, the reason I called is because I could use your help with a story I'm working on."

"Sure. How can I help?"

"I'm trying to get a line on this guy who calls himself CJ?"

"The only CJ I can think of is some lunatic bus driver named Charlie Johnson I busted in a barroom murder investigation."

"Murder?" Meka said more to Angie than to him, her eyes widening with excitement. "You don't say." Burke explained that they hadn't found enough evidence to charge him, but Meka's mind didn't even register that part. All she heard was, "murder." Covering the phone with her hand, Meka opened her mouth in a silent scream, stomping her tiny Manolo Blahniks on the floor in excitement. "Tell me something, Carlton. You ever heard of this guy doing anything bizarre, like claiming to be a faith healer or something?"

"Wait a minute," Burke said, finally catching on. "You're thinking this guy is Reverend CJ, the one they're calling the ghetto prophet?" She told him that was what she was hoping to prove and he laughed, advising her to forget it. "I've worked on the west side

148

of Chicago for over five years and trust me; I haven't seen anything good come out of there yet."

"You're probably right," she said. But could you just e-mail me whatever you have on him? I'd really appreciate it." Burke assured her that he would. "Thanks Carlton. You're a doll." Meka gave him her e-mail address and hung up. "And that's how you do that," she said to Angie, bowing her head ever so humbly.

CHAPTER 22

That evening, Reverend Thomas and Bishop Hanks fought their way through the throng of people gathered in front of Teddy's house. When Thomas rang the bell, Teddy peeked out of the window at the top of the door to make sure it was them. He then snatched the door open and pulled them in, slamming the door quickly behind them. The determined reporters began beating on the door, demanding that CJ come out and speak to them.

Once safely ensconced in Teddy's living room the bishop told CJ and his crew about the mandate from New York. "I can't tell you how sorry I am, CJ. But it's out of my hands. There's nothing I can do."

"I understand," CJ said, disappointed, but not surprised.

"Well, I don't," said Thomas. "I think we should demand a meeting with Rev, I mean Reverend Bradshaw. Once he sees how many people you've helped . . ."

"I don't think so," said Hanks. "He's already heard the news reports and as far as he's concerned . . . I'm sorry, CJ, but he thinks you're a con man. And once Rev makes up his mind, anybody trying to sway him with the facts is going to have hell to pay." Turning to

Thomas, he said, "Trust me; you don't want to look like you're questioning his word."

"We could take it in front of the AACC," said Thomas.

"Rev *is* the AACC," said Hanks.

"But why would he want to keep CJ out of the churches?" Sebastian asked.

"He thinks CJ's making black preachers look bad," replied Bishop Hanks.

"Bad?" Sammy said, leaping up from his seat. "He's out there healing people. You're talking like he's some kind of mass murderer or something." Cheyenne patted him gently on the thigh and he sat back down, fuming.

"God never closes a door without opening a window," said CJ, rising from his seat. Thomas stood as well, realizing the meeting was over. "I appreciate everything you've done, Reverend. You too, Bishop, but I wouldn't expect y'all to go up against Bradshaw. He's a very powerful man." CJ placed his hand on Thomas' back and walked them to the door.

"Call me if you need me, CJ. This isn't right. If I have to stand up against the AACC, I will."

"Let's hope it doesn't come to that, CJ said." He shook hands with the two preachers and opened the door. As they stepped out a swarm of people descended upon them.

"CJ! CJ! Reverend CJ!" They flew back into the house and slammed the door.

"Man!" CJ said. "I forgot they were out there."

After a while, Teddy peeked out the window and said, "Looks like they're breaking up. The TV vans are gone, but there's still some people hanging around."

Reverend Thomas stood. "Maybe if I go out there and talk to them . . ."

"Oh, man!" Teddy exclaimed, bursting out in laughter.

CJ ran to the window and peered out. "Oh man," he echoed, holding his hands to his head as he watched Dee and Sherman climbing out of a cab – with luggage.

"You knew it was just a matter of time," Teddy chided.

"What's the matter?" the bishop asked, jumping up in alarm.

"It's my mother," CJ said. Just then, the doorbell rang.

"I'll get it," Teddy said, still laughing. He opened the door a crack, peeked out and then pulled Dee and Sherman inside, quickly slamming the door behind them. "Mama Dee!" he exclaimed, swooping her up in his arms.

When Teddy released her, Dee said, "Hello Theodore. Where's Chucky?"

"Here I am, Ma?" CJ said, crossing the room to greet her.

Sammy turned to Cheyenne and mouthed the word, "*Chucky?*" Cheyenne smacked him on the arm and stifled a laugh as CJ embraced his mother and brother.

"What are y'all doing here?" CJ asked, giving Sherman a hard look.

"It was all her idea," Sherman said, holding his hands up in a show of faultlessness. "She was coming whether I came along or not." What he didn't say was that he had to see first-hand what his big brother was up to. As much as he loved CJ, Sherman had always been a little jealous of him. As if being his mother's favorite wasn't enough, now he was supposed to have some kind of magic power.

"We came to see about you," Dee said. She then stepped back and gave him a critical look. "When's the last time you had a haircut?"

CJ's hand went to his bushy hair. He couldn't remember when he'd had his last haircut. Usually fastidious about his grooming and appearance, CJ realized that he hadn't given it much thought since he'd arrived in L.A. The only new article of clothing he'd purchased was the jersey he wore when he preached – and that had been at Teddy's insistence. He didn't care how he looked. All he cared about was spreading the Word to the people and getting them to believe.

"Where you get them gym shoes from, big brother? Payless?" Sherman asked with a snicker.

"I beg your pardon," said Teddy. "This man does not shop at Payless. He purchased that fine footwear at Kmart."

"Oh," Sherman said. "My bad." He and Teddy burst out in uproarious laughter, leaning on each other for support.

CJ watched them like a tolerant parent waiting for his children to realize they were misbehaving. When the laughter finally stopped, he said. "Y'all through? Have you got it out of your system?"

"I'm sorry, man," Sherman said. "I don't think I'm gon' ever get that out of my system. What are you made up for? You look like a refugee from a 1930's labor camp."

"Excuse me," said Bishop Hanks, giving a nod to Dee as he addressed CJ, "I think Reverend Thomas and I are just going to slip on out." Dee eyed him curiously.

"Forgive me, Bishop," CJ said, remembering his home training. "I'd like you to meet my mother, Mrs. Deanna Johnson and this is my brother, Sherman. Ma, these are my good friends, Bishop Hanks and Reverend Thomas.

Thomas rushed over and grasped Dee's hand. "Mrs. Johnson. I am so glad to meet you."

"Thank you," Dee said. "Nice meeting you too, Reverend."

As Thomas shook hands with Sherman, the bishop clasped Dee's tiny hand between both of his, his well-practiced smile beaming down on her in genuine admiration. "Mrs. Johnson. I can't tell you how pleased I am to meet you. You've raised a fine son. Bless you."

"Why, thank you," Dee said, clearly impressed.

Hanks kissed her hand before heading toward the door. At the mouth of the foyer, he turned. "Call me, CJ. Let me know what's going on."

"Yes, sir. I will," CJ replied as Teddy followed them to the door. He pushed back the little curtain at the top of the door and peered out. Most of the people had gone. Teddy opened the door and the two men slipped out.

"That bishop is a very charming man," Dee said. "Where is his church?"

"You're a married woman," Sherman reminded her, only half joking. Sherman, like CJ, was very protective of their mother. Sometimes he went a bit overboard, attempting to prove to Dee that he was just as deserving of her love as CJ was.

"Oh, hush." Dee said, looking around at the roomful of strangers. "You're gonna make these people think I'm some kind of hoochie mama or something."

CJ chuckled. The possibility of the sun forgetting to shine was more likely than anyone ever mistaking his churchy little mother for a hoochie mama. "Let me introduce y'all to everybody."

After CJ had made the introductions, Cheyenne gave Dee a hug and said, "Welcome to L.A., Mrs. Johnson. Can I get you some tea or something?"

"Thank you, darlin'. Tea would be lovely." Dee plopped down on the couch and patted the seat beside her. CJ took a deep breath and slumped down next to her. "So, what's all this stuff I've been hearing about you on the news?" CJ looked around at his friends who quickly got the hint and began to disband.

Sebastian stood first. "It was nice meeting you, Mrs. Johnson. You too, Sherman," he said, shaking Sherman's hand, "But I really have to run. I'll call you later, CJ." He quickly made his exit, followed by Hawk and the twins.

When Cheyenne emerged from the kitchen with the tea, she found Sammy bidding the newcomers good-bye. "Are we finna leave?" she asked, placing the tea on the table in front of Dee.

"Thank you, baby," Dee said, standing to give her a hug.

"Yeah," Sammy said. "We got some things to take care of at the club."

Cheyenne looked surprised, but only said, "Call me if there's anything I can do for you, Mrs. Johnson. CJ has the number."

"Okay, honey." Dee replied. "But you call me Mama Dee."

"Yes, ma'am," Cheyenne said as they headed for the door.

Once they'd gone, CJ took his mother's hands in his and said as gently as he could, "Ma. I need you to go home."

Dee snatched her hands away, "Fine. But if I go, you're coming too."

The news accounts she'd heard had frightened her and she'd come to take her boy home. "I didn't want to say anything in front of those people," she continued, "but if you just had to run off after you got out of the hospital, you could have at least called me. I didn't know if you were living or dead until I saw this lil' Chinese looking girl on TV making all her lil' snide remarks. She's a nasty lil' thing," she said with a shiver and began to dig in her purse for a tissue to wipe the tears that were beginning to spill.

"If you didn't want to talk to me, you could have at least called your daddy and let him know where you were. He's been worried sick. We all have. At least you could have had somebody send you your clothes. You look like some old homeless person.

You ain't homeless, Chucky. You got a family that cares about you."

"I know, Ma," said CJ as she continued to rag on him.

Teddy, struggling to keep from laughing, gave Sherman a nudge. "How about a beer?"

"Cool," Sherman said, following Teddy to the kitchen.

Interrupting Dee's continuous reprimands, CJ finally said, "Ma. Don't you see what's happening?" Dee froze. She knew what was happening and it scared her to death. "I'm doing the work I was put here to do," he said. "Isn't that what you wanted?"

"I don't know," she admitted. "All I know is that you are more precious to me than the air I breathe and I'm scared for you."

CJ wrapped his arms around his mom and kissed her on the head. "You're a trip, you know that?"

Dee smiled. "That's all right. I'm your trip and ain't nothing you can do about it." And that was that. Dee was there to stay and there was nothing anyone could do about it.

The next day, CJ and the guys sat on the patio discussing the news the preachers had delivered. The confident face CJ had shown for the ministers was gone. He wondered how he was going to get his word out to the people without going into the churches.

"We could do infomercials on TV," Sammy suggested.

"Yeah, right," Snorted Sebastian. "You got a couple of million bucks to spend?"

"It was just an idea," Sammy said.

After kicking around a few more ideas, none of which seemed feasible, Teddy said, "I don't know about y'all, but I'm hungry."

"Me too," said CJ. "What do y'all want to eat?"

"How about some soul food?" said Hawk, "One of my partners been bugging me about bringing you around to his restaurant. But, I didn't think you'd . . ."

"Cool," said CJ. "Let's go"

"I know you're not going to some greasy spoon one of Hawk's friends owns," said Sebastian.

"You ever hear of a place called Le Chitter-Ling?" said Hawk.

"Le Chitter-Ling!" Sebastian was incredulous. Le Chitter-Ling was the hottest new restaurant in L.A. and he had been trying for months to get a reservation. "That's pretty upscale, isn't it?"

"Maybe for you," Hawk replied.

"I've been wanting to check that place out. They say the shrimp is this big," said CJ, making an estimate of the size with his fingers.

"Cool. I'll give him a call."

"So, you're trying to tell me Clarence Prescott is a friend of yours," said Sebastian. He knew that Clarence Prescott, the infamous drug kingpin, secretly owned Le Chitter-Ling.

"I'm not trying to tell you nothin'," said Hawk. "You can come with us or not. I don't care one way or the other."

"I've got plans," said Sebastian. As badly as he wanted to go to the exclusive new restaurant, he wasn't about to be seen in public with this motley crew. He stood and clasped CJ's hand. "I'll talk to you later. Have fun."

As the door closed behind Sebastian, Hawk muttered. "Punk ass nigga."

"Say what?" CJ said, although he'd heard him perfectly well.

"That nigga's just as full of shit as he was in middle school."

"You went to school with Sebastian?" said the twins simultaneously.

"Man, we used to take that punk's lunch money every day. Now, he gon' pretend like he don't know me. Bet if I whupped that ass like I did in school, he'd remember who I am." They all chuckled at the thought.

CHAPTER 23

Sebastian was bursting with excitement as he maneuvered his Jaguar down the Hollywood Freeway. He'd been reluctant to let his friends know that he was involved with CJ until he was sure he was the real deal. But now that CJ had agreed to meet with Clarence Prescott, it was time for him to rally his troops. Everybody knew that Prescott's father had been a stone radical back in the day, and Prescott had no love for the establishment. With him in the picture, Sebastian knew that the revolution was about to be on.

"Call Marcus," he said into his phone. Marcus Benoit was Sebastian's longtime friend and the regional leader of an underground revolutionary group called Mama's Children. Created by a 1970's radical and funded by affluent blacks, the group kept an exceptionally low profile. While other groups were yelling, Black Power and getting infiltrated by the FBI, Mother's Children had been quietly educating and indoctrinating their young to obtain high paying jobs such as doctors, lawyers and politicians, several of which held sensitive government positions.

They'd encouraged their youth to join the military and many of them had gone into intelligence or elite special ops groups such as the Navy Seals. There were also pilots and military strategists among them. And under the guise of programs to keep inner city youths off the streets, Mother's Children had been conducting paramilitary training camps for decades. They now had a formidable army and an intricate system of multigenerational operatives planted everywhere from the school house to the White House, just waiting for the call. Whoever said that black folks couldn't get together and do something, had never heard of Mama's Children.

When Marcus, a popular rapper with a degree in economics answered his cell phone, Sebastian, not bothering with unnecessary greetings said, "You home?" Marcus replied that he was and Sebastian told him that he was on his way there with news that would blow his scalp back. When they disconnected the call, Sebastian slapped his steering wheel, threw his head back and shouted, "Yes!" as he gleefully steered his Jag toward the Hollywood hills.

A short while later, Sebastian leaned forward on Marcus' black leather couch and said, "I'm telling you, man, this dude CJ is the truth. You know me, I don't believe in nothing. But this guy is righteous."

"I hear what you're saying," said Marcus. His voice was as smooth as a mother's caress, but a look of skepticism showed on his attractive face. Marcus had the kind of boyish good looks that never faded. At thirty-five, he looked nearly the same as he did at twenty-one. That same bad boy smile still drove the ladies insane. "But the paper said . . ."

"Since when did you start believing that propaganda they write in the papers?"

Marcus chuckled and took a sip from his cocktail. "All right. So what is he supposed to be, the second coming or something?"

"I don't know," Sebastian admitted, taking a long swig from his own glass of amber liquid. "All I know is that the man has some serious powers. I've been hanging out with him for a while now and some of the stuff he's done . . ." He took a deep breath and blew it out, shaking his head. "I'm telling you, Marcus, I've seen him heal people with cancer, AIDS."

160

Marcus lifted one eyebrow incredulously. "And how is curing AIDS supposed to help with the revolution?"

Sebastian rubbed his hand over his face in frustration. "Look, I just met the man. I don't know what all he can do. But I do know that the first time I saw him I felt something. I can't really explain it, but he told me stuff about myself that he didn't have any way of knowing. Now, if he could do all that who knows what else he can do. I'm telling you, Marcus, he's got that revolutionary spirit and he's all about helping the black man. I've seen him cure a lot of people and none of them were white." He paused for a moment and freshened his drink from the crystal decanter on the coffee table. He took a long swallow of his drink and leaned forward, his hands clasped together in front of him. "I know you heard about the dude down in South Central who had been in a wheelchair for ten years. CJ is the one that healed him.

"Don't' tell me you believe that shit," said Marcus.

"I know the man," replied Sebastian. "I know him and his wife, Cheyenne. They own a little hole in the wall joint called Shenanigans."

Suddenly Marcus' expression changed and he seemed to be taking what Sebastian was saying more seriously. "What's this dude's name?"

"Sammy. Sammy Rocquemore. Why?"

Marcus picked up his glass, strolled to the sliding glass doors and gazed out on the lights of the magnificent homes scattered about in the surrounding hills. "What's his wife look like?"

Confused by this transition, Sebastian replied, "She's cute. A little dark for my taste, but she's got a body on her that won't quit."

"Yeah," Marcus said, nodding his head and smiling to himself. He turned to face Sebastian. "Does she have a little beauty mark right there?" he asked, pointing to the corner of his mouth. "Like that model, uh, Cindy What's-her-face?"

"Cindy Crawford? Yeah, she does. Don't tell me you know her."

"We kicked it for a minute back in the day. That was before I got my first big hit. Cheyenne. Yeah. She was sweet. She was real sweet."

"What happened?"

Marcus gave him an uncomfortable smile and slumped back down into his chair. "She dumped me for some ol' thug ass nigga fresh out of the penitentiary. Nigga named Sammy. All this could have been hers," he said opening his arms to encompass his lavish home. He then shrugged and made a face that said what the hell as he reached for the decanter and refilled his glass. "Not long after that, somebody told me the cops had shot him in the back and he was gon' be crippled for life. I know it sounds cold, but when I heard about him getting shot, I was glad. I was glad that she was going to have to spend the rest of her life taking care of some crippled ex-con."

"Well, he's not a cripple anymore," said Sebastian.

CHAPTER 24

When CJ, Teddy, Sherman, Herc, Sammy and Hawk strolled into Le Chitter-Ling, the elegance of the place overwhelmed them. Crystal chandeliers hung from the beamed ceiling and floor to ceiling windows graced the brick walls. Exotic looking plants, subdued lighting and soft, piped in music added to the ambience as a gorgeous hostess in a sleek black evening gown escorted them through a sea of tables adorned with glistening white tablecloths, where sat the crème de la crème of Hollywood society; among them were famous actors, producers, directors and studio bigwigs.

The hostess led them to a table in a discreet corner of the swank restaurant and Hawk introduced CJ and his entourage to their host Clarence Prescott, a big time drug trafficker said to have ties to the Columbian drug cartel. Prescott rose to shake their hands as did his two associates, Lorenzo the pimp who thought he had class, but didn't know enough to remove his bowler hat in a restaurant and Wesley, a violent street thug upon whom Prescott relied to handle his day-to-day operations.

Clarence Prescott stood about six foot, five and weighed over three hundred pounds. All muscle. Dressed in a tailor made suit with a "V" neck cashmere sweater underneath, he sported an ostentatious diamond ring on his pinky finger, a thick gold chain around his neck and a chunky gold Rolex Presidente on his wrist. Prescott hadn't gotten to where he was by being trusting. And despite what Hawk had told him about CJ, he was skeptical and anxious to find out exactly what his game was.

Surrounded by the sounds of polite laughter and controlled conversation, CJ said, "Thank you for inviting us to dinner, Mr. Prescott. This is a fantastic place you have here."

"You're welcome," Prescott said proudly. "I figure after all those hundreds of years with us taking the scraps off the white man's table and making them not only do, but do very well, it's about time we slap a fancy name on it and sell it back to him." Everyone laughed, agreeing wholeheartedly with the cleverness of his theory.

CJ looked around at the sophisticated, mostly white diners and smiled as they gorged themselves on such delicacies as chitlins Florentine, hog maws in a savory wine sauce and delicately grilled filet of catfish elegantly arrayed on small plates and sold at exorbitant prices.

Sensing the distrust in his fellow diners, CJ kept the conversation light. Turning to Hawk, he said with a smile, "So, you went to school with Sebastian, huh?"

"Yeah. He was a punk then and he's a punk now."

"Who's that?" Prescott asked.

"You remember Gabrielle St. John's lil' brother, Sebastian," Hawk said.

"Gabrielle St. John . . . Yeah," said Prescott, smiling at the fond memory. "So, what's up with her little brother?"

"He's been sniffing around CJ ever since that first thing in the church I told you about."

"What's he want?" Prescott asked.

"I don't know." Hawk answered. "I ain't seen the nigga in years. Thought he was the shit back in high school 'cuz he could play basketball. Once he got that scholarship and went off to college, nigga never looked back."

"Would you?" asked Teddy, eliciting laughter all around.

After a scrumptious meal washed down by a few bottles of Cristal the conversation flowed more easily, but CJ could still feel the uncertainty among them. Finally, Prescott asked CJ point blank, "Why did you agree to have dinner with us?"

"Because you invited me." CJ replied.

"Do you know who I am? Have you read what they write about me in the papers?" "I know exactly who you are."

"And . . .," Prescott said.

"And you ain't never done nothing to me."

Prescott stared at him for a beat and then laughed loudly, ignoring the reproachful looks cast on him by his refined patrons. "You're all right, man. You're all right," he said. "Most preachers wouldn't have nothing to do with us, especially these degenerates," he said half-jokingly, waving a hand toward his companions.

"I'm not most preachers," CJ replied, scraping the last of his delectable flambéed banana pudding from the dish with his spoon. He wiped his mouth with his napkin and patted his stomach. "My compliments to the Chef." He surveyed the faces of the men around him and reared back in his chair, sucking his teeth. "Ever hear the one about the prophet and the 'ho?" he asked. The men started grinning, prepared to hear a lewd after dinner joke.

"Hosea was this prophet in the Old Testament," CJ began. "He fell in love with a chick named Gomer."

"Gomer? Wasn't that the dude that used to be on the Andy Griffith show?" said Wesley.

"The name Gomer means perfect", CJ said, "and she was – on the outside at least. She had the face of an angel and the body of a goddess. But she was a 'ho." The guys were really grinning now, anxious to hear the story. "Now, God knew Hosea was crazy about this girl, so He told him to go ahead and marry her."

"I don't believe in God," Lorenzo announced.

"Well, He believes in you," CJ replied, staring straight into his eyes. Lorenzo looked like CJ had slapped him in the face with a dirty diaper.

"So why would God want a prophet to marry a 'ho?" asked Wesley.

"Because He wanted to show the people what unconditional love was all about," CJ said.

"Yeah, right," Prescott scoffed. "So, the 'ho gave up her evil ways and they lived happily ever after."

"Can I finish?" CJ said. Prescott leaned back, throwing up his hands as CJ continued. "Now, Gomer was fine. No doubt. But she didn't have a moral bone in her body."

"Can't make a 'ho into a housewife," said Sammy, shaking his head.

"But Hosea tried," CJ said. "He set her up in this beautiful crib, bought her fine clothes and expensive jewelry. But the sister still had to get her swerve on. I mean, she didn't give the man no respect. She'd flirt with men right up under his nose. She'd

disappear for days at a time and he wouldn't know where she was."
"I used to have a bitch like that," said Lorenzo.

"I'm telling you, man, she made a laughingstock out of my man in front of the whole town," CJ continued. "She wound up having three babies while she was with him and wasn't none of 'em his. But he took care of 'em anyway."

"Homeboy was a chump," said Wesley. "I woulda had me a DNA test."

"They didn't have no DNA back in them days, fool." Hawk said.

"Man, I woulda stomped a mud hole in that bitch's ass," said Lorenzo.

"Hey, he went into that relationship with his eyes wide open," said CJ. "He knew the girl wasn't no good from the jump, but he probably thought the love of a good man might turn her around," He shook his head and said, "That brother couldn't have been more wrong if he took classes in it. If anything, she got even worse after they got married."

"He shoulda knowed that." Lorenzo said.

"Now, these are the Jews we're talking about. They were the Lord's chosen people. God did everything for these people, but they had a bad habit of going off worshipping other gods. And you know God don't play that."

"Thou shall have no other god before me," said Wesley. When he saw the surprise on their faces, he said in his own defense, "What? I went to Sunday School."

CJ chuckled, he knew that they all had some type of religious training in them; he just had to make it relevant to their own lives. "Sometimes God would have a prophet like Hosea, warn the people about the judgment He was planning for them, so they could give up their sinful ways. He'd have the prophets tell them about His love for them and how much He wanted them to come back home to him. And sometimes, He'd give the prophet a message to act out."

"You mean like a play?" Sammy asked.

"Exactly," CJ said, pointing a finger at Sammy. "Only it would be like a living drama playing out God's message in a dramatic way. That's what He did with Hosea when He told him to marry Gomer. It represented God's marriage to the unfaithful Jews. See, God figured that when people saw Hosea married to Gomer, a woman everybody knew was low-down, they'd get the message that there was a similarity between Hosea's relationship to Gomer and God's relationship to them."

Prescott sat back in his chairs and rolled his eyes. "That don't even make no sense."

"If love always made sense, it wouldn't be love," CJ replied. "Yeah, God's love for Israel was unreasonable. I mean, if He wanted to make a commitment to a nation of people He shoulda chose people He knew would be faithful. People who would appreciate His love and be thankful for His blessings. Right?"

They nodded in agreement. "But then the Bible says that if we are faith-less, He will remain faith-ful. See what I'm saying?"

CJ could see that they were confused, so he tried to explain. "See, where we make our mistake is thinking that God only loves good people. But God loves sinners. In fact, He chases after 'em, just like He had Hosea run after Gomer. He goes looking for 'em. I'm telling you, them Jews used to cheat on Him with other gods every chance they got. They worshipped wooden statues, gold statues, Baal, the Queen of Heaven. All that. Some of 'em even went so far as to burn their own children in sacrifice to some of these man-made gods."

Ignoring the shocked looks on his listeners' faces, he said. "But even that didn't stop God from loving 'em."

"Damn," said Sammy.

Sherman was seeing CJ in a whole new light. His wimpy older brother seemed more confident and authoritative than he'd ever seen him before and these hardcore criminals were eating up every word he said. "Now, getting back to Hosea," CJ said. "After Gomer got everything she could outta my man she wanted out. She thought like so many fine women do, that her beauty would see her through."

"That's just how them whores think," Prescott said.

CJ held up an admonishing finger. "Now let's not confuse a 'ho with a whore."

"What's the difference?" Prescott asked.

"Allow me to elucidate" Teddy said, resting his hand humbly on his chest and assuming an authoritative air. "Although the terms are often used interchangeably, a 'ho is just a low-life skank who be givin' it up on G.P. (general principles)."

"But a whore," CJ added, "is a prostitute. She gets paid for her favors. Well, Gomer was a straight up 'ho, calling her a whore would be an insult to hard working hookers everywhere. Not only was she not getting paid, she was spending my man's money on these niggas she was laying up with. So what's a brother supposed to do?" he said with a shrug.

"I'd break my foot off in that bitch's ass," Lorenzo said.

"I'd give her plenty air and a whole bunch of letting alone," said Hawk, evidently cured of his woman beating ways.

"And that's exactly what he did," CJ said. "When she just insisted on running the streets, he didn't have no choice but to let her go. I mean, iron wears out."

"I heard that," said Teddy.

He went on to tell them how God had told Hosea that He was going to block Gomer's path with thorn bushes; wall her in so she can't find her way out. "Then she'll say . . ." He jumped into the character of Gomer, speaking in a falsetto home girl voice. "Chile, I'm going back to my husband. I was better off then, than I am now." Just as quickly, he's CJ again. "And we're just like Gomer. Sometimes we have to take some hard knocks before we learn that God's way is the best way." He leaned forward, making sure they understood where he was coming from. "Sometimes we have to bump our heads up against a wall, until we just can't take it anymore. That's when we say I'm going back to God. I was better off with God than I am now."

The men stared at him, transfixed as he continued, "Remember how beautiful Gomer was in the beginning? Well, after a while that beauty was gone. "Now, you think these niggas out here in these streets are cold – Man, them Jews was like ice. When they got tired of her they stripped her naked and put her up on the auction block. But she was so diseased and run through by then that didn't nobody want her. They started laughing at her, throwing stuff at her. And when they was just about to stone her, guess who jumps up and buys her for himself."

"Hosea." They all said in unison.

"She was cheap," CJ said in a humorous attempt to mitigate Hosea's boneheaded move. "Only cost him 'bout twelve bucks. That's half the price they usually got for a female slave."

"Hmph, he still got beat," said Lorenzo.

"When she became a slave he bought her back and took her home. That's the predicament we're in right now," he said leaning in closer. "We've become slaves to sin."

"Damn," Hawk muttered.

CJ gave them a minute to let it sink in. Then, in words that flowed like honey he said, "But in spite of that, God still loves us

170

and wants to bring us out of our slavery to sin. The Bible says that it was not with perishable things like silver or gold that you were redeemed, but with the precious blood of Christ. Now that's some good stuff right there." This brought smiles and confirming nods from everyone at the table.

"That's why the Bible can say, 'You are not your own; you were bought at a price.' Dig that. You were bought at a price. See, there's a natural, logical kind of loving that loves lovely things and lovely people. That's just . . . logical. But there's another kind of loving that doesn't look for value in what it loves, it creates value in what it loves. Like Earth, Wind and Fire says, 'It's all about love.' Have mercy! Now, that's coming from a hip place," he said, leaning back from the table and giving them a big smile.

"That's how God's love works – unconditional, inescapable love," he said emphatically. "His kindness leads us home. He don't care what we've done. He don't throw us in the garbage just because we've screwed up."

Prescott felt himself choking up. He gulped down the champagne in his glass and refilled it, taking a long swig as CJ continued. "God don't save you because you're so good and righteous. He saves you because of His mercy and His grace." CJ looked around the table at each of them and said softly, "You might think it's too late for you, or that you could never be forgiven for some of the stuff you've done. But all you have to do is say: Lord, I want to come home. I give myself totally and completely to you. When you do, you'll find his arms open wide," he said, opening his arms to them as God would.

The hardened group of criminals, ex-cons and felons sat staring at him in silence, overcome by the words he had spoken. CJ could see that for the first time in their miserable lives, they believed that they might actually be worth something – if only to God.

Sniffling, Lorenzo quickly wiped a tear off his cheek with the back of his hand. "It's getting hot in here," he said, lifting his hat and wiping the sweat from his head with his napkin.

Hawk leaned over to Prescott, who sat stoically, his massive chest rising and falling with the effort it took to maintain his composure. "I told you man. This cat is deep," Hawk whispered.

As they left the dining area CJ turned to Prescott and took his hand between both of his, "I want to thank you for a wonderful dinner, Clarence. I really enjoyed meeting you guys." CJ's touch made Prescott feel as if he was about to cry. He wanted to snatch his hand away and run, but having a rep to maintain, he just nodded and tried to smile.

As the others made their way out of the restaurant Prescott caught Hawk's eye and jerked his head toward his private office. Hawk followed him wordlessly. Once inside the elegantly appointed office Prescott flopped down in the big chair behind his desk and nodded toward a couple of red leather armchairs sitting in front of the desk. "Sit."

Hawk sat as Prescott opened a box of cigars and took one out. He removed a cigar cutter from the box and with slow and deliberate movements clipped the end off of his cigar, lit it and took a deep puff. After taking a moment to get himself together he asked, "Where you get that dude from?"

"He just walked up to me one night and said 'Come with me.'"

"And you just went?"

Hawk hadn't really thought about it before. "Yeah," he said. "I just went."

"Was he looking to buy some dope?"

"Naw, man," Hawk said, squirming in his seat. He hated having to explain himself – especially since he didn't know himself why he'd followed CJ. "It wasn't nothing like that."

"You just went off with a nigga you never saw before. Were you planning on robbing him or something?"

"Naw, man. What's up?" Hawk said, holding his hands out to the side.

"Look, Hawk, I know you, man. You ain't one them ol' rinky-dink ass niggas that go runnin' off behind somebody you don't know just because he says come on." He eyed Hawk quizzically for a moment before asking, "You ain't into none of that sissy shit, are you?"

"Hell, naw!" Hawk said, leaping out of his chair, appalled that Prescott would even ask him something like that.

"Alright. Okay," Prescott said, holding his hands up. "I'm just trying to figure out why you went off with the nigga. See, I'm thinking he might be CIA." Prescott was grasping at straws, desperately seeking any explanation for the affect CJ's words had had on him."

"CIA?"

"Yeah, CIA. You know they're into that mind control shit." Hawk had to chuckle at the incredulous idea. "You ever heard a nigga talk like that before?" Prescott asked.

"Naw."

"That's what I'm saying. I've seen that shit on PBS."

Hawk looked at him as if he'd just realized he was talking to a crazy man. "Hey, man, I was just trying to put you up on something. You think what you want," he said, turning to leave.

"Wait." Prescott said, opening his desk drawer. He pulled out a stack of hundred dollar bills still in its bank wrapper and slapped it down on the desk.

Damn! Hawk thought. Prescott had gotten his attention big time, but Hawk remembered his ABCs (Always Be Cool) and maintained his nonchalant demeanor. He resumed his seat, crossed his legs and propped his elbow on the arm of the chair, his hand stroking his chin. "What's that for?" he asked, nodding toward the money.

Prescott slid the cash across the desk to him. "That's ten grand. Give it to CJ."

Hawk's gaze went from Prescott to the money and back to Prescott. "For what?"

"I don't know," Prescott said with a shrug. "Whatever." I ain't seen a preacher yet that didn't need money. What's so cool about it, he didn't ask." If he had, Prescott would have turned him down flat. He then threw in a quick disclaimer just to make sure he wasn't looking like a punk. "I ain't saying I think he's no prophet or nothing like that. I just like the way the man carries himself. Go on," he said, nodding toward the money. "Take it to him." Hawk reached for the money, keeping a wary eye on Prescott. Sure enough, as soon as his hand touched the money Prescott's manicured paw slapped down on top of it. "One stipulation." Hawk smirked. He knew Prescott wasn't going to just get up off of ten stacks without some kind of conditions. He was too good of a businessman.

Prescott removed his hand and leaned back in his chair. "What kind of stipulation?" Hawk asked.

"You can't tell nobody where this money came from," Prescott said, picking at the hairs of his neatly trimmed van dyke.

"Not even CJ?"

"Especially not CJ," he said. "Hmph. He probably wouldn't even take it if he knew it came from me. Just tell him it's from an anonymous benefactor." He then turned away from Hawk, picked up the phone and started to dial, an indication to aw

Hawk that the meeting was over. Hawk picked up the money, stuffed it into his inside jacket pocket and left the office without attempting any further conversation.

When the door closed behind Hawk, Prescott hung up the phone, closed his eyes and clasped his hands in prayer and said softly, "Lord, I want to come home. I give myself totally and completely to you."

CHAPTER 25

Carla thought that if she came to a more affluent part of town she might be able to do some panhandling. But, she looked so nasty and germy that people turned away in disgust when she approached them. *I need to get to a doctor,* she thought as she crept down Melrose holding her hand to her aching stomach. She hadn't returned to the free clinic since the doctor diagnosed her with AIDS and syphilis. She was afraid they might put her in the hospital and then how would she get her drugs.

As she started down the block where Le Chitter-Ling was housed she saw a huge crowd gathered outside the restaurant and heard people shouting, "CJ! CJ! That's Reverend CJ!" When word got out that CJ was inside, everybody and his mama had flocked to Le Chitter-Ling.

"Reverend CJ," she whispered, focusing her eyes on the entrance of the restaurant across the street. There he was, standing at the top of the four steps leading up to the chic eatery. There were other men with him who tried to hold back the stampeding horde. The frenzied crowd crushed in on them, shouting outlandish requests.

"Hey, Reverend CJ. Can you put a spell on my husband's girlfriend?"

"I need a new car, CJ."

"Can you get me a part in the Princess Di movie?"

CJ had never sought celebrity and he didn't like it when they mobbed him like this. But this was what he encountered every time he went out in public. They all wanted to see him. They all wanted something from him. "Calm down. Calm down," he said, holding his hands up. But the excited crowd drowned out his words.

Chewing nervously on her grimy, nubby fingernails, Carla thought of asking CJ for help and quickly dismissed the notion. *He'd probably have me arrested just for talking to him,* she thought. However, she'd seen what this man could do. More importantly, she'd looked into his eyes and known instantly that this was a man of God – and God was the only one who could help her now. Before she could think further, her feet decided for her and she found herself skirting traffic in her attempt to cross the wide street. A plan formulated in her mind as she fought her way through the dense crowd. *I don't even have to talk to him,* she thought. *If I could just get close enough to touch his clothes, I know I'll be healed.*

Pain gnawed at Carla's insides as the massive crowd pushed and jostled her frail body like a leaf in the wind. However, she hadn't survived on the streets this long without knowing how to think fast. She started coughing intentionally, knowing that it would make people step away from her, allowing her to slip into the space they'd vacated. It worked perfectly and she plunged forward with an overwhelming determination, until a man pushed her aside and she fell to the ground where people stepped over her as if she were just so much trash in the road.

Undaunted, Carla began to crawl through the crowd on her hands and knees. Her head was reeling from the chaos around her and she felt like a campfire was burning in her belly. Suddenly a huge, booted foot smashed down on her hand and she heard her bones crunch like peanut shells. She had to close her eyes and bite her lip to keep from screaming out in pain, while frantically punching the leg belonging to the offending foot until its owner removed it from her hand. Through blinding pain, Carla continued her arduous journey. She tried to protect her injured hand by holding it up and using her good hand and her elbow to scoot along the ground on her belly, continuously inching her way toward the stairs. Toward CJ.

CJ now stood on the second to the bottom step with Sherman and Herc on either side of him attempting to hold back the rapidly increasing crowd. Teddy grabbed the parking valet and slipped him his parking ticket along with a twenty-dollar bill.

When Carla spotted Hawk standing behind CJ, she froze, wondering why CJ would be with a trifling nigger like him. She knew that if Hawk saw her, he'd run her off for sure. Weighing her options, Carla decided that she had nothing to lose – and everything to gain.

As CJ stepped down to the bottom step the onslaught of people closed in on him even more, pressing against him as Carla, concealed among the legs of the assemblage, continued to inch forward. When she got as close as she dared, she balanced herself on her good hand and stretched out the dirty, bony fingers of her injured hand straining to reach him. *If I could just touch his clothes*, she thought. When she touched the hem of his pants, she felt a spark race through her body like an electric shock. At that same instant, a chill shot from CJ's head straight down to his toes. Suddenly he felt scared, invaded. "Who touched me?" he demanded, scanning the crowd with his eyes. Carla quickly shrank back into the sea of legs.

"Whatchu mean, who touched you?" Sammy whispered. "We're smashed in with wall to wall people."

The anguish showed on CJ's face. "Somebody deliberately touched me. I felt the power leave my body. Who touched me?" he shouted, his voice cracking through the air like thunder.

The startled crowd fell back, parting like the Red Sea to reveal Carla crouched on the ground with her head tucked between her arms, trembling like a wet dog. A wave of despair washed over her and she wanted to disappear, but it was too late – she was already exposed. She lifted her head slightly and whimpered, "I did." Relief swept over CJ as he recognized her. He gently gripped her by the shoulders and helped her to her feet.

Carla felt strange. Pain had been her companion for so long that she didn't recognize the feeling of it being gone. Suddenly she realized that there was no pain anywhere in her body. She covered her face with her hands and began to laugh hysterically, tears pouring from her eyes – tears of joy, tears of relief.

CJ gently removed her hands from her face and stared into her eyes. The transformation was astounding. The gaunt face ravaged by drugs and disease now radiated health and vitality. Eyes that had been red and vacant were bright and clear, glistening with tears as they stared up at him.

Sammy whispered to Hawk. "Is that Carla?" Staring wordlessly at the ravishing beauty, Hawk could only nod his head.

The Italians call it "The Thunderbolt." And it struck CJ hard the moment he looked into Carla's big brown eyes. Yes, she was beautiful, but it went far beyond that. He felt an immediate connection with this woman, something he'd never felt with anyone before. The feeling was so intense that it unnerved him.

"I'm sorry," Carla said, fighting to control herself. "I was so sick. I knew that if I could just touch your clothes I'd be healed. I didn't mean no harm."

"Why didn't you just come up to me and ask for my help?" CJ said, touched by the enormity of her faith.

"Look at me," she said, unaware of her outer transformation. "I wouldn't even disrespect you by coming up in your face."

Just then, Teddy's SUV pulled up, scattering the crowd. The valet jumped out of the vehicle and threw the keys to Teddy who climbed into the driver's seat with Sammy riding shotgun. Herc opened the back door for CJ who grasped Carla's elbow and to her surprise ushered her into the back seat. He then climbed in beside her, followed by Sherman and Herc. Hawk stood on the steps next to Clarence, watching as they drove away.

A short time later, Carla gazed at herself in the mirrored wall of Teddy's music room. "Oh my God!" she exclaimed in disbelief, touching the lovely, flawless face that stared back at her. She then stared at her hand; it looked as though it was never injured. Tears filled her eyes and all she could do was repeat, "Oh my God!"

She stepped back to get a full view of herself in the mirror and was amazed at the Marine Corps tight body she found there. She barely remembered the healthy looking woman in the mirror. It had been so long since she'd looked like that. She turned to CJ beaming with appreciation and wonder. "Thank you, Reverend CJ." She started to hug him and pulled herself back. "I'm sorry," she said, looking down at her filthy clothes self-consciously.

"Call me CJ," he said, wrapping his arms around her in a warm embrace. Carla clung to him, her face buried in his chest, tears flowing. She allowed herself to relax in the comfort of his strong arms, inhaling the clean masculine scent of him as she cried for old and new.

Teddy wondered how CJ could touch her. She looked good, true enough, but her clothes were deplorable. "Look here." Teddy said. "Why don't you come on up to my sister's room and take a shower and what not? I know she's got something up there that'll fit you."

Reluctantly, Carla released CJ and stepped back. "No," she said, shaking her head and wiping her eyes. "I couldn't do that." "It's cool," Teddy said reassuringly. "She's out of town." Carla looked at CJ, wondering what to do. Lord knows she could use a shower, but she knew how women were about other women invading their space.

CJ knew what she was thinking and said, "Go ahead. She won't mind."

With a hesitant smile, Carla allowed Teddy to lead her up the stairs and into Dusty's bedroom. "You have to excuse the mess," he said. Discarded shoes and clothes cluttered the floor and the bed.

When Teddy left, Carla stepped into the lavender and white bathroom and gasped. A tub. A big, beautiful bathtub. "Well," she said, eagerly shucking her filthy clothing, "If I'm gonna get cussed out for taking a shower, I might as well have me a bath."

CHAPTER 26

"Mmm," Carla moaned, sinking down to her chin in a tubful of fragrant bubbles, luxuriating in the warmth of the water as it caressed her body. She couldn't remember the last time she'd felt so relaxed. "If God made anything better than water, he must have kept it for himself," she said.

After lounging in the bath for what seemed like hours, a dark sadness began to encroach on her joy. "Oh, God," she said through tear filled eyes, "Something so simple shouldn't feel this good." She had to laugh at herself. *Damn girl, it's just a bath.* But she knew it wasn't just the bath. It was the healing. The transformation. Most of all, it was the feeling she'd experienced when CJ held her in his arms. She'd felt safe for the first time since who knows when, like she was being held by the man who loved her. "Dream on, sister," she said, snapping herself out of her fantasy with a harsh chuckle. "As if anybody could ever love a worthless bitch like you. Especially him."

Carla stood up in the muddy water and let it drain out as she turned the shower on. Taking a bottle of shampoo from the shower caddy, she washed her hair. After climbing out of the tub, she dried herself off with one of the big, fluffy towels hanging on the rack and wrapped a second towel around her hair. She cleaned the tub immediately; making sure no one ever saw the amount of filth and grime that had come off her body.

After her bath, Carla took her time smoothing lotion all over her body, savoring the silky soft feel of her skin and the enticing fragrance of Dusty's expensive body lotion. *Now, for something to wear*, she thought, stepping into Dusty's walk in closet. She was astonished at the racks of beautiful clothes crammed into the huge closet. There were hats, belts and scarves hanging from the walls and rows upon rows of shoes. But she dared not touch any of it.

Instead, she went to the dresser and searched the drawers looking for something worthless to wear. She opened a drawer filled with panties, some of which still had the tags on them. Even though she'd fallen to the bottom of the barrel, Carla couldn't bring herself to wear panties someone else had worn. A girl had to draw the line somewhere. She chose a pair of brand new pink bikinis and slid them on. The panties gave her an unexplainable feeling of security. She opened another drawer that held bras; she held one up and saw immediately that it was too small for her. She discovered some cut off shorts and an old T-shirt in the bottom drawer and put them on. She found a shirt that looked like it probably belonged to Teddy and slipped it on to cover the fact that she wasn't wearing a bra.

Carla stood in front of the dresser mirror blow drying her hair. She was amazed at how the hair that had been so brittle and matted was now long and lustrous. She rooted around among Dusty's massive array of cosmetics and perfumes until she found a ponytail holder. She brushed her hair back in a ponytail and smiled at her reflection in the mirror. "Thank you, God." She stuck her feet into a pair of Dusty's flip-flops and checked herself out in the full-length mirror. "Not bad," she said, smiling at her reflection."

Carla started down the stairs with her dirty clothes tied up in a plastic bag and froze at the sound of Hawk's slow, sneaky voice coming from the kitchen. Terrified, she made a quick dash toward the front door and stopped abruptly. "*Where am I going?* She had no family and had long since alienated all her friends. And the flophouses and shelters she'd frequented in the past were out of the question. Besides, CJ and Teddy had been too good to her for her to just slip out like that. Gathering all her reserve, Carla took a deep breath and marched toward the kitchen.

"Aw, there she is." Teddy said. All eyes turned toward Carla as she entered the room smiling bashfully. "I thought we were gonna have to come up there and rescue you."

"Sorry I took so long," she said meekly.

"Don't pay any attention to Teddy," CJ said with a smile. "He's just talking. Come over here and sit by me." He pulled a chair out for her and as she started towards it, she saw Hawk perched on a stool in a corner and her stomach tightened.

"Hey, Carla," he said with a sly smile.

"Hey," she said softly, her body stiffening in preparation for the onslaught of insults that never came. Once again, she wondered what Hawk was doing there.

"We ordered a pizza." Teddy said, pointing to the gigantic pizza sitting in the middle of the table. "Better get some before these greedy niggas gobble it all up."

The delightful aroma of the pizza caused Carla's empty stomach to growl. Hoping no one heard it she slid into the chair next to CJ, still clutching the bag of dirty clothes.

"What's that?" Teddy asked, eyeing the bag suspiciously, as he placed two large slices of pizza on a paper plate.

"My clothes," she said. "I was gonna wash them if you don't mind. Then I could put them back on and wash your sister's clothes. I hope she won't be mad at you for letting me use them."

"Don't even worry about it," CJ said, taking the bag from her and throwing it over his shoulder. "Dusty's not like that." Teddy handed Carla the plate he'd fixed for her. "Want some *soda*?" CJ

184

asked flashing a smile at Teddy as he picked up the bottle and filled a plastic cup for her.

"Thank you," she said shakily, taking a bite of her pizza.

"Well, hello there," Said Dee, entering from the patio, a robe covering her bathing suit and a towel tied turban style on her head. "You must be Carla." Carla stared at the petite beauty in surprise.

"This is my mom," CJ explained.

"Nice to meet you, Mrs. . . ."

"Call me Mama Dee," she said, wrapping Carla in a warm embrace. She liked the young woman immediately and felt a certain protectiveness toward her.

Carla smiled tentatively, "I really . . . I really appreciate . . ." Tears the size of young golf balls tumbled from her eyes and she began to sob uncontrollably.

"Hey," CJ said, wrapping his arm around her shoulders and giving her a little squeeze. "It's all good." He spoke to her gently, his voice reassuring.

"I'll go up and clear out some of my sister's junk, so you'll have somewhere to sleep," Teddy said.

"Don't mess with that girl's stuff," Dee said. "Carla can bunk with me. I got that big old chaise lounge in my room. She can have the bed and I can sleep on that."

"Oh, no," Carla protested. "I couldn't intrude on you like that."

"Intrude? Honey, you're looking at the queen of the party crashers. Right, Theodore?"

"*Mi casa es su casa*," Teddy said with a slight bow.

185

"But, but . . ."

"No buts," CJ said. "You get yourself a good night's sleep and tomorrow I'll get Sammy's wife to take you shopping."

"I don't have any money to go shopping," she quickly objected.

"Don't worry about it," he said, whipping a gold credit card out of his wallet and placing it on the table in front of her.

"No," she protested, backing away from the card like it was a venomous snake. "No, I can't let you do that."

"You can't wear those shorts for the rest of your life," he said, giving her an irresistible smile.

"I know," she said. "I was gonna wash my clothes and . . ." His doubtful smile told of the improbability of ever getting those clothes clean again and she had to smile. "Okay. But I'm going to pay you back as soon as I get on my feet. I promise."

"I know you will," he said, pushing the card closer to her plate.

Unaccustomed to even the smallest kindness, Carla slowly picked the credit card up, looked at it for a moment and flung her arms around CJ's neck. "Oh, thank you, CJ. Thank you for everything." She burst into tears again. "I'm sorry. I'm just so emotional tonight. I think I do need to go lay down."

"Come on, baby," said Dee, wrapping her arm around Carla's waist. "I'll show you were you're gonna sleep."

"Thank you, Teddy," Carla said, sniffling as she wiped snot from her nose with the back of her hand. Sammy held out a paper napkin which she took and blew her nose. "I'm sorry. I just can't seem to get it together."

"That's all right," CJ said. "You go on up and get some rest. We'll see you in the morning." Nodding tearfully, she let Dee lead her out of the kitchen and up the stairs.

Hawk rubbed at his chin with his hand, attempting to hide the smirk that had appeared on his face. "What's up, Hawk?" CJ asked.

Hawk had never been one to blow another player's game, but he felt that CJ had a right to know who he was dealing with. "You can kiss that credit card goodbye."

"What do you mean?" Teddy asked.

"Man, when y'all get up in the morning, Carla and that gold card gon' be long gone."

"What makes you say that?" CJ asked.

"I know the broad," Hawk said. "Been knowin' her since she first started coming around in her lil' Audi. Just got out of the service and had a habit a mile long. She was fine too, man. All the niggas wanted to hit that."

"Including you." Sammy said.

"Pussy don't excite me," Hawk drawled. "Money's what gets my dick hard. And she was spending plenty of it. Had a nice lil' ol' office job, be coming through lookin' slick with her lil' suits and high heels. At first, she just came through on the weekends with this dude. Then she started coming more often, by herself. Next thing I know, she out there every day. Started turning tricks, looking bad – Man she went from sugar to shit in less than a year. It's been all downhill since then. The broad is scandalous, man. She'll steal the sweet out of ginger cake and won't even crack the crust."

As everyone laughed at Hawk's remark, CJ just shook his head. He wasn't worried about Carla running off with his credit card. He knew what she had been, but he also knew who she was.

He pulled a card from his pocket and picked up the cordless phone. They all watched as he dialed a number and waited for someone to answer. "Hey, Chad," he said, after a few seconds. "This is CJ, Dusty's friend."

"CJ! How good to hear from you." Chad had heard about the mysterious Reverend CJ and wondered if this friend of Dusty's could be him. The thought occurred to him because he'd felt some disturbing energy coming from CJ when they met. Not negative, but disturbing. Once the customary greetings and inquiries into each other's health were out of the way, CJ said, "I need to ask you a favor."

"Just name it," Chad replied.

"I got this friend," CJ said, "who could use a total beauty overhaul."

"You mean a makeover?"

"Yeah, a makeover."

"Sure, no problem," Chad said. "When would you like her to come in?"

"Tomorrow," CJ said.

"Tomorrow?" Chad said in a doubtful voice as he consulted his Blackberry.

"Is that a problem?"

"Oh, no. No," Chad lied. The salon was booked solid for the next month and he had a growing waiting list. "I'm sure I could squeeze in one more."

"Well, actually, there'll be two," CJ said, unapologetically. Another lady's coming with her. I want them both to get the full treatment, hair, nails, facials – all that stuff."

"I see," Chad said, scratching his head. "No problem. Can they come early?" They set an appointment for eight o'clock the next morning.

"You think that'll be okay with Cheyenne?" CJ asked Sammy as he hung up the phone.

"Yeah. She love all that beauty shit."

Teddy placed his hand on CJ's forehead, a look of concern on his face. CJ pushed it away. "Don't start none, it won't be none," he warned, pointing a finger at him.

Teddy fell out laughing. "I'm just trying to see if you got a fever, Nigga." Since when did your cheap ass become Big Papa?" CJ chuckled as Teddy started singing, taunting him with Tina Turner's prophetic words. "You're just a fool. You know you're in love."

"You're the fool," CJ said, laughing it off. He opened the refrigerator and grabbed a bottle of water, hoping no one could see that Teddy's crack had hit perilously close to home. CJ had known from the moment he looked into Carla's eyes, that she was his. It was as natural for him to take care of her as it was for a mother to nurse her child.

Hawk watched as CJ opened the glass sliding door and stepped out onto the patio. Finally, a chance to talk to him alone, he thought.

"Why you always messing with him, Teddy?" Herc asked, obviously perturbed.

"Down boy," Teddy said. We play like that all the time. That's my boy. We grew up together."

"Oh," said the big man, settling back in his chair.

"But you know something. I like that in you."

189

"What?

"That guard dog thing you got going on. I like that. You really got his back don't you?"

"Yeah." Herc answered. "Don't you?"

Teddy's face broke into a huge smile. "Man, I've had that nigga's back since Chicago was a cow pasture."

Unnoticed by the others, Hawk followed CJ out to the patio. "Hey," he said, interrupting CJ's thoughts. "Got a minute?"

"Sure," CJ said, gesturing to the seat opposite him. "What's up?"

"I got something for you," Hawk said, removing an envelope from his pocket as he sat.

"What?"

Hawk took the money from the envelope and placed it on the table. "Ten grand."

"Whoa!" CJ exclaimed. "What's that for?"

"For you. For your ministry," Hawk shrugged. "It's a donation."

"From who?" CJ asked. But he knew who it was from. *Clarence Prescott*, he thought with smile. Prescott had constructed such a strong emotional shield around himself that CJ hadn't been sure if he'd connected with him or not.

"He wants to remain anonymous," Hawk said. "He said you could think of him as your anonymous benefactor."

"Hot Dog!" CJ exclaimed. Hawk thought he was excited over the money, but he was overjoyed about the soul he'd won.

CHAPTER 27

The following morning, CJ awoke to the tantalizing aroma of coffee and bacon. He jumped out of bed, threw on his jeans and padded barefoot down the stairs. He followed his nose into the kitchen where he found Teddy and Carla having coffee as she prepared breakfast. "Good morning," Carla said with a brightness she didn't feel.

"Good morning," he said, taking a mug from the cabinet and pouring himself a cup of coffee. "Sleep well?"

"Like a log," she lied. She didn't tell him how she had lain awake in the fresh, clean sheets afraid to go to sleep for fear she'd wake up and find that it had all been a dream. She averted her eyes from his bare chest as she placed their breakfast of french toast, bacon and eggs on the table. *Put a shirt on*, she thought, barely able to keep from hurling herself at his broad shoulders and six-pack abs or running her tongue down the enticing little line of hair that trailed from his navel down into the mysterious recesses of his jeans. *Lord, why did you let him leave the top button of those jeans undone?*

"Cheyenne called," Teddy said as CJ slid into the chair across from him. "She's on her way over."

"Cool," CJ said, snapping Carla out of her reverie. "Sammy's wife is coming to take you shopping, Carla. I want you to get whatever you need. You hear? And you've got an eight o'clock appointment with Chad to get your hair and all that other stuff done."

"Chad?" she said incredulously. "I know you're not talking about *Mr. Chadwick*."

"Yeah, that's him."

"The Mr. Chadwick?"

"The only one I know," CJ said, drowning his french toast and eggs in syrup. "He's got a shop somewhere in Beverly Hills."

"Mr. Chadwick's House of Style is not a shop. It is the most incredibly exclusive beauty spa on the west coast.

You sure you can afford that, CJ? It's expensive."

"Don't worry about it," CJ said, looking up from his plate. "I got you."

Carla wanted to turn it down, tell him no way. But she was too ecstatic. She leaped up from her chair and threw her arms around his neck. "Oh, thank you, CJ," she said, showering him with kisses. "Thank you so much."

"You're welcome," CJ said with a smile. "You better hurry up and eat, if you're gonna make that appointment." He was glad that he'd been able to put a smile on her face.

Carla was too excited to eat. She jumped up and started cleaning the kitchen. When the men finished eating, she emptied the scraps into the garbage disposal, rinsed the dishes and piled them into the dishwasher. As she was sweeping the kitchen floor, the doorbell rang. "I'll get it," Teddy said, starting for the door. A moment later, he returned with Cheyenne at his heels.

Sammy had told Cheyenne all about Carla's miraculous transformation, but she couldn't wait to see it for herself. When she stepped into the kitchen, she mistook Carla for Dusty, Teddy's sister whom she had never met. "Hi," Cheyenne said, extending her hand as she crossed over to the other woman. "I'm Cheyenne, a friend of CJ's."

"Hey, Cheyenne. It's me, Carla."

Cheyenne peered closely into her face. Seeing a vague resemblance, she said, "Carla?"

"Yeah. It's me," Carla smiled. She almost fainted from shock when Cheyenne pulled her into a warm hug. Although they had often crossed paths, the two women had never been friends. Cheyenne held Carla at arm's length and looked her up and down, "Girl, you look good. You look so . . ."

"Healthy?" Carla supplied.

"Yes. Healthy."

They laughed and hugged again. When the ladies left, Teddy leaned back on the counter staring at CJ with a funny little grin on his face.

"What?" CJ said.

"I was just wondering when you started treating folks to shopping sprees and what not?"

"Give it a rest, Teddy. What good is money if you can't use it to help somebody?"

Teddy's eyes widened in surprise. Was this his old pal, Cheapskate Charlie talking?

That night when the gang gathered at Teddy's, everyone complimented Cheyenne and Carla on their new hairstyles and professionally made up faces. In fact, Sammy couldn't keep his hands off of Cheyenne and CJ couldn't keep his eyes off of Carla. She looked amazing. Her hair was styled in a bouncy bob and she sported a lavender pants outfit with shoes to match.

When Sebastian breezed into the music room grinning like the cat that swallowed the proverbial canary, he froze at the sight of Carla. "Hello, there," he said, instantly turning on the charm. "I don't think we've met. I'm Sebastian."

"I'm Carla," she replied, giving him her prettiest smile.

"Nice meeting you, Miss Carla," his gaze lingering a moment longer than necessary before turning to CJ.

"Good evening, gentlemen. How is everyone doing this fine evening?" "You're in pretty good spirits," CJ said. "What's up?" Sebastian slid onto the keyboard bench next to CJ. "I've been thinking about what Bishop Hanks said about the AACC not letting you preach in his church anymore."

"And . . ."

"He didn't say you couldn't preach in any other churches."

"That goes without saying," Teddy said. "Bishop Hanks is one of the most powerful preachers in this state. If he has to bow down to the council so does every other black church in California."

"Who said we have to stay in California?" Sebastian replied.

"What do you have in mind?" CJ asked.

"You said you wanted to get your message out to all the black people in the country, didn't you?" CJ nodded. "Well, we need to take this show on the road?"

"Like go on tour?" CJ asked.

194

"Exactly. *Reverend CJ's Gospel Revue,*" he said, using his hands to show an imaginary marquee in the air. "Reverend Thomas said he'd contact some of the preachers he knows around the country. Bishop Hanks said he didn't want his name involved because he's on the Executive Committee of the council, but he promised to help us any way he could on the QT. We could hit one church in each town and be gone before the sun comes up. By the time the council's stool pigeons know we've been there – we're already gone."

"Guérilla style salvation," CJ said. "Sounds good . . ."

"But?" Sebastian added.

"But, I don't want to bill myself as *Reverend* CJ. I'm not a preacher, you know."

"You can call it whatever you want. The name's not important."

Herc said, "How about *CJ's Soul Saving . . .*

"Crusade," added Jimbo.

Everyone liked the name. "How are we supposed to finance this grand crusade?" asked Teddy.

"I've got a few irons in the fire," replied Sebastian, turning to CJ. "I wanted to run it by you before I made any commitments."

"Let me pray on it," CJ said, even though he already knew that CJ's Soul Saving Crusade was the window he'd been waiting for.

A few nights later, CJ gathered his crew together and told them that he thought the tour was an excellent idea.

"Yes!" Sebastian said, slapping his hands together.

As the excitement of the impending road trip spread throughout the room, CJ laid out the rules. "Now, we're only going to black churches," he said to Sebastian who began taking notes. And then to the group at large, he said. "We're gonna do this guerrilla style. Hit 'em hard and hit 'em fast. We'll be gone before anybody realizes we've even been there. I'll still heal the sick, but my main goal is to let the people to know about the nation of God – that it is available to them," he said, walking among them like a general giving orders to his troops. "If anyone doesn't welcome us or want to hear what I have to say, we leave that town quick, fast and in a hurry. But I'll tell you one thing, it'll be better for Sodom and Gomorrah on Judgment Day than it will for that town." They all laughed.

"I'm serious," he continued in a grave tone. "This might sound like fun right now, but you can trust and believe it's gonna get nasty before it's over with."

"What do you mean?" Sammy asked.

"I've been spoon-feeding the people up until now, but I'm 'bout to start giving it to 'em straight – no chaser. I'm gon' be pulling the masks off of some people and bringing some truths to light. I've been praying on this and the truth is that not every black face you see is gon' be your friend. Some folks might even start hating *you* because of the things I say You know we still got plenty house niggas out there."

"I heard that," said Sebastian.

"Even people you thought were your friends might turn on you, just because you're with me." He was about to take his mission to a whole new level and he had to be sure that these people, people who instinctively rejected authority, would follow him. "I ain't gon' lie to you," he said. "This could get dangerous. But if we're gonna do it, y'all gon' have to trust me and follow my lead no matter what."

"You're talking like somebody might try to kill us or something," Sammy said warily.

"So what if they do," CJ snapped, his eyes blazing with fury. "All they can do is kill your body. The one you need to be worried about is the one who can destroy your body *and* your soul. – in hell." They all stared at him, confused by his sudden burst of anger. They would soon learn that these bouts of anger and frustration would become even more frequent as CJ transitioned into his God-self.

"Ain't nobody playing with y'all. You think I came to bring peace to the world?" No one answered. "Naw," The Brother Man," he said, slapping his chest, "comes swinging a sword."

They were seeing a whole new side of CJ now – the warrior side and they liked it. These were radical men and what he was saying sounded like revolutionary talk to them. Sebastian's heart was about to leap out of his chest. He couldn't wait to call Marcus and tell him to spread the word. Things were getting ready to jump off.

"That's what I'm talkin' 'bout," Hawk said, whipping out a big ominous looking gun.

"You ain't gon' need that," CJ said, waving the gun away. Reluctantly Hawk put his pocket cannon away. He didn't understand how CJ could be talking about revolution and then say they didn't need their guns. "Anybody who welcomes me welcomes the one who sent me. And anybody that harms a hair on your head will suffer the wrath of God. You dig?" They nodded as though they understood, but they didn't. CJ could tell by the way Sammy's face was twitching that he was scared, "What's up, Sammy?"

"It's just that uh, you know, I got a business to run. I got a wife to think about."

"You don't have to worry about me," Cheyenne stated calmly. "I'm going too."

197

Sammy tried to stifle her with a look, but she stared right back, not fazed in the least. "Who gon' run Shenanigans?" Sammy asked through tight lips.

"We might have to shut it down for a while," Cheyenne said nonchalantly.

"Shut it down!" Sammy said. "We're making money hand over fist. People been flocking there, hoping to see CJ."

"Well, CJ ain't gon' be there, is he?"

Sammy leaped to his feet. "Look here, woman . . ."

"See what I'm saying?" CJ interjected, nodding toward the squabbling couple. "I'm about to shake up the world. Turn a husband against his wife, a man against his father and a daughter against her mother. Before I'm through, a man's worst enemies could be the members of his own household," he said with a boldness they hadn't heard before. "So, anybody who thinks he can't cut it better speak now or forever hold his peace. Because once we get started ain't no turning back."

CJ had to know where they stood, right then. He couldn't take a chance on going out on the road with anyone he couldn't count on. He glanced around the room checking for dissenters, but no one spoke. "All right," he said. "Let's do this thing." He then went around the room giving them all the traditional soul brother handshake.

CHAPTER 28

As CJ sat on Teddy's Patio gazing up at the starlit night sky he could have sworn that a face was looking down on him from the full moon. He wondered if it was God, trying to tell him that he'd bitten off more than he could chew by taking on this grand crusade. "Earth to CJ," said Sebastian.

Startled out of his reverie, CJ said, "What?"

"It's your move," Sebastian said, pointing to the chessboard. "What were you so deep in thought about?"

"How's the fundraising going?" CJ asked as he made his move.

"Not as good as I hoped." Sebastian admitted. "I thought people would be jumping at the chance to be a part of something this important."

"But they're not," CJ said.

Sebastian shook his head. "Those big corporations like Pepsi and MacDonald sponsor charitable events all the time. But they say we don't qualify. They think it's just another gospel show and we should sell tickets." He shook his head in dismay. "I've set us up as a non-profit organization, but they still won't bite. Nike said they might consider sponsoring us if we had an actual church – which we don't."

"Well, you tried."

"I haven't given up. Maybe the corporate angle didn't work out, but we still have to do this," Sebastian said emphatically. "Maybe we need to go directly to the black community. There's a lot of black folks out there with money."

"How much do you think we're going to need?" CJ asked as Teddy stepped out onto the patio with a four-pack of Heineken in his hand."

Sebastian exhaled. "I don't know. If we want to do this thing right, we're going to have to put on a show they'll never forget."

"I think performing miracles is a pretty good act," Teddy said, placing the beer on the table next to the chessboard.

"True," said Sebastian opening a beer and handing it to CJ, then taking one for himself. "But it's not so much about what you're cooking as how you serve it up. We need singers, musicians, praise dancers . . ." Sebastian noted a hint of amusement on CJ's face. "I'm serious," he said as Teddy took a seat and opened a beer for himself. "This is going to be a once in a lifetime event. We have to set it out. But it won't be cheap."

"You think ten grand might do the trick?" CJ asked.

"It would definitely be a start. Maybe I could get ten different people to cough up a thousand bucks each."

"We don't have to do that."

Sebastian was so busy brainstorming with himself that he didn't even hear CJ. "Some of them might even give more. It's tax deductible."

"We already got it," CJ said.

"Yeah, it's doable, but it'll take some. . ." CJ slapped the money down on the table and Sebastian's eyes nearly popped out of his head. "Where'd you get that?"

"A donation," Teddy said with a smug look on his face, CJ having already discussed the donation with him. He resented CJ's growing reliance on Sebastian and was glad to be privy to information that he didn't have.

"Really," Sebastian said. "Who's it from?"

"That's on a *need-to-know* basis, homeboy. And you don't," Teddy said.

Turning to CJ, Sebastian asked. "How much is it?"

"Hawk says it's ten thousand dollars," CJ replied.

"Hawk? You told Hawk about it before me?"

"He's the one who brought it in," Teddy said.

"Hmmm," said Sebastian, slipping the wrapper off the money. "Wonder how much he took." CJ watched as Sebastian counted out the hundred dollar bills. Ten thousand dollars exactly. Sebastian looked up in amazement. "It's all there."

"You're surprised?" CJ asked calmly.

"Yeah," Sebastian said, sliding the wrapper back on the bills. "I am."

CJ chuckled, "I want you to put this in the bank."

"First thing in the morning," Sebastian said. "If Hawk's low-life friends can come up with ten grand, think what kind of donations we'll get from good upstanding Christians."

"Yeah," CJ said, knowing that the good upstanding Christians would be the most critical of all.

Sebastian tucked the money into his inside coat pocket, saying, "After I come from the bank, I'll get started on the audition notices."

"Auditions?" Teddy said.

"Yeah, auditions." Sebastian replied, beaming with excitement. "This is going to be a Hollywood extravaganza. I'm telling you, CJ, this is gonna be a gold mine."

CJ's forehead creased with concern. "This ain't about the money, Sebastian."

"Oh, I know that," Sebastian said with a cheap grin. "But even God's work has to be financed. I figure this ten grand will get us started and we should raise enough in donations to keep us going." Teddy just glared at him. CJ didn't have to be a mind reader to know that he was wondering how long it would be before Sebastian absconded with all the money.

When CJ returned from walking Sebastian to the door he found Teddy sitting on the edge of the pool with his feet dangling in the water. He slid his shoes and socks off and sat down beside him. "What's up?"

"Nothing." Teddy said in a terse tone.

CJ knew that when Teddy started answering in one word sentences he was too angry to speak. "Talk to me." Teddy turned to face him, an incredible look of solemnity on his face. "I don't trust this dude, CJ. He's too slick. Now, you wanna put all that money in his hands. I don't like it."

"Hmph," CJ said, shaking his head. "Sebastian doesn't trust Hawk and you don't trust him. Ain't none of us nothing but sinners saved by grace. I thought you had my back."

"I do." Teddy said.

"Well, trust me then. Can you do that?"

"Yeah, man. You know I trust you – It's that nigga Sebastian I don't trust."

As CJ prepared for bed, the constant infighting and dissention that existed among the men nagged at him like a persistent toothache. He could understand their distrust, coming up as they had with everybody trying to get over on everybody else. They'd had to think like animals in the jungle just to survive, always on the alert, fearful of being meat for the stronger animals. At one time he'd felt that way himself. But not anymore. Now he felt absolutely fearless.

CJ knew he was about to embark upon a dangerous undertaking and he was ready. He was ready to do or die. And he was beginning to feel that the latter might be a distinct possibility. Putting a target on his own back was one thing. But did he have the right to risk the lives of his friends?

CJ prayed that night like he'd never prayed before. He asked God to give him wisdom, knowledge and discernment so that he could guide these people in the way He wanted them to go. He asked God to protect them and to let them come together in complete unity and love for each other. "Let them be one, Lord – like I am one with you and you are one with me."

The only ones who seemed content in the niche they'd carved out for themselves were Herc and Carla. Herc had become CJ's self-appointed bodyguard and stayed constantly by his side. He felt an undying love and commitment for him as did Carla who had made CJ the center of her world. She lived only to please him and had taken upon herself the responsibility of seeing to his comfort and well-being. They could listen to him talk for hours – and often did. CJ spent countless hours teaching them as well as the others about the will of God and the nation of God. As he taught them, he himself continued to grow in wisdom and knowledge. As time to leave grew closer, CJ began to fast, spending more time alone in prayer. Yet he couldn't shake the consuming depression and sense of utter futility that had overtaken him.

One night as the melodious voice of Nina Simone saturated Teddy's music room, CJ sat at the bar brooding over the predicament he found himself in.

"You want another beer, CJ?" asked Carla as she leaned across the bar and placed a fresh one in front of Teddy.

"Naw, I'm good," said CJ, taking a swig from his barely touched beer. His smile did little to disguise the sadness and depression that were eating away at his very core.

"What's wrong?" she asked?

CJ shook his head. "Tell me how this sounds. To the best of my understanding, I'm supposed to somehow undo a systematic mind whuppin' off these niggas that they been suffering under for hundreds of years."

Teddy laughed. "You can't even keep these niggas up in here from trying to kill each other?"

"That's what I'm saying," said CJ. "I mean, Y'all would tell me if I was just running around here on some kind of delusional trip, wouldn't you?"

"Of course, we would," Carla said, grasping his hand. "It's obvious that God is using you, CJ. Just look at me. Look what you've done for me. You just need to chill."

"All jokes aside, man. You know I'd tell you. But, it's all good. God done put his stamp of approval on you. We got this."

Teddy's faith was unshakeable. CJ slapped him on the back and they did their special handshake.

Carla laughed. "I know y'all ain't got no secret handshake." The guys looked at each other, then at her and they all fell out laughing.

A few nights later, the Spirit led CJ to take Teddy, Herc and Carla with him to a room at the Roosevelt Hotel. He didn't know why and he didn't question it. All he knew was that God wanted him to seclude himself with his closest companions and pray.

As they kneeled in prayer CJ, dressed in a gray hoodie and blue jeans, underwent a startling transfiguration. The interior shining of his divinity burst forth before their eyes producing an incredible luminescence which emanated from his body, filling the room with a blinding light and turning his clothes a dazzling white, whiter than any bleach could ever have gotten them.

CJ's friends leaped to their feet staring at him in awe. Suddenly, Moses and Dr. Martin Luther King, Jr. appeared before them. The terrified trio fell to their knees and covered their faces, afraid to look on these holy apparitions.

The Prophets proceeded to tell CJ that they recognized and adored him. They told him that they knew he had become discouraged, but that they were proud of him and encouraged him to continue with his mission.

CJ told them that the people didn't seem to understand why he was there. He told him how the media made him out to be a joke or a con and how some even seemed to hate and despise him. "All they're interested in is the miracles," he said.

Moses told him that he knew all about stubborn and ungrateful people, reminding him of how God had parted the Red Sea for the Jews to escape from Egypt and even after hearing the voice of God, they had still taken it upon themselves to make a golden calf to worship because they felt like he, Moses was taking too long with his face-to-face meeting with the Lord.

Dr. King informed CJ that God never intended for a prophet's walk to be pleasant. He spoke of having white folks spit in his face and set dogs on him. He reminded him of how those who had followed him had suffered persecution, beatings, arrest and in many cases, murder.

They encouraged him to continue to spread the word of God and not let the obstacles and opposition that would inevitably obstruct his path, discourage him. They told him that Elijah and all the other prophets that had gone before him were rooting for him and had faith that he would fulfill his task. They warned him of the trials which awaited him in New York and assured him that God was with him and would strengthen him. Their words bolstered CJ with confidence and determination. He felt infused with a renewed sense of purpose and a profound commitment.

Suddenly, the room grew dim and an awe-inspiring voice resonated throughout the room, "This is my Son, whom I love. Listen to his words!" Teddy, Carla and Herc quaked with unimaginable fear. *Was this the voice of God proclaiming CJ His Well-loved Son?*

Just as suddenly as they had dimmed, the lights returned to normal. "You can get up now," CJ said. The petrified trio slowly raised their heads to find CJ standing there alone. His clothes were back to normal, but his face shone with radiance the color of copper. Carla clutched onto Herc's arm as they all stared at CJ in silent wonder, frightened beyond all comprehension. They had witnessed a unique display of CJ's divine character and a glimpse of the glory of God. This glorious manifestation strengthened the faith of these three friends and prepared them for the terrible struggle which lay ahead.

CJ was amazed at how calm and in control he felt. He told them that they had witnessed the glory of God and warned them not to mention what they had seen to anyone. From that day forward, these three regarded CJ with a new reverence and awe. He had become more god than man and on some level, they knew it.

For three days, CJ remained in his room fasting and praying. When he emerged the change in him was shocking. Although his face had returned to its natural color, he had lost weight to the point of looking emaciated and had a far off look about him, an otherworldly look that made many uncomfortable in his presence. No longer focused on the things of this world, CJ became increasingly moody and reclusive. Dee realized that something momentous had occurred, but remained silent. She knew that God was now in possession of her child and that events must proceed as they were ordained.

A week or so, before the tour was to begin Marquita Phillips, the singer from CJ's church arrived at Teddy's door in response to CJ's summons. Although CJ left the major planning of the tour to Sebastian, in whom he had complete confidence, he knew that if they were going to have singers Marquita was the one to lead them. She was a staunch woman of God whose singing could touch the heart of anyone within the sound of her voice.

Marquita had always had good chemistry with CJ and had quit Mt. Zion church when they turned on him. She sincerely believed that if CJ said God had called him to do a work, then God had called him. So, when he phoned and said he needed her she'd left for California immediately – No questions asked.

Before leaving California CJ called everyone together and baptized them in Teddy's pool. Aside from his friends, he baptized Reverend Thomas, Bishop Hanks, Clarence Prescott, Chad and several others that had shown themselves to be true believers.

When CJ asked Bishop Hanks to baptize him the renowned preacher balked at the idea, saying that he was not qualified to baptize him. CJ explained that *anyone* hoping to see the nation of God must be baptized into the new covenant of Christ.

When CJ told the bishop that it would be an honor to have such a God-fearing man of integrity baptize him, Hanks felt obliged and privileged to perform the task.

CHAPTER 29

"I don't see why we couldn't at least wait 'til spring," Sammy complained as Teddy's Escalade pulled into the driveway where the crew was busily loading the other vehicles. "It's gon' be cold in some of them places."

"Then we'll just have to get some coats," Cheyenne said, pushing past him to put a suitcase into the van.

All action stopped when CJ stepped out of the SUV decked out in new dress pants, button down shirt, sport coat and leather shoes, looking like a million bucks.

"Oh, CJ!" Carla cried, running up to him and fingering his short haircut and neatly trimmed goatee." You look amazing."

As the others crowded around CJ telling him how good he looked, Teddy hauled shopping bags out of the Escalade. "Y'all can thank me for that," he said. I told him I wasn't going nowhere with him looking like something the cat spit up." Even CJ had to laugh at that one.

Early the next morning, CJ's Soul Saving Crusade left Los Angeles with the blessings of Bishop Hanks and Reverend Thomas.

The impressive caravan consisted of Teddy's Escalade, Hawk's Lexus, Sebastian's Jaguar and the Shenanigans van which carried Marquita and the other performers.

Their first stop was Houston, Texas where the Reverend Jeremiah Jenkins, pastor of the New Hope Missionary Baptist Church awaited their arrival.

When Reverend Jenkins, a blustering old school preacher who scared his congregation into salvation with visions of hellfire and damnation met CJ he was not impressed. Was this average looking, soft-spoken man accompanied by what looked like a ragtag band of hooligans and roughnecks the one Elijah Thomas had raved about? He wondered if he'd made a mistake in inviting him. However, his doubts were eradicated the moment CJ began to speak.

Marquita and her troupe prepared the crowd with a rousing praise and worship service that had them on their feet praising the Lord with gusto. Dressed in an Alexander McQueen pin striped power suit, Hermes tie and hand stitched Turnbull and Asser shirt, CJ sat at the piano playing along with the other musicians. The congregation had no idea who he was. When he got so full of the spirit that he couldn't hold back any longer he grabbed the mike and burst into song. Together he and Marquita tore the roof off that church.

When the song ended, the congregation responded with a resounding round of applause. As the applause died down Marquita stepped to the side, threw her arm out toward CJ with a flourish and announced, "I give you Reverend CJ." She then bowed gracefully to him and took her seat in the front row.

CJ took his place behind to the podium smiling confidently as he opened his Bible. "Praise the Lord," he called out vigorously. The church responded back with enthusiasm.

CJ scanned the faces in the large congregation and asked, "Are there any righteous people in the house tonight?" Although everyone there considered themselves to be righteous, only a few

210

hands went up. Most of the people, thinking it a trick question just looked around at everyone else. "You don't have to raise your hands," he said. "I'll answer for you. No." The hands went down immediately, some of their owners looking a little bent out of shape. "The Bible says that none of us are righteous. No, not one. So, how can a man get right with God?"

He paused a moment and then said, "This is the essence of the gospel and the heart of the Christian message. I'm going to speak to you tonight from the book of Romans where Paul discusses the universal sinfulness of mankind." He took the microphone from its stand and stepped out from behind the podium.

"I want to paint y'all a picture of the human condition," he said, stepping down and talking to them as if they were old friends. He told them how the human condition was deteriorating more each day. "I'm not talking about what's going on in Afghanistan and around the world. Let's talk about what's happening in our own backyard." He looked around at the confused faces of the parishioners.

"You holler about *Black Lives Matter* when the police kill your kids and get away with it. But black folks are killing each other left and right. Why should the cops value your life when you don't? Don't black lives taken by other black folks matter?" The church got eerily quiet as he continued walking down the center aisle.

"Then you got the politicians, stealing from the people to finance their adulterous affairs and exorbitant lifestyles. Preachers yelling about the evils of homosexuality on Sunday when they know they were out there Saturday night trolling the streets for young boys." This statement scorched a few nerves and he heard the rumblings of discontent from some of the pseudo righteous preachers seated in the pulpit.

A heavyset sister in the amen corner leaped to her feet and shouted, "Tell the truth, preacher! Tell the truth."

"The truth is that we are all infected with a virus called sin," CJ said. "Not only are we infected with this deadly disease, we're *contaminated*. And without a miracle there's no hope for any of us."

"I told you he was the one that be doing them miracles," one member whispered to another.

CJ continued as though he hadn't heard. "I'm talking about the miracle of God's love and His capacity for forgiveness. In Romans 3 Paul tells us that a righteousness that comes from God has been made known. And if you ever hope to see the nation of God, that's what you're going to need. A righteousness that comes from God."

He then asked, "What is God's answer to the depravity of the human race? Does He turn His back and damn us all to hell?" Some heads nodded yes. "No," he said. "God's grace and mercy are given to anyone who believes and has faith in His son, Jesus Christ." This doctrine was quite beyond the scope of the vengeful God this church was accustomed to hearing about.

CJ went on to tell them about the righteousness of God, quoting scriptures to back up his words. They stared at him in amazement when he said, "We have all sinned and fallen short of the glory of God and we're all justified by His grace through the redemption that came through Christ. God presented Jesus as a sacrifice of atonement through the shedding of his blood." As soon as those words left his mouth, CJ felt a heaviness in his chest, the stark realization that this same fate was to be his as well.

Momentarily stunned, he rallied quickly. In fact, the conviction of his fate seemed to strengthen him and set him free. Acceptance of the inevitability of his own death immediately released him from the grip of fear. And when a person has no fear of death, nothing can stop him.

Suddenly CJ was on fire for the Lord. He preached with a courage and conviction that he'd never shown before. The people were mesmerized. The only sound in the church was the sound of his voice; it rang throughout the sanctuary, enveloped them and consumed them with its power and authority.

"In God's eyes none of us are righteous. We all need salvation. See, when we think about our own sinfulness we like to measure ourselves against somebody we feel isn't quite as good as we are, that way we end up looking pretty good in our own eyes. *Well, I might not be perfect*," he said in his other man voice. "*But I'm a lot better than old Smith over there*." This elicited chuckles throughout the church. When the laughter subsided, he said, "That may be fine for you, but that's not how God sees it. God says, stop looking at Brother Smith and take a look at my son. How do you stack up next to him?"

He looked around at the silent crowd before continuing. "How does your life measure up when it is compared to Jesus?" he asked in a gentle voice. "Jesus never committed a sin. He never had an evil thought, never said an evil word or committed even one evil deed. He never cheated, lied or stole. Jesus never lusted after a woman. Can you say that? I know I can't. Jesus lived a life of perfect holiness, perfect purity, perfect kindness, truth and goodness. He was the one perfect person that ever lived on this earth. Now, how are you gon' stack up against that?"

He paused, allowing the silence to reign. It wasn't for dramatic effect; CJ wanted them to get the full impact of what he was saying. "The answer is clear, brothers and sisters. You can't. But the good news is that you don't have to. God doesn't save us because of our good works, inner beauty or great moral achievements." He shook his head, still walking the aisle. "God saves us in spite of the fact that we really don't deserve it. It's called grace – pure and simple. Hallelujah! Praise the Lord!" he shouted, throwing his hand up in the air.

"Amen!" "Hallelujah!" replied the church. And he continued to teach.

"Don't you know that you've been redeemed? To redeem means to set free by the payment of a price. God paid that price with the blood of His son. When a sinner trusts Christ, God releases him from the chains of sin and accepts him on the basis of that bloody sacrifice. Whooo!" CJ exclaimed as a shiver shot through his body. The Spirit was moving in him so strongly that he could hardly contain himself.

One good sister jumped up waving both hands in the air and shouted, "The blood, the blood. Nothing but the blood!"

Walking back toward the front of the church, CJ looked from one side of the aisle to the other, his voice soft and inviting as he told them of God's love and His grace. The people listened with rapt attention. They had never heard a man speak like this before. The power of his words had them enthralled.

Returning to the pulpit, CJ looked out on the congregation and said, "Think about it. God's gift of salvation doesn't cost us anything, even though it cost His son everything. God is saying, 'Take it by faith! It's yours for free. I've already paid the cost.' The only option we have," he said, holding out first one hand and then the other, "is to accept it or reject it."

As Marquita's angelic voice rose in a heart rending spiritual the people praised the Lord without restraint. Their response touched CJ's heart. Overflowing with the Holy Spirit, he once again left the pulpit and walked among them, healing the afflicted with just a touch of his hand. In some cases, he just pointed to people and said, "You are healed in the name of Jesus." And they were.

After the service, CJ felt as if he had given his all and the only thing left was his mortal shell. Herc and the women escorted him back to the hotel. This left Teddy and the others to baptize all who wished to be baptized into the new covenant of Christ. Sebastian and Jimbo raised the offering, taking in buckets full of money and leaving scripture cards behind that listed a Los Angeles post office box where they could send further donations.

CHAPTER 30

Word of CJ's Soul Saving Crusade spread like wildfire. It was the most spectacular show in town, whatever town that happened to be. The people came in droves to see sight brought to the blind, hearing to the deaf and the cripple made to walk. Some of them even followed CJ from town to town. Stronger than their desire to hear the Word was the curiosity, the titillation brought on by this mysterious preacher who could perform miraculous tricks. However, many that came with a skeptical mind left with a changed heart.

The troupe traveled constantly and CJ found himself relying more and more on Sebastian, who handled every aspect of the tour with incredible skill and kept things flowing smoothly. Carla was constantly at CJ's side, making sure he ate, attending to his wardrobe, often anticipating his needs and tending to them which was fortunate for CJ, because he was driven by one obsession, to do the will of the Lord. Food and clothing were the furthest things from his mind. He would have preached in his blue jeans if they'd let him. He wasn't about showing the people how cool or slick he was. His focus was on leading them to the glory of the Lord. However, the part of him that remained a mortal man was in constant turmoil over the love and desire he felt for Carla, a desire he fought mightily to control. Carla, on the other hand, made no secret of her love and devotion to him.

After several weeks on the road, CJ's ever-growing closeness to Carla began to cause dissention among some members of the crew. One day in a motel outside Biloxi, Mississippi, the group waited impatiently in Sammy and Cheyenne's room for CJ and Carla to return from a walk on the beach. "It doesn't look right for him to be spending so much time with a woman like that," Sebastian confided to Sammy.

"A woman like what?" Cheyenne snapped, coming quickly to Carla's defense.

"A whore," Sebastian said snidely. "Anybody with half an eye can see she's just out for what she can get."

"He ain't got nothin'!" Teddy exclaimed. "CJ put every dime he had into this crusade. And you know it, Sebastian."

"I'm talking about fame and opportunities to make money. Do you know how much TV shows and gossip rags would pay for her story? She could wind up with her own reality show."

"And that just galls you, doesn't it?" Cheyenne said.

"And why shouldn't it?" Sebastian shot back. "I'm the one who's been displaced. Before she wiggled her little ass in front of his face, I was the one he relied on. I was his right hand man."

"How you figure?" Teddy said, standing to confront Sebastian.

"I know you and CJ go way back, but a fact is a fact," Sebastian said. "If it wasn't for me, there wouldn't even be a crusade."

As the two men stood with their faces only inches apart, chests heaving and testosterone pumping, Sammy stepped between them. "Y'all acting like two kids fighting over who Mama loves the most," he said. "That's just plain stupid." As Teddy and Sebastian began to consider the childishness of their behavior, Sammy

216

continued. "I don't even know why y'all trippin'. I'm the one he healed, so ain't no question about who's gon' be second in command in the nation of God." At this, both men turned on Sammy and a turbulent shouting match ensued.

In the meantime, CJ strolled on the beach with Carla, enjoying the warmth of the balmy autumn day. He felt more content than he had in a long time. The calmness of the gulf soothed his frazzled nerves and the warmth of the sun seemed to be shining only on them.

"I think the people are responding very well. Don't you?" Carla asked, smiling up at him.

"Mmm," CJ said, shifting his head from side to side. "I guess. I just wish they'd focus more on the Word and less on the healings."

"Give 'em time. They will."

He stopped walking, taking her hand in his. "You are such a cheerleader."

"I got something to cheer about," she said, gazing lovingly into his eyes. "I feel so relaxed out here. Just you and me. I wish it could be like this forever."

"Well, I can't promise you forever," he said with a mischievous smile. "But we could play hooky today."

"We can?" she asked, her eyes gleaming like a child's at Christmas.

"Why not? Church doesn't start until seven thirty. Let's have us some fun. What do you want to do?"

She pointed to a Ferris wheel in the distance. "Can we go to the carnival?"

"Only if you promise we can get some cotton candy," he laughed.

"You have to catch me first," she said, playfully. Shoving him in the chest, she took off like she was Flo Jo.

CJ lit out behind her. Surprised at the effort it took to catch up with her, he leaped forward and tackled her around the waist. They fell to the sand laughing hysterically. "Girl, you must be part racehorse," he said breathlessly, gazing into sparkling brown eyes so dark that they looked almost black. The love he saw there mirrored his own. His arm slipped easily around her waist and he pulled her close.

"You too," she whispered snuggling up even closer. CJ felt her heart beating in sync with his own and caressed her tenderly. There was no need for words. The heat flaring between them spoke volumes. His lips drew toward hers as if pulled by magnets. As their lips touched Carla's sensuous moan ignited a spark in CJ that told him he'd danced too close to her flame. He leaped to his feet, running his hands through his hair. "I'm sorry."

"For what?" Carla asked, reaching her hand out to him.

CJ took her hand and pulled her to her feet. "Don't start none, it won't be none," he warned jokingly.

"What if I want to start something?" she said, plastering her body against his.

"You're killing me, Carla," CJ moaned, brushing his face against her hair before reluctantly pushing her away. "Look, we can't be doing this."

"Why not?" she asked.

"Because I've got a job to do."

"So. I love you, CJ."

"No," he said. "You can't love me. I won't let you."

"Oh, really?" She said, flashing him a smile that would grow roses on barbed wire.

"Really," he said. "Don't confuse gratitude with love, Carla." The seriousness of his tone wiped the smile off her face and a look of embarrassment took its place. "Hey," CJ said, hoping a change of subject might lighten the mood. "I thought you wanted to go to the carnival." She tried to smile, but he saw tears forming in the corners of her eyes. "Well, come on, then," he said, grabbing her hand and taking off down the beach.

"CJ . . .," Carla called, forcing herself to laugh as disturbing thoughts ran through her mind. *Did I read him wrong? Maybe I came on too strong*, she thought as they raced toward the carnival.

While at the carnival CJ did something he hadn't done in a long time, he let himself relax. It did Carla's heart good to see him so carefree. As they ate hot dogs and cotton candy, rode the Ferris wheel and the merry-go-round, CJ wished as Carla had earlier, that this day could last forever. He won Carla a big pink bunny rabbit with his basketball skills and they laughed and played like two kids until it was time to return to the motel and get ready for the service. Carla had never enjoyed herself more. *No,* she thought. *This is far more than gratitude.*

Vast crowds flocked to see CJ wherever he stopped. By the time they reached Atlanta, the whole country was buzzing about Reverend CJ's Soul Saving Crusade, calling him the ghetto prophet and talking about his "show." The Lord was with CJ in Atlanta. He turned many hearts to Christ and they baptized people in droves.

As CJ's fame skyrocketed, Meka Maxwell's unrelenting attacks intensified, sending her station's ratings through the roof and earning her a nationally syndicated talk show.

Meka attacked, condemned and defamed CJ with such vehemence that it seemed to be a personal vendetta. She'd made up her mind that he was a fake, a fraud and a phony and promptly dismissed any facts to the contrary. Meka took the information she received from Detective Burke and painted CJ as a former mental patient wanted by the Chicago police for questioning in a murder. The fact that the cops had cleared him of any involvement in the murder was of no consequence to her. What was sensational about that?

Meka tried to catch up with CJ on the road, but everywhere she went; he'd already been and gone. Failing to ascertain CJ's whereabouts, she decided to go to Chicago and interview people that knew him. Tony told her in no uncertain terms to take her mike and shove it, but the Johnsons' neighbors were more than willing to talk. Most of them had only praise for the enigmatic man of God. But snarky Lena Wilson told her with a self-satisfied smirk, how she had lived next door to the family for years and had always known there was something not quite right about, "That boy," meaning CJ.

Claude Wilson, Lena's soft-spoken husband told Meka that CJ had always been a nice, polite kid and that he had obviously fallen in with a bad crowd. "I'm gon' pray for him," Wilson said.

When Meka returned to L. A., she brought religious pundits onto the show who sought to analyze the effect CJ's *antics* were having on the American people. She hoped this would force CJ to appear on the show to defend himself.

"People are scared to death," snarled Father Maggioli, a hard faced Catholic priest from the Bronx who, with his slicked back black hair and lean physique, looked more like a mafia hit man than a priest. "If this guy does have some kind of power, he could just as easily use it to hurt as to heal. What's his real agenda? That's what I wanna know."

"The man is obviously mentally ill," stated Mason Dupre, a pompous televangelist with a mega-church in Washington D.C. Dupre's snake oil charm made him a prominent face on the D.C. social scene. "What they need to do is . . ."

"It's just a test," droned Rabbi Judah Wiesenthal with a wave of his hand, his yarmulke covering the onion part of his wreath and onion head. "God is testing us just like He did in the Old Testament. Don't you see that?" He leaned forward to explain. "Okay, say he does have supernatural powers . . ."

"That's a ridiculous assumption, Rabbi," Reverend Dupre cut in. The Rabbi winced, not accustomed to having his opinions questioned. "The man is obviously crazy."

"Like a fox," snapped Father Maggioli, cutting Dupre down with a look so cold it defied opposition. "This guy's making out like a bandit. I got people coming to confession telling me how their church offering was light because they sent money to this mutt. I wanna know who he's working for," he said, shooting Dupre the stink eye.

"Why are you looking at me?" barked Dupre, his forehead creasing into a frown.

"Whassa matter?" Maggioli replied, infuriated by the aggressive bass in the preacher's voice. "Guilty conscience?"

Dupre sprang to his feet, his ghetto instinct for fight or flight momentarily overshadowing the years of education and polishing. He was ready to get it on. "Who the f . . ."

Thank God for the ten-second delay. Quick thinking technicians quickly cut the mikes of Reverend Dupre and Father Maggioli who also leaped to his feet, having no shortage of street creds of his own. Rabbi Wiesenthal pushed his chair back, half smiling as he watched the two glib gladiators engage in a verbal joust, waving their arms and pointing their fingers at each other in righteous indignation.

"Well," said Meka, her smiling face taking focus from the enraged men of the cloth. "As you can see, the topic of Reverend CJ makes for stimulating conversation. But on a more serious note," she said peering somberly out at the audience, "My three guests

221

today are some of the most distinguished clergymen in the country. Giants in their field and yet . . .," she said, her voice reflecting a sobriety she did not feel. For in truth, this mêlée couldn't have gone better if she had scripted it. "Even they can't sit down and talk about this man without getting into a heated confrontation. What's going on, America?"

Meanwhile, CJ and his crusade continued to take the country by storm, preaching the good news of Jesus Christ and baptizing thousands into the nation of God. The more Rev Bradshaw heard about the nation of God, the more he became convinced that it was a religious retreat that CJ was planning to build to rival his City of Solomon. *I've worked too hard and too long putting this thing together to let some weirdo screw it up,* he thought.

Rev issued a nationwide ban, forbidding any church affiliated with the AACC to allow CJ access, thinking that this would surely stop him. But it didn't. Undaunted, CJ continued to spread the Word. He used schools, union halls, even private homes to get his message across.

As the New Year began, CJ's following was stronger than ever and the news reported that the murder rate of blacks by blacks was at an all-time low. Of course, the police were quick to take credit for this phenomenon. However, Rev had no doubt that the dip in crime as well as in his donations could only be attributed to one man – CJ. He wondered if CJ was indeed, imbued with supernatural powers from God. It even occurred to him that he might be the reincarnation of Jesus, a thought he quickly dismissed.

When Saunders stepped into Rev's office he found him seated on the couch holding Ashton, his seven-year-old godson on his lap. "You wanted to see me, Rev," Saunders said, pretending not to notice Rev's hand under the little boy's shirt, massaging his stomach as Ashton played with a hand-held video game.

"Yes," Rev said, giving Ashton a kiss on the head and sitting him on the couch. "Just give me a minute." He went to his desk and spoke to his secretary through the intercom. "Regina, will you please let my driver know that Ashton is ready to go home."

"Yes, sir," came Regina's disembodied reply.

"Thanks," said Rev, removing an envelope from his desk drawer. He folded it and stuffed it into Ashton' pocket. "You give that to your mother," he said. "Tell her to take you shopping and get you whatever you need. Okay?"

"Okay," the sad eyed little boy replied as he started toward the door.

"Hey," Rev called after Ashton. "Don't I get a goodbye hug?" Ashton turned obediently, returning to Rev's outstretched arms. Rev scooped him up in his arms, kissed him on the forehead and set him back on his feet. "Okay, you can go now." As Ashton once again started for the door, Rev said, "Love you, Ashton."

"Love you, too," the little boy replied in a dry tone, shutting the door behind him.

"That's one sweet kid," Rev said, smiling lovingly at the closed door.

"Yeah, sweet," Saunders replied. *Not as sweet as he's going to be,* he thought.

"You know it does my heart good to be able to help kids like him."

"You wanted to see me about something, Rev?" Saunders interrupted. Even though Rev spent a lot of time and money on sports teams and summer camps for boys, it made Saunders' skin crawl to hear him patting himself on the back.

"Oh, yeah," Rev said. "You know I get so carried away with these kids, 'til I forget what's on my mind."

"Yes." Saunders said with an insincere smile. "You're one in a million, Rev."

"Heh, heh, heh. Just doing God's work, Saunders. But the reason I called you in here is because I have a special assignment for you. I've been thinking about this Reverend CJ character," Rev said, taking a seat behind his desk. "He's building up quite a name for himself."

"Yes, sir. He is," Saunders agreed, sliding into a chair across from Rev's desk.

"He's making us look bad."

"How so?"

"He's got people thinking he's this big holy man, healing people and what not. Now, they're saying he's responsible for the drop in crime. How? We've had meetings, prayers, marches and it hasn't helped. I want to know how he's doing it."

"You and about fifty billion other people," Saunders said, eyeing him with quiet concern.

"Well, I want you to talk to him. See what he's about."

"How am I supposed to do that? Nobody knows where he might hit next."

"I have it on good authority that he's heading here. I want you to cut him off at the pass. We need to embrace this guy. Let the world know that everything he's doing is under the auspices of the AACC."

"That way, we'll get the credit," Saunders said with a sly smile.

"See where I'm going? Tell him I want to meet with him. Offer him whatever it takes to get him on board. I don't know who he's working for, but let him know that we can make him a better offer." A snakish smile spread across Saunders' gaunt face as he nodded in compliance. Rev's underhanded brilliance never ceased to amaze him.

Reverend Saunders found CJ preaching in a community center in Baltimore and the intensity and the authority with which CJ spoke captivated him. When CJ started healing people, Saunders could only gaze at him in amazement, astonished at the power that exuded from the man.

CHAPTER 31

Saunders followed CJ to the hotel where he was staying. Unable to get CJ's room number from the front desk, he hung around the lobby until he spotted a bellboy who was hustling harder than all the others. The young man kept up a pleasant stream of conversation, spliced liberally with "Yes, sirs" and "No, ma'ams" as he hauled bags, escorted guests and graciously pocketed tips left and right. Saunders stationed himself near the elevators and when the enterprising bellhop shot out of one of the cars, he snagged him, offering him fifty bucks for CJ's room number, which he readily supplied.

Still shaken by what he had witnessed, Saunders stood outside CJ's room too frightened to knock. He knew that Rev would say that what he'd seen was a trick or a con game. But he'd been there. He'd seen and he'd heard. More importantly, he'd felt the energy in that room, the palpable energy ignited by this man. This enigmatic CJ. And he'd been awestruck.

Nevertheless, Saunders knew which side his bread was buttered on, so he took a deep breath and knocked on the door. When Sebastian opened the door, Saunders said, "I, uh . . ."

Sitting out of sight of the door, CJ said, "Come in, Reverend Saunders." How does he know who I am? Saunders wondered, shooting a fearful look at Sebastian who only smiled and stepped back to allow him entrance. After a beat, Saunders stepped into the room, his heart pumping like a Texas oil well.

"I've been expecting you," CJ said. Rising to greet his guest, he extended his hand. Saunders grasped CJ's fingers, giving them a quick shake. As CJ led Saunders to a seat at the small dining table, he turned to Sebastian and said, "Why don't you go see what Sammy and them are up to, Sebastian."

"You sure?" Sebastian said, casting a suspicious eye on Saunders. Despite Sebastian's arrogance, he did truly love CJ and was very protective of him.

"Yeah." CJ said. "It's cool." Saunders watched Sebastian go, wishing he'd stay. He didn't want to be alone with CJ. CJ took a seat opposite Saunders and asked, "What can I do for you, Reverend?"

Saunders pulled a handkerchief from his pocket and wiped the sweat from his severely receding hairline. "I uh, I was hoping to speak to you," he stuttered.

"I'm listening." CJ said with an amiable smile. He knew why Saunders was there and enjoyed watching him squirm. "Would you like a cold drink?" CJ asked, taking a bottle of water from a nearby cooler. Saunders shook his head, rubbing one hand over the other fist and then reversing the motion repeatedly.

As CJ opened his water and drank it in silence, Saunders nervously explained that he represented the AACC and that as the leading religious organization of the black community, they wanted to extend the hand of fellowship to him. "Take you under our wing, so to speak." He assured CJ that if he affiliated himself with the council he would have their full protection from anyone seeking to do him harm. "Why would anyone want to hurt me?"

"I'm not saying they do," said Saunders. "I'm just saying if they did, you'd be protected." The distrust in CJ's eyes was unmistakable.

Realizing that he was digging himself into a pit, Saunders decided to let the AACC's deep pockets speak for him. He pulled out a notebook and wrote a figure, tore the page out and slid it across the table to CJ. "This will be your guaranteed annual salary." CJ glanced at the figure and slid it back to him, unimpressed. "Of course, nothing is written in stone," Saunders said with a cheesy grin. "We're willing to negotiate. But don't forget. You'll also get a church of your own anywhere you want. A nice house to live in. Rent-free, of course. And a car and driver. All you have to do is, come on board with us. We could fly you out to New York tonight." And then, as if it were the grandest inducement of all, he said, "Rev Bradshaw has agreed to meet with you personally."

"How magnanimous of him."

Confident that he'd made an offer no logical man could refuse Saunders began to relax. "There's no reason for us to be working at cross-purposes, CJ," he said, flashing a smile that bordered on a wink. "If you play this thing right you could have wealth beyond your wildest dreams."

This was the final insult. CJ sprang out of his seat, disgust dripping from his very pores. "And you call yourself a man of God. You tell that slime you work for that I don't associate with pedophiles.

Saunders' jaw hit the floor. *How did he know?* "I beg your pardon!" he said, springing to his feet in feigned indignation. CJ's eyes held his and Saunders dropped his head.

"You tell that nigga that I would eat dog crap with a fork before I'd step foot into the same room with the likes of him." Saunders cringed under CJ's harsh words. CJ went on to inform him that he had come to bring souls back to the Lord, to establish the nation of God and to expose the corruption and moral depravity of so-called religious leaders stealing in the name of the Lord. "And I'm not just talking about money," CJ said, looking deeply into Saunders' eyes. "I'm talking about the theft of innocence. The stealing of lives."

There had long been whispers of Rev having a fondness for young boys. Although there had never been any public accusations, Saunders knew it to be true. He had been Rev's henchman for the past twelve years and was often tasked with procuring boys for Rev's enjoyment and paying off the parents when they became suspicious.

Together, Saunders and Rev had bamboozled both the congregants and the public for years, having them believe that Rev's intensive fund raising efforts had been to spread the Gospel to people in foreign countries. When in reality the money had lined the pockets of a select few council members known as the Executive Committee. These ill-gotten gains had also gone into building The City of Solomon, a monument not to God, but to Reverend Thaddeus P. Bradshaw.

CJ loved children and the thought of what Rev was doing was utterly repugnant to him. He told Saunders that if he had any hopes of ever seeing the nation of God he had some serious repenting to do. "Do you know how much God loathes a man that defiles the innocence of a child?"

This statement hit Saunders straight in the heart. His bottom lip began to tremble and he fell to his knees before CJ, blubbering uncontrollably. He didn't admit his sins or beg for forgiveness. But CJ could see that he was suffering a tremendous crisis of conscience.

Saunders returned to New York convinced that CJ was surely a prophet of God. But he knew he couldn't tell Rev that, so he simply told him that he had presented the offer and CJ had rejected it. "Is that all?" Rev asked. "Who's he working for? What does he want?"

Saunders hemmed and hawed, skirting around the truth with the grace of a prima ballerina. "He's nobody. Just some bus driver from Chicago trying to make a name for himself."

"Did he do any tricks while you were there?"

"Yeah, a few," Saunders said, sitting down on the sofa and thumbing aimlessly through a magazine on the table. "I don't think we need to worry about him. He'll get his fifteen minutes and before you know it he'll be yesterday's news." Although Saunders' voice was calm, Rev could see his leg shaking like crazy.

"Bullshit!" Rev bellowed, snatching the magazine and hurling it to the floor. "Has this joker gotten to you too, Saunders? I heard he was supposed to be some kind of Pied Piper."

Saunders jumped up to his feet. "Come on, Rev, you know me better than that." Rev remained silent, waiting for Saunders to come clean. Finally, unable to stand up under Rev's scrutinizing gaze, Saunders told all, including the fact that CJ knew of his closeted perversity.

Rev's face turned an unhealthy shade of red, his breathing became erratic and Saunders feared he was having a heart attack. "Get out of my sight," Rev whispered, his voice hoarse and unrecognizable. He didn't have to tell Saunders twice. He was gone in a flash. Rev slumped down into his chair, devastated at the thought of being exposed.

When his mind finally began to function, Rev picked up the phone and called his old golfing buddy Pete Petrocelli, Chief of Police. He told the chief that CJ was running an interstate confidence game headed for New York. When the chief expressed little interest in CJ's activities, Rev told him that he believed CJ to be an agent for a foreign government seeking to undermine the American way of life. He knew this would get the chief moving.

Petrocelli immediately instituted a complete investigation that included the FBI. They looked into the allegations made by

Meka Maxwell and found them to be a pack of half-truths, exaggerations and downright lies.

Nonetheless, they kept their eyes on CJ, labeling him the new black leader and a potential problem for the U.S. government.

When news of the FBI investigation reached CJ, he confided in Sebastian that the persecution he feared had begun. Sebastian assured him that everything they were doing was perfectly legal and that they had nothing to fear from the law. What he didn't say was that he saw this move on the part of the government as the opening shot of the revolution. A revolution that would enable the black man to overthrow the government and stake his rightful claim to the country built on his blood, sweat and tears.

Unfortunately, the white community saw things much the same way. Protest groups sprang up all over the country. White supremacists railed against CJ, making wild accusations that a foreign government had sent him to destroy the American way of life. They had no idea what CJ's agenda was. But when perceiving a threat their rallying cry through the ages and their justification for committing whatever heinous actions they deemed necessary had always been, "They're trying to destroy our way of life." All they knew for sure was that black-on-black crime had gone down an astounding eighty percent. Whatever he was doing was galvanizing the black community and they wanted it stopped.

But CJ's fame continued to grow to astronomical proportions. His likeness graced magazine covers, newspapers and TV all over the world. His name was on everyone's lips when the biggest scandal since that of Reverend Jim Bakker hit the news.

Several young men came forward, publicly accusing Rev of molesting them when they were children. And every one of them stated that he had gotten the courage to speak out after listening to CJ speak.

The media vilified Rev from coast to coast. The public demanded that he step down from his position and his mayoral nomination was hanging precariously by the slenderest of threads.

Rev, in a state of absolute panic ordered Reverend Mason Dupre, one of his devoted flunkies to get something on CJ that would take the spotlight off him. By the time CJ arrived in Washington D.C., the plan was set.

Exhausted from their non-stop pace, CJ sat on the edge of the bed in yet another hotel room holding his head in his hands. Carla crawled onto the bed behind him and began to massage his shoulders. Her touch sent sparks of desire racing through his body. He tried to shake her off, but she slapped his shoulder and said, "Be still. You're so tense. You gotta learn how to relax, CJ. Do you meditate?"

"You mean like meditating on the Bible?"

"No," she said. It's a relaxation technique. Here, let me show you." She propped a pillow up against the headboard of the bed and patted it, indicating for him to sit with his back against it. "Now, close your eyes and try not to think of anything. Just clear your mind."

He rested his back against the pillows and closed his eyes. After a few seconds, they popped back open. "How do you not think of anything?"

"Just focus on your breath." She patted his solar plexus. "Bring it up from here, hold it for ten seconds and let it out slowly. It'll help your body relax and then you can relax your mind."

CJ closed his eyes and began breathing deeply. After a few breaths, Carla noticed the tightness in his face relaxing. Soon his head fell forward and his shoulders slumped as he gave in to the relaxation.

When CJ opened his eyes he felt so calm and relaxed that he just sat there for a while smiling. He turned his head and saw Carla lying on the bed propped up on her elbow. "Hey," he said, stretching languidly.

"Hey, yourself," she smiled. "How do you feel?"

"Wow. That must be what they call a fifteen-minute power nap."

"Try forty."

"Get outta here," he said incredulously. "No way was I out for forty minutes."

"You don't know how tired you were. Now that you know how to do it promise me you will."

"I promise," he chuckled. "Boy! Forty minutes?"

"Umm, hmm," she nodded as someone knocked on the door. It was the special code knock they had agreed upon so that they would always know if it was one of their crew. Nonetheless, Carla asked cautiously, "Who is it?"

"Sebastian," replied the voice from the other side of the door. Carla opened the door and plopped back down on the bed crossing her legs Indian style. Sebastian strolled in and said snidely, "Hope I'm not interrupting anything."

"What's up?" CJ said. He caught the implication in Sebastian's voice, but chose not to acknowledge it.

Sebastian pulled a smallish blue envelope from his jacket pocket and handed it to CJ. "They gave me this at the front desk," he said. "I think it's an invitation. It was hand delivered." When CJ flung the envelope on the bed dismissively, Sebastian snatched it up and opened it. As he read the invitation, his lips turned up in a big smile. "Looks like you've finally hit the big time. *The Reverend and*

Mrs. Mason Dupre cordially invite you and a guest to attend a dinner party in your honor," he read. How about that?" he said, holding the invitation out to CJ.

"Toss it," CJ said.

"No. You've got to go. Mason Dupre is one of the most influential black men in D.C. You need people like that on your side."

"I don't need nobody on my side but God."

"Yeah, I know that," Sebastian said. "But you have to be practical. If you make a good impression on this guy it could cement us with the black religious leaders and make us that much stronger."

"No," CJ said, shaking his head.

Carla said, "I think you should go."

That's when it hit him. God wanted him to go to this party. "Okay," he replied. "I'll go."

Sebastian's mouth dropped. One word from Carla had caused CJ to do an about face. Quickly regaining himself, he smiled, "Great."

And don't worry about a thing. I'll be right there with you."

"No, you won't."

"But, it says *and guest.*

"I'm taking Carla," CJ replied.

With shocked looks on their faces Sebastian and Carla said simultaneously:

"Carla!"

"Me!"

"You can't take her," Sebastian warned. "These are high class people."

"And . . .?" CJ asked, his look a definite challenge.

"Nothing," Sebastian shrugged. "Nothing."

"Yeah," CJ said. "That's what I thought."

CHAPTER 32

The snow-covered trees outside Dupre's impressive Victorian style townhouse looked like a scene on a Christmas card to Carla. "I'm not sure about this," she whispered clutching CJ's arm as they strolled up to the door. Although she looked like a queen in her black sequined cocktail dress and fur trimmed coat, Carla dreaded the thought of mixing with such high-class people.

"Don't worry," CJ said, ringing the bell. "I got this." Within moments, a snooty looking butler opened the door. He looked at them as if they were cats coming home with dead rats in their mouths. CJ handed him his invitation.

The butler stepped aside allowing them into the foyer. He then shut the door saying, "One moment please," and left them waiting in the entrance hall. Carla marveled at the elegance of the home. "Do you think that's their real butler or did they just hire him for the party?" she asked.

"Who, Smugly?" CJ asked, pinching his face up in a constipated looking grimace and imitating the butler. "One moment please. I'm smugly the butler and I have to go take this stick out of my butt."

Carla couldn't help but laugh. "Don't make me laugh, Smugly. I'm trying to be serious."

"Just be yourself," CJ said helping her off with her coat. "They're just people. They belch and fart like everybody else."

Carla laughed; glad to see him in such an upbeat mood. Putting on her southern belle charm she adjusted his bowtie, "Might I say that you clean up right nicely, Mr. Johnson."

"Well, thank you, ma-am." CJ said removing his cashmere overcoat. He threw the coat over his arm and tugged at the cuffs of his Hugo Boss tuxedo. "And may I tell you how stunning you look this evening, Miss Carla."

"Why thank you, kind sir," She said with a hint of a curtsy.

CJ leaned back in a pimp pose and rubbed his goatee, eyeing her hungrily. "Yeah. Very nice. Very nice, indeed."

"You're so crazy, CJ," Carla said loving every minute of it.

After waiting several minutes, CJ's good humor began to fade. "I didn't come here to stand around in the hall all night. Come on, we're outta here."

He grabbed Carla's coat and was helping her into it when he heard a loud bombastic voice. "Reverend CJ." They turned to see Reverend Dupre walking toward them with a cigar in one hand and a cocktail in the other. His wife, Zeriah dressed in an African inspired dress and matching head wrap trotted along behind him, her short legs hustling to keep up with his long strides. "I'm Mason Dupre. This is my wife, Zeriah," he said, boldly eyeing Carla's curves.

"How good of you to come Reverend," Zeriah said. "I've been looking forward to meeting you.

"This is Miss Carla Cantrell," CJ said. "Carla, Reverend and Mrs. Dupre."

"How do you do?" Carla said with a tense smile.

"Welcome to our home," said Dupre, clasping her hand between both of his.

"Carla Cantrell," Zeriah said, taking an instant dislike to the ravishing young woman who looked to her like a caramel Jessica Rabbit. "Is that a stage name?"

"No," Carla replied, her nervousness quickly turning to anger at the condescending tone in her hostess' voice. "Is Zeriah your stage name?"

Zeriah flashed an icy smile. "Heavens no. I've never been on the stage."

Carla looked her up and down disparagingly, giving the nice/nasty smile right back to her. "How silly of me." Zeriah puffed up like a little pigeon. Just when it looked as if the scratching and hair pulling was about to begin, Smugly appeared.

"Take their coats, Ridgeway," Dupre said.

As Ridgeway/Smugly disappeared with their coats Zeriah slipped her arm through CJ's. "Come, CJ. Everyone has been dying to meet you." She led him toward the living room, totally ignoring Carla who fell in behind them followed much too closely by Dupre.

As they entered the living room Dupre announced, "Ladies and gentlemen, our guest of honor has arrived." The affluent party quests quickly besieged CJ, bombarding him with questions.

"I hear you're not from around these parts, Reverend. Where did you go to school?" asked Wayman Boggs, a swaggering brown skinned reporter for the Washington Times. Having thoroughly researched CJ, Boggs knew that his education didn't go any farther than a couple of years at UIC. But he wanted to humiliate him.

"John Marshall high school," CJ replied.

"No, silly," Zeriah laughed, playfully slapping his arm. "He means what college. What divinity school. My husband, the Reverend Dupre graduated from Loyola University in Chicago," she said proudly. "It's one of the most prestigious theology schools in the country, you know."

CJ knew exactly what Boggs had meant, but had answered as though he didn't. "Yes, I know," he said returning her patronizing smile.

"Chicago. Beautiful city. That's your hometown, isn't it, CJ?" Dupre' asked.

"I understand you had a little trouble back in Chi-town," Boggs said. "What was that all about?"

Before CJ could answer, which he had no intention of doing, Linda Sinclair, inebriated, cocktail totin' wife of Jackson Sinclair another high-ranking church official better known as Pastor Jack, latched on to his other arm. "Are you going to do any of your tricks for us tonight, CJ? I just love magic tricks," she said, slurring her words. Apparently, Linda knew a few tricks of her own as she had miraculously stuffed her size fourteen self into a size ten cocktail dress. A former Miss New Jersey, Linda had once been quite beautiful. But those days were long gone.

As the other guests joined in with assenting voices, Carla pulled CJ to the side and whispered through clenched teeth, "You don't have to put up with this, CJ. Let's get out of here." Just then, Smugly announced that dinner was served.

"You heard the man," CJ said, linking his arm with hers. "Dinnah is served," he said in his Smugly voice.

As they entered the dining room, Zeriah whisked CJ off to the far end of the elegantly set table where he held her chair out for her as she took her place. She then waved a dainty hand toward the seat to her right indicating for CJ to sit. Carla took a seat on the other side of CJ ignoring the daggers shot at her from her hostess. Carla found the dinner of grilled veal chops, vegetables with roasted ginger and cumin, new potatoes in chive butter and warm cherry tomato salad delectable. But she noticed that CJ hardly ate a bite. "How's your veal?" she asked.

"It's all right," he said, taking a sip of his wine and surveying the table. Dupre stuffed his face while his vicious little wife prattled on. "So, what church are you affiliated with, CJ?"

"I'm not connected to any particular church."

"Really," Zeriah said incredulously. "So, you're more of an evangelist like our Andrea."

Hardly," the immaculately coifed Andrea Fine said haughtily.

The elite dinner guests then set upon CJ like a pack of ravenous wolves, trying to trip him up with their questions and thinly veiled allegations which CJ turned back on them with perplexing answers. Finally, CJ pushed his plate away, wiped his mouth with his napkin, folded it neatly and laid it on the table beside his plate.

"Something wrong with the food?" Dupre asked.

"No, CJ said, "It's not the food." He was full – But not from food. He was full of their spiteful, childish game playing. He was full up to the gills with these pretentious, hateful people who held themselves out to be better than the rest.

"So it must be the company then," said Jackson Sinclair. He was an intimidating presence, tall with a head full of white hair and a white beard set off by thick black eyebrows that looked like two caterpillars had crawled up on his yellow, aging face and died. "Perhaps we're not decadent enough for you. I understand you prefer to socialize with pimps and drug dealers." Muffled laughter tittered from behind crisp linen napkins. Dupre stopped chewing, choosing instead to feast on Pastor Jack tearing this sucker a new one.

CJ lifted one corner of his mouth in an antagonizing smile and gave a humorless chuckle. "I can see where you'd think these people are beneath you," he said. "It's like the dope dealers and pimps of the world are down at the bottom of the morality mineshaft. While you stand up at the top of Mt. Everest. Right?"

"That's one way of putting it," said Pastor Jack with an affirming nod.

CJ leaned back and crossed his legs. "That reminds me of a story I once heard."

Uh, oh. They're in for it now, thought Carla smiling to herself.

"Some TV show was offering a million dollars to anyone who could swim from California to Hawaii," CJ began. "On the day of the race ten swimmers lined up on the beach at Santa Monica and took off swimming toward Honolulu. They swam for six hours before one of them caught a cramp and had to quit. Four hours later two more dropped out," he said, oblivious to the bored expressions on the faces surrounding him. "Twelve hours passed then fifteen, then eighteen. After twenty-four hours, there was only one man left and he was determined to win that money. He swam for forty-eight hours before his body finally quit on him." He looked around the table and asked, "So, does he get the million dollars?"

After a brief pause, Andrea said, "Yes. He won."

"Wrong," CJ said. "The prize wasn't offered to the one who swam the farthest, but to the one who made it all the way to Honolulu. Since no one went the distance, nobody won the money."

241

Andrea rolled her eyes thinking it had been a stupid story. "Some did better than others," CJ continued, "but they all fell short of the goal. It's the same way when it comes to serving the Lord. Some do better than others, but ultimately they all fail because they just can't go the distance." He turned to Pastor Jack. "That's why there's absolutely no difference between that dope dealer and you."

The caterpillars on Pastor Jack's face arched in righteous indignation, "I beg your pardon!"

"It doesn't matter if you're high up or low down. You're still a sinner in God's eyes. And as sinners, we all fall short of the glory of God. So you ain't no better than any criminal out there in the street. In fact, you're worse." Pastor Jack cringed at this bold accusation. "They're just doing what criminals do. But you call yourself a man of God and your shirttail is dirtier than theirs."

"How dare you come to my house and insult my guest!" Dupre said, springing up from his seat. "Pastor Jack has been preaching the gospel longer than you've been on this earth. He has degrees from respected universities and more awards for the good works he's done than he can count. But you'd rather spend your time in the company of drug addicts and low-lifes. How is that when *you're* supposed to be a man of God?"

"It's the sick who need the doctor," CJ said calmly. "Not the righteous."

"Watch it now," Leonard Fine, Andrea's Jewish husband and the council's attorney said only half joking. "You don't want to get sued for impersonating a doctor."

"Oh, Lenny," laughed Andrea. "You're always trying to sue somebody." The pre-maturely balding lawyer shrugged guiltily, saluted CJ with his wine glass and took a sip.

Zeriah tapped her finger against her cheek as though thinking, "Carla Cantrell," she said. "Now, where have I heard that name before?" CJ knew full well that Boggs, a diligent reporter, had researched Carla's background as soon as they received his RSVP with her name on it.

Boggs leaned in toward Carla, a devilish glint in his eye. "You wouldn't be the same Carla Cantrell that was arrested for prostitution and drug possession in California would you?" Carla's face dropped and the sophisticated dinner guests burst out laughing.

"Don't be silly, Wayman," said Andrea with a snakish smile. "No one in his right mind would dare bring a loathsome creature like that into a religious home."

Boggs slapped a mug shot photo of Carla looking wild-eyed and nappy headed down on the table. "Is that you?"

Carla burst into tears, covering her face with her hands as Dupre picked up the picture and passed it around. "Don't tell me," he said to CJ with a smirk, "she found God."

CJ wanted to leap across the table and rip out Dupre's heart. Instead, he said, "Let me ask you something, Dupre."

"What's that?"

"Say a man had two people owing him money. One owed him five hundred dollars and the other owed him fifty. And it turned out that neither one of them could pay, so he says, 'Forget it.' He lets them both slide. Now which one of them is going to love this man more?"

Dupre answered, "The one who owed him the most, I guess."

"You're right." CJ said. Then gesturing toward Carla he said, "This woman has more love in the tip of her little finger than you do in your whole pseudo-religious body. You invited me here to your home and didn't even shake my hand when I came in or offer me a drink. And who are these people you got interrogating me? You were so anxious to humiliate me and use me for entertainment that you didn't even bother to introduce me to any of them. But this lady has had my back since we walked through that front door. You think she didn't know you people would snub her and disrespect her? But she came anyway because she wanted to be there for *me*. Yeah. She's had some issues. But she has given her soul to Jesus and she loves the Lord."

He stood up, took Carla's hand in both of his and declared, "Your sins are forgiven, Carla. Your faith has set you free."

"Oh no!" Andrea gasped. "I know you're not trying to say you can forgive sins."

"Why? Do you have something you need to be forgiven for?"

"I most certainly do not."

"So, you really don't have any reason to love God; do you?" Andrea looked dumbfounded as CJ continued, "See, the more the Lord forgives you for, the more you love Him." He then turned to Carla and said, "Let's get out of here."

As they strolled out, Linda whined, "You said he was going to do some tricks, Jackson."

"Shut up, Linda," he snapped, giving her a hard look.

Dupre was on the phone before CJ and Carla reached Teddy's waiting Escalade. "He just left. No. It looks like we're going to have to go to plan B."

When CJ and Carla climbed into the SUV Teddy asked, "How was dinner?"

CJ ripped off his tie and undid the top button of his shirt. "Those sniveling, lying hypocrites . . . Drive." Without any further questions, Teddy sped away from the elegant home, the whitewashed mausoleum that housed dead men's bones.

As they drove, Sammy looked out of the back window and spotted a van a couple of car lengths behind them. When they turned the van turned also. "I think somebody's following us."

Without turning around, CJ said, "I know. Lose 'em, Teddy." Teddy hit the gas and the Caddy took off. He zoomed up and down the unfamiliar streets leaving red lights and stop signs in his wake. But the van was hot on their tail.

When they turned down MacArthur Boulevard Teddy looked back and gave a sigh of relief. He'd lost them. "Heh, heh, heh. Now that's some Hollywood driving – Chicago style."

Teddy held his hand up for CJ to hit and Herc shouted, "Watch it!"

Teddy screeched to a stop at the sight of a van parked directly in front of them blocking the street. Another car pulled up behind them and masked men dressed in black leaped out of both vehicles brandishing guns. They yanked open the doors of the Escalade and snatched everyone out. "On the ground," ordered one of the men. CJ noted the military precision of their movements.

"What the fuck?" Teddy shouted, stepping forward. The one who seemed to be the leader jabbed the butt of his gun into Teddy's face, knocking him to the ground.

Herc broke for the man and stopped when he felt cold steel in the back of his head. "Take another step and you're a dead man," said the second gunman. "Down!" Herc hesitated for a moment before lying face down on the ground. Sammy quickly joined him.

"We don't have any money," Carla shouted.

"Shut up, bitch, "snarled one of the gunmen drawing his hand back to strike her.

CJ grabbed the man's wrist. "You want that arm to fall off?" he said through clenched teeth.

One of the other assailants sneaked up behind CJ and clocked him upside the head with the butt of his gun, knocking him out cold.

Carla screamed and ran to CJ's side, but one of the gunmen grabbed her, holding her as the other two bound CJ's wrists and ankles with zip ties, threw him into the trunk of the car and jumped into the driver's seat. The attacker holding Carla slung her to the ground, jumped into the van and both vehicles sped off into the night.

Later, in CJ's hotel room, Teddy lay on the bed with an ice pack on his swollen jaw as Dee paced the floor, wringing her hands. "They gon' kill him. I know it. They gon' kill my baby."

"Come on, Mama Dee," Cheyenne said in a vain attempt to console her. "Sammy and them are going to find him." Dee just slumped down on the side of the bed and wrapped her arms around herself, moaning and rocking.

"We need to call the cops," said Carla.

"No cops," Sammy replied. "We have to find them ourselves."

"The cops are probably in on it," Teddy mumbled, barely able to open his mouth.

"What we need to do is go up to that preacher's house and kick some ass. I know he's got something to do with it," Sammy said.

The kidnappers pulled up to a deserted warehouse and jumped out. As two of them lifted the door to the warehouse, the third man opened the trunk of the car and froze. "Hurry up and get him out," said one of the other guys. "You want somebody to see us?" When the man at the car made no response, the others went to see what he was staring at. "Oh, shit!" said one of the men as they gazed into the trunk. It was empty, except for the zip ties they'd used to bind CJ's wrists and ankles.

Back in CJ's hotel room, his entire crew froze at the sound of their secret code knock on the door. They wondered who it could be. Everyone that knew that knock was there. They whipped out their guns and Jimbo went to the door. He peeked through the peephole and turned back to the group with a look of astonishment on his face. He opened the door and CJ stepped into the room.

"Oh, my God! You're alive," screamed Carla as she and Dee threw themselves into his arms sobbing hysterically. Everyone else stared at him in disbelief.

"I almost shot you, man," said Sammy, returning his gun to the back of his waistband.

"Where were you?" Herc asked. "How'd you get away?"

CJ looked around at all of them and said, "Maybe one of these days, y'all gon' realize who I am."

CHAPTER 33

"*CJ Boffo in Gotham!*" *The Daily Variety* raved about CJ's sermon in an off Broadway theater the previous night. "Mind explaining this?" Rev asked, slamming the paper down in front of Saunders.

"That damned Dupre. He was supposed to take care of him. I'm calling him right now." As Saunders reached for the phone, it rang and he snatched it up immediately. "Reverend Bradshaw's office," he answered. "One moment please." He covered the mouthpiece with his hand. "It's the governor," he whispered holding the phone out to Rev.

Rev stared at the phone like it was a snake. Finally, he took it. "Bradshaw here." After a few seconds, a big cheesy grin appeared on his face. "Governor. How good to hear your voice. What can I do for you, sir?" His smile slowly faded. "Yes, sir. I realize that. Of course, I want what's best for the party. See, my assistant . . . No, sir. It won't happen again. Yes, sir. Thank you, Governor. You can count on it. Okay. Okay. Good-bye, Governor."

Rev hung up the phone, opened his desk drawer and pulled out a bottle of liquor and a glass. He poured himself a nice little jolt and downed it. "That was the governor," he said in a voice that was much too calm. "It seems that those imbeciles Dupre hired let that nigga get away from them. Said he just vanished out of the trunk of a car. Whoosh! You ever heard of any shit like that?"

"That's incredible," said Saunders.

"Oh, that's not the best part. Two more boys came forward with accusations against me. It's a conspiracy. They're trying to ruin me with their lies. After all I've done for them."

Saunders didn't know what to say, so he remained silent. "It's that damned CJ. The governor's threatening to pull my name from the ticket if I don't stop this sucker and clear my name." He plopped down at his desk, a world of torment showing in his face. Finally, he said, "You need to find this freak and put a stop to his bullshit once and for all. You understand?"

"What am I supposed to do?" Saunders asked.

"I'll leave the details up to you. All I want is results."

Meka glared at the TV, watching as reporters mobbed CJ outside a New York hotel. "If one of those New York reporters gets an interview with CJ before I do, I'm going to pull my hair out by the roots," she said, running her fingers through her lustrous mane. "This is my story. I found it." Suddenly she heard gunshots coming from the TV set. She watched in amazement as the crowd scattered like ants.

A shot whizzed past CJ's head barely missing him as Herc knocked him to the ground and covered him with his immense body. Teddy and the others dashed into the hotel for cover as the shooter, a leathery faced white man in army fatigues ran toward CJ and Herc firing a semi-automatic weapon.

"You goddamn black devil!" he screamed.as the blaring of police sirens filled the air. The would-be assassin stopped shooting and took off running, jumped into his car and peeled out just as several police cars came to a screeching halt in front of the hotel.

The cops jumped out with their guns drawn. As soon as they spotted CJ and Herc grabbed them, slammed them up against the wall and started searching them.

Two women who had been hiding behind a car, jumped out screaming at the cops. "Them ain't the ones," shouted one of the women. "Some white man was shooting at them."

"There he goes," the other lady yelled, pointing at the gunman as his car sped off.

A big burly young cop grabbed the woman by the arm and shouted in her face, "Get back. We'll handle this."

He shoved the woman roughly into her friend and both women started screaming, "Help! Help! Police brutality." People started running out of their hiding places, cell phones recording the offending officers.

Teddy saw a cop twisting CJ's arm behind his back and shouted, "Hey! What are you doing?"

"Just back off and no one will get hurt," yelled one of the cops, pointing his gun at Teddy. A white shirted sergeant got out of one of the cars and strolled up to the cop holding CJ. "What's going on here?" asked the sergeant.

"Shots fired," said the hyped up young cop.

"This the shooter?"

"No!" Teddy snapped, "This is Reverend CJ. He's the victim."

"He looks alright to me," the sergeant said. "If nobody's hurt, we'll just let you guys off with a warning."

"A warning?" Shouted Sammy, incredulous. He started toward the cop but Cheyenne pulled him back.

The sergeant turned toward Sammy and sneered, "You got a problem with that home boy?"

"No," Cheyenne piped up. "He doesn't have a problem with it." Sammy was boiling, but he knew it was in his best interest to remain silent.

Later, in CJ's hotel suite Sammy paced the floor while the others sat around looking shaken and scared. "That was some bogus shit," he said. "Them cops didn't even try to catch that dude."

"So, what else is new?" Hawk replied.

CJ sat on the couch rubbing his head. Even though he had accepted the fact that this mission would likely cost him his life, this brush with death had rattled him more than he cared to admit.

"Are you okay, CJ?" Carla asked in a voice filled with concern. CJ nodded, but said nothing.

"I'm still shaking," Cheyenne said. "Somebody tried to kill you. Who'd want to do something like that?" Hearing a knock on the door, they all nearly jumped out of their skins.

After a long silence, Teddy eased toward the door. He stopped before reaching it and stepped to the side. "Who is it?"

"Room Service," the voice on the other side replied.

"We didn't order no room service," Teddy said harshly. CJ shot an apprehensive look around the room and the twins moved quickly to Teddy's side. Sammy and Hawk's hands went automatically to their guns. "Compliments of the hotel, sir," said the voice on the other side of the door. Teddy approached the door slowly. Putting his eye to the peephole, he saw a nervous looking young waiter holding onto a cart filled with covered serving dishes, a bottle of wine, plates, glasses and silverware.

Teddy cautiously opened the door. The waiter smiled politely. "The hotel wants you to know how sorry they are about . . . You know, what happened," he said.

Teddy stepped aside, allowing him into the room. When the waiter finished unloading the food onto the table, Teddy reached into his pocket for a tip. "That won't be necessary, sir," said the young man. Teddy shrugged and moved toward the door. "But I would like to say one thing to Reverend CJ – if I could," the waiter said, timidly.

"What do you want to say?" CJ asked.

Awed by CJ's presence, it took him a moment before he could speak. "Uh . . ., my name's Jason."

"What's up, Jason?"

"I . . . I just want you to know that I think you're awesome. And that dude that tried to shoot you is probably crazy. I mean, why would anybody want to shoot *you*? I mean . . . You're awesome."

CJ smiled, touched by Jason's words. "Thanks, Jason." He stood, extending his hand to the young man. "I appreciate you saying that." A big grin spread over Jason's face and he grasped CJ's hand shaking it enthusiastically. When CJ eventually freed his hand, Jason grabbed his cart and hurried out of the room.

After shutting the door, Teddy shot CJ a smile. "At least you've got one fan left."

"Hey, one fan for me is another soul for my Father," CJ said.

Sammy walked over to the table and poured himself a glass of wine, "Cheap ass hotel. They could've sent something stronger than this," he said. "After all we've been through."

"They didn't have to send that," Sebastian said. "It's not the hotel's fault that some idiot decided to take pot shots at CJ."

"How do you know he was shooting at CJ?" Hawk drawled. "He could've been trying to kill you, for all we know."

"Me?" Sebastian said. "Why would anyone want to kill me?"

"You tell me. We don't know what kind of shit you're hooked up in."

"That's the stupidest thing I ever heard, Sebastian flared. "You're the one that's got him out there partying with hoodlums, *Carlos*."

"Oh," said Hawk. "So you do remember me, huh?"

"Carlos Hawkins. I recognized you the first time I saw you. I just didn't want to acknowledge you."

"Naw," Hawk said stepping up to him. "Because then you'd have to acknowledge who you are."

"Was that supposed to be profound?" Sebastian deadpanned.

"Hey!" Teddy shouted. "We don't need this right now. Somebody's trying to kill CJ. I think we need to get back to L.A.," he said to CJ. "They might not miss next time."

Knowing his friend was worried about him, CJ smiled and said, "Those suckers can't kill me." All motion in the room ceased and every eye fixed itself on CJ.

"They can't?" Carla asked in amazement.

"Not yet," CJ answered. "My time hasn't come yet." Displaying a newly found confidence, even arrogance, he said, "They think they can shut the Brother Man up. Hmph. They better think again. They ain't done nothing but make me mad." He strolled over to the table and poured himself a glass of wine. He took a long swallow and said, "Yeah. They might kill me. But, I'll be back," he said in his best Schwarzenegger impression, laughing at his own personal joke.

Thrown by CJ's grim pronouncement, everyone just stared at him blankly. They didn't know if he was serious or joking. Therefore, they chose to believe the part about no one being able to kill him and dismiss what he said about coming back.

CHAPTER 34

"Sebastian, call that TV chick and tell her I'll do her show." The assassination attempt had really shaken CJ's crew and he needed to do something to bolster their faith.

"What show?" Sebastian asked. "Every talk show in the country has been trying to get you to make an appearance."

"What's-her-face. The one from KBDJ. I want to go on her show."

"Meka Maxwell?" Sebastian laughed, shaking his head. "Nooo. You don't want to do that. That woman hates you. She'll tear you to shreds in front of a nationwide audience."

"A wise man once told me that I couldn't hide. And he was right."

"Okay," Sebastian said, shaking his head. "It's your neck."

"Y'all get your stuff together," said CJ. "We're going back to L.A. tonight."

"Cool," replied Sammy. "But we need to get the cars serviced first though."

"We might not be able to get them all done on such short notice," said Sebastian.

"Just the van," CJ said. "We can send the performers back in that. Call Bishop Hanks, first. He said we could use the council jet anytime we wanted to, didn't he?" Sebastian nodded. "Cool. Tell him to have it pick us up at Teterboro tonight around midnight."

"But what about our rides?" Hawk asked.

"We can get some of the brothers here to get them serviced and drive 'em back to L.A." As they continued to discuss their return to California, they heard a loud banging on the door.

Teddy ran to the peephole and peeked out at a dead eyed white man in a cheap gray suit. With him was a tall woman with equally dead eyes – cop's eyes, a short haircut and a much nicer suit. Teddy turned to CJ and whispered, "Cops." He knew it the moment he set eyes on them. To the door he said, "Who is it?"

"NYPD," the man said gruffly. "Open up."

Teddy opened the door wearing his best fake smile. "What can I do for you officers?"

"Detectives," Fiona Pontrain snapped, shouldering her way past him and into the room. "Mind if we come in? That's Sergeant Kostas and I'm Detective Pontrain." Her partner sauntered in behind her, taking a quick inventory of the occupants of the room.

"Which one of you calls yourself Reverend CJ?" asked Kostas.

CJ stood, "I'm CJ. What's this all about?"

256

As the Detectives walked toward CJ, Carla jumped up, placing herself between them and CJ. "May we see some ID?" Kostas gave her a disdainful look and whipped out his badge, as did Pontrain. Sebastian stepped forward. "I'm afraid there's been a mistake, detectives. We didn't call the police."

"Nobody said you did. We've been assigned to protect the reverend here and see that he gets out of New York safely." He then strolled over to the table and began lifting the tops to the various serving dishes. "Mmm, shrimp," he said, taking a shrimp from the dish with his big sausage fingers and popping it into his mouth.

"Assigned by who?" Sammy asked, jumping up from his seat.

Pontrain's hand went immediately to the gun riding on her hip. She held the other hand out toward Sammy like a stop sign. "Easy now. What's your name?"

Knowing that Sammy was carrying a gun, Cheyenne jumped up, successfully diverting the cops' attention away from him. "I demand to know who sent you here," she shouted. "Nobody here asked for any police protection. I want to know what this is really about."

"Look, lady," Kostas said gruffly, "You can either, sit down and shut up or we can haul your ass down to the station and charge you with interfering with an officer in the performance of his duty. What's it gonna be?" Cheyenne took a deep breath and flopped down into her chair.

"Let's get one thing straight," Kostas said. "We don't want to be here anymore than you want us here. For all I care that screwball could have shot the whole fucking lot of you. But, our job is to protect and serve," he said with a put upon sigh. "So, you might as well get used to us being a part of this happy little family as long as you're in our fair city. Just consider it a courtesy of the New York Police Department. When are you planning on leaving?" he asked CJ.

257

"Tonight!" Sammy blurted out.

"Well," said Kostas, "That makes my life a lot easier."

"So what time are you leaving out?" Pontrain asked, looking at Sammy.

"We're planning on flying out from Teterboro around midnight," said CJ.

"Great," said Kostas, eyeing Sebastian warily as he approached.

"Can I speak to you for a minute, Sergeant?

"And you are . . .?"

"St. John," Sebastian said, pulling a business card from his pocket and handing it to him. "Sebastian St. John. I'm Reverend CJ's business manager and I have some things to take care of before we leave. Do you mind if I go? It should only take me a couple of hours."

"Sure," the detective said. "Go take care of your business."

"Thanks." Sebastian said, heading for the door.

"Pontrain. Go with him."

Sebastian flashed Kostas a look, then sighed and opened the door. "After you, Detective," he said gallantly allowing Pontrain to precede him out the door.

That night, Kostas, Pontrain and four uniformed NYPD officers escorted CJ and company to Teterboro Airport where the AACC's private jet awaited. As they prepared to board the plane, CJ pulled Teddy off to the side and told him that they should go on ahead and he would catch up with them later.

Overhearing his instructions, Kostas bellowed, "What the hell is this?"

"I just need some time alone," CJ said. "Is that a problem?"

"Hell yeah, it's a problem." Kostas said. "I was supposed to see you on that plane."

"I didn't say I wasn't going." CJ said. "I'm just not going now."

Sebastian saw them squabbling and quickly intervened. "What's the problem?" he asked.

"Your boss doesn't want to get on the plane." Pontrain said.

"What's wrong?" Sebastian asked CJ.

"Nothing," CJ replied." Y'all go ahead. I'll catch up with you later. I need to pray."

Reluctantly, they all got on the plane. Sebastian was fuming. He had arranged for several groups to meet CJ at the Los Angeles Airport. He'd even given the media a "heads up."

CJ rode back to the hotel with the two detectives in silence. When CJ unlocked the door to his suite, he stepped in and turned abruptly almost bumping noses with Kostas who was dead on his heels. "Do you mind?" he asked, blocking the cop's way.

"What are we supposed to do?" Kostas asked, "Stand out here in the hall all night?"

"Of course not," CJ said, shutting the door in his face. A few seconds later, the door opened. CJ set two chairs in the hall and said, "Good night, detectives." He then closed the door, leaving the angry cops standing in the hall.

Kostas snatched his phone out and called his chief. "Yeah. It's me. Just left the airport. No. Everyone got on the plane except him. Says he needs some time alone to *pray*. Don't worry. He's not going anywhere. Pontrain and I are camped out in front of his hotel room. He'll have to go past us to get out of this hotel tonight." He ended the call and stuck the phone back into his pocket. "Better go get us some coffee, Pontrain." He parked his wide butt on one of the straight back chairs, extending his legs and crossing his ankles. "This is gonna be a long night."

The elevator doors opened and Detective Pontrain stepped out into the hotel lobby, cell phone in hand. She immediately hit a speed dial number. "Meka, it's me, Fiona. The plane just took off. Guess who's not on it."

CHAPTER 35

Ensconced in plush leather seats that rivaled furniture in the finest hotel lobby, Teddy and the gang reclined in aeronautical splendor aboard the AACC's luxuriously appointed private jet. Sammy sat next to a window with Cheyenne beside him. He'd never flown before and was as excited as a kid by this new adventure. When Jasmine, the shapely flight attendant stopped her cart in front of them and served him his double shot of Jack, he grinned like he'd won the lottery.

As Jasmine pushed her cart toward Hawk who sat alone in the rear of the cabin, she noted how handsome he looked in that black Patrick James silk linen sport coat over a form fitting Dior Homme black polo. Those Raf Simmons skinny black jeans he was rocking gave him an air of the *bad boy* that intrigued her.

Jasmine's frozen professional smile turned warm as she served Hawk his drink. "Double shot of Courvoisier on the rocks," she said, embracing him with her smile.

As Hawk took the drink, her hand brushed lightly against his. "Will there be anything else, sir?"

Hawk slowly removed his shades, revealing eyes so deep and soulful that Jasmine had to hold onto the cart to keep from falling into them. He licked his lips and said softly, "I'll let you know."

As Jasmine pushed her cart toward her station, she turned to get another quick glance at Hawk. Just then, Sebastian came barreling in from the cockpit where he had been conferring with the pilot. He smashed into the cart, causing Jasmine to lose her balance. Hawk leaped from his seat and caught her before she hit the floor. "You okay?" he asked, holding her a moment or two longer than necessary before letting her go.

Hawk returned to his seat and Sebastian plopped down next to him. "Clumsy bitch." he said. Hawk gave Jasmine a look and shrugged as if to say, *he's a jerk. What can I say?*

As Jasmine started back up the aisle with her cart Sebastian turned, snapping his fingers imperiously. "Hey, stewardess. Bring me a double scotch and soda." Not anxious to share the next few hours of his life with his childhood tormenter, Sebastian glanced around the cabin to see if there was another seat available. There was not. Resigned to the seating arrangements, he stretched his legs out, kicked off his Italian loafers and loosened his tie and shirt collar. "Man," he sighed shaking his head in frustration.

Hawk just stared out at the near empty airfield.

When Jasmine returned with his drink, Sebastian drank half of it in one swallow. However, the liquor did little to settle his jangled nerves.

As the flight got underway and the lights dimmed, the chatter died down and they all settled in for the flight. Cheyenne snuggled up against Sammy, resting her head on his shoulder as he peered out the window entranced by the luminous night sky. Hawk, pretending to be asleep could feel Sebastian fidgeting in the seat next to him.

Sebastian turned on his overhead light and pulled a magazine from the rack. He flipped through the magazine, but he couldn't concentrate. He needed to talk to somebody. However, everyone had either gone or was going to sleep. He glanced at the man sitting to his left. *What the hell*, he thought. He didn't like the dude, but if he didn't talk to someone soon he was going to burst. He shot Hawk a sharp elbow to the ribs. Hawk jumped as though startled from a deep sleep. "Are you asleep?" Sebastian asked.

"Yeah," Hawk replied dryly, settling back into his seat.

Sebastian continued, "What's up with CJ?"

"I don't know," Hawk muttered.

"Why didn't he come back with us?"

Hawk refused to answer, but Sebastian never noticed. "Don't you think he's been acting strange lately? Maybe he's getting ready to make that move."

Hawk realized that playing sleep was not going to save him from the displeasure of Sebastian's company so he lowered his sunglasses and asked, "What move?"

"The revolution," Sebastian said. "When is he supposed to set it off?"

"Look man," Hawk said, impatiently. "These are things you need to be asking the man himself. I don't know nothin' about nothin'."

"That makes two of us. I'm supposed to be his right hand man, but he's starting to confide in that whore more than he does me," he said with a derisive nod in Carla's direction, unaware that she was peering at him through half-closed eyes and listening to every word he said. "I think his fame is going to his head. That's what it is. If it wasn't for me, he'd still be back on the block spreading his pearls among winos and crack heads." Anger raged within Carla as Sebastian continued to put CJ down. "He's got this country in the palm of his hand right now. He could make any demand he wanted and they'd go for it. But he's just faking the game. If I had the powers he has . . ."

"But, you don't!" Carla shouted, springing out of her seat. If anyone on the plane had actually been asleep, they woke up then. "And you never will. So, why don't you just shut your stupid mouth and give everybody a break."

"Shut up, bitch!" Sebastian hurled back at her. "Just because you're screw . . ."

Before he could get that lie out of his mouth, Carla was on him like a Tasmanian devil. She snatched him out of his seat and laid a punch on his nose that dropped him to his knees. By the time Sebastian realized what was happening, he was flat on his back with Carla straddling his chest and slapping his face like it was the latest Olympic sport.

"Who's the bitch now?" she asked, grasping his collar with one hand and slapping him cross-handed with the other. "What's my name?" she snarled. Sebastian glared at her defiantly as the others watched in amusement. Carla demanded that he, "Say my name, bitch. Say my name." But Sebastian stubbornly refused. "Say my name! Say my name!" she repeated, banging Sebastian's head against the floor until blood ran from his nose. She wanted to smash his smug face through the floor of that plane and ride him all the way down to hell.

Strangling on his own blood, Sebastian shouted, "Carla!" Carla. Your name is Carla," he said. Everyone on the plane cracked up laughing as Carla stood up and gave him a sharp kick to the ribs.

She pointed down at him and said, "Don't you *ever* let me hear you say anything against CJ again. You hear me?" He glared up at her, rising to his knees. A quick palm of her hand to his forehead sent him sprawling onto his back again. Pinning him there with her foot, the heel of her boot digging into his stomach Carla asked through tight lips, "Did you hear what I said?"

264

Mortified, Sebastian dared not look around at his howling companions. He just wanted to get off that floor, off that plane. "Yes. Yes, Carla. I heard what you said." Carla swept her hair out of her face and stepped back. Sebastian stared up at her, afraid to get up.

As Carla strode back to her seat, Sebastian pulled himself up into the seat next to Hawk. He took his handkerchief from his pocket and wiped the blood, snot and tears from his face. Hawk, grinning so broadly that deep dimples showed in his handsome face said politely, "You were saying?" Sebastian shot him a contemptible look and continued to wipe his face.

Jasmine smiled at Sebastian as she walked past him to bring Carla a bottle of water. "You okay, honey?" Carla nodded with a grateful smile, taking a big sip of the water.

Sammy laughed. "Looks like you picked the wrong sister to mess with, Sebastian."

As they all settled into their seats, Sammy glanced out the window and did a double take. "What the . . ." he said gazing out the window in astonishment. "It's CJ!" he shouted in alarm. "It's CJ!" They all flew to Sammy's window and were amazed to see CJ – walking alongside the plane as if he were on solid ground, his form illuminated by the stars sparkling in the night sky. He smiled and waved at them. Then a cloud floated past him and he was gone.

"Ho-ly Fuck!" exclaimed Teddy.

"Oh, my God. CJ's dead!" Carla screamed.

"No," Said Teddy. "He can't be dead,"

"How else could he be walking on thin air?" Cheyenne countered. Teddy shook his head refusing to believe that his dearest friend was dead.

"Well, where is he then, Teddy? Where is he?" Carla shouted hysterically.

"I'm right here."

They all turned to see CJ standing behind them with a big smile on his face. Nobody moved. Nobody breathed. They just gaped at him in absolute terror. CJ's appearance filled Sebastian with dread. CJ had just transcended the laws of gravity and matter. Sebastian wondered if he had also heard the things he'd said.

CJ had not intended to frighten them by this display of power. He did it to strengthen their faith and to confirm to them once and for all that the power of God was indeed, in his hands. Carla took a step toward him and passed out cold.

When Carla opened her eyes, she saw CJ's face hovering over her. "Hey you," he said, rubbing her hand.

"They killed you," she whimpered.

"No," he said, flashing a devastating smile. "Not yet."

CHAPTER 36

A massive crowd waving signs that said things like, I love you CJ and CJ for President waited outside LAX to greet CJ. The media was out in full force. Meka Maxwell, who had no idea that CJ had decided to do her show, went over her game plan with Darnell and Angie. "Okay. I got word that CJ isn't on the plane. But his friends are. He'll probably be coming in sometime this afternoon. We'll find out exactly when so we can get to him before anybody knows he's back in L.A. In the meantime, maybe we can get somebody in his camp to talk." She looked around in disgust at the sea of reporters and laughed. "Look at those vultures. Won't they be surprised when CJ doesn't get off the plane."

Suddenly, the crowd began shouting and cheering uncontrollably. CJ stepped off the plane and waved to the adoring crowd. Filled with the Holy Spirit and empowered by his most recent miracle, he walked with the confidence and authority of a man under divine protection.

"What's he doing here?" Meka asked incredulously. "My police contact in New York called me the minute the plane took off. And CJ wasn't on it."

"Well, there he is." Darnell said.

Reporters hurled questions at CJ as he strolled toward the waiting limousine flanked by Teddy and Herc with Carla and Dee following close behind. But CJ didn't respond.

Once Meka recovered from the shock, she darted through the crowd like a greased snake, weaving a path for Darnell and his camera to follow. "Excuse me. 'Scuse me," she said, maneuvering bodies out of her way until she was close to CJ. "Do you know who tried to kill you, CJ?" she asked, shoving her mike in his face. CJ ignored her, never breaking his stride.

"No comment," Teddy replied curtly.

Undaunted, Meka jumped in front of CJ and coldly spat out her vicious accusation, "You're afraid for your life, aren't you, CJ? Isn't that the real reason you left New York so suddenly?" CJ stopped abruptly, giving her a steely-eyed glare.

"You think I mind dying in my Father's name?" he said through clenched teeth. Teddy tried to pull him away but he snatched his arm free. "Listen. I'll lay my life down willingly and I'll take it back up again. But ain't nobody gon' take it from me. God is in me," he said, pounding his chest. "God and I are one!"

A collective gasp went up from the astonished masses, who only a moment ago was celebrating him as if he were a rock star. Outrage thundered through the crowd as they began to close in on CJ, screaming curses and obscenities. Teddy and Herc quickly hustled CJ into the limo. The irate crowd threw down their signs and began beating and kicking on the car as it slowly made its way through the throng of hostile citizens.

Meka stared into the camera with an exaggerated look of shock on her face and asked, "Did I hear what I thought I heard? Did rogue preacher, Reverend CJ just say that he was God? Stay tuned to KBDJ TV for more on this explosive development. I'm Meka Maxwell; live at LAX."

At the end of Meka's broadcast, Rev clicked the TV off in disgust. "Who does this moron think he is?"

"Apparently, he thinks he's God," replied Saunders.

Rev shot him a hateful look. "This sucker's gotta go," he said with an ominous tone of finality.

"What do you mean, 'go'?" Saunders asked.

"I mean," Rev glowered, "I *will* be the next mayor of New York City. And no lousy bus driver with delusions of grandeur is going to stop me."

Later, Sebastian arrived at Teddy's house freshly dressed in a tan suit and a brown and white silk shirt. He found CJ and the others in the music room watching Meka on TV. She played the clip from the airport, adding, "People are up in arms over Reverend CJ's bold and blasphemous statement. Does he really think he's God? Or is this just the latest volley in this arrogant con man's grand scheme to manipulate the people? How much of this are we going to stand, America?" she implored, brushing a wayward curl off her face. "Give me a call and let me know what you think." The phones lit up with furious callers castigating CJ in terms so vile that almost every other word had to be bleeped out.

Teddy clicked off the TV and Sebastian dropped his head in defeat. "Why, CJ? Why did you have to say that?" When CJ didn't respond, he continued. "I hope you know you alienated a lot of people with that crack about being God." CJ gave him a reproachful look. He didn't feel that he owed Sebastian or anyone else an explanation.

Realizing he'd overstepped, Sebastian adroitly changed the subject. "I stopped by the post office to get the mail, but it was too much for me to carry so they're sending it over."

CJ glanced around the room and asked, "Where's Big Jimbo?"

269

"He split," Baby Herc said, looking embarrassed. "He took off as soon as we got off the plane; said shit was getting too freaky for him. I'm sorry, CJ."

"Is that how the rest of y'all feel?" CJ asked. "If you do, speak up. I ain't got time to be fooling around with no half steppers. You're either in it or you ain't." When no one responded, he turned to Sammy. "Sammy?"

"I'm with you, CJ. Ride or die," he declared. The others vowed similar commitments.

"Teddy. CJ. Where y'all at?" Dusty called as she opened the door to the music room. She stepped in and froze, shocked to find a group of strangers in her house staring at her as if she were the intruder.

Teddy scooped up his sister, giving her a big hug. "Hey, baby girl, I didn't expect you back until next week."

Dusty clung to her big brother, "Thank God you're all right." She released Teddy and ran to CJ. "The news said somebody tried to kill you," she said, nudging Carla out of the way so that she could give him a hug.

"I'm alright," he said dryly. Carla felt her whole body grow rigid as Dusty clung to CJ.

Dee could see that those brown eyes were turning green and she quickly intervened, grabbing Dusty away from CJ. "Dusty!" Dee said, wrapping her in a big hug. "Look at you, all grown up and pretty as you wanna be."

"Miss Dee? What are you doing here? Who are all these people?"

"Oh, my bad," Teddy said, introducing her to the crew, saving Carla for last. "And this is Carla. She's gonna be staying with us for a while." Carla smiled and slid closer to CJ.

"Can I talk to you for a minute?" Dee said, grasping Teddy's hand and pulling him toward the door. Once outside the room, Dusty asked. "What's going on, Teddy? I've been hearing all this stuff on TV. And when I heard that somebody tried to kill y'all up in New York, I got somebody to cover for me and jumped on the first thing smokin'. Are you sure you're all right?" she said, placing her hand on his cheek.

"I'm fine," he said, holding his hands out to the side. "See, no holes."

"What about CJ?" she asked. "He looks strange." Since last she'd seen him, CJ had become moody and introspective. His eyes, always his best feature now seemed to shine with a brightness that bordered on madness while his countenance was otherwise subdued.

"He's cool."

"Tell me the truth, Teddy. People at the airport were talking about him claiming to be God. What's going on? Is the stuff they're saying about him true? He's got some kind of magic healing power?"

Teddy took her arm, leading her away from the door, "Baby girl, the stuff you saw on TV don't even start to tell the story. CJ done turned into some kind of . . .," He couldn't think of a word that would describe what CJ had become. "He says he's on a mission for God."

"So, he doesn't really think he *is* God?"

Teddy shrugged. "I don't know. He keeps referring to himself as the 'Brother Man,' whatever that means. But I'll tell you this, I've seen him do some stuff that would blow your mind. He's even healed some of those people in there," he said with a nod toward the music room. "Sammy, the dude behind the bar was paralyzed. Been in a wheelchair over ten years. I mean the man was dead from the waist down. One night, CJ told him to get up and walk and he *did*. Been walking ever since."

271

She stared at him in amazement. "Who's that Carla chick? Did he cure her? Why is she staying here, anyway? Don't tell me that's his girlfriend."

"Carla?" He nodded toward the kitchen, indicating for her to follow. Teddy grabbed two bottles of beer from the fridge and Dusty followed him out to the patio.

"Carla was a mess," said Teddy, sipping his beer. He then proceeded to fill her in on Carla's story, as well as many other extraordinary things he'd seen CJ perform. "People been saying he's the son of Jesus. Some are even saying he's the second coming of Jesus or the reincarnation of Dr. Martin Luther King. I don't know," he said, throwing up his hands. "I just know that he's my boy and I got his back."

"So, what else is new?" she said with a smile, clasping her brother's hand. "What can I do to help?"

"First thing you gotta do is get baptized."

"I've already been baptized."

Teddy laughed, "It's a long story, baby girl. Get CJ to explain it to you." Before she could respond, the doorbell light flashed.

When Teddy opened the front door, he saw a mail carrier standing there holding two large sacks of mail. He looked past the man and spotted three mail trucks parked in front of his house and two other mail carriers lugging mail and packages up the walk.

Later that night, CJ and the crew sat around the dining room table opening the massive influx of mail. Stacked up around them were sacks and sacks of mail as well as numerous packages. "Every one of these letters has a check or some cash in it," said Sebastian, paper clipping a check to its accompanying letter.

Cheyenne tore open a box and held up a pair of gigantic panties. "Why are these women sending you their underwear? This is like the tenth pair of panties I've seen already."

"You sure that's not ten pairs rolled into one?" Sammy joked, giving them all a good laugh.

Cheyenne read the accompanying letter, "*Dear Reverend CJ, I am a healthy twenty-five-year-old mother of six. I am looking for a good man to help me raise my children. I asked the kids and they said that they would love to have you for a father. If you are ever in the Tuscaloosa area, please give me a call*." She then folded the letter and returned it to its envelope. "Want me to hold onto it in case you ever get to Tuscaloosa?" Cheyenne laughed.

Dusty pinched CJ's cheek playfully, "Aw, another marriage proposal," she said, throwing her arms around his neck. "Can I be the best girl?" Everyone laughed except Carla who wanted to slap the taste out of Dusty's mouth. She did not appreciate her putting her hands all over CJ.

"Don't worry about the panties," CJ said half joking. "Look out for the letter bomb." All motion stopped as fearful looks spread around the table. CJ gave them a sly smile and ripped open another letter. They all seemed to release a shared breath. Laughing nervously at his not so funny joke, they returned to work.

"Check this out," Sebastian said, peering at a letter in his hand. "This guy is a designer who wants you to wear his clothes." He stood up, removing a beautiful black pin striped suit from the box and holding the jacket up in front of him. "This is sharp, CJ. If you don't want it, I'll take it."

CJ chuckled. "Carla, get my suit from that man before I have to hurt him." When Carla started to rise, Sebastian quickly threw the jacket back into the box and shoved it toward her. Smiling, Carla took the box and placed it on the floor next to her chair.

Teddy waved a letter in the air. "This store wants to develop a line of men's suits called the CJ Collection."

"I don't think I should be endorsing anything," said CJ. "That's all that Maxwell woman would need; to have the Brother Man come on her show doing a commercial for some store."

A look passed between Dusty and her brother. CJ had not explained to anyone, not even Teddy why he referred to himself as the *Brother Man*. He did it because he saw himself as the brother of *the man* – the man, being Jesus.

"You're going on Meka Maxwell's show?" Dusty asked.

CJ nodded, "Yeah. But I'm beginning to wonder if that's such a good idea."

"It's a great idea," she said. "Then people can see that you're not the monster she's making you out to be. But be careful, CJ. I've seen her show and the woman is vicious."

"Told you," Sebastian said.

CHAPTER 37

CJ was sharper than piranha's teeth when he stepped onto the set of *The Meka Maxwell Show* in his new suit. And Meka was as excited as a young girl on prom night to have him on the show. Meka had wanted to do a one-on-one interview with CJ in front of her live studio audience, but her producers insisted she bring on other guests to incite controversy.

Meka smiled graciously into the camera and introduced her guests. "With us today on The Meka Maxwell Show is the controversial preacher, Reverend CJ." CJ received a spattering of applause laced with a generous chorus of boos. He wasn't surprised. His popularity had taken an enormous hit after his shocking statement at the airport. Meka held her hand up for silence. "Let's be nice now," she said through a thinly veiled attempt at neutrality.

"We're also pleased to have Reverend Jackson Sinclair representing the AACC. You may know him better as Pastor Jack of the long running TV show, *The Salvation Hour*." Pastor Jack received a respectable round of applause to which he nodded his wooly head. CJ could see that he was chomping at the bit to get at him. "Next we have syndicated columnist and author, Addicus Bankhead," Meka said extending her hand toward Bankhead, a

275

pretentious little man in a large white hat who thought that the best way to earn acceptance from the white establishment was to trample blacks at every opportunity. He flashed a smarmy grin and nodded his head.

"And last but certainly not least, Father Sean O'Shaunessy, the outspoken Catholic priest who first came to prominence in the 1950's when he took an unprecedented stand in defense of Brown vs. The Board of Education." The white haired grandfatherly looking priest looked as though he'd come straight out of Central Casting. "Father Sean has been a staunch supporter of civil rights for over sixty years," she said, starting off the applause which quickly grew to a crescendo. When it died down, she said. "Welcome to our show, Father. We're honored to have you with us."

"It's an honor to be here, Meka," Father Sean said with a cherubic smile.

"Now," Meka said to the audience, "I know you're all as anxious as I am to hear what Reverend CJ has to say for himself, so let's get this party started." Taking her seat, she crossed her gorgeous legs and gave CJ her sweetest smile. "Let me start by saying how glad I am that you agreed to join us today, Reverend CJ."

"Thank you," CJ said cordially. "It's a pleasure to be here." And he meant it. He was as anxious as she was to get this party started.

"Reverend CJ, you've been attributed with healing people across the country of various ailments and diseases. What exactly is your medical experience?"

"I don't have any."

"I see," she said, pursing her lips. "Then, can you tell us how you came to perform these alleged healings?"

"I haven't healed anyone," CJ said, shocking both Meka and her audience. When the buzz of confusion died down, he continued. "Everything I've said or done has come from God."

"You said you *were* God," she accused. "Are you backing down from that statement?"

"I don't back down from anything I say. I said that God and I are one. And if I said anything less I'd be a liar just like some of your esteemed religious leaders."

"Who are you calling a liar?" Pastor Jack asked.

"Anybody that bends the word of the Lord to make it say what he wants it to say," CJ replied. He was coming out of the gate swinging. He hadn't come there for polite conversation or collegiality. He came to confront and to condemn. And that's exactly what he did.

"I will not be called a liar by some blaspheming nut case with a God complex," Pastor Jack protested.

"What would you call a person who preaches one thing and does another? Who stands up in his big fancy church or on the TV hollering about family values when all the time he's got a chick on the side? What would you call that man, Pastor?"

That struck a little too close to home. Pastor Jack's jaw tightened and one caterpillar jumped up high on his brow. *How does he know?*

"I'd call that man a liar. Wouldn't you, Mr. O'Shaunessy?"

"You can call me Father," the kindly cleric corrected.

"No. I can't," CJ said bluntly. "The only one I call father is my Father in heaven."

It took the outraged priest a moment to regain his composure. Finally, he said, "To answer your question, Reverend – I call you Reverend because I find it prudent to afford a man the courtesy of addressing him by his official title."

"Official title," Bankhead snorted. "Hmph."

"I agree," O'Shaunessy continued. "There are some members of the clergy that preach the Ten Commandments yet find themselves drawn into adultery and other covetous behaviors. That's why we in the Catholic Church take a vow of celibacy in order to avoid such sexual improprieties."

"Yes," CJ said, disgusted by the priest's air of virtuous superiority. "I'm familiar with your vow of celibacy. In order to become a priest a man must vow not to marry or form any personal, lifelong, secret, exclusive, intimate and emotionally fulfilling relationships with women. Is that right?"

"Yes, that's correct," the priest said piously.

"That's quite a sacrifice for a man to make," CJ said. Father O'Shaunessy nodded in agreement, glad that CJ understood the grave sacrifices priests made.

"But we both know it's just a crock, don't we?" The priest's head jerked as if someone had slapped him. "This priestly vow of celibacy doesn't mean a priest has to refrain from sex," CJ continued, "only sex with *women*. But since so many Catholic priests are homosexuals, vowing to refrain from sex with women is hardly a sacrifice. Am I right?"

"Well, yes . . ., I mean no"

"And this makes their priestly vow of celibacy an easy, though utterly pointless promise for them to make. Doesn't it?"

"Well, well . . . I, uh . . . No!" the priest shouted.

"Who are you kidding?" CJ said in derision. "Your so-called vow of celibacy is just a front for your duplicitous moral standards. Not only does the church advocate homosexuality and pedophilia, it condones it."

"Reverend CJ!" Meka broke in. "You're making some very harsh accusations."

"Am I? I think raping children is harsh." Father O'Shaunessy clasped his hand to his chest, his face looking like a Stop sign with eyes. "But maybe I'm just funny that way," CJ said.

"We're not here to attack the church," Meka said pointedly.

"Who are we here to attack?" CJ asked. Knowing she wouldn't answer, he went on with his diatribe. "The power structures in the Catholic Church have routinely protected pedophiles and helped them conceal their despicable actions from the public under the cloak of *celibacy*. Celibacy's just a front, a curtain for perverted priests to hide behind."

"I see what you're doing," snarled the infuriated priest, his condescending attitude obliterated under CJ's brutal attack and the surprisingly intelligent and articulate way in which he presented it. "You're trying to use the church to advance your own anti-gay agenda."

"I'm not anti-anything. Homosexuality isn't new. It's been around since Sodom and Gomorrah. What I'm against is the endemic sexual abuse of children that has been overlooked and underplayed by the Catholic Church for decades."

"Don't try to change the subject," Meka snapped. "We're here to talk about you and your agenda."

"No. I can see where he's coming from," said Pastor Jack, glad to help beat up on the priest if it will keep CJ's focus off him. "Sexual abuse has always been a well-known secret of the Catholic Church."

But CJ didn't want Pastor Jack's help. "I'm not just talking about Catholics. I'm talking about anybody who claims to be a man of God and intentionally preys on the innocent and the helpless. You got more predators in the church than any one organization in the world. It's just more systemic in the Catholic Church," he said with contempt. "But *any* man who causes harm to a child might as well strap a cement block around his neck and jump in the ocean, because his fate is already sealed."

"Ooooo," the audience responded, amazed at the boldness with which he spoke.

Pastor Jack and Father O'Shaunessy just glowered at CJ. Neither man could say anything because they knew he was telling the truth.

"Excuse me, Reverend CJ," Meka cut in with a smile so slippery it's a wonder it didn't slide right off her face. "Allow me to play the devil's advocate."

"Play?" CJ said reproachfully.

Ignoring the obvious dig, Meka continued. "So, what you're saying Reverend CJ, is that all preachers are hypocrites."

"I said what I meant," he replied, refusing to let her twist his words. "And anyone it doesn't apply to doesn't have any reason to be offended."

"First of all," Pastor Jack interjected, "I take exception with the constant referral to this man as 'Reverend.' There's no evidence that he has ever been ordained as a minister in any Christian denomination. And anybody that has the audacity to claim that he is God Almighty is displaying the height of sacrilegious behavior as far as I'm concerned."

"Pastor Jack makes a good point. If you really are *God,*" Meka said, rolling her eyes. "Why don't you give us some kind of sign? Rain down some fire and brimstone, part a sea."

CJ gave her a wry smile as the audience burst into applause. He knew that if the things he'd already said and done hadn't won them over, nothing he said now would convince them. When the applause subsided he crossed his legs and said, "The only sign I got for you is the sign of Jonah."

While the others tried to figure out what he meant, Bankhead said, "It all goes back to the slavery experience. Blacks in this country still need someone to tell them what to do. And obviously, this person has seen that need and decided to fill it. What I want to know is who's pulling his strings. Who are you working for?" he shot at CJ. "Who's behind all this crap you're spouting?" Not waiting for the answer, he continued with a catty smile. "Now I'm not naming any names, but I have it on good authority that you've been seen in the company of members of the Black Muslims. Can you explain that?" He sat back smugly and crossed his arms over his chest.

"Whoa!" Meka said, feigning shock at this revelation which was no surprise to anyone on the panel, since CJ had arrived at the studio with two of the Fruit of Islam's most capable and impressive officers in his entourage. "We'll be right back after this message and see if the good reverend can defend himself against this startling new revelation."

CHAPTER 38

"Bombshell!" Meka announced beaming into the camera. "Before the break, author Addicus Bankhead accused Reverend CJ of being in league with the notorious Minister Louis Farrakhan. Now as you know, we like to hear all sides on this show. So let's give Reverend CJ a chance to defend himself in light of this devastating new development. How about it, CJ?" she said, honing in on him like a jungle cat zooming in for the kill. "Is the controversial Muslim leader really the wind beneath your sails?"

"Minister Farrakhan is a brother who loves the Lord just as I do," CJ said. When he saw how intent the AACC was on shutting me up, he graciously offered to provide security for me. He thought my life might be in danger. Initially, I turned the offer down. But as you've seen, his assessment turned out to be correct."

"Are you insinuating that the council had something to do with that so-called assassination attempt in New York?" Pastor Jack spouted angrily.

"It wouldn't be the first time corrupt preachers set out to murder one of God's prophets."

"Make up your mind," Bankhead snickered. "Are you a prophet or are you God?"

"What are you?" CJ asked, snapping on the man with such ferocity that even the audience jumped back in fear. "A sellout? A pitiful little man, so hungry for the spotlight that you have to stand on the backs of your brothers to make yourself look tall?" The audience roared as Bankhead's face turned from a pale shade of brown to an unhealthy looking red.

"Who are you calling sellout?" Pastor Jack snarled. "Whatever happened to all that money you collected on your so-called crusade?" He smirked into the camera, "I can tell you for a fact the church didn't see a dime of it."

"Is that why you're so mad?" CJ replied with a shrewd smile. "Because the *Christian Mafia* didn't get its cut?" The audience laughed as Pastor Jack fumed. "That money was donated to *Feed the Children* and other organizations dedicated to helping the poor and indigent in this country. That's where it went. And you're right. The Church didn't get its paws on a dime of it."

"You sure you didn't give it to your low-life friends, the Association of Murderers and Thieves?" Pastor Jack sneered. "Who gave you the authority to call yourself a minister of the Lord, anyway?" he asked in an imperious tone.

"You tell me who gave Dr. King the authority to stand up for the rights of black folks in this country and I'll be glad to answer your question. Was he a prophet? Or was he just some nigga running around flapping his gums?"

This caught Pastor Jack off guard. "Well, I, uh . . ." He knew that most black people believed that King was a prophet and if he said anything to the contrary, he'd be done for. "I don't know," he finally admitted.

"Okay, then," CJ said with a nod, indicating that since Pastor Jack had not answered his question he need not expect an answer in return.

"Ooooo!" the audience chorused, amused at the out done look on the pompous preacher's face. After that, what could he say? CJ had shut him up sufficiently.

Although it may have seemed like CJ had cleverly evaded the question, he hadn't. He wasn't trying to dodge the question. He'd told them repeatedly that his teaching and all his miracles came from the power and authority of the Lord. However, Pastor Jack was trying to corner him into admitting that he had an agenda of his own. In answering him as he did, CJ flipped the script on the learned theologian's attempt to ensnare him, thereby discrediting him in the eyes of the televiewing audience. It was this knack for dealing with his adversaries that made them so afraid of him.

Infuriated over the way CJ had just verbally trounced his strongest orator, Rev clicked the TV off, picked up the phone and dialed Chief Petrocelli's number. "Hello, Chief? Bradshaw here. Look. I need you to get the LAPD to issue an arrest warrant for this CJ character." When the chief asked what they should charge him with, Rev said, "Charge him with practicing medicine without a license, public nuisance, jay walking . . . I don't care. I just want him off the streets. Yeah. Okay. Thanks, Pete." Rev hung up the phone and leaned back in his chair smiling maliciously.

CJ, Teddy, Herc and Sebastian left the TV studio with the two stalwart FOI officers following close behind. As they entered the station's parking garage, a limousine pulled up in front of them and stopped. Herc immediately stepped in front of CJ and the Muslims whipped out their Glocks so fast you'd think they'd spent the whole night greasing them down. The back door of the limo flew open and Annemarie, a wild-eyed white woman in a pink Donna Karan pants suit sprang out. "Reverend CJ!" she called, grasping frantically at his arm. "Thank God, I found you. You've got to help me." CJ glanced at her with disdain and shook himself free.

"You need to get out of here lady," Herc warned.

He was a fly on the wall to Annemarie as she poured her heart out to CJ. "When I heard you were appearing here today, I

284

flew all the way from New York to see you. You've got to help my daughter, Melissa. Please. She's only five years-old and she's dying of leukemia. The doctors have done all they could. But it's no use. They've given up," she sobbed.

Unmoved by her pleas CJ said in an uncharacteristically cold voice, "Sorry, lady. I ain't got nothin' for you." He turned abruptly and Annemarie grabbed his arm spinning him around.

"Who the hell do you think you are?" she screamed. "God gave you the power to heal and you're just gonna let my baby die? You don't get to choose who lives and who dies. God gave you a job to do, so why don't you just do your stinkin' job and heal my baby!" she cried, poking him in the chest with her finger. Without saying a word, CJ turned to leave. Annemarie dropped down to her knees, clutching his leg as he tried to walk away. "Please," she pleaded tearfully, "Please heal my child. I'll pay you any amount you want. Just come back to New York with me. Please. You're the only one that can help her."

CJ stopped, blown away by her incredible show of faith. He'd insulted her, dismissed her and still she believed. Up until this point, he had firmly believed that God had sent him to save the black man. However, the unmitigated faith of this woman was opening him up to a whole new reality. He stooped down and helped her to her feet. "Go on home," he said gently. "Your daughter is healed."

"Thank you," she said, not questioning his statement for an instant. She grabbed his hand with both of hers and kissed it, her heart overflowing with gratitude. "Thank you, Reverend. Thank you, so much," she repeated, clutching his hand to her chest. "How can I ever thank you?"

"You already have. Now go on home and take care of your daughter," he said, opening the back door of the limo for her. Annemarie snatched a large diamond ring from her finger and pressed it into his hand. "Here Take this."

"No, "he said, trying to give the ring back to her. "I can't accept this."

"Then sell it and give the money to charity," she said, jumping back into her limo. She stuck her head out of the window, tear smudged mascara giving her the look of a happy raccoon. "God bless you, Reverend," she said confident that her daughter would be cured. How was she to know that little Melissa had been healed the instant the words left CJ's mouth.

CJ stared after the car as it drove away. "Now that's what I call faith," he said. His companions gazed at him in amazement, obviously troubled by this latest turn of events.

CHAPTER 39

When CJ and the others returned from the television studio, Carla and the gang surrounded CJ, lavishing praise on him for the job he'd done. "Thanks, guys. Look, I'm going upstairs and lie down for a while," he said, heading for the stairs. He needed to pray, needed to gain a clearer understanding of his mission. The faith Annemarie exhibited had compelled him to help her. It had also given him food for thought.

CJ wondered if he had misunderstood his task. *Did God send me to save just black people – or am I supposed to save the world, starting with the black man?*

"Want me to fix you something to eat?" Dee asked.

"I'm not hungry," he said and proceeded up the stairs.

"What's he so down about?" Sammy asked. "I thought he'd be happy, the way he put them suckers in check."

"I better go see about him," Carla said. Dusty shot her a venomous look as she started up the stairs.

287

"He's all right," said Sebastian. "He probably just realized how stupid it was to give away all that money. "I'm not saying he's stupid," he quickly added, shooting a quick look at Carla. "I just don't see why he gave *all* the money away. We worked hard for that money." Carla just glared at him through squinted eyes and continued up the stairs. They heard her knock on CJ's door and enter.

"She's got her nerve," Dusty said.

"She's not the only one," said Sebastian. "Do you know CJ healed a white girl today?"

"That's a dirty lie!" Dee exclaimed.

"Am I lying, Herc?"

"Well . . . He said she was healed, but we don't really know for sure. The girl wasn't even there."

"How could he heal somebody that wasn't there?" Sammy wanted to know.

"If he said she was healed, she's healed," said Teddy, always CJ's staunchest defender.

"Her mother, this rich white chick pulls up in a limo begging CJ to heal her little girl who was dying of cancer. And he's like, *Cool, she's healed*," Sebastian said.

"But why would he do that?" Cheyenne asked. Sebastian shrugged.

"He said she had a lot of faith," Herc replied. Refusing to listen to any more lies about her son, Dee stormed out of the room.

"I love CJ to death," Sebastian said, "But let's face it he's not the brightest bulb on the tree. Just because he's got this power, doesn't mean he knows what to do with it."

"I suppose you do," Sherman said, giving him a harsh look.

"I sure couldn't do any worse," Sebastian said. "He's made some dumb moves, but that was the stupidest one yet."

Teddy made a break for him, but Herc held him back. "You better watch your mouth, punk. I guess having a woman kick your ass wasn't good enough for you," Teddy growled.

Sebastian, quick on the lip, but a coward at heart, backed away from the enraged man. "I was just saying . . ." His cell phone rang, interrupting him. "Hello," he said into the phone. He listened for a few minutes and said, "What! Yeah. I see. Thanks a lot." He clicked the phone off and plopped down on the couch, a troubled look on his face.

"Who was that?" Sammy asked.

"Sergeant Wallace," Sebastian said, rubbing his chin with his hand.

"Who?" Cheyenne asked.

"Remember the cop whose son CJ healed of AIDS? Him. He wanted to give us a heads up. They've put out an APB for CJ's arrest."

"For what?" Dusty asked, incredulous.

"They're accusing him of fraud, creating a public nuisance, practicing medicine without a license and felonious disregard for the public safety."

"I ain't never heard of no felonious disregard for public safety," Sammy said.

"They probably made it up just for him," said Sebastian. "These people aren't playing. You don't mess with the Catholic

Church and get away with it." He rose from his seat and headed for the door.

"Where are you going?" Sammy asked.

"I've got to make some arrangements. Tell CJ not to leave the house until I get back."

As CJ soaked in the tub, the rejuvenating powers of the warm water did little to ease the tension created by the day's events. He knew the guys were upset because he'd healed the white girl. He wondered if they'd ever just trust him and know that whatever he did was the will of God. God didn't distinguish between black and white and CJ had finally realized that the only way to save the black man was to save mankind in general.

"Carla," he called through the closed bathroom door.

"Yeah?"

"Will you come wash my back?" Stunned by the request, Carla remained seated on the edge of the bed staring at the TV with unseeing eyes. She wondered what he was doing. She had massaged his back many times – but never in the tub.

Ordinarily, he would never have made such a request. However, in his newly evolved state, the impropriety of it never crossed his mind; he just needed the comfort of her touch. After a long beat, he called again. Carla walked slowly to the bathroom door, pushed it open and stepped in. "Will you wash my back for me?"

Carla kneeled down beside the tub. CJ handed her the wash cloth and she proceeded to rub the soapy water over his broad shoulders. "Ahhh, that's good," he said. "You know, when we were little my mama used to throw me and Sherman in the tub together. I hated that. Lil' sucker used to pee in the tub. Thought it was funny." "My sister, Carmen used to do the same thing," Carla said. "I was

290

scared somebody was going to tell me I smelled like pee." They both laughed.

"Where's your sister now?"

After a moment of silence, Carla said. "She died."

"Oh, wow." CJ said. "I'm sorry."

"Actually, she was murdered," said Carla. "By my stepfather. Her father."

"Aw, man," CJ replied, too stunned to say anything else.

"My mother married Benny when I was about six." She stopped washing his back and wrung out the towel, tears settling in her eyes. "Seems like he started molesting me the minute he moved in," she said more to herself than to him. CJ's head whipped around in shock. "I was just a little girl," she added, justifying the guilt she still felt.

"You don't have to talk about this," he said.

"Yes. I do," she said, unable to stop now. "He told me that if I told anybody, he'd kill my mother and my little sister. So I kept quiet. But my teacher, Miss Stapleton noticed the change in me, I guess. I'd started acting depressed, hardly talking. My grades just hit the floor. When I started wetting my pants at school, Miss Stapleton called my mother in. When she explained to my mother what was going on, she seemed totally surprised. But even then, as young as I was I wondered how Miss Stapleton had noticed that something was wrong, but my mom hadn't. Anyway, when my mother asked me what was making me sad, I told her in spite of Benny's warnings. I thought that with both my mother and my teacher on my side, they could make him stop."

She chuckled coldly, "Surprise. My mother called me a liar right there in front of the teacher. She told Miss Stapleton that I was always making up things and that I was just having trouble adjusting to our new family situation."

"Did the teacher buy it?"

"I don't know. I never went back to that school again. We moved right after that and I went to a new school. Guess nobody noticed the change in me there, since I'd been sad and standoffish since I came."

CJ knew that Carla had lived a hard life, but he had never imagined the extent of the suffering and abuse she had endured. "Let me get out of this tub," he said. Carla walked back into the bedroom and CJ climbed out of the tub. He took a big, fluffy towel from the rack, dried himself off and draped the towel around his waist. He joined her in the bedroom, plopped down on the bed beside her and wrapped his arm around her shoulders.

She shrugged his arm off of her. With the memories of her stepfather's hands all over her abruptly resurfacing, Carla couldn't stand the thought of being touched – not even by CJ. "When we got home my mother beat me until I had blood running down my legs. She told me that I was just jealous because Carmen's daddy was there with her and mine had run off. She told me that if I ever said anything to make Benny leave that she would put me in the orphan's home where all I would get to eat is one bowl of soup and they'd beat me every day."

"Naw," CJ said incredulously.

She couldn't bear the pity she saw on his face, but she couldn't stop talking. The floodgates had opened. She picked up a bottle of lotion from the nightstand and said, "Lay down." CJ lay on his stomach and Carla poured lotion into her hand and began rubbing it onto his back. She told him how the molestation continued all the way through high school. How she believed Benny was abusing Carmen as well, but they never discussed it. Theirs was a house of secrets and distrust. "Know what was funny," Carla said. "I hated my mother more than I did him. I guess it was more of a betrayal thing with her, you know. He was just a sick creep, but she was my mother. She was supposed to protect me."

"Yeah. She was," he said. He knew that his own mother would fight a lion with only a toothpick in her hand to protect him and Sherman.

"When I graduated," Carla continued, "I went straight into the military. My plan was to do my time and after I was discharged, I'd get an apartment and bring Carmen to live with me."

"So, what happened?"

"Evidently Carmen had more guts than I did. She eventually told what he was doing and they arrested him. When Mama got him out on bail, Children's Services put Carmen in a foster home. But I guess he must've been stalking her or something, because one day the people she was staying with came home to find her raped and murdered."

"Oh, my God."

"But she fought him," Carla said proudly." They found his DNA under her nails and arrested him. I testified how he had abused us for years and my mother had known about it, but didn't do anything to stop him. He got life without the possibility of parole. She got twelve years for contributing to the sexual abuse of a minor."

"They should have shot him up with battery acid," CJ said. "Her too."

"When my time in the Marines was up, I didn't have anywhere to go or anyone to go to, so I re-upped. Signed up for Special Ops."

"That's a pretty dangerous gig."

"I didn't care. I think I wanted to die. The guilt and the grief were eating me up. I kept thinking that I should have done something to get her out of there," she said, unable to hold back the tears any longer. "I was her big sister." Carla dropped her head into her hands and wept unrestrainedly. "I should have done something," she lamented. "I should have protected her."

"You couldn't even protect yourself," he said, sitting up and taking her in his arms. You were just a kid." He held her close, her tears washing his bare chest. She felt safe in his arms. When she lifted her head, he kissed her, gently at first and then the pent up emotion they'd been fighting overtook them bursting forth in an explosion of unrestrained passion. He explored every inch of her body with his hands . . . with his mouth and she came with abandon. It was as if she were being reborn. As their bodies became one, moving together in synchronized bliss CJ felt a rightness, a completeness that he'd never experienced before.

When CJ strolled into the music room the next morning, he was surprised to see Sebastian there. He looked frazzled as he spoke into the phone. "But if you have a vacant apartment why can't . . . Yes, I know, but this is an emer . . . Hello? Hello?" Sebastian let out a frustrated sigh and clicked the phone off.

"What's up?" CJ asked, taking a sip from the cup of coffee in his hand.

"They've put a warrant out for your arrest."

"For what?" he asked, taking his seat at the piano.

"They got a whole list of crap. Bottom line, we've got to get you out of L.A. I've been trying to find someplace we can lay low for a while, but nobody wants to help us. All these people you've helped and not one . . ." His phone rang and he quickly answered, "Hello." He listened for a moment and said, "Thanks, man. You're a true brother." He ended the call and smiled. "That was Sterling Brown."

"The actor?"

"Yeah. He's got this houseboat down in Palm Beach. Said we could use it as long as we need to."

"Cool," CJ replied. "Have the cars arrived from New York yet?"

"No. I was thinking about flying out there and getting mine."

"I need you here," CJ said. "I'll send Teddy and Hawk. Teddy can drive your car and they can hire somebody to drive his." Reluctantly, Sebastian agreed.

Within an hour, they were all in the Shenanigans van headed for the airport. They dropped Hawk and Teddy off for their flight to New York and took off for Florida.

CHAPTER 40

Ominous storm clouds were roiling in the darkening Florida sky as CJ and company climbed out of the van fighting against gale force winds. "Hurry up and get that stuff out of the van," Sebastian ordered, grabbing his suitcase and racing toward the blue and white houseboat.

"Looks like we made it just in time," Cheyenne said, running for the shelter of the houseboat as the rain began pouring down. CJ and the other guys hauled out the rest of the luggage as Sebastian retrieved the key from under the welcome mat. To their surprise, the door opened and there stood a tall cinnamon colored Adonis. It was Sterling Brown America's latest heartthrob, but he wasn't wearing his trademark smile.

"Sterling," Sebastian said, "I didn't expect to see you here." He tried to push past Sterling to get in out of the rain, but Sterling's muscled arm barred the doorway.

"I'm sorry, man," he said, purposely avoiding looking at CJ who was getting soaked along with everyone else. "I, uh . . ." He rubbed at his throat as though coaxing the lie out. "I forgot that I was uh . . . having some work done on the place. Y'all gon' have to find somewhere else to stay." CJ could see that he was scared to death. "Somebody done got to this dude," Sammy shouted.

"Come on, man," said Sebastian. "It's raining cats and dogs out here." Sterling's lip trembled as if holding back tears, but he didn't budge.

"Sorry, man," Sterling said in a sincere tone. As he started to close the door, Sammy sprang forward and plowed his fist into the actor's pretty face, dropping him like a sack of wet cement. He then whipped out his gun and commenced to pistol-whipping him.

"Stop it Sammy! You're gonna kill him," Cheyenne screamed, spurring Sherman and Herc into action. They pulled Sammy off the man and hustled him back to the van; leaving Sterling sprawled in the doorway with rain pouring down on his blood-spattered face. He looked down at the two bloody teeth lying beside him and started to bawl.

Huddled in the van like wet rats, the group tried to decide what to do. "Can't we just go to a hotel?" Dusty asked.

Sebastian shook his head. "They've got a nationwide alert out for CJ. If anybody recognizes him they're bound to call the cops."

"Don't you have some more friends you could call?" Sherman asked.

"Nope. The word is out. Did you see how scared Sterling was?"

Cheyenne sneezed. "Turn the heat on, Sammy, I'm freezing." As they continued to throw around fruitless ideas, they heard someone tapping on the window. Sammy lowered the window to see a little round Cuban woman. She appeared to be about sixty and was fighting to hold onto an umbrella that seemed determined to get away from her.

297

"Hi," Sammy said, curious as to why this woman was out in such a bad storm. Yelling over the wind and rain, the woman whose name was Esperanza told them in her heavy accent that she had seen them sitting in the van for a long time and graciously offered to let them wait out the storm at her house.

The small, two-bedroom house that Esperanza shared with her two young grandsons was little more than a shack, but it was warm and dry. The furnishings were old and shabby, but the house was immaculately clean. When Esperanza realized who CJ was, she was elated. "Oh, Padre," she said as she crossed herself, "I am honored to have you in my home. Are you hungry?"

"I could eat," he said. Esperanza immediately began cooking as they took turns changing out of their wet clothes in the small bathroom.

The meager meal she sat before them consisted of a chicken and rice dish and flour tortillas. Esperanza looked embarrassed as she apologized for the simplicity of the meal, explaining that it was all she had in the house. "It's not much," she said. "But at least there is enough for everybody to get a little." CJ assured her that it was plenty and prayed over the food. After they had all eaten their fill, Esperanza was amazed at how much there was left. She carefully stored it in the refrigerator with plans to serve it for breakfast.

As the violent storm raged outside, Esperanza put the boys to bed and the others crowded around a small TV that sat on a rickety table in the living room. The wind howled like a demon from hell and the windows rattled as though they were about to come flying out at any minute. Esperanza offered her bed to CJ who refused. She then gathered up blankets and quilts to distribute among her guests. "I'm sorry I don't have more room for you to sleep," she said.

"Don't worry about it," CJ said, wrapping his arm around her shoulder. "We appreciate everything you've done for us."

She smiled and handed him a small flashlight. "Sometimes the power goes out in a big storm," she said before bidding them goodnight and retiring to her bedroom.

CJ grabbed a blanket and curled up on the floor in a corner of the living room. While the others claimed their spots, Carla spread a quilt on the couch for Dee and stretched her blanket out on the floor near CJ.

"Are you all right, CJ?" Carla asked. He had been trying to appear upbeat, but Carla could tell he was troubled.

"I'm cool," he said with a smile he didn't feel. He wanted to pull her close and lose himself in her warmth, but he forced himself to keep a respectable distance between them.

The storm outside raged with such ferocity that they feared it might rip the tiny house from its foundation. Suddenly, the loud peal of the emergency warning system sounded from the TV and a weather alert warning appeared on the screen. A grave, disembodied voice announced that due to high winds and severe flooding in the coastal areas of Florida, the governor had ordered the evacuation of Palm Beach and surrounding counties.

"Oh my God," Dee said. "Are we safe here?"

"About as safe as we're going to get," replied Sebastian.

As if on cue, a bolt of lightning flashed outside the window, followed immediately by a loud crack of thunder and the terrifying sound of a tree being ripped from its roots and crashing to the ground. The house shook violently, knick-knacks flew from shelves and pictures fell off the wall. Only the picture of Jesus remained undisturbed. Suddenly, the TV and all the lights blinked out.

"Oh, shit!" Sammy shouted.

"Sammy!" Cheyenne called out in the darkness, reaching for her husband.

Carla grabbed the flashlight and clicked it on as Esperanza and her terrified grandchildren ran into the room. They all sat in silent terror with only the beam of the flashlight between them and total darkness as the fierce storm shook the little house as though it were a baby's rattle.

"CJ!" Sammy shouted as he felt water seeping through his blanket. "The water's getting in."

"What do you expect him to do?" Sebastian snapped. "He can't control the weather."

Without warning, the door flew open, blowing rain and debris into the house. "We gon' die! We gon' die!" Cheyenne screamed. The kids began screaming and crying as Herc and Sherman struggled to get the door closed. CJ just glared at them without saying a word.

"Do something, Chucky!" Dee screamed.

Moved to action by the fear in his mother's voice, CJ stood in the middle of the room and raised his arms high above his head. "Be still!" he commanded in a voice that resounded throughout the house. The wind instantly died down and the storm ceased.

The lights came back on and CJ, his eyes blazing and chest heaving, glanced around the room at his friends who stared back at him in shocked amazement. What kind of man is this? Even the wind and the rain obey him.

"Don't you know who I am?" His voice was so low and frightening that it sent chills through them. Sherman cringed; he'd never seen his brother this angry before. The others cowered in fear. "What is it gonna take for you to believe that the Brother Man is who he says he is?" Appalled at the extent of their dimness his face twitched with unleashed fury. "You got eyes, but you just won't see. You got ears, but you don't hear." Shaking his head in disgust, he stormed out of the house, slamming the door behind him. Esperanza fell to her knees and began to pray in Spanish.

Alone on the quiet beach, CJ talked to God as if he were right there with him. "Why are you playing me like this, God? How am I supposed to get the world to believe that what I'm saying is coming from you, if I can't even get these knuckleheads you gave me to believe?"

He walked back and forth, waving his hands and gesturing to make his point. "The people hate me. My crew's falling apart. I don't know how much more of this I can take, God. I've done everything you've asked me to do. And here I am hiding out like some kind of criminal. Is it over? Is that what you're saying?"

Mired in frustration and misery, he leaned his back against a tree and closed his eyes. "Why am I going off on you, Lord? I know you do all things in your own time. I know you won't desert me," he said. "I'm just tired Father. You gotta tell me what to do. How can I make them believe that it's you, Lord? It's all you."

CJ prayed until the brilliant sun started peeking over the horizon. He'd never seen such a magnificent sunrise, so bright and so promising. He took it as a sign. He felt as though God were saying, "Don't worry, I got this."

As CJ walked along the beach surveying the devastation left by the storm, he saw huge uprooted palm trees lying on the ground and roofs torn from houses. Sterling's beautiful houseboat was a pile of rubble. However, Esperanza's little shanty had weathered the storm. It stood like a lone soldier among the fallen. A survivor. Yes, he thought. This is definitely a sign.

CHAPTER 41

It was a few days before the roads were cleared and they could get to the store, but those stranded in the little shack ate well on the chicken and rice that never ran out.

One evening as night descended over the blissfully balmy Atlantic, CJ and the guys sat on the front porch playing poker. CJ was in uncommonly good spirits joking and jiving with his friends. As Herc dealt the cards Sammy turned to CJ and said, "Must be nice having women fighting over you."

"What?"

"Dusty and Carla. Don't tell me you haven't noticed them swiping at each other. Dusty acts like she's scared to leave Carla alone in a room with you. Maybe she thinks home girl's gon' jump your bones."

"I wouldn't put it past her," Sebastian cracked.

"My money's on Dusty," said Sherman. "She's got the advantage of youth."

"Y'all crazy," CJ chuckled

"CJ could have any woman he wants," said Herc. "You read that mail."

"Yeah," Sammy said. "Don't forget about Big Bertha and her tribe waiting for you in Tuscaloosa." This elicited laughter all around.

"Gimme a break," said CJ. "Are we gonna play cards, or what?"

Unaware that they were the topic of conversation Carla, Dusty and Cheyenne had turned Esperanza's kitchen into a makeshift beauty parlor. Dusty snipped and curled Cheyenne's short new hairdo to perfection while Carla sat before a mirror propped up against a flour canister, flat ironing her hair.

After fingering Cheyenne's thin bangs to her satisfaction, Dusty sprayed a cloud of hairspray over her client's head. "There," she said as she reached into her humongous bag and pulled out a large mirror which she handed to Cheyenne.

Dusty smiled proudly as Cheyenne gazed into the mirror patting her hair and admiring the chic new style. "Girl! I love it. I like this even better than when Mr. Chad did it."

"Yeah, right," Dusty laughed gathering her equipment and stuffing it into her bag. "Like you could afford to have Chad do your hair."

"I beg your pardon," Cheyenne said, highly offended. "I'll have you know Carla and I both went to Mr. Chad's and not only did he personally do our hair, but we didn't pay a dime." Cheyenne slapped Carla a high five.

"Was he doing some kind of charity work or something?" Dusty asked.

"No, dear. In fact, when Carla tried to give him CJ's credit card he wouldn't even take it," Cheyenne said, hitting her with a smile that only one woman can give another. The smile that says, take that, bitch.

Dusty exploded. "What was she doing with CJ's credit card?"

"That's not your business," Carla said with a taunting smile.

"Remember that foot bath?" Cheyenne said.

"Oh, that uh, aqua citrus . . . Whatever. Girl. That was to die for." Carla knew they were getting under Dusty's skin, but she was enjoying it.

Dusty stopped her packing and twirled around grasping a pair of curlers in her hand. "I know you're not talking about Mr. Chadwick's European Aquamarine Citrus Foot Relaxer."

"Yeah," Cheyenne said. "That's it."

"Now I know y'all lying," Dusty said, waving the curlers at them. "That's Chad's own personal formula. He only uses that on his most important clients. He doesn't even sell it."

"Oh, we didn't buy it," Cheyenne said.

"He gave it to us for free," Carla added, pulling a jar of the miraculous ointment out of her purse and waving it in the air. "Never leave home without it." She and Cheyenne fell out laughing as Dusty's jaw dropped in amazement.

"Y'all just lying," Dusty said, shaking her head and scrunching her face up like a spiteful five-year-old. Her petulant behavior caused the other two ladies to laugh even harder. Dusty slammed the curlers into her bag not even bothering to zip it up. She wanted to get away from these lying tramps as quickly as possible. "I'm getting cabin fever up in here," she said. "I should have stayed in L.A."

"They got planes leaving out every hour, Boo," Carla volunteered.

"Yeah, you'd love that wouldn't you? Then you could have CJ all to yourself."

"Where did that come from?" Cheyenne asked looking around.

"Don't tell me you haven't noticed how she be hanging all up under CJ like a second skin. Stevie Wonder could see she's in love with him."

"Girl, you're crazy," Carla said with a wave of her hand.

As the guys continued their game, Sebastian asked, "How does it feel to have all that power, CJ? It's got to be awesome knowing what everyone is thinking."

"I don't always," CJ said. Some things He reveals and some He conceals. I just go with the flow. I wouldn't even want to know what everybody was thinking. Can you imagine walking into a room full of people and getting bombarded by all their thoughts?" He made a face and gave a little shudder, remembering how disconcerting it had been to him as a youth. He then laughed, pretending to be the thoughts of others, *My girdle's too tight. Soon as he turns his head, I'm gon' pick his pocket. She don't know I'm screwing her husband.* Forget about it, man," he said in his own voice shaking his head as the others laughed. "I don't even need that." They were still laughing when Sebastian's cell phone rang. It was Hawk.

"Hey, man, you back in L.A.? I've been trying to call Teddy, but he doesn't answer. I hope he hasn't crashed . . ." He stopped talking and a look of dread came over his face.

Back in the kitchen, Cheyenne, the instigator tried to make peace. "Come on Dusty. Give the girl a break." But Dusty was in full attack mode.

305

"Break? I wouldn't pour cold cat piss down that bitch's throat if her heart was on fire"

Never one to mince words, Cheyenne said, "You act like he's your man." When Dusty hesitated to respond she asked, "Well, is he?"

"He'll never be hers. I've known CJ all my life and I don't care how much he's changed, he could never go for trash like that," Dusty said, turning to Carla with contemptuous amusement. "That's right. I know all about you."

"So the answer is no," Cheyenne said. "He's not your man."

"Not yet," Dusty said, with supreme confidence. "But you better tell your girl to back off."

Tired of Dusty's crap, Carla got up in her face. "You tell me."

Dusty flung her bag to the floor, stepped out of her shoes and began removing her earrings. Just then, Dee and Esperanza rushed into the kitchen. "What's going on in here?" Dee demanded to know.

"Nothing," Carla said her cold gaze still fixed on Dusty.

"Let's see what CJ has to say about it," Dusty said, storming past Dee and out of the room. The other ladies trailed her out to the front porch.

Dusty marched out on the porch and froze when she saw the tense looks on the guys' faces. Sebastian was chewing on his bottom lip with the phone pressed to his ear. "Okay," he said into the phone. "Yeah. We'll be there as soon as we can. Okay."

As soon as he clicked the phone off, Sammy asked, "What's up?" Sebastian gave Dusty a look that stopped her heart.

"What's wrong?" she asked.

"You better sit down."

"No," she snapped. "What do I got to sit down for?"

"It's Teddy," Sebastian said taking her hands in his. The pity in his eyes ripped through her soul and she snatched her hands away from him.

"What about Teddy?" Dusty demanded, knowing it was something she didn't want to hear, but enraged at the torturous way he was dragging it out.

"What are you waiting for man, a drum roll?" Sammy said springing up out of his chair. "What the fuck happened?"

Sebastian took a deep breath and said, "Teddy's been shot."

"Oh, my God!" Dee exclaimed. Dusty clamped her hands over her mouth and slumped down into a chair, shaking her head in denial. The women gathered around Dusty as she began to weep inconsolably.

"Who shot him?" asked Herc.

"Hawk doesn't know," Sebastian said. "He thinks they got set up. When they went to pick up the cars somebody ambushed them."

"They kill one of us they gon' have to kill us all," Sammy said.

"I didn't say he was dead."

Carla grasped the back of Dusty's chair leaning on it for support. "Well, is he?" she asked, praying that Teddy would be okay.

"Hawk says they're not telling him anything," Sebastian answered.

All the guys were now on their feet expressing their outrage and anger – All except CJ who seemed to have receded into a state of unnatural calmness.

When Sebastian picked his phone back up, CJ asked, "Who are you calling?"

"The airport," he said. "We have to get to New York."

"Hang up," CJ said. "We're driving."

Sebastian looked at him as though he'd just grown a second head. "Driving? It'll take us days to get there."

"Not me," Dusty said, leaping to her feet. "Book me on the next flight leaving for New York," she told Sebastian as she started back into the house. "I gotta go see about my brother."

"Wait! I'll go with you," Cheyenne said, shooting a quick look at Sammy who gave her an approving nod. She then hurried into the house after Dusty.

Sebastian spoke to CJ as though he were talking to a slow child. "CJ, we need to get to New York as quickly as possible. If we drive, Teddy might be dead by the time we get there."

CJ gave him an enigmatic look and said softly, "Teddy's already dead."

Everyone fell into a shocked silence. Carla closed her eyes as tears flowed down her grief stricken face. A whimper of pain escaped from Dee's lips as she sank down in a chair, her head resting in her hand as she sought to accept the unacceptable. Teddy was like a son to her.

"And for your sakes, I'm glad I wasn't there," CJ said, looking around at all of them. "Now, maybe you'll believe that I am the son of God." Sebastian and Sammy exchanged looks of astonishment. CJ had never before stated openly who he was. "This had to happen so that the world would know God's glory. And so that the Brother Man would be glorified through it."

They exchanged quizzical looks, but nobody said a word.

CHAPTER 42

By the time the Shenanigans van pulled up in front of The Rock of Sharon Baptist Church, Teddy's funeral was already underway. Cheyenne had called them with confirmation of his death, explaining that the city officials had forbidden them from shipping his body to Los Angeles as Dusty had wanted to do. The only reason they had given was that in situations such as this, they had to bury the deceased person immediately. The truth was that they hoped Teddy's funeral would lure CJ back to New York so they could arrest him, as evidenced by the presence of dozens of FBI agents in dark suits and sunglasses strategically stationed outside the church as well as in.

When CJ stepped out of the van, he saw Cheyenne, Hawk and a tall ghoulish looking man, obviously the funeral director attempting to console Dusty. Her woeful sobs tore at his heart as he noticed one of the FBI agents whisper into his collar, "The eagle has landed."

When Dusty saw CJ, she charged at him like a raging rhino. Eyes that once shone with love now burned with fury. "Murderer!" she screamed pounding his chest with her fists. "You killed him, CJ. You killed my brother. He loved you and you let him die."

CJ grabbed both her wrists firmly. "Dusty," he said through clenched teeth, his face close to hers. "You're going to see your brother again. You hear me?"

"Yeah," she said sarcastically, snatching away from him. "On Resurrection Day."

"I am the resurrection! And the life," he whispered fiercely, "Anybody who believes in me will live even if he dies." The intensity of his gaze stilled her, but it didn't quell her anger. "Do you believe that, Dusty?"

"Teddy's dead, CJ. Don't you get it? You're too late."

CJ could see that her faith was shattered, but he persisted, "Didn't I tell you that if you believe in me you'd see the glory of God?"

"Yes, but . . ." CJ dropped her hands and stalked toward the church. The icy finger of fear ran down Dusty's back as she realized what he intended to do. "No, CJ!" she screamed running after him. "No!" She grabbed onto his coat and CJ turned to face her. "No, CJ. No," she pleaded shaking her head violently. "I know God'll do whatever you ask. I know that. But don't do it, CJ. Please. He's been dead for days. He's been embalmed." Without another word, CJ shook her off and marched into the church. Sammy and Cheyenne walked behind him, holding the hysterical Dusty up between them. Carla and the others followed them into the packed church.

A soloist stood in the pulpit above Teddy's casket, singing Trouble of the World, the heart-wrenching spiritual made famous by Mahalia Jackson in the movie Imitation of Life. CJ marveled at the enormous number of people in attendance, seeing that Teddy had hardly known anyone in New York. But the mourners were nothing more than an assemblage of curiosity seekers and the media, all hoping to get a look at the great man himself. Among the alleged mourners were Reverend Saunders, Meka Maxwell and of course, her ever-present cameraman Darnell.

At the sight of CJ striding down the center aisle, the singer stopped cold. Everyone in the church turned to see what she was gazing at and immediately started hurling insults at CJ.

"You're kinda late, ain't you, CJ?" someone cracked.

"Where were you when your friend needed you?"

"He's got a lot of nerve, showing up here." someone else scoffed.

Ignoring their taunts, CJ stepped up to the casket as Dusty and the others solemnly took their seats in the front row. Dee wrapped her arm around Dusty, but her sorrowful moans were more heartbreaking than comforting.

CJ looked down on the dead, pasty face of his beloved friend and an unbearable pain clutched his heart like a fist. Tears fell from his eyes and a pitiful sound somewhere between a snort and a moan escaped from his throat. "It's gon' be alright, man," he whispered, stroking Teddy's cold lifeless hand. "Oh, Heavenly Father," he prayed. "I thank you for hearing me, Lord. I know you always hear me, but I'm saying this so that these people will believe that you sent me. Use me, Father. Let them know that you're working in me and with me, Lord."

He then raised his arms skyward and said in a loud voice, "I command you to rise, Teddy. In the mighty name of Jesus Christ, I command you to come back now!" An audible gasp sprang from the shocked crowd. Since CJ was standing in front of the casket no one saw the color coming back into Teddy's face or his eyelids beginning to flutter. No one but CJ saw Teddy open his eyes.

When Teddy sat up in the casket, Dusty's piercing scream catapulted the stunned mourners into mass hysteria. Shrieks of horror filled the sanctuary as they stampeded out of the church ripping the doors from their hinges in their frantic efforts to escape.

Saunders bolted toward the door knocking a little girl to the floor in his desperate attempt to flee the church. Darnell's camera continued to roll as Meka stood frozen unable to believe her eyes. Suddenly she knew in her heart that this was no ordinary man. Her legs became like water and she slumped down in her seat sobbing uncontrollably. Bishop Hanks fell to his knees in the pulpit and began to pray.

"Get him out of there," CJ said. Sherman and Herc hurriedly helped a confused looking Teddy climb out of the coffin.

When CJ stepped out of the church with Teddy at his side, what he saw was bedlam. People running and screaming; cars crashing into each other as they all tried to flee the scene at once. The terrified FBI agents scattered like a bag of dropped marbles.

CJ spotted a black BMW parked across the street and ran toward it. "Come on," he shouted to Teddy and Herc. The diminutive driver, a shady lawyer called Shorty Long gulped in surprise as CJ jumped into the seat next to him and the others climbed into the back. Shorty panicked wondering if CJ had come to punish him for his life of crime and misdoings. "Drive Shorty," CJ ordered.

Trembling in fear, Shorty took off as though the devil himself were after him. The Shenanigans van was right behind them. When they were clear of the pandemonium raging outside the church, Shorty asked in a timid voice, "Where are we going?"

"Your house." CJ replied.

"My house!" Shorty exclaimed.

"We're gonna need to crash there for a while," CJ said. "Is that cool?"

Shorty was dumbfounded. "Yeah. Yeah, that's cool. Y'all can stay as long as you want. I got plenty of room."

Teddy sat in the back seat next to Herc looking dazed and confused. "Where are we going?" he asked. "What am I doing in this suit?" CJ assured him that he would explain it all to him later and they continued to ride in silence.

CHAPTER 43

"Yeah. Sure," Rev said into the phone, "Let me get six tickets. Hey, what's six hundred dollars when it comes to a great charity like The Make a Wish Foundation? I just wish I could do more. In fact, go ahead and put me down for ten," he chuckled as Saunders stumbled into the office looking sweaty and disheveled. His eyes were wide with terror and he was breathing as if he'd run all the way from the church. Rev jumped up in alarm. "I'm gonna have to call you back, Bill." The phone was back in its cradle before he finished speaking.

Heading straight to Rev's desk, Saunders yanked open the desk drawer, took out Rev's bottle of booze and his glass and poured himself a drink. He gulped the liquor down in one swallow and immediately poured another. Rev grabbed his arm before the second drink could make it to his mouth, "What in the hell is wrong with you, man?" Saunders just stared at him and burst into tears.

Rev released Saunders' arm, deciding that if anyone ever needed a drink this man surely did. Saunders gulped down the liquor and slid down into Rev's chair. He leaned his head back against the soft leather and closed his eyes.

"What's wrong, Saunders? What happened?" Rev asked again.

After a long moment, Saunders spoke without opening his eyes. "He raised the man up from the dead."

Rev's heart froze in his chest. "What?"

Saunders opened his eyes, reaching again for the bottle which Rev snatched out of his grasp. "What did you say?"

"The man was dead, Rev. He was dead. He was in the casket. Dead."

"Okay. I got that part."

"Then CJ came. He told him to get up – and he did. I'm telling you, Rev when that man sat up in that casket I thought my heart was going to jump right out of my chest. I've never been so scared in my life." He leaned his head back on the chair shaking it from side to side. "He was dead, Rev. The man was dead."

"That's impossible, Saunders. Pull yourself together. It had to be some kind of trick," said Rev nudging Saunders out of his chair. He grabbed the remote and clicked the TV on. Meka Maxwell's face appeared on the screen. Beneath it a chyron reading, Breaking News.

The usually calm and collected beauty now looked wild-eyed and crazy. With a heart thumping so hard in her chest that she wondered if the television viewing audience could see it, she fought to maintain her composure. "For nearly a year now I have been reporting on the activities of a man known as Reverend CJ," she sniffled, tears filling her eyes. "I told you that he was a fraud and a con man. I warned you that he was up to no good." Unable to hold herself in check any longer, she began sobbing hysterically. Wiping the snot from her nose with the back of her hand, she bawled, "But, I was wrong. This man . . . He . . . Oh, God forgive me," she said, collapsing on the desk. "I was so wrong."

The camera quickly shifted from Meka's on-camera breakdown to a clip of the pandemonium in the church as people trampled one another in their frenzied efforts to escape. Over a shot of Teddy sitting up in the casket, looking bewildered a male announcer reported that during the funeral of Theodore Montgomery, the man known as Reverend CJ is alleged to have said something to the dead man that caused him to rise up in his casket. "Needless to say," the announcer continued, "the church erupted in mass hysteria and several mourners were taken away by ambulance suffering from injuries and severe emotional disturbances. Four people were reported to have suffered heart attacks. Law enforcement believes this to be an elaborate hoax perpetrated by this Reverend CJ whose real name is Charlie Johnson, a Chicago bus driver with a history of mental illness."

Rev clicked the TV off and stared at the dark screen for an interminable few seconds. "It's voodoo," he whispered.

"Say what?"

"Voodoo!" he shouted, launching out of his chair.

"Come on, Rev," said Saunders, shaken out of his shocked state by Rev's bizarre pronouncement.

"How else can you explain it?" Pointing a finger at Saunders he said, "Contact everybody on the Executive Committee. I'm calling an emergency meeting. I want everyone here 9 o'clock tomorrow morning."

"What if they can't make it on such short notice?"

"Did I say, ask them if they could make it, or did I say tell them to be here?" Rev said giving him a hard look.

CHAPTER 44

Sammy's van followed Shorty's car through an array of exotic trees which lined the long winding driveway leading to Shorty's sprawling mansion on the Hudson. When they stepped out of the cars CJ and his friends stared in awe at the magnificent fountains and exquisite gardens. Teddy let out a long whistle at the sight of the magnificent Mediterranean style, three-story home. "Damn! This is your house?"

"Yeah," Shorty said with a shame-faced grin. "Welcome to Villa Lewaro. This used to be Madame C.J. Walker's home."

Villa Lewaro had been the envy of American royalty in its day and had incited no small amount of jealousy and controversy over how a black washerwoman from Louisiana could peddle enough hair grease to afford such sumptuous luxury. Moreover, Madame C. J.'s detractors were stricken by the sheer elegance and style of the home. Villa Lewaro was the epitome of sophistication and elegance. There were bronze and marble statues, sparkling cut glass candelabra, paintings, rich tapestries and countless other accoutrements that made the place into the extraordinary showplace that it was. But the moment CJ stepped inside; the cold, uninhabited feel of the place overwhelmed him.

"Oh, my God!" Dusty said, gazing at a gold framed portrait of Madame C. J. Walker that graced the foyer wall, "I can't believe I'm in Villa Lewaro. I can feel Madam C.J.'s presence."

"It took some doing," Shorty said. "But I tried to replicate the original look of the place even down to her gold-plated piano."

As the others marveled at the grandeur and opulence of the house, CJ thought that the palatial estate may as well have been a museum for all the warmth and love it possessed. He felt an intense sadness at the realization that no one had ever been truly happy in this extraordinary showplace. For that is what it was, a grand showcase devoid of the love and joy it took to make a house into a home.

A short time later, Shorty escorted CJ and his friends into the drawing room where Consuela, the maid was putting the finishing touches on a lavish buffet. "This calls for a celebration," Shorty said with the swagger of a little rooster. "Help yourselves. There's plenty more where that came from." Beneath the obvious giddiness Shorty felt at having CJ in his home, lurked an overwhelming fear that he couldn't shake. Why is he here?

"Get Teddy something to eat," CJ said to no one in particular.

Dee started toward the buffet and Dusty placed a restraining hand on her arm. "I'll get it," she said rushing to fix the plate. She'd been a bundle of nerves ever since the reincarnation or reanimation – or whatever it was. She didn't know what to call the miraculous return of her brother from the dead. All she knew was that CJ had done it and she loved him more than ever.

Carla tried to get CJ to eat, but he told her that he wasn't hungry. "But you haven't eaten anything since yesterday," she said.

CJ smiled mysteriously, "I've got food you don't even know about," he replied, his eyes fixed on Shorty. Carla shot a look at Dee wondering if she knew of CJ having eaten. Dee shrugged, shaking

319

her head in confusion. What they didn't realize was that CJ's nourishment was coming from the prospect of winning yet another soul for the Lord.

"If you don't see anything there you like, I can get Consuela to fix you whatever you want," said Shorty.

Consuela had not taken her eyes off CJ since he came into the room. "Are you really Reverend CJ?" she asked timidly.

"Yes, Consuela. I am."

"Ay Dios mio!" Her eyes grew wide with fear as she backed away slowly, crossing herself before turning abruptly and running out the door.

"There goes your cook," Sammy said in amusement.

"I know how she feels," Shorty said staring out the window at the maid as she raced toward the immense garage.

"You want to run away too?" CJ asked.

"I don't know what I want to do," Shorty said scratching his forehead. "See, I don't think you know who I am."

"You're Darias Longwood," CJ said. "The infamous Shorty Long, lawyer to the mob." Shorty's eyebrows arched in amazement. Had CJ googled him? "No, I didn't google you," CJ chuckled, reading his thoughts. "But I do know that you've been accused of drug trafficking, political fixing and many other crimes. But thanks to your association with the Francioso family, you were never charged. Should I go on?"

Shorty dropped his head shaking it from side to side. "Did you come to get me?" he asked tentatively. CJ just looked at him and said nothing. "I mean; why else would you be here if you know who I am? What I am."

"Why do you think?" CJ asked.

"I don't know," Shorty said. "Are you mad because you think I was stalking you? I wasn't. But I saw you in Charlotte and I never heard anyone speak the way you do. So when I heard you might be at that funeral, I had to come. I had to see you, had to be near you."

"Why didn't you just come up to me?"

"For what? I'm not sick or crippled," he said pulling himself up to his full five feet, two inches.

"You're not?"

"No," he said resolutely. "Besides, you wouldn't have talked to me, anyway. You just said it yourself. I'm a criminal."

"We're not exactly a bunch of choir boys," Hawk said.

"I've been on my own since I was ten years-old," Shorty said, compelled to explain himself. "Mr. Francioso caught me breaking into his house when I was thirteen. After he kicked my ass, he asked me why I tried to break into his house. I told him that I had seen him on TV and that he was the coolest white man I'd ever seen. I told him that I only wanted to get one of his suits so that people would respect me the way they did him." He paused, catching CJ's smirk. "I know. What I saw as respect was really fear. Anyway, I stayed at his house that night and never left. Not like anyone was out looking for me or anything," he shrugged. "Papa Tony treated me like I was one of his own kids, sent me to school and got on my ass if I didn't do well. He was the closest thing I've ever had to a father. If it wasn't for him, I wouldn't be where I am today."

"And where are you?" CJ asked.

"Look around you." Shorty said opening his arms to encompass his lavish digs. "This is just one of my homes. I've got one in California and another one in Puerto Rico. I have a law degree from Harvard, bank accounts in the Caymans, investments all over the U.S. and . . ."

"And what good is it?" CJ asked, "What good is having all the money in the world, if it's gon' cost you your soul?" Shorty felt his heart stop. "You have this big old mansion here and nobody in it but you and the maid."

"The maid's gone," said Sammy.

That statement struck Shorty harder than anything else. He had no one. Since the death of Antonio Francioso, there was no one who cared whether he lived or died. At least the maid had counted on him for a paycheck. He began crying like a tortured child – The child he'd once been, crying for the man he had become.

CJ placed his hand gently on Shorty's shoulder and said, "Don't you know that the Lord loves you, Shorty?"

"Yeah, right," Shorty said through his tears. "I don't even love myself."

"But God loves you and so do I."

Shorty looked into CJ's honey colored eyes and saw pure love. No one had ever told him that they loved him before. Covering his mouth with his hands, he let out a heartbreaking moan and slithered down to the floor sitting on his haunches rocking back and forth. "I'm so sorry. Oh, God please forgive me. I'm so sorry. Lord, I'm sorry for everything I've ever done wrong. Please forgive me."

CHAPTER 45

When Rev and Saunders entered the conference room, Bishop Hanks, Reverend Dupre and Pastor Jack and several others were already gathered around the large conference table.

Rev took his place at the head of the table, looked from one of them to the other and said softly, "I called you all here to discuss a certain disciple of Satan called Reverend CJ." Hanks crossed his arms in front of his chest and leaned back in his chair waiting to see what nefarious plot Rev had concocted. "The Lord has revealed to me that this man is a false prophet, an emissary of the devil pretending to be a man of God."

"The Bible says that the Anti-Christ would come in the guise of a man of God," said Pastor Jack.

"Exactly," Rev said. "And we as guardians of the souls of black folks have to defend our people from this malevolent spirit by any means necessary. Somehow, he's managed to convince people that he has raised a man up from the dead. Now they think he's some great deity or something. The man's obviously out of control."

"Yeah. Well, that little stunt is going to cost us," Dupre said. "I just got word from my contact in the White House that the Feds are putting together a task force to investigate him. Somehow they got the idea that he represents a risk to national security."

"Wonder where they got that idea," Rev said.

"Who cares," said Saunders. "Let them deal with him. Once the government puts a target on a man's back he's done for."

"It's not that simple," Dupre said. "See, if the government has to intervene in what they call a 'religious arena'; that affects how they deal with the church – financially."

"And 'the church' in this case just so happens to be black," Rev said. "So you know that presents a particular problem." He glanced around the table at the prosperous and respected men and said, "I don't know about the rest of you, but I'm tired of this man damn fooling the people and stealing money out of my . . . I mean, the church's pocket. Do you know that church donations have gone down over sixty percent since this character came on the set?"

"The way I understand it the tithers are still tithing, they're just giving it to him instead of us," Pastor Jack snarled.

"Oh, yeah. He's slick," Rev said. "If we don't do something about this sucker soon we could lose everything."

"Including your bid for mayor," Hanks interjected. Rev shot him a look of pure venom.

"What do you propose we do, Rev?" asked Dupre.

Rev leaned back rubbing his chin as though deep in thought. "Now, we're all men of God." The members readily concurred on that point. "But," he said holding up one finger, "we are also business men and this is about survival. Why should a whole race of people have to suffer because of one man? Wouldn't it be more productive to just sacrifice that man?"

Bishop Hanks eyed him suspiciously and asked, "What do you mean, sacrifice?"

"You're familiar with the Old Testament, Bishop. What does sacrifice mean to you?"

"You must be out of your rabid mind!" exclaimed the bishop, springing up from his seat. "Is this what we've come to?" he asked, looking around at the stern faces surrounding him. "You're ready to kill a man of God?"

Rev eyed him with suspicion. "You sound like you're buying into his game, Bishop. Has he gotten to you too?"

"No," he said. "But you have. I've gone along with a lot of crap since you've been in charge of this council, Bradshaw. But here's where I get off. I will not be a party to the murder of any man, particularly a man so obviously anointed by God. Why does he scare you so much? Huh?" When Rev's only answer was a detestable glare, Hanks waved his hand in disgust, "I'm outta here." He started for the door and then turned giving Rev one last parting shot. "CJ was right. You're turning this council into a Christian Mafia."

When the door slammed behind Bishop Hanks, Rev looked around the table and asked, "Anybody else feel that way?" No one spoke. "Okay then." he said, rising from his seat and leveling a steely-eyed gaze on the high-ranking men of the cloth. "How are we going to kill this mother fucker?"

From that day on these hypocritical, unrepentant men plotted CJ's demise. They hated him because he spoke with authority and they feared him because he enlightened the people with his doctrine. Yet no one laid a hand on him because his time had not come.

Bishop Hanks went directly to Villa Lewaro. "You have to get out of New York right now," he told CJ. "The council is putting a hit out on you. I tried to talk them out of it, but Rev wants you dead. He's not listening to anything anyone else has to say."

"I came here to die," CJ said calmly. Taken aback Hanks looked at him as if he'd just eaten a roach. "They are going to kill me, Bishop – But not yet. My time hasn't come yet. So you can tell that sucker that I'm gon' be healing the sick and raising the dead – today. Tomorrow. And on the third day I will be glorified."

Word of Teddy's resurrection spread like a brushfire. People around the world began to believe that CJ was indeed, sent from God. Some thought he might even be the second coming of Christ. Due to the intensity of the public's reaction, CJ no longer came out in public. Instead, he mysteriously appeared in hospitals during the night, curing terminally ill children, AIDS patients and others on whom the medical profession had given up hope. This only added to his fame and his mystique.

The AACC announced a one-million-dollar reward for information leading to CJ's arrest. What they didn't announce but had spread through the grapevine was that they wanted him dead or alive – preferably dead. But, those that knew anything about him were not talking and those talking didn't know anything. False sightings flooded the police hot lines in response to the reward. But none of them led to CJ's whereabouts.

As the time for the grand opening of The City of Solomon grew near, Rev became as nervous as a baby-daddy waiting for the results of a DNA test. Although he'd managed to pay off the men accusing him of sexual abuse, he needed this event to go off without a hitch. His financial and political future hinged on it. However, CJ's crew looked forward to the grand opening as the opportunity for CJ to kick off the revolution.

"You know the grand opening of The City of Solomon is this weekend," Sherman reminded CJ.

"Yes, I know."

"Well? Are you going?"

"Why?" CJ asked.

326

"Because it's time to shit or get off the pot," Sherman said tired of tiptoeing around his own brother. "All this sneaking and hiding ain't gon' cut it. You need to step up and make your demands. Let them know where you're coming from."

"I know," CJ said.

"Bishop Hanks has reserved a suite for us at The City of Solomon hotel," said Sebastian.

CJ just nodded. "Y'all go on. I'll catch up with you later."

Sebastian remembered the last time CJ had told them to go ahead, but he said nothing.

On the day of the grand opening, Rev stood at the floor to ceiling window of his sumptuous new office located on the top floor of the spectacular Grace Chapel. The chapel was an architectural wonder made of smoked glass and steel. The magnificent structure spanned two square blocks and stood three-stories high with a thirty-foot steeple adorning the top of the church. It was truly a thing of beauty. Rev felt a burst of pride as he looked down on the main thoroughfare of The City of Solomon and saw thousands of people strolling along the gold encrusted sidewalk imprinted with Biblical Scriptures in the tradition of the famous forecourt of Grauman's Chinese Theater. Street vendors hawked everything from souvenirs and T-shirts to a wide variety of foods, creating a festive atmosphere surpassed only by Rio's Carnival.

Tourists from all over the world had been streaming in all week, anxious to experience the exquisite amusement/water park, extravagant four-star restaurants and the luxurious Bradshaw Plaza Hotel. However, the main reason they'd come was to see CJ. The fire that fueled the undeniable air of excitement was the expectation that CJ would make an appearance. An army of TV news crews filmed the flow of visitors as they swarmed in and out of the various shops, attractions and restaurants. But they're vigilant eyes were on constant alert for a sighting of Reverend CJ.

327

"What a turnout." Rev said as he turned from the window.

"It's amazing, Rev," Saunders replied. "Nobody could have pulled this off but you. The hotel is full and people are still coming. We've sold a hundred and fifty percent of the senior citizen cottages," he grinned. "That idea you had about the VIP cottages was a stroke of genius – Mr. Mayor."

"From your mouth to God's ear," Rev said, eating up the praise as he strolled toward a large portrait of himself that hung on the wall of the opulent office. He smiled at the portrait for a moment before pushing a button on his remote that caused the picture to slide to the left, revealing an elegant bar complete with cut crystal decanters and glasses. Rev poured cognac into two glasses and held one of them out to Saunders. Saunders readily accepted the drink grinning from ear to ear. "To The City of Solomon and all it entails," Rev said, hoisting his glass.

Saunders clinked glasses with Rev and said, "I'll drink to that."

As they drank to their success, they heard a knock on the door. "Come in," Rev said.

The door opened and Captain Jeffrey James of Rev's personal security team stepped in. "Captain Jeffrey James reporting, sir?" James said, standing at attention. Having failed at his dream of becoming a policeman, James took his job as a private security officer very seriously.

"Any word on CJ yet?"

"No, sir. As you instructed, I have secured the perimeter of the city and placed armed guards at every entrance. The only way he'll get in here is if he turns himself into a fly and buzzes his way in," James smiled.

Don't put it past him, Saunders thought draining the last remnants of his drink. Suddenly, they heard earsplitting shouts and

328

cheers coming from the street below. They all raced to the window and what they saw immobilized them.

There was CJ riding down the street in a slow moving red Mustang convertible they'd borrowed from one of his followers. Rev and his cohorts had made every attempt to keep CJ out of the celebration and there he was, bigger than life.

With Herc seated next to him and Sammy at the wheel, CJ stood in the back of the Mustang wearing a humongous smile and waving to the adoring crowd as a shower of confetti and balloons rained down on him. At last, he felt appreciated. Although the ecstatic crowd shouted out his name, CJ gave all the glory to God. How he wished Teddy was here to enjoy this momentous experience with him. But he had warned Teddy to stay out of sight for fear of the uproar his presence might create among the people.

Suddenly, drowning out the cheers of the crowd the mysterious voice spoke once more, "Your close trusted friend, whom you love, will betray you and turn you over to be killed."

CJ felt as though someone had dashed cold water in his face. His gaze fell immediately on Sammy and he wondered if this impetuous man to whom he had given legs would be the one to turn him in. Although CJ had many incredible powers, omniscience was not one of them. As he had said earlier, "Some things God reveals and others He conceals." One of the things not yet revealed to him was the identity of the traitor.

Rev turned on James in a rage, "That's the biggest fly I ever saw in my life."

"I . . . I, uh . . ." James stuttered, attempting to explain.

"Just get the hell out of my sight," Rev growled. James slithered out of the office without another word. "Son of a bitch," Rev said, glaring out at the exuberant crowd. "Get down there and put a stop to this right now, Saunders."

"How?" Saunders asked.

"I don't care. Shoot him if you have to."

CHAPTER 46

Teddy, Carla, Dee, Dusty and Cheyenne threw confetti at CJ from the balcony of their lavish hotel suite, cheering and screaming ecstatically as Saunders plowed through the crowd and trotted alongside the slow moving Mustang. "Please, Reverend CJ," he pleaded. "You've got to stop this display immediately. We have some very dignified guests here and . . ."

Consumed by the Holy Spirit CJ looked at him like he was talking out of the side of his neck, "Even if I could stop these people from cheering, the hills and mountains would burst out singing and the trees would clap their hands. This is the day of the Lord!" He raised both arms high in the air basking in the adoration and love flowing from the masses, allowing himself to embrace the honor and praise bestowed upon him despite the agonizing knowledge that one of his friends was about to betray him. Saunders froze in his tracks watching helplessly as the one car parade passed him by.

Teddy and the women waited impatiently for CJ and the others to return to the hotel suite. "I wonder where they are." Dee worried aloud. "I hope Chucky's all right."

"He's all right, Mama Dee. If he wasn't, I'd know it. I'd feel it," Carla assured her, resting her hands on her chest. Dusty shot her the stink eye but said nothing.

Cheyenne tried reaching Sammy on his cell phone, but it went straight to voice mail. "He must have turned his phone off," she said, keying in another number. "I'm going to try Sebastian. He never turns his off." Sebastian told her that he was in a meeting and didn't have time to talk. He assured her that CJ and the others would be there shortly. Sebastian had taken advantage of the international interest in The City of Solomon to arrange meetings with various foreign businessmen and political leaders in the hope of gaining support for what he believed would be the most phenomenal coup the world has ever known.

After a while, they heard the secret knock on the door. Carla flung the door open and disappointment showed on her face when Hawk rushed into the suite. "Y'all seen CJ and them?"

"No," Carla replied. She too was becoming concerned though she tried not to show it. "Weren't you with them?"

"We lost 'em." Where's Sebastian?"

"He's in some meeting." Cheyenne said. "You know Sebastian. He's always got some kind of deal going."

The door flew open and Sherman burst in. "Did you find 'em?"

Hawk shook his head, "Not yet. I don't know where they could be."

No longer able to mask her anxiety, Carla took charge. "Sherman, you and Hawk get back out there and track them down."

"You got it," Sherman said darting out the door with Hawk on his heels.

Dee's anxiety grew as the day wore on with no word from CJ. "Lord, have mercy Jesus. They done killed my child," she moaned rocking back and forth on the couch.

"Don't say that, Mama Dee," Carla said displaying a confidence she didn't feel. "They wouldn't dare do anything to him today. There's too many people around. Did you hear how they were cheering for him? These people love CJ. They'd tear this place down if anything happened to him.

He's probably just off somewhere praying. He does that."

Carla didn't realize how right she was. CJ sat parked in the borrowed convertible in plain sight. However, no one saw him as he prayed with Herc and Sammy for protection from his enemies and the strength to continue his mission.

That evening as beautiful music wafted from the sanctuary Rev prepared for his twilight service, the highpoint of the day. Dressed in a burgundy robe with gold trim he stared into a full-length mirror nervously blotting the sweat from his face and hair with a towel. Turning slowly so that Saunders could get the full effect he asked, "How do I look?"

"You look amazing Rev," Saunders said. "Just relax." He plucked a piece of towel lint from Rev's hair and said, "There. Perfect."

"How can I relax with that maniac running around loose? Do you see what I have to put up with?" he said with a martyred sigh. "Where's James?"

"He's got the whole security team scouring the grounds. If he's still here, they'll find him. If he's smart, he took off right after his little exhibition," Saunders said hoping with all his heart that it was the truth.

"Oh, he's smart all right." Rev said. "Smarter than that stupid rent-a-cop James. This idiot's got one job, keep that sucker

333

out. And he can't even do that." He turned to Saunders, "I can't have any screw ups tonight, Saunders. You understand what I'm saying?"

"Sure, Rev," Saunders said wondering what Rev expected him to do.

The cathedral was resplendent, with highly polished wood, fresh flowers and stained glass windows. But it was more like a gigantic theater than a sanctuary, fully equipped with light and sound equipment and jumbo monitors positioned throughout the arena.

The house lights dimmed and a display of colored lights hit the stage. Rev stood in the wings rolling his shoulders like a fighter preparing to step into the ring. His adrenalin was pumping.as he waited for the music cueing his entrance. Suddenly, Sammy's resonant voice filled the packed auditorium.

"Ladies and gentlemen. May I present the man we've all been waiting for? He's the Alpha and Omega. The beginning and the end. The anointed man of God. The holy one sent from above. He's the sun in the morning and the moon at night." The audience burst into spontaneous applause.

"He's the divine son, faithful and true. I'm talking about the revealer. A righteous and upright man." Rev didn't know who this new announcer was, but he certainly liked what he was saying about him even if he was putting it on a bit thick. "Y'all know who I'm talking about," said Sammy. "He's God's anointed one. The great I am. He's the healer, the king of kings and the lord of lords. I'm talking about that mighty man of God."

Rev was so excited over the buildup Sammy was giving him that he couldn't wait for the music. As Sammy continued the intro, Rev strode onto the stage like the emperor with no clothes. The colored flashes of light hitting him from all directions gave him a cartoon-like appearance.

"The man of holiness, y'all. The Lamb of God, messenger of God's new covenant. He's the Messiah." The word stopped Rev in his tracks and the crowd exploded. Glancing up at the huge monitors, Rev saw his own bewildered face staring back at him and stood like a deer in headlights as the disembodied ringmaster continued.

"He's the beloved son of the Most High God. The author of eternal salvation and the bread of life. He's the second comforter, chosen by God. The deliverer and the shepherd of the Lord. The physician and the prince of peace. He's the redeemer, the resurrection and the life." The crowd grew more frantic with each word Sammy spoke. "The savior and the servant of the Lord. He's the son. He's my rock. He's a teacher and a preacher. The truth and the way. The Word. They call him the wonderful counselor of God, for he is worthy to be praised. Let's give it up for the man of the hour, the Brother Man himself. I give you Reverend Ceeee-Jay!"

The crowd erupted in outrageous cheers and applause. As the lights went up, Rev stood in the middle of the stage watching as CJ's solemn image replaced his own on the monitors, simultaneously appearing on every channel of every TV across the country and around the world. The audience sprang to its feet. The applause was like thunder. Whistling. Screaming. Saunders ran out onto the stage and led his befuddled boss off.

CJ looked straight into the camera and said, "The Lord has given me all authority in heaven and on earth." His voice reverberated throughout the auditorium stilling the crowd. He paused momentarily before continuing. "The word of God says, '*I will raise up among you a prophet, a man just like yourselves; I will put my words in his mouth and he will tell you everything I command him to say. Then the eyes of the blind will be opened and the ears of the deaf unstopped. The lame will leap like a deer and the mute tongue will shout for joy.*' This promise has been fulfilled before your eyes."

After a brief pause he continued. His handsome face was serious, unsmiling. "I have revealed myself to people who didn't ask for me; I was found by those who weren't looking for me. I held my

335

hands out to pigheaded people who continued in their sinful ways."
After a beat he said, "Your religious and political leaders have the
authority to tell you what's right and what's wrong. And you should
do what they say – but not what they do, because so many of them
do not practice what they preach."

The high-ranking political and religious officials sitting in
the VIP section sat up straight in their seats looking around as if they
smelled something rotten. People around the world watched in utter
amazement, each country hearing CJ's words in its own language.

Mrs. Wilson, CJ's neighbor turned to her husband with tears
in her eyes and said, "See, Claude. I told you that boy had the Spirit
of God on him."

Claude just rolled his eyes and said, "Yeah baby." He knew
that to call her on her hypocrisy would lead to an argument and he
didn't want to miss a word CJ had to say.

"Your religious leaders tell you to 'Do this and do that.'
Meanwhile; they're out there indulging in every kind of licentious
behavior imaginable," he said.

Then he told them how the preachers give beautiful sermons,
dress in expensive suits and fine-looking robes, seeking honor and
respect all the while feathering their nests from the pockets of the
poor and preying on the young and defenseless with their perverted
and despicable desires.

"I'm telling you the truth," he said, his light eyes ablaze with
fury. "Anyone who defiles one of God's innocent children will burn
in the hottest part of hell. They want you to call them Reverend,
Pastor and Father," he sneered. "But I'm telling you that these men,
who set themselves up on high, will soon be brought low. They are
so consumed with their own self-righteousness that they don't even
fear God. But, now God has made his righteousness known to you."

In his office, Rev lay on his soft leather couch with a cold
compress on his head while Saunders, Captain James and several

336

other men stared at the TV in rapt amazement. "I'm talking to you foul and contemptuous preachers," CJ said. The men shot a quick glance at Rev and quickly turned their attention back to the TV. "You're just a bunch of hypocrites! You want to shut the door of heaven in the faces of the people. You know you're not getting in, so you try to stop those who are trying to," CJ accused.

"Why is he doing this to me?" Rev muttered repeatedly. The men were so engrossed in what they were watching that they paid no attention to his ramblings.

"Lord, have mercy on your fraudulent and decadent souls," CJ said his voice dripping with contempt. "You prey on the weak and the innocent, turning them into twice the child of hell that you are. But when you lead the upright along the path of evil, you're bound to fall into your own trap. You build fine churches and elaborate cathedrals, not for the glory of God, but for your own vainglory, to line your own pockets with ill-gotten gain. You blind fools. You're like greedy dogs that don't never get enough of nothing."

He glared into the camera, his eyes filled with scorn. "You are such hypocrites! You think that just because you can spout Scripture like a trained actor you can ignore the laws of God – justice, mercy and faithfulness. You're just blind guides! And when the blind leads the blind, we all know where they end up. You're like ravenous wolves. You get up there and rail against homosexuality, but nobody knows where your nose goes when the doors close." This elicited a smattering of laughter from the audience.

"Turn that shit off!" Rev shouted holding his head in both hands. "I can't think." CJ's words were killing him softly. I'm not like that, he thought shaking his head as if to dislodge the torturous truth. I love children.

"You wrap yourselves with pomp and circumstance and put on pretty smiles," CJ said, continuing his blistering denunciation of the clergy. "But inside you are full of greed and self-indulgence. Do you think a designer suit or a priest's collar is going to hide your despicable habits from the Lord?" Guilty tears slid down Saunders' face as he slumped down in his chair, holding his hand over his mouth.

CJ shook his head in dismay. "You hypocrites! Before you start dressing up on the outside, you better be sure you're clean on the inside. You present yourselves to the public as being righteous and sincere while your inner-man is overflowing with hypocrisy and wickedness."

But CJ's scorn was hardly reserved for the religious elite. "And you wretched and corrupt politicians," he said shifting gears.

"You're so quick to shed blood. You build statues honoring Dr. Martin Luther King and tell your constituents that if you had lived in his day, you would never have taken part in the atrocities perpetrated on him. You are such hypocrites! All you're doing is testifying against yourselves. Your fathers were the ones that murdered the prophet! Devastation and misery follow you everywhere you go." His forehead creased into a frown when he said, "You're just a bunch of belly crawling snakes. And you will never escape the condemnation of hell!"

Rev snatched the cloth from his head and shot up from the couch. "Turn it off, I said!"

James turned to Rev with an impatient, "Shhh."

"Who the hell do you think you're shushing?" Rev shouted grabbing the remote and clicking the TV off.

"Come on, Rev," Saunders pleaded.

"Get out of here!" Rev shouted. "Find that sucker and kill him!" The men looked at him as if he was crazy. "Now!" he screamed and they all hustled out the door.

"You can kill me, but you can't shut me up," CJ continued. "The ones I leave behind will become prophets and teachers. Yeah.

You'll kill some of them; others you'll lock up in your prisons, hoping that'll quiet their voices, but it won't. You can't keep 'em quiet any more than you can keep the wind from blowing."

Then to the amazement of his followers and all those who had labeled him the Black Messiah, he said, "In God, there is no difference between black and white, rich and poor, Christians, Muslims or Jews, because we have all sinned and fallen short of the glory of God and we have all been justified by His grace through the redemption that came through His son Jesus Christ."

People around the world stared at their TV sets transfixed as CJ peered out at them, his face awash with sadness. His voice softened as he said, "You are a hardheaded and disbelieving people. If the signs and wonders I've performed across this country had been done in Sodom and Gomorrah, they'd still be standing today. I came into this world as a light so that those who believed in me would never have to walk in darkness. Walk in the light while you have it," he pleaded.

"Because you won't have it much longer. You'll look for me, but I'll be gone and where I'm going you cannot follow," he said. Many were horrified, taking this to mean that he intended to kill himself.

"When my mission on earth is complete, you won't hear from the Brother Man again until that great morning when we all stand in front of the one true Judge. The one who sees what you do in the dark. The one who knows your innermost sins and perversions. Then you'll know that I am he that was sent from God and that God's love is everlasting."

As CJ stared out at the world with sad and weary eyes all the screens of all the TV's around the world went black for a second before returning to their regularly scheduled programs.

While Rev's guards searched the grounds for CJ and his friends, they were already on their way back to Shorty's house. When they arrived at the mansion, the general feeling was one of triumph and excitement. However, CJ was in one of his more pensive moods.

As the others celebrated, Sebastian strolled in wearing the proverbial Cheshire cat grin and carrying a magnum of champagne. He thrust the champagne out to Sammy saying, "Open this." He saw CJ sitting alone in a chair by the big bay window and grabbed his hand, clasping it between both of his.

"You were awesome, CJ. Awesome. I could feel the hairs standing up on the back of my neck. You've got them scared now. You can demand anything you want. I talked to representatives from several countries that are willing to give you asylum, as well as all the land and money you need to set up the nation of God. We don't even have to stay here. We can go anywhere in the world and call our own shots. But we can talk about that tomorrow. Tonight we celebrate!" he said jubilantly.

"I can't leave New York," CJ stated simply.

"Why not?" Sebastian demanded to know, his high-flying balloon suddenly deflated. "They already tried to kill you once."

"I came here to die," CJ replied calmly.

"You're talking crazy, CJ," Sammy interjected. "Can't nobody kill you."

"Shut up!" CJ snapped, convinced that Sammy was the traitor. "Ain't nobody talking to you." Sammy jumped back, shocked by the fierceness of his tone.

"But what about the nation of God?" Sebastian asked.

"The nation of God isn't a place, Sebastian. The nation of God is in your heart." Sammy's face contorted with anger and disappointment.

Dumbfounded, Sebastian said, "But you said you came to save the black man."

"That's what I thought at first," CJ admitted. "Now I realize that God didn't send me just to save the black man. He sent me to save the world. And my body is to be the ransom, the living sacrifice."

"Screw the world!" Sebastian shouted. He stared at CJ in utter disbelief. "How can you do this to me? I've worked my ass off to get you where you are. And you're just going to lie down and quit? Now? Talking about some abstract notion of saving the world. What's wrong with you?"

"Didn't you hear a word of what I said tonight, Sebastian?"

"Oh, I heard what you said – And I hear what you're saying," he shot back, burning with uncontrolled fury. Sammy, too upset to speak watched in uncharacteristic silence as Sebastian stormed out of the house incensed over having spent so much time and energy with CJ, only to find out that he'd been running around behind a loony who led him to believe one thing and then changed the game in midstream.

CJ's televised statement rocked the entire world. Nations across the globe went on Red Alert. They saw in CJ an American plot to rule the world, while U.S. leaders viewed him as a terrorist threat. They thought their worst fears had finally come to pass. The long oppressed black man had finally risen up in retaliation. The President initiated the suppression plan the pentagon secretly referred to as, "Operation Tar Baby," which they had prepared in the seventies when the fear of a black reprisal was at its peak. The National Guard stood ready to squelch any sign of aggression on the part of America's black citizenry and the hunt for CJ became more intense than ever.

The people of America were riveted to the news. CJ's name and likeness were splashed across the newspaper pages and the airways daily. Some quaked in terror, while others cheered him on. Reports of CJ sightings came in from all over the country, but in reality, he never left New York.

"How do I know you're telling the truth?" Chief Petrocelli asked the man seated across from his desk. The man did not respond. "Reverend Bradshaw is on his way. If he believes what you're saying, we can take it from there."

A few minutes later, Rev stormed into the Chief's office. "What's this about somebody claiming the reward, Pete? Is CJ in custody?"

"Calm down, Rev. This gentleman says he can deliver him."

For the first time, Rev noticed the other man. "Who are you?"

"He just might be the answer to your problems," said Petrocelli. They both stared down at the man and smiled.

CHAPTER 47

Easter Sunday. CJ was in a better mood than he'd been in for quite a while. He even helped prepare Easter dinner for the crew. As he sat at the gold plated piano diddling on the keys, Carla slid onto the bench next to him smiling mysteriously.

"What's up?" he asked with a bashful smile. Although they tried to downplay their relationship, the love between them was apparent.

"I just want to thank you."

"For what?"

"For everything," she said, flashing a conspiratorial smile at Teddy. "A little birdie told me how much you like the Stylistics, so . . ." She began singing You Make Me Feel Brand New.

As she sang the words to one of CJ's all-time favorite songs, his hands went automatically to the keyboard and he began to play, his love issuing forth like a spigot as he sang along with her. When the song ended, Carla threw her arms around CJ's neck and said, "I love you, CJ." CJ smiled and gave her a kiss on the nose.

Cheyenne grabbed a bottle of wine from the ice bucket and began filling glasses. "This calls for a toast."

Teddy raised his glass high, "Here's to CJ, a true friend to the end – And then some," he chuckled. "I love you, man."

"To CJ," they all said in unison, drinking to him.

CJ raised his glass, "Here's to all my rowdy friends," he laughed. As they again raised their glasses to drink, a sudden flash of revelation struck CJ. He knew who the traitor was and it broke his heart.

"Wait," CJ said, holding up his hand. "I'm not finished." Taking a moment to assimilate the devastating knowledge he raised his glass again. "To all my friends," he said through eyes clouded with pain and sadness. "You've gone through so much with me and I love you all."

"Aww," Cheyenne said touched by his words.

"Even though one of you is a turncoat. A snake and a rat." He downed his drink while the others stood staring at him like stone statues, drinks in hand. The festive mood fell like a lead balloon and silence engulfed the room like a cold fist. "Drink up," CJ said refilling his glass, "Because the Brother Man won't be tasting of the grape again until he drinks with his Father in heaven."

"It wasn't me," Sammy declared. "You know I'd die for you, CJ."

"Would you, Sammy? Really?" CJ said with a wry smile. He then prophesied, "Before this thing is over you will have denied me three times." The Spirit had shown him that the devil was continuously working to reclaim Sammy's soul.

Sammy shook his head violently, "No way. I'm with you, man. Ride or die."

The others quickly added their vows of allegiance, assuring CJ that they were not the traitor. Sebastian looked hurt, "I know you're not talking about me." CJ just stared at them, wondering how he hadn't seen it before. Perhaps he hadn't wanted to. Obviously, it was part of God's plan, he conceded. But he still couldn't understand it.

When CJ entered the kitchen, the first thing to hit him in the face was Carla's voluptuous backside as she bent over to remove a pan of cornbread from the oven. He eased up behind her as she stood. "Need some help?" he asked slipping his arms around her waist.

"Oh, CJ. You scared me," she said plopping the pan of bread on top of the stove.

"Sorry," he said, kissing her on the neck. He then strolled over to the table and began chopping celery.

"You okay?" She asked.

"Yeah. Why wouldn't I be?"

"You tell me. After that toast you made, I don't know what to think. You might think I'm the rat for all I know," she said, with a forced laugh.

"Don't even joke like that," he said. "You know I would never think anything like that."

"You wouldn't?" she said, moving closer to him.

He put the knife down on the table and turned to face her. "No. I wouldn't."

"Do you really think one of the guys turned you in?"

"I know it."

"Who?"

"You'll see. He'll be the one who sticks his fork in the last piece of meat at the same time I do." He then reached into his pocket and pulled out the diamond ring the distraught woman in the parking lot had given him. "This is for you," he said, slipping the ring on her finger.

Carla's eyes brightened with delight as she stared at the enormous sparkler. "Oh, CJ!" she squealed throwing her arms around his neck. "Are you asking me to marry you?"

CJ gently removed her arms from his neck and held her hands firmly in his. "No, Carla. I'm not." He could feel her heart breaking along with his. "I wish I could," he said. "But it's just not in the cards." Carla just stared at him, her eyes filled with confusion.

"I love you, Carla. I love you more than I ever thought I could love any woman. But I can't marry you."

Fighting to hold herself in check Carla whispered, "It's because of my past, isn't it?"

"You know better than that," he said lifting the hand that bore the ring up to his lips. "This ring is worth a lot of money. I gave it to you so that when I'm gone . . ."

She shushed him by placing two fingers over his lips. "Don't say it."

"You don't understand," he said gazing into her upturned face.

"I understand that I love you and I want to spend the rest of my life with you," she said pressing her body close to his. "It's the oldest concept in the world."

"Oh, God," he moaned rubbing his face in her hair, inhaling the sweetness of her.

"We could go away," she said resting her face on the hardness of his chest. "We could go where nobody knows us." He had to chuckle at the utter implausibility of her statement. "I'm serious. We could get married and . . ."

"And before long you'd be a widow. You can't escape the inevitable, Carla."

"But I love you," she said through trembling lips, tears spilling down her lovely face.

"I love you too," he replied, kissing her tears away. "But, God's will must be done." He then took her mouth in a kiss so fraught with fire and desire that it ignited their passion to a whole new level. When the kiss finally ended, she clung to him desperately afraid to let go.

While feasting on a dinner of chicken and dressing, ham, greens, macaroni and cheese and other delectable dishes, everyone tried to make bright conversation, but CJ's cheerful attitude had been obliterated.

"You put your foot in it this time, Mama Dee," Teddy said, helping himself to more mac and cheese.

"This dressing reminds of the kind I wish my mama used to make," said Herc.

"Well, you can thank CJ for that," said Dee. "He made the dressing."

"Ooo," Cheyenne said, eyeing Carla. "Not only is he handsome, the man can cook too." They all laughed, CJ's toast all but forgotten.

A few minutes later, CJ took his fork and speared the last piece of ham on the platter. Carla's fork froze midway to her mouth when Sebastian's fork claimed the same piece of meat. CJ removed his fork and gestured graciously, "Go ahead." A pall fell over the table as Sebastian plopped the telltale meat onto his plate and began to devour it ravenously, unaware that all eyes were fixed firmly on him.

"Slow down," Dee teased, feeling suddenly uncomfortable at the abrupt change in the atmosphere. "There's more in the kitchen."

As Sebastian continued to gorge himself, Satan entered his heart. When he lifted his head from his plate, his handsome face contorted into a visage of pure evil. His mouth skinned back in a hideous grimace, revealing pointed fang-like teeth. To the others he looked the normal, only CJ saw his features change. Sebastian wiped his mouth on his napkin, pushed back his chair and stood. "I have to go," he said, suddenly desperate to get out of there.

"Sebastian," CJ called as he started to leave. Sebastian turned to face him and CJ saw the hatred and discontentment within him. But his unwavering love for his friend was extraordinary. Even though he knew Sebastian had already betrayed him, he gave him one last chance to repent. "Do what you think is right."

Realizing that his cover was blown, Sebastian hurried out of the dining room and straight out the front door without saying a word. CJ stared after him, the pain of betrayal gnawing relentlessly at his soul.

"What's his problem?" Cheyenne asked.

"He didn't even wait for dessert," Dee added.

"He probably went to volunteer at the soup kitchen or somewhere. You know how conscientious Sebastian is," said Dusty.

"We need to get out of here," CJ said, throwing his napkin down on the table as he stood.

"Why?" Dee demanded to know. "What's going on?"

"Sebastian is the one who turned CJ in," Carla said.

"Oh, my God!" Dee said, running to CJ.

"Don't worry, Ma. Everything's gon' work out for the glory of God," he assured her. However, anger over Sebastian's treachery eclipsed everything else in his friends' minds.

"That dirty bastard," Teddy said.

"I told y'all that nigga was a snake," said Hawk.

"We need to roll on that nigga, right now," Sammy said.

"We ain't got time for that," CJ said. "They'll be here soon."

"Who?" Shorty asked. "

The cops."

CHAPTER 48

"If you got any guns, bring 'em." Although CJ had admonished them not to carry weapons, he knew they had them and he knew that they might have to defend themselves against trigger-happy cops when the deal went down.

He immediately heard a series of clicks as everyone except Herc whipped out their guns, checking them to make sure they were ready. Hawk pulled a gun from an ankle holster and offered it to Herc who shook his head, "I don't need no gun." Hawk shrugged, returning the pistol to its holster.

As Teddy stuck his Glock into the back of his waistband and reached for his jacket, CJ placed a restraining hand on his arm. "Not this time, brother. They're looking for you too."

"Hey, they say you can't die but once," Teddy said with a lop-sided grin. "I got you, man."

CJ looked deeply into his friend's eyes. "I know you do," he said. "And I love you for it. But I need you to stay here and make sure the women are safe. Please."

Realizing that he was relegating her to the ranks of the left behind, Carla spoke quickly, "I'm going with you." CJ saw the fierce determination in her eyes and nodded, knowing that arguing with her would be fruitless.

He hugged his mother and she clung to him sobbing softly. After a long moment, CJ kissed the top of her head and held her at arm's length peering into her tear-filled eyes. "I gotta go, Ma. You know that." She closed her eyes, nodding in acceptance. Over her head, he said, "Teddy, take care of my mama."

"You know I will," Teddy said, wrapping a protective arm around Dee's tiny shoulders, his other hand grasping CJ's in their private handshake.

Sherman gave Dee a kiss on the forehead saying, "It's gon' be all right, Ma. I promise." She watched as both her sons left with their companions and wondered if she would ever see either of them alive again.

After leaving Shorty's house, Sebastian drove directly to Rev's Park Avenue apartment. Rev opened the door to his lavish home and led Sebastian directly to his study. Rev took a seat behind his desk and motioned for Sebastian to sit. He perched on the edge of one of the buttery soft leather chairs in front of Rev's desk. "There better be a damned good reason for you to be coming to my home, St. John."

"He's at Madame C.J. Walker's mansion out on the Hudson," Sebastian blurted.

"Who?"

"Who do you think?" Sebastian snapped. "I'm turning him over just like I promised. Where's my money?"

"Not so fast," Rev said. "How do I know you're not lying, just trying to beat me out of my money?"

"I just left him. If you get the cops over there right away, you can still catch him. I need that money tonight. Cash."

"You'll get your money when that maniac is safely behind bars," Rev said. He picked up the phone and called Chief Petrocelli. "Hey. Rev here. It's going down tonight. Yeah. He's at the old Anne Poth house," as the Italianate villa was now called. "Yeah. Great. I'll have St. John meet you there. He knows the layout of the place. Yeah, good enough. And Chief," he added as an afterthought. "I want that damned zombie he raised up from hell too." He smiled wickedly and hung up the phone.

Sebastian sprang to his feet, "I'm not going back there!" he said adamantly, knowing how Teddy and the others must despise him. He knew they'd want to kill him. Not only was he disloyal, but he was a real coward at heart.

"Oh, you're going. If you think I'm just going to hand over a million bucks on the word of a stool pigeon," Rev said, flinging the words at him like a handful of feces, "you got another think coming." He had no doubt that Sebastian was telling the truth, but he hated a snitch almost as much as he hated CJ and wanted to make it as uncomfortable for Sebastian as possible. He then called Saunders and ordered him to get to his house immediately.

The police chief arrived shortly after receiving Rev's phone call, as did Saunders. When Saunders learned why he was there, he freaked. "This is a matter for the police. You don't need me."

"I need you to keep an eye on our friend here," Rev said, shooting a hard look at Sebastian.

"Naw," Saunders said, shaking his head. "Not me."

"You scared?" Rev challenged.

"Yes," Saunders readily admitted. "I'm scared to death."

"I don't blame you," Sebastian said. "If I were you, Chief, I'd call in the SWAT team."

"I thought he was non-violent," said Rev.

"He is. But the men with him aren't."

By the time CJ and the others got to their secret hideout, a suite they'd kept on reserve in a Harlem hotel, CJ was in a state of deep depression. He knew his time had come. "This is the final come down," he told them. "And if you believe in God, I'm asking you to believe in me. You all have stuck with me through thick and thin. But like I said the other night, where I'm going now you can't go. But don't worry; you'll be there with me one day. Y'all know the way."

"We don't even know where you're going," Sammy said. "So how are we supposed to know the way?"

"I am the way," CJ said. "The only way you can get to the Father is through me. If you really know me, you know my Father too, because you've seen Him."

"When?" Sammy asked. "I ain't seen nobody. You need to show Him to us."

"After all this time, you still don't know me?" CJ answered in frustration. "If you've seen me, you've seen Him. So how you gon' say, 'Show Him to us'? Don't you believe that I'm in the Father and He's in me?"

"Yeah," Sammy said, "But I just thought . . ."

"I'm not making this stuff up!" CJ snapped. "If you don't believe me when I tell you that I'm in the Father and the Father is in me, at least believe in the miracles you've seen. I'm telling y'all the truth and if you believe in me, you'll keep doing my work after I'm gone, because I'm going to be with my Father."

"So, you're just going to desert us?" asked Shorty.

"You'll see me again. Then you'll realize that I'm in my Father and you're in me, just like I'm in you. Whoever loves me, will follow my instructions and I'll love him, and my Father will too. But, if you don't obey my teaching, you don't love me. And if you don't love me you don't love the Father that's in me." The men were confused. He was talking crazy.

CJ sat down on the couch, rubbing his hands over his face and hair. The wild look in his eyes frightened them. "You heard me say that I'm going away, but I'm coming back. I'm telling y'all this now before it happens, so that when it does happen you'll believe." They stared at him in bewilderment.

"See, it's like I'm the vine," he said, rising to his feet and tapping his chest with the fingers of both hands, "And my Father is the gardener. He cuts off every branch in me that doesn't bear fruit. But every branch that does bear fruit He prunes back, so that it'll produce even more." He was rambling now, pacing the room and the guys were looking at him like he was a crazy man. "You have to stay in me, like I'm in you. See, it's like you're the branches. But a branch can't bear fruit by itself; it has to remain in the vine."

Again with the fruit, Sammy thought.

"I'm the vine and you're the branches," he said, desperate to make them understand. "If you remain in me and me in you, you will bear an abundant crop, but separated from me you can't do nothing. Nothing. If you don't remain in me, you'll wither up like a dead branch," he said nervously wiping the sweat from his face. "But if you remain in me and my words remain in you, you can ask my Father for whatever you want and He'll do it for you. This is for the glory of God. I've loved you just as He loves me. Just stay in my love," he pleaded.

Carla could see CJ's anxiety mounting. His breathing was erratic; his eyes darted from one of them to the other as he paced, alternating between rubbing his hands together and massaging his forehead. "I'm telling you all this because y'all gotta love each other, just like I've loved you. I'm not gon' have time to say much more to y'all, because the law is on its way. Y'all know they don't have any power over me, but I'm going to let them arrest me anyway, so that the world will see how much I love the Lord and that I'm doing what He commanded me to do."

He shook his head slowly from side to side, the awesomeness of his responsibility bearing down on him like a two-ton weight. "A man can't show any greater love than to lay down his life for his friends," he said. "You all are my friends and I've shared everything that I learned from my Father with you. You didn't choose me, I chose you and I anointed you. So if the world winds up hating you, remember it hated me first. See, if you belonged to the world, it would love you. But I plucked you out of the world. That's why they'll persecute you just like they've persecuted me. Because they don't know the one who sent me."

Carla, alarmed by his inane mutterings wrapped her arm around his waist and nodded toward the bedroom. "Why don't you go lay down, CJ? You need to rest."

But he couldn't lie down. How could he rest when his heart was so heavy? When his soul was so distraught. He shook her off and flopped down on the sofa, his hands rubbing one another vigorously as he rocked back and forth tormented by what he knew was about to transpire. "If I'd never come and spoken to them," he mumbled shaking his head in despair, "they wouldn't be guilty of sin; but they don't have no excuse now." He sprung up from the couch and resumed his pacing. "If they hadn't seen me do things that no one else has ever done before, they wouldn't be guilty of sin. But, they've seen the works of God and they still hate me. And if they hate me, they hate the one who sent me." He chuckled at the irony of it. "But it had to come down like that so that the Scripture would be fulfilled, 'They hated me without cause,'" he quoted.

"I'm telling y'all this so that you won't be shocked when people you thought were your friends turn on you like mad dogs," he warned. "Folks claiming to be Christians will rip you apart. In

355

fact, the time will come when anyone who kills you will think they're performing a public service. That's because they never knew me or my Father." He groaned as if in physical pain. "I know this is bringing y'all down. But I'm just telling you for your own good, so that when it happens you'll remember I warned you. I didn't tell you any of this before because I was here with you and I could protect you. But now I'm going back to the one who sent me."

He stalked the room like a caged tiger, rubbing his hand over his head, "I've got so much more to say to you, more than you can take right now," he said. "In a little while you won't see me anymore and then after a little while you'll see me again."

"What's that supposed to mean?" Sammy whispered to Carla.

"Why are you asking her?" CJ shouted. "I'm standing right here. Truth is, while you're weeping and mourning the rest of the world will be shouting with joy. But your grief will turn to joy. Just like a woman suffering through labor," he explained. "Once her baby's born she forgets all about the pain she's been through, because she's so happy over the birth of her child. That's how it's gon' be with you. You might grieve at first, but when you see me again, you'll be rejoicing and can't nobody take that joy away from you. And that's the truth."

"I know I be talking around in circles sometimes, but now it's time for me to give it to you straight. God loves you because you have loved me."

"Now, we can believe that," said Sherman.

"Oh, so, now you believe," CJ replied sardonically. "Let me tell you something; a time is coming, in fact has already come when every one of you will abandon me." Sherman gave him a shocked look, offended that his own brother would include him in such a statement. "But I won't be alone, because my Father will be with me." After an uncomfortable moment of silence, CJ fell to his knees and said, "We need to pray." The others exchanged looks before going down on their knees as well.

"Oh, heavenly Father," CJ prayed. "You have granted me the authority to give eternal life to those you gave me. And I have revealed you to them. They were yours, Father; you gave them to me and they have obeyed your word. I'm praying for them, Lord. I'm not praying for the world right now, but for those you have given me, because they're yours. I know my time in this world is over and I'm coming home to you, Lord. But they'll still be here. None of them has been lost except for the son of perdition, who was doomed to destruction so that the Scripture would be fulfilled. While I was with them, I protected them and kept them safe by the power of your name. Now, I'm asking you to protect them, Almighty God, so that they may be one as we are one."

When CJ paused Sammy started to stand up, rubbing his aching knees. But CJ continued to pray, "Righteous Father, . . ." Carla shot Sammy a look and he fell back into position.

CJ prayed hard and long, consumed by such anguish and despair that his words became incomprehensible. When he dissolved into tears, Carla rose to her feet. Standing behind him, she placed her hands on his shoulders and completed the prayer for him, "In the name of Jesus Christ, we pray. Amen." Helping him to his feet she said, "Come on, CJ. You need to rest." Carla could see that he was suffering. She had never seen him so sorrowful and overwhelmed.

CJ turned his tear-stained face to her, grasping her shoulders with both his hands and peering deeply into her eyes, "This grief is eating me up, Carla. All I can think about is dying. Dying for sins I didn't even commit."

CHAPTER 49

There is nothing more heartbreaking than wasted suffering. CJ dreaded the prospect of dying for sins that others deserved to pay for. He could see the future and knew that his death would be a gross miscarriage of justice. He felt unappreciated and rejected. And he thought that the suffering he was about to endure would all be in vain.

Carla hugged him close and whispered a firm reprimand in his ear, "Pull yourself together, CJ. Don't let them see you like this."

He tried to get it together, but the sorrow and the love he felt at the thought of leaving them bore down on the humanity of his heart with such crushing intensity that it made it even more difficult to face the certain death he knew awaited him.

"Promise me you'll stay here and keep watch with me," he begged Carla. Before she could answer, he turned to the others, anxiety spilling from his very pores. "Can y'all do that for me? Just watch and pray," he said before rushing out onto the terrace, suddenly desperate to be alone.

On the terrace, the full moon shone conspicuously bright and the cool night air wafted over CJ as he fell to his knees and prayed,

"Oh, heavenly Father, I came into this world to do your will and I have. I know that the time has come for me to lay down this life in the flesh and I'm not trying to punk out. I'm not. I just need to know that I will please you in my death as I have in my life." Unable to continue he burst into tears, his hand rubbing at his forehead and clutching the front of his hair. The pain and torment in his soul were unbearable. No longer able to conceal the thought that had been lurking in the back of his mind; he moaned in anguish, "I don't wanna die! I know all things are possible for you, Father and I'm asking you to spare me. Don't make me drink this bitter cup."

CJ suffered through an intense spiritual battle that night, struggling with the natural instinct to save himself, rather than following through with the mission handed to him by the Lord. But his struggle to accept God's will only illustrated the human aspects of his nature. His agony wasn't due to rebellion, but to man's natural instinct for self-preservation.

"I've done everything you told me to do," he prayed. "I've tried teaching them, pleading with them, warning them, but these are hard-headed people Lord, so jaded that even the miracles you've shown them don't have any affect. Even the ones who are willing to believe have to deal with leaders who would rather see me dead than let the truth be known." CJ wiped the sweat from his face and to his horror, found his hand covered in blood. "What the . . .?"

He was sweating blood!

CJ was experiencing an extremely rare phenomenon called hematidrosis. This condition causes hemorrhaging of the sweat glands and only occurs when a person is suffering the most extreme levels of emotional agony. The more sensitive the nature, the more intense the suffering and CJ's very nature elevated his suffering to an excruciating level. Every drop of blood that poured out of CJ's body that night was divine. It stood for the personified Son of God and his suffering for our sins.

CJ stared at the blood on his hands in horror and suddenly his purpose on earth became perfectly clear; his ministry was to culminate by sacrificing his own life to make it possible for sinful people to connect to God through him.

He fell face down on the floor and cried, "Forgive me Father, for the weakness of my flesh. But this is just such a hard pill to swallow." Then, girding himself with strength he never knew he had, he sat up and said, "Nevertheless, it's not my will, Lord, but your will that must be done." With these words, he surrendered his own desires to that of the Almighty. God saw CJ's anguish and sent an angel from heaven to strengthen him.

As CJ begged God's forgiveness, a familiar fragrance captured his attention. Lifting his head, he saw Ariana smiling down on him in all her angelic splendor. She wiped the tears and the blood from his face and gently stroked his head, speaking words of encouragement to him.

"God has heard your prayer, CJ. He knows your pain and He wants you to know that He's with you and he'll never leave you." Her comforting words strengthened him for the arduous journey that lay ahead. She told him that God wanted him to complete his earthly task by passing through the experience of death just as all mortal creatures must. She explained that he had to experience physical termination in order to pass from the existence of time into the progression of eternity. And she reminded him that God always empowered people to do whatever he called them to do.

CJ benefited tremendously from Ariana's help that night. The angel strengthened him, preparing him both physically and emotionally for the intense demands that awaited him. Encouraging him to stay strong, she said, "The Lord is with you, CJ." Her words lingered in the air as she dissolved into nothingness. "The Lord is with you. The Lord is with you . . ."

As Ariana's words faded into the atmosphere, CJ rose to his feet feeling refreshed and looking revitalized. He radiated an aura of power and was ready to face whatever lay ahead. He took a deep breath and raked his hands through his hair. When he looked down from the terrace, he was not surprised to see police cars, sheriff's cars and SWAT vans surrounding the hotel. He knew that once Sebastian realized they weren't at Shorty's, he'd lead them to this hotel.

CJ stepped back into the suite and looked around in disappointment at his sleeping companions. They'd been too exhausted to stay awake. "Wake up," he shouted, shaking Sammy roughly. "Can't you even watch with me for an hour?"

"I'm not sleep," Sammy said, sitting up quickly. "I was just resting my eyes."

"Get up," CJ told him. "The cops are here." The others awoke at the sound of his voice and rallied around him.

"Oh, my God!" shouted Carla at the sight of his bloody shirt. "What happened?"

"Nothing." CJ said, peeling off the soiled garment and flinging it to the floor. Carla sighed with relief at the sight of his unblemished chest. She fished a fresh shirt out of her bag and handed it to him, still wondering where the blood had come from. CJ slipped into the clean shirt and as he buttoned it, he was suddenly compelled to tell Sammy, "The devil has his eye on you, Sammy." Sammy stared at him in alarm as he continued. "I need you to be strong. I'm counting on you."

Sammy nodded, "Yeah, CJ. I will."

CJ smiled, knowing that he had done his best for them. Even though the humanity of his heart wished that he could have done more, for he truly loved these people, they had been like family to him.

CHAPTER 50

By the time they heard the secret code knock on the door, CJ had regained his usual composure. The Brother Man was prepared to face his enemies with poise and wholehearted dedication to his Father's will. He had met and successful passed the supreme test of his human nature. The spirit had triumphed over the flesh; faith had asserted itself over all human tendencies of fear and doubt.

"It's Sebastian," Shorty said, his face brightening with unsubstantiated hope. "He didn't rat us out after all." But CJ knew better. He remained silent as Shorty opened the door and Sebastian strolled in. He went straight to CJ, giving him the traditional handshake.

As Sebastian clasped CJ's hand, the police swarmed into the room, weapons drawn. "Police! Freeze!" shouted Lieutenant Stiles, the leader of the raid. Saunders slunk into the room behind them, quaking with fear. Sebastian tried to free his hand from CJ's grip, but CJ held him fast, his penetrating gaze causing the traitor to drop his head in shame.

After a long beat, CJ dropped Sebastian's hand in disgust and turned to Lieutenant Stiles. "Who are you looking for?" he asked as Sebastian slid out of the room.

"We're, we're looking for uh . . . Reverend CJ," Stiles stuttered, overwhelmed by the sheer essence of the man. He knew he was talking to CJ, but didn't know what else to say.

"I'm CJ," he said, stepping forward boldly. Stricken by the magnificence of his presence, the cops all fell back, stumbling over one another in terror. "I said, I'm CJ," he repeated. "What do you want?" The cop trembled in fear, incapable of making a response.

When Stiles eventually found his tongue, he said, "You, you are . . . You're under arrest." Turning quickly to a sandy haired young cop, he ordered, "Cuff him, Petrosky."

"Me!" Petrosky said, looking terrified. Stiles just jerked his head in CJ's direction. As Petrosky made a hesitant step toward CJ, Sammy whipped out his gun. The bullet tore through the cop's forehead and he was dead before he hit the floor.

"No!" CJ shouted.

"I told you I had your back," said Sammy.

"Don't you know I could call on my Father right now and he'd send a whole battalion of angels to fight my battle?" CJ snapped, bending down over the fallen officer. He placed his hand over the gaping hole in Petrosky's head. Within seconds, Petrosky's eyes fluttered open and CJ stood. When Petrosky scrambled to his feet, many of the policemen threw down their weapons and fled in horror.

CJ then turned to Saunders, who stood trembling like a dog trying to pass broken glass. Getting right up in his face, CJ said, "Am I such a dangerous criminal that you had to have all these cops sneak up on me in the middle of the night? Why didn't you have me arrested when I was out there preaching in public?"

Saunders was so scared that he soiled his pants. As the disgusting odor filled the room, he fell to his knees sobbing like a tortured child. CJ looked down on him in contempt and turned to

Lieutenant Stiles unfazed by the massive show of force. "I'm the one you want," he said, presenting himself to the terrified policeman. "You can let these people go. They haven't done anything." When it dawned on them that CJ was actually surrendering, Sammy, Hawk, Sherman and Shorty eased quietly out of the room. However, Carla and Herc refused to budge, standing by CJ like mismatched bookends. "You guys go on," CJ said.

"I'm not going anywhere without you," Carla said, standing her ground.

"Me neither," Herc chimed in.

CJ looked into Carla's eyes and the love he felt for her was unfathomable. "You have to go, Carla. I've got to do the rest of this by myself."

"They don't have any right to arrest you," she said, tears glistening in her lovely eyes.

"This is how it's got to be."

She threw her arms around his neck and he closed his eyes against the pain in his heart. "Get her out of here, Herc," he said, prying himself loose from her grasp.

But Herc didn't move, "I'm with you, CJ. I go where you go."

"Not this time, big man," CJ said, clasping his hand. Reluctantly, Herc ushered a tearful Carla out the door. CJ turned to the lieutenant, thrusting his wrists out for him to put the cuffs on. "Well?" he said. "What are you waiting for?"

Once outside, Carla and Herc hid themselves from view and watched as the army of police vehicles pulled out. By the time Stiles and another beefy cop hauled CJ out in handcuffs, there were only two squad cars left. "Now," Carla whispered as they lead CJ toward one of the cars.

Herc leaped out, spun Stiles around and smashed his fist into the policeman's face, knocking him out cold. The other cop whipped out his gun and Carla kicked it out of his hand with a quickness and precision that startled him. The cop lunged at Carla, wrapping his meaty hands around her throat. Carla shot a sharp knee to the cop's groin and his scream caught the attention of the other two cops who jumped out of their car to find him on the ground writhing in pain. One of the cops grabbed Carla as his partner viciously attacked Herc with his nightstick. Herc shook the man off his back and spun around like an enraged bear, pummeling him into unconsciousness as Carla flipped the other unsuspecting cop over her shoulder and onto the ground, delivering a fierce kick to his head.

CJ winced as one of the cops whacked Carla over the head with his nightstick, knocking her to the ground. He averted his eyes, barely able to restrain himself from slipping his handcuffs and rescuing her, but having surrendered himself to the process, there was nothing he could do. For once put in motion, this vile charade had to play itself out.

When the cop drew back his foot to kick Carla, Herc snatched him up and began bludgeoning him with fists of iron. Suddenly, cops were coming from everywhere, racing to their brother's defense. Several of them attacked Herc with their nightsticks, but the blows bounced off him as if the sticks were made of rubber. He flicked the cops off like flies, his one thought being to protect Carla, whom CJ had left in his care.

One of the cops pulled his gun and shot Herc in the back. Growling like a wounded animal, Herc turned and charged the shooter. The terrified cop continued blasting away, but Herc kept moving forward, oblivious to the bullets tearing into his body. He clasped his huge hands around the man's neck, choking the life out of him. The other cops whipped out their guns and pumped Herc full of even more lead.

At that very moment, Big Jimbo in Los Angeles sat straight up in his bed covered in a cold sweat. "Nooo!" he screamed, feeling the life force ebbing out of his twin.

Herc fell to the ground like a mighty redwood, his hands frozen in a death lock around the cop's neck. Carla lay near them struggling to maintain consciousness and fighting back the rising panic that threatened to strangle her.

As the cops threw CJ into the back of the car and sped off, Carla managed to raise her bloodied head. At the sight of Herc's bullet-ridden body she let out a piercing scream as darkness engulfed her and she descended into the refuge of unconsciousness.

CHAPTER 51

"Well, well," said Rev as four cops pushed the handcuffed CJ into the interrogation room where he and the chief had been waiting. "So this is the legendary Reverend CJ." He walked around CJ, eyeing him up and down "He doesn't look like much to me. I thought he'd be bigger."

"I don't have to be big, CJ replied boldly. The one I'm with is Big."

"And who's that?" asked Chief Petrocelli. CJ met his look with a cold and defiant gaze, but did not reply. One of the cops leaned over and whispered into the chief's ear, informing him about what had happened to Petrosky. The smug smile on the chief's face vanished as the frigid hand of fear gripped his heart in its icy grasp. "Are you really the second coming of Christ, like they're saying?" he asked.

"Evidently you think I am, or I wouldn't be here." CJ said, staring him straight in the eye.

A brash young cop hauled off and punched CJ in the mouth, "Watch your mouth, nigger."

As blood trickled from the corner of his mouth, CJ gave the cop a look that chilled him to his very core. "You're going to wish that hand had shriveled up and fallen off." The frightened cop stepped back, plunging his hand into his pocket as though for safekeeping.

They grilled CJ for several hours, but he refused to say another word. Finally, the exasperated chief said, "Take him to Rikers. I'll decide what to charge him with in the morning."

When the cops grabbed CJ to take him away, Rev hocked a big glob of spit in his face, laughing in contemptuous amusement. As the thick globule slid down his face, CJ gave Rev a withering gaze that forced him to back away.

Instead of locking CJ in a cell, the guards at Rikers Island blindfolded him, kept him in handcuffs and led him to a hidden soundproof room designed specifically for interrogating prisoners. They then formed a circle around him and one of them started off the festivities by punching him hard in the face. "Prophesy who did that, prophet," he said with harsh laugh. He then pushed CJ toward one of his fellow guards who slapped him so hard that CJ thought his head might fly right off his neck.

The guards had a grand old time punching and slapping CJ around their little circle, until Mike Kelly the captain of the guards sauntered into the room. Kelly's shaved head sat atop a body as compact as a stack of bricks.

"All right," Kelly shouted. "Playtime's over." The guards obediently backed off. The unsmiling captain snatched off CJ's blindfold and got right up in his face. "Who are you working for?" he demanded.

CJ turned his head, offended by the man's fecal smelling breath. Kelly smashed his powerful fist into CJ's jaw and repeated the question. "Who are you working for, goddammit?" CJ just glared at him with the utmost contempt.

"Let me finish this punk off, Cap," said, Dickens, a feisty little female guard with a pixie haircut and a perverse lust for blood. "We can say he hung himself."

"No," said Kelly. "They wanna do this by the book. He'll be dead soon enough. Right now, they want to know who's behind him. No way a nigger can pull off the crap he's been doing all by himself. There's got to be a white man behind him somewhere and I intend to find out who that son of-a-bitch is. You gonna talk, nigger, or do we gotta get rough?"

CJ's steely-eyed gaze never faltered. If this redneck thought he could break him, he had another thought coming. "Strip him." Kelly ordered, angered by CJ's defiance. As they stripped CJ naked, Kelly went to a control panel on the wall and flicked a switch that activated pulleys which lowered chains from the ceiling.

They strapped CJ's ankles into the leather straps connected to the chains and hung him upside down like a hog going to slaughter, hoisting him up so that his body hovered inches above the ground. A look akin to ecstasy shone in Dickens' eyes as she zapped his genitals with her stun gun. A scream of agonizing pain died in CJ's throat yet he refused to utter a word.

"Oh, you're a tough nigger," said Kelly, snatching off the thick leather belt he'd had specifically designed for beating obstinate prisoners. The belt had holes cut in it at strategic intervals in order to inflict the most excruciating pain. "I got something for tough ass niggers like you." He then began beating CJ on his back and buttocks with the heavy strap, the holes in the belt painfully sucking in CJ's flesh with each resounding blow. CJ's body bucked and wriggled in a vain attempt to avoid some of the blows. Overcome by the severity of the pain, he closed his eyes and prayed silently.

Kelly continued to thrash CJ until his arm gave out. Fearing that CJ was near death, he ordered that he be let down. Reluctantly Dickens lowered the chains. CJ fell to the floor and they removed the straps from his ankles. He tried to stand, but his legs were numb and would not respond.

369

One of the more humane officers, repelled by the bloody stripes on CJ's body, said, "He's not gonna talk, Cap. We might as well just put him in a cell."

Kelly shot him a vicious look while putting his belt back on. "This son-of-a-bitch is gonna talk tonight, or my name ain't Michael Patrick Kelly."

Dickens glared at the tortured man, her cornflower blue eyes alive with excitement, "I bet the Gitmo treatment will make him talk, Cap."

Kelly smiled at the bloodthirsty blonde and said, "Dickens, you got more balls than any man here."

Dickens' face lit up with pride. "Thank you, sir."

Kelly snatched CJ up from the floor and half carried/half drug him to an inclined table rigged with restraints for the hands and feet. While Dickens filled a bucket with water from the sink, Kelly threw CJ onto the table and strapped him down on his back with his feet elevated above his head. They threw CJ's discarded shirt over his head and Kelly proceeded to pour water over his face. CJ felt like he was drowning. Struggling to free himself from his confines, he choked and gagged as the water clogged his breathing passages. When the bucket was empty, Kelly raised the table so that CJ was in a sitting position. Coughing and spitting water, he shook his head trying to get the water out of his lungs.

"You ready to talk?" Kelly asked. Breathing hard, CJ looked at him with such cold defiance that it set the experienced torturer's teeth on edge. "Naw, he ain't ready yet." Kelly said, lowering the table. The ever-reliable Dickens was right there handing him another bucket of water. After five minutes of this exquisite torture, CJ still refused to talk. Unable to endure the torment any longer, he prayed silently for the gentle release that death would bring, but it was not to be. Finally, darkness closed in around him and he slipped into blessed unconsciousness.

Amazed at CJ's endurance and frightened that he may have gone too far, Kelly called a halt to the inhumane water torture. He'd seen hardened terrorists begging to confess after two minutes of this barbaric interrogation technique. Yet CJ had endured it for over five minutes and still had not spoken a word. What kind of man is this?

CHAPTER 52

"Hello," said Teddy, anxiously answering his cell phone. It was Carla. He could hardly understand her as she tried to speak between sobs. Finally, he got it. The cops had killed Herc and she and CJ were in jail. Teddy assured her that he would get someone down there right away to bail them out.

He raced to Cheyenne's room and burst in without knocking. Cheyenne, still fully dressed leaped to her feet. Teddy informed her of Carla's call and told her to go down to the police station and get them out. "What about Sammy?" she asked frantically.

"I don't know." He replied. "Just get down there as quick as you can." Cheyenne grabbed her purse and hurried out; terrified that something awful had happened to her husband.

When Cheyenne arrived at the jail, the desk sergeant told her that she could bail Carla out, but they were holding CJ at Rikers Island without bail. "On what charge?" Cheyenne asked. The sergeant replied that the charges were pending. *Whatever that meant.*

A short time later, Cheyenne and Dusty huddled around Carla's bed as Dee nursed her wounds, "They could have at least had a doctor look at you," Dee said, shaking her head.

Teddy knocked on the door and poked his head in. "Okay, if I come in?"

Not waiting for an answer, he stepped into the room and handed Dee a bottle of pills. "These are the strongest pain killers I could get without a prescription. I hope they help."

"I started to take her to the hospital," Cheyenne said, defensively. "But I was scared."

"You did right," said Teddy. "We can't trust nobody."

"Carla," Cheyenne said soothingly, "Do you think you can tell us where Sammy and the other guys went?" She'd been dying to inquire about her husband in the car, but Carla had been drifting in and out of consciousness.

"Herc's dead," Carla croaked, her neck so badly injured that she could barely speak. "They killed him," she said as tears poured from her eyes. "I tried to help him, but there was so many of 'em. They just kept shooting him and shooting him," she said burying her face in her hands.

"Shhh," Dee said, cradling her in her arms. "That's all right."

"Sammy?" Cheyenne asked in a desperate voice. "What happened to Sammy?"

"I don't know." Carla replied. "They all ran when the cops came."

"Sherman too?" Dee asked in disbelief. Carla nodded.

CJ awoke in a windowless jail cell dressed in an orange jumpsuit. His mind was swirling with confusion. He didn't know if it was day or night, or if he had been unconscious for hours or even days. He wondered if the visions of horrific torture had just been a terrible dream. But he still felt like he had water in his head and when he tried to move, the jumpsuit stuck to the oozing cuts on his back and buttocks causing him unbearable pain. No. It was no dream, he concluded, examining the bloody gouges in his ankles where the restraints had cut into his skin.

As his mind cleared CJ realized that the reality of his ordeal was even more chilling than the dream that had not been a dream at all. The real nightmare, he feared was just beginning.

The following morning as Rev and Lenny Fine met with District Attorney Dominick DeStefano and Mark Carter, DeStefano's blond headed young ADA, Rev stated what he wanted in no uncertain terms. "We've got to get this guy in front of a judge as soon as possible."

DeStefano, tall and handsome with a head full of thick, black hair wore an outrageously expensive suit and had a condescending air that made Rev's blood boil. "What's the rush?" he asked reclining behind his mahogany desk. "He's locked up. What harm can he do?"

"Don't you read the papers?" said Fine. "This man has uncanny abilities. Who knows what he might do, even locked up in jail."

DeStefano knew all about CJ, he just loved watching Rev sweat. This self-important nigger had been a thorn in his side for far too long. And Fine, Rev's greedy little Jew lawyer, didn't care who he represented as long as he got big bucks for it. "I think you're giving this guy more credit than he has coming, Lenny. Sure, he's a gifted illusionist. I'll give you that. But he's not some superhuman god as you're making him out to be. He's just a man. We've got him on twenty-four-hour lock down. He's not going anywhere. Besides, we don't even know what to charge him with yet."

"I don't care what you charge him with," said Rev. "As long as he gets the death penalty."

"Whoa! New York doesn't even have a death penalty."

"We will," said Fine with a smirk. "Reinstatement is already in the works."

"Well aren't we the busy little bees," said DeStefano. "And what do you propose to charge him with?"

"Murder one," Fine said. "Two counts actually, for the death of Officer Hernandez and for his friend," flipping through his notes, he continued, "Erik Strong."

"I thought Strong killed the cop and the police shot him," said Mark.

Annoyed by the young man's ignorance, Fine's cold, gray eyes locked in on DeStefano. "If I'm not mistaken counselor, any participant of a crime can be charged with any murder committed during the commission of said crime."

"I know the law," DeStefano said. "But it's my understanding that Mr. Johnson was handcuffed at the time Strong attacked the officers and had no hand in the crime."

"Says who?" Fine replied with a challenging gaze.

"Why are you so anxious to have this man executed?" DeStefano asked.

Before Fine could answer, Rev jumped in. "Because he's a criminal. He could be working with some foreign power to overthrow this country for all we know."

"He has been linked to Louis Farrakhan," Fine added, the loathsome name like garbage in his mouth.

DeStefano rubbed his chin, "Don't you think that's stretching it a bit, Lenny? I mean, we have no proof . . ." "Proof my ass!" Rev shouted, tired of this legalistic ballet. "Look, DeStefano," he said, rising from his chair. He slapped his hands flat on DeStefano's desk and leaned forward threateningly. "You're coming up for re-election and we both know that without the black vote, you don't stand a snowball's chance in hell. Now you know I can deliver that vote. But I need some assurances that the concerns of the black community will be addressed."

Leaning back in his chair, DeStefano said with a hint of humor, "And you feel that the black community will be best served by executing this man?"

"Yes," Rev said emphatically.

"And what if the people don't agree with you? We could have a race riot on our hands."

"You just take care of the legal end of it. I'll handle my people. If you're afraid of getting your hands dirty . . ."

"That's never stopped him before," Fine cracked.

DeStefano shot Fine an acrid look as Rev continued, "If you're scared of getting your hands dirty, you can put it off on the AACC. We'll take the rap. Just get it done."

"We can't just execute a man without due process," DeStefano said, reveling in Rev's desperation.

"Come on, Dom. We both know that due process can be sidestepped in cases of national security," Fine said.

"Do I need to call the governor?" Rev threatened.

"Okay," DeStefano said, holding his hands up in surrender. "I'll see what I can do." Rev smiled, pleased at his ability to wield the power he wasn't sure he still held. "But I'm not promising anything," DeStefano added.

"We're counting on you to do the right thing," Fine said, rising to leave. The men shook hands and Rev and Fine strode confidently out of the office.

When the door closed behind them, Mark turned to his boss and asked, "Do you think he'd really go to the governor?"

"Who gives a shit?" DeStefano said. "The trial is just a formality. Johnson is a dead man. They can break his plate."

"But you said . . ."

"Look, kid, if you plan on playing the game of politics, you'd better learn the rules. And the first rule is there are no rules. I got word from Washington this morning. The trial starts tomorrow."

"Tomorrow!"

"Hey, you gotta try 'em before you can fry 'em."

"So, you're really going for the death penalty?"

"Who, me?" DeStefano said innocently, placing his hand on his chest. "You heard the man. The African American Council of Churches is going to do that." Mark grinned at the wily veteran attorney in admiration.

DeStefano propped his feet up on the desk and leaned back in his chair, a satisfied smile spreading across his face. "Did you honestly think the United States Government would let a black man with that kind of power live?" he asked, chuckling at the naiveté of his young colleague. "Oh, he's going to die all right. But it won't be me asking for the death penalty, it'll be his own people." They both laughed at the beauty of the plan.

CHAPTER 53

"The state of New York vs. Charlie Johnson. Judge Daniel Caparelli presiding," announced the bailiff as the judge took the bench. CJ shuffled into court with a deputy clutching each arm. He was still dressed in the orange jumpsuit and shackled hand and foot; his handsome face disfigured and his hair matted with blood.

The judge took one look at CJ and his eyebrows shot up in astonishment. One of his eyes was swollen shut with a purplish bruise surrounding it. The other eye was barely open and showed blood red. His head and face, covered with knots and lacerations had swollen to twice their normal size – and that was just the parts of his body they could see.

Carla's hand flew to her mouth and she fought to hold back the tears as she watched her brutalized love stumbling into the courtroom, his movement severely hampered by both the shackles and the intense pain he suffered with each step he took. Dee sprang from her seat and rushed toward him. "Oh, my God! What have they done to you?" One of the deputies quickly grabbed her, forcing her to return to her seat.

Tony's heart broke at the sight of his son. As per their agreement, CJ hadn't called him, but Tony had come as soon as he heard of his arrest.

"What happened to this man?" asked the judge.

DeStefano stood and said with a straight face, "He resisted arrest, Your Honor."

"This case is continued until one week from today," said the judge pounding his gavel. "I'll see counsel in my chambers."

Inside his chambers, Judge Caparelli removed his robe, carefully placing it on a padded hanger and hanging it on a hook on the back of the door. Fine, followed by DeStefano almost knocked him down as they barged into the office. "This trial was supposed to start today, Judge," said Fine in a fit of rage.

Judge Caparelli went to his desk and sat down before responding. "I can't try that man in the shape he's in. The media would eat me alive. No. We've got to wait until he at least looks human. He should be more presentable by next week. I'm not putting my career on the line to satisfy whatever twisted arrangement you have with the prosecution."

This rattled DeStefano's cage. "Look, Judge . . ."

The door opened and Judge Caparelli's six-year-old daughter Melissa, a beautiful little girl with dark ringlets of curls surrounding her angelic face charged into the room followed by her mother. "Hi, Daddy," she chirped, jumping onto the judge's lap.

"I'm sorry Dan," said the judge's wife, standing in the doorway dripping in diamonds and furs. "Come on, Missy. Daddy's still working."

"That's okay." Caparelli said, waving her in. "These gentlemen were just leaving. You remember my wife Annemarie and my daughter Melissa." Yes, this was the same Annemarie that accosted CJ in the parking garage, begging him to cure her terminally ill daughter.

"Good to see you again, Mrs. Caparelli," DeStefano said, shooting a baleful look at the judge as he reached for the doorknob.

"Dominick," she said with a nod. Fine gave her a nod and a smile as he followed DeStefano out the door.

As soon as the door closed, the judge gave a sigh of relief, "That was perfect timing, honey."

Annemarie stared daggers at him, "Don't you honey me, you stupid ass."

The judge gave her a shocked look and Melissa chided, "Ooo, Mommy. You said a bad word."

"You can't try this man," Annemarie said. "You're risking your immortal soul."

"Don't be so melodramatic," he said.

"Melodramatic? The man is an angel from God."

"Now you're being ridiculous. He's just a man."

"Tell that to your daughter!" she said, pointing to the precious child who sat cradled in her father's arms. "Are you forgetting what he did for her?"

"He never even met Missy. You told me that yourself."

"That's the point. He healed her from three thousand miles away, Danny," she said, lowering her voice to a whisper. "You know as well as I do that if it wasn't for him, she wouldn't be here today."

The judge's eyes fell on the happy and healthy child who sat on his lap playing with his tie. "Daddy, you said you were going to take us to lunch. I want to go to Sardi's. Maurice always gives me a Shirley Temple. He says it's a cocktail for big girls like me. Cocktail's a funny word, isn't it, Daddy?"

The judge hugged his beloved child for a long moment, remembering how sick she'd been, how the best pediatric oncologists in the country had given her up for dead and how she had miraculously recovered while Annemarie was in L.A. "Sure, baby. We can go to Sardi's," he said, near tears. He kissed her head lovingly before releasing her and sliding her off his lap. "But first, I need to talk to Mommy." He buzzed for his clerk who immediately appeared. "Janet, will you take Melissa into your office and give her something to do while I speak with my wife?"

"Sure, Judge," answered the plain looking law student as she held her hand out to the girl. "Come on, Missy. Wanna draw me a picture?"

"No," Melissa said, running past her. "I want to use your computer." Janet rolled her eyes in mock consternation and followed the precocious child out of the office, shutting the door behind her.

"Now, where were we, Mrs. Caparelli?" said the judge, springing from his chair and taking her into his arms.

"Forget about it, Danny," she said, pushing him away. "You can't sweet talk me. I'm too damn mad."

"What are you so mad about?"

"You!" Annemarie said, stabbing him in the forehead with her finger. "How can you be so incredibly stupid? You can't try this case. I forbid it."

"You can't forbid me to do anything. I'm a judge."

"Judge not, that ye might be judged."

381

The judge chuckled, "Since when did you start quoting the Bible?" Although they had both been raised Catholic, it had been some time since either of them had attended mass.

"Since that day I got down on my knees in a filthy parking lot and begged this man to save my baby's life. That's when."

He took her hands in his and tried to console her. "If he's innocent it'll come out at trial."

"Don't make me laugh," she said, snatching away from him. "You know as well as I do that the outcome of this trial is a foregone conclusion."

"That's ridiculous," he said, averting his eyes.

"I'm telling you, Danny," she said, shaking a warning finger at him. "Whatever happens to this man is gonna be on your head."

CHAPTER 54

"Nobody's willing to defend him," said Shorty, clicking off his phone. "I've called every lawyer I could think of. They wouldn't touch this case with a ten-foot pole."

"Why don't you defend him?" Carla asked. "You're a lawyer."

"I'd be doing him more harm than good. They'd use my ties to the Froncioso family as more evidence against him."

"Well, what are we going to do?" Dee asked.

"I don't know," Shorty said. "Trial starts Tuesday. We might have to go with a public defender."

They called it the trial of the century. Thousands of people crowded the streets outside the courthouse. Some carried signs reading Free CJ and We Love you CJ, while other placards said things like CJ is Guilty and Burn the Witch. TV news trucks lined the streets and reporters from around the world set up tent cities. Cops in full riot gear tried to manage the crowd that was fast becoming a mob.

As Sammy and Cheyenne approached the courthouse, one of the reporters shoved a microphone in Sammy's face. "Aren't you a member of CJ's gang?" he asked.

"Hell no! Now get that damned thing outta my face," Sammy shouted, shoving the mike away and storming into the building.

Judge Caparelli peered out on the packed courtroom. "Seeing that the defendant has been unable to secure counsel, the court appoints Leonard Fine to the defense," he said. "Is that all right with you, Mr. Fine?"

"Yes, Your Honor."

Carla remembered this little twerp from Dupre's dinner party. "I object!" she shouted, springing out of her seat. "What kind of kangaroo court is this?"

The judge pounded his gavel. "Sit down Miss. And if you can't control yourself, I'll have you removed from my courtroom." Turning to the deputy, he said, "Bring in the defendant."

Two deputies escorted CJ into the courtroom in shackles. Although the swelling had gone down, he still bore traces of the horrendous beating he'd suffered at the hands of the jail guards.

CJ watched in silence as the prosecution's first witness, a jailhouse snitch named Willie McDaniels took the stand. Although Willie had never met CJ he testified, in exchange for the D.A. dropping the charges in his own case that CJ had confessed to him that he was part of a grand conspiracy to overthrow the government. He even said that CJ had tried to get him to enlist in the plot, but that he, being a loyal American had turned him down. Infuriated by these vicious lies, Carla tried to stand but Teddy's firm grip on her arm held her in place.

CJ remained stoic as one prosecution witness after another took the stand, lying about things he had said or done. Leonard Fine had no questions for any of these witnesses. As the lies and false accusations mounted, CJ steadfastly refused to free himself from the cruel clutches of this wicked conspiracy. He realized that the scene, dire as it was, was playing out as it was supposed to. He knew that God wanted him to finish his career on earth naturally. So he just let nature take its course.

Finally, the persecution called its last witness. "The people call Samuel Rocquemore." CJ closed his eyes, saddened that his friend had to testify against him. As Sammy took the stand Sebastian, drenched in guilt and shame slumped down in his seat in the back of the courtroom, hoping no one would notice him.

DeStefano asked Sammy if he was a member of the gang that had traveled around the country with CJ. And Sammy, fearing that any connection between CJ and himself might land him back in prison vehemently denied knowing CJ and swore he had never gone anywhere with him.

Cheyenne couldn't look at him. She was too embarrassed. How could he? She dropped her head in disgrace tears rolling down her face as she listened to her husband perjure himself.

Undaunted by Sammy's volatile response, DeStefano continued. "May I call you Sammy?"

"No."

"Okay, Mr. Rocquemore. Aren't you, in fact, a close friend of the defendant?"

"What you call close, I might not call close," Sammy countered.

"I see," said DeStefano menacingly. He picked up a police report from his table and leafed through it. "Ah, here it is." He paused, pretending to read the report. "This arrest report lists you as one of the people in the hotel room with the defendant when the police apprehended him. Is this report true, Mr. Rocquemore?"

"How do I know? I didn't write it," Sammy said belligerently.

"I'll rephrase the question. Would you say that if one man killed a policeman in order to stop him from arresting another man, one could categorize that person as a close friend?"

"What? You're crazy, man," Sammy said, rubbing his face with his hand, his knees knocking together nervously. CJ silently prayed for Sammy. Even now, he knew that Sammy had love for him. But he also knew that Sammy had been under Satan's control for a long time and the devil wasn't letting go so easily. CJ prayed that this ordeal would make Sammy strong.

"Didn't you in fact, shoot and kill a New York City police officer when he tried to arrest this murderous, traitor?" DeStefano said, pointing an outraged finger at CJ.

"Say something," Carla whispered harshly, giving Fine's shoulder a sharp poke. His back straightened and he continued to stare straight ahead.

"Well, how come I'm not the one on trial for murder?" Sammy snapped.

"Because you ran," DeStefano said, glaring at him. "When the police finally tracked down the defendant and cornered him in that hotel room, you ran. Didn't you, Mr. Rocquemore?" Sammy tried to speak, but the glib lawyer rolled right over him. "When push came to shove; when you saw that you were outnumbered, outmanned and outgunned you ran like a scared little girl." He got all up in Sammy's face. "You loved this man so much that you'd kill a policeman to protect him, but when your closest friend needed you the most, you turned tail and ran." He stepped back, a look of

386

revulsion on his face. "All you were thinking about is saving your own ass. Isn't that right, Mr. Rocquemore?"

"That's a goddamned lie!" Sammy shouted, leaping out of his seat. "I told you already. I don't even know the man!"

Upon this third denial, CJ's prophetic words hit him like a Mac truck speeding through the dead of night. *"Before this thing is over, you will have denied me three times."*

Mortified at what he had done, Sammy slumped back down into the witness chair. His eyes fastened on CJ, who lifted the corner of his mouth in a half smile. This was more than Sammy could bear. He broke down on the stand, sobbing sorrowfully.

When the defense was to present its case, Lenny Fine stood, stating simply, "The defense rests, Your Honor."

Carla shot up from her seat, "What do you mean, 'The defense rests'? You haven't even called a single witness."

"We have not been able to locate any witnesses willing to testify on the defendant's behalf, Your Honor," said Fine.

"I'll testify," Carla shouted. As she started toward the witness stand deputies grabbed her.

"Take that woman out of here," the judge ordered. The deputies carried her out kicking and screaming.

DeStefano sprang to his feet. "In view of the defense's inability to put on a substantial defense, the people move for a directed verdict of guilty."

"This is an outrage, Your Honor!" Shorty said, leaping to his feet. "The defendant has a constitutional right to be judged by a jury of his peers."

"You have no standing in this trial, Mr. Longwood. Take your seat or I'll cite you for contempt." Shorty sat down fuming. Despite his many trickerations and side stepping of the law, he held the constitution dear and was appalled at this blatant miscarriage of justice.

The judge tugged at his collar, clearly uncomfortable with his role. "Does the defense object to Mr. DeStefano's motion, Mr. Fine?"

"We do not, Your Honor."

"Motion granted," Caparelli said, turning to the jury. "Ladies and gentlemen of the jury, in light of the overwhelming evidence against this prisoner and the defense's failure to present its case, I have no choice but to order you to presume that this failure is indicative of guilt and to render a verdict representative of that fact. We will resume at ten o'clock tomorrow morning. At which time, I will pronounce sentence. Court is adjourned." He banged his gavel on the desk, wishing it was the defense attorney's head.

CHAPTER 55

The judge stormed into his chambers ripping off his robe. He threw it onto the couch and went straight to his credenza where a decanter of scotch and four glasses sat on a tray. He poured himself a stiff drink, gulped it down and stalked into his private bathroom. As the judge washed his hands, the door to his chambers flew open and both attorneys floated in on a cloud of exhilaration.

"That was a fucking stroke of genius," DeStefano said, giving Fine a high-five.

"Thanks," said Fine, looking around for the judge. "I was hoping you'd pick up on it and you came in right on cue. Judge?"

"Here I am," said the judge, drying his hands on a towel as he entered the room.

"I was just congratulating Lenny on his brilliant tactic. He set it right in my lap," DeStefano said as the judge threw the towel on the desk and took his seat. The attorneys dropped into the two chairs opposite the desk. DeStefano crossed his long legs, while Fine perched on the edge of his seat waiting to hear praises from the judge.

"Are you sure that was the right move?" asked the judge.

The attorneys looked at him in dismay and then at each other. "This is exactly what we need," said DeStefano. "Juries can't be trusted. Look at O.J."

The judge held up his hand, halting him. "That was over twenty years ago and I'm sick of hearing about it. I thought the AACC was supposed to be asking for the death penalty, Mr. Fine. Whatever happened to that?"

"They don't have any legal standing, so I . . ."

"I think it would have been better to take our chances with the jury," interrupted the judge. "Maybe then it wouldn't look like such a put up job. People aren't stupid, you know."

"Sure, they are," DeStefano said. "They'll believe anything you tell them, if you tell it to them right."

"Well, I'm not comfortable with it," Judge Caparelli said. "This guy hasn't done anything. Forgive me for not jumping at the chance to execute an innocent man."

"With all due respect," DeStefano said, "This isn't about your comfort. We've all got our marching orders."

"This man has to die," said Fine.

"New York hasn't executed anyone since they fried Eddie Mays back in sixty-three," the judge said. "Let 'em try him in Texas."

"He wasn't arrested in Texas. And besides, those holy rollers down there would probably think they were indicting Jesus," DeStefano quipped.

"How about this?" said the judge. "Why don't I sentence him to fifty or sixty years in prison? That way he'll be out of your hair and he can't do any harm."

Lenny Fine stood, leaned over the judge's desk and spoke slowly, "He raised a man up from the dead, Your Honor."

"That's just speculation," the judge said unconvincingly.

"It's a fact," DeStefano said. "We've got hundreds of eyewitnesses to corroborate it, plus we have it on tape. They were in the middle of his funeral, for Christ's sake. How much deader does a man have to be?"

"In People v. Stephen LaValle," the judge cited, "The Court of Appeals ruled that it was unconstitutional to impose the death penalty on a defendant who didn't deserve it just because they were scared he might get out of jail one day."

The two lawyers just glared at him. The judge shot up from his seat. "I can't do it. Think what it'll do to my career."

"Look, Dan," said DeStefano in a deadly tone, "If you flake out on us now, your career will be the least of your worries."

"Are you threatening me?"

DeStefano shrugged and turned toward the door. "Call it what you want," he said as he flung the door open and strolled out.

Fine felt sympathy for Judge Caparelli who had obviously dredged up something resembling a conscience. "I'm sorry, Judge. But this is how it has to be." He followed his so-called opponent out and closed the door. The judge collapsed into his chair, holding his head in his hand.

CHAPTER 56

Lenny Fine stared straight ahead, refusing to look at his client as the judge delivered his sentence. "In the case of The State of New York vs. Charles . . ."

"Charlie," Janet whispered to the judge. "His name is Charlie, not Charles."

"Whatever," the frustrated judge said, looking down on the already condemned man. "Having been found guilty by a jury of your peers . . ."

"He ain't got no peers," shouted one of CJ's supporters from the back of the courtroom.

Ignoring the outburst, the judge continued, "It is my solemn duty to impose sentence. But first, I'd like to question the defendant. Will the defendant please stand?"

CJ rose to his feet, staring defiantly at the judge. "Is it true that you consider yourself to be some kind of black Messiah?" CJ stared back at him without saying a word. "I'm speaking to you, Mr. Johnson," the judge said, annoyed by CJ's impertinent demeanor. "Are these allegations are true."

"What do you think?" CJ said.

The judge stared at him through squinted eyes. "Who do you work for, Mr. Johnson? Who's behind all this?" CJ stared him straight in the eye and said nothing. When it became obvious that CJ had no intention of answering, Judge Caparelli said through clenched teeth. "Do you realize that I hold the power of life and death over you?"

CJ held his head high and gave the judge a look that chilled him all the way to the marrow of his bone. "The only one that has any power over me is God," he said boldly. The spectators responded with a collective, "Ooooo!"

Outraged and outdone, the judge banged his gavel. "Order! I'll have order in this court." He peered down at CJ and declared, "Having been found guilty of murder and conspiring with person or persons unknown to overthrow the government of these United States of America, I hereby, sentence you to death by lethal injection." CJ shut his eyes as Dee's tortured howl pierced the ensuing silence of the room.

CJ's supporters exploded in screeches of rage, while his detractors shouted out in joy. Sebastian's mouth dropped open in shock. What have I done? It had never occurred to him that they would sentence CJ to death.

Judge Caparelli shouted over the cacophony, "I am remanding you to Sing Sing Prison until such time as you are put to death for your crimes. Court is adjourned." He slammed the gavel down in disgust and stormed off the bench.

Unable to bear the horrendous outcome of the events he had set in motion and terrified at the thought of facing his former companions, Sebastian bolted out of the courtroom steeped in guilt, shame and remorse.

CHAPTER 57

Although Judge Caparelli had not allowed cameras in his courtroom during CJ's trial, his execution was another matter altogether. The execution would be televised.

During the days leading up to the execution, CJ sat in his cell fasting, praying and reading his Bible sustaining himself only on the word of God. He tried to do the relaxation exercise Carla had taught him, but the noise in the cellblock made it impossible for him to concentrate. He picked up his Bible; the beautiful white Bible the angel Ariana had given him. This Bible had brought him a mighty long way and like its owner, was now in pretty bad shape. The cover was dirty and torn, but the Word was still intact. The word of the Almighty God.

CJ tried not to dwell on the times God had tested someone and spared him at the last minute. How He had let Job sink into the depths of despair before giving him relief or how He had spared Isaac from the sacrificial fire. Every time one of these thoughts invaded his mind, he reminded himself that it was God's will for him to drink the full cup of mortal experience from birth to death.

"Hey, Rev," shouted Peterson, the dreadlocked inmate in the cell to CJ's left.

"Please don't call me that," CJ said, cringing at the commonly used abbreviation of "Reverend," a name he had come to associate with the despicable Rev Bradshaw.

"Oh, so you're a sensitive con, huh," Peterson sneered. "Well you better get with the program, son. Up in here you're just another inmate."

"Leave him alone, Peterson," shouted Ramirez, the severely tattooed convict in the cell to CJ's right.

"Fuck you, Ramirez," Peterson spat back. "Hey, Rev. If you so tight with God, why don't you get him to bust you outta here? Hell, all of us for that matter. We're all innocent. Right, Ramirez?" His laughter was vulgar and mocking.

"Knock it off, Peterson. Ain't you got no respect?" Ramirez shouted. "Don't pay him no attention, Reverend CJ. I went to one of your services before. And I got baptized too." He paused momentarily, building up the nerve to ask, "Do you think God could ever forgive somebody like me? I mean . . ., I've done a lot of bad stuff, you know. Stuff I'm really sorry for. Know what I'm saying? I wish I could take it all back. But I can't," he said, gripping the bars. "I know you got your own problems right now." CJ had to smile at the gross understatement. "But I was just wondering . . . You know, I was just thinking like maybe you could pray for me or something. You know, put in a word for me with the Man upstairs?"

This simple statement of faith, coming from a truly repentant man was a sign to CJ that he was doing the right thing. "Don't worry, brother," CJ said through the bars of his cell. "Your sins have already been forgiven."

Ramirez, a lifelong criminal broke down and cried. "Thank you," he said, making the sign of the cross on his chest. "Thank you."

As six a.m., the hour of CJ's execution grew near; a hefty, red-faced priest came to pray for him. The priest looked on CJ with disdain as he recited the twenty-third Psalm. The evil emanating from the man was so pervasive that CJ was relieved when he finally said, "May God have mercy on your wretched soul."

A guard brought CJ a fresh set of clothes to put on, a new pair of denim trousers and a blue work shirt. They wanted to make sure that he looked nice when they killed him. After all, it would be on television.

At precisely 5:30 a.m., a guard entered CJ's cell and cuffed his hands behind him. "Dead man walking," a second guard shouted, grabbing CJ's arm and pulling him through the open cell door.

With a guard on either side of him, CJ walked across a long walkway enclosed in bulletproof glass. When the hordes of people surrounding the prison saw CJ, they began hurling taunts and insults at him, not to mention rocks, shoes and any other throwable object they could get their hands on. Even though the missiles bounced off the impenetrable glass, their intent was clear. They wanted to hurt him – because he had hurt them.

Most of the crowd was not mad because they hated CJ. They were mad because they felt betrayed, particularly the black people among them. They felt that if he really was this God-sent Messiah as many had come to believe, he wouldn't allow mere mortals to execute him? *Why couldn't he use his magical powers to free himself?*

As they approached the door of the death chamber, CJ felt the angels that had protected him, pulling away. "Oh, God," he moaned. "You said you'd never abandon me." His knees buckled as the last vestiges of his humanity instinctively fought to preserve his mortal life. The guards grabbed him under his arms to keep him from collapsing.

Suddenly he heard a familiar voice:

"You've done all you can – Now, stand."

The words imbued CJ with renewed strength and determination. He knew God hadn't deserted him. He shook off the hands that supported him and stood. Standing firmly on the Word of God, CJ stepped over the threshold and marched into the death chamber with his head held high, prepared to meet his doom.

White garbed attendants strapped CJ to a table and inserted an IV into his arm. They also hooked him up to a heart monitor that showed an electronic graph of his heartbeat; it was strong and steady. On a table next to him lay three syringes on a sanitary white towel. The first syringe contained 5.0 grams of sodium pentothal in 25 cc of diluent, a diluting agent, to insure the easy flow of the poison through his system. The second one held 50 cc of pancuronium bromide and the third contained 50 cc of potassium chloride.

CJ concentrated on his breathing, forcing himself to relax. He looked out on the glass encased witness areas. On one side were the warden, Rev Bradshaw, Dominick DeStefano, Meka Maxwell and several other reporters and witnesses.

However, CJ fixed his gaze on his loved ones seated on the other side. The look of pain and devastation on his mother's face cut through his heart like a hot knife through butter. Dee looked as though she had aged ten years since last he'd seen her. Teddy and Sherman stood behind Dee, while Carla and Tony sat on either side of her. Bishop Hanks was there as well. These were the people he was dying for, them and all those like them. Not for anything he had done, but to appease the anger they had provoked in God through their ignorance and weakness, to spare them from destruction and eternal damnation. He experienced an awesome peacefulness at that moment, knowing that his death was not in vain.

Tony stared helplessly at his son, wondering if he had helped CJ more would he be in the terrible situation he was in now. Teddy and Sherman remained stoic; pokerfaced and unemotional. Silent tears flowed down Carla's face as her eyes sought his. "I love you," she mouthed.

His reply to her was simply, "It's finished." Words that echoed throughout the entire angelic realm: "It's finished. It's finished. It's finished . . ."

At the warden's signal, the grim faced executioner administered the sodium pentothal into the IV and then the line was flushed with a sterile saline solution. As the cold poison infiltrated his body, CJ felt a sense of relief. "Father, I commit my spirit into your hands," he said as he began to drift into a state of delirium.

It is said that one's life flashes before him at the time of death, but CJ saw visions of all the people he'd healed, their elated faces and their tearful gratitude. He saw the mass baptisms they'd performed and the loving faces of his parents. And he saw Carla, his one true love. He saw visions of Sherman, Herc and Sammy. And he saw Teddy awakening in his casket.

As they administered the pancuronium bromide, followed by another saline flush Carla's smiling face embedded itself in his mind. As the executioner injected the finishing dose, the potassium chloride, CJ's chest rose and fell in one final exhalation – and the beloved Brother Man breathed his last.

When the lines on the heart monitor went flat, the morning sky went dark. The sun refused to shine and the lights of the prison blinked out, throwing the occupants of the death chamber into a panic.

"He was sent from God!" shouted one of the terrified guards.

After a while, the prison's generator kicked in and the lights came back on. Carla turned to the viewing window and screamed, "He's gone! What have they done with him?" All eyes fixed on the gurney where CJ had lain. It was empty, except for the straps they had used to fasten him down.

Dee clutched Carla's hand and said a silent prayer. She knew that CJ's disappearance wasn't the work of the guards – It was the work of God.

"Oh, my God!" DeStefano shouted. "Where did he go?"

Later, after hours of interrogation Teddy, Carla, Dee, Tony and Sherman emerged from the prison. Besieged by reporters, they fought their way through the crowd to their rented car refusing to answer any questions. They piled into the car and drove straight to JFK Airport where they boarded a plane for Los Angeles, shaking the dirt of the Big Apple from their feet.

That evening, they all gathered in Teddy's music room to watch Meka Maxwell deliver a special report. She looked ashen and stunned, shock and dismay still evident in her face. "This morning," Meka said, "the man known around the world as Reverend CJ was executed in New York by lethal injection. Shortly after the execution, officials at Sing Sing prison reported that the body of Reverend CJ had been stolen from the death chamber by his co-conspirators."

Suddenly, Meka's lips began to tremble and her eyes grew moist. She couldn't read any more of those carefully crafted lies. "That's what they want you to believe," she said, staring straight into the camera. "That way they won't have to answer the hard questions: Who was this man? Was he really an emissary from God? If so, what have they done?" she asked incredulously. "And where is he now?"

As those watching with her pondered this same question, Dee remained inexplicably quiet.

"What do you think they did with him?" Sherman asked no one in particular. Receiving no answer, he kneeled down in front of his mother, taking her hand in both of his. "We need to go home, Ma."

Dee closed her eyes, shaking her head back and forth. "I can't go. Not yet."

"But there's nothing we can do here. When we get home we can hire a private investigator and . . ." Dee continued to shake her

399

head. "Wasn't killing him bad enough?" Sherman whimpered, dropping his head on his mother's lap. "Why did they have to steal his body?"

Stroking his head, Dee said, "Don't worry, baby. He'll be back and I'm gon' be right here waiting for him." Sherman lifted his head, giving her a stunned look.

Disturbed by Dee's refusal to accept reality, Tony said gently, "I'm gonna have to be getting on back to Chicago, Dee. I want you to come with me. There's nothing you can do here." Although Tony believed that CJ had come from God, he also believed that when you were dead you were done.

"You know I can't go, Tony. You take Sherman back with you. I'll be all right."

Teddy said, "Don't worry, Pops. I'll take care of her."

Tony reluctantly agreed. "Okay," he said, pressing a kiss against Dee's cheek. He knew that once she made up her mind there was little anyone could do to change it, especially when it came to CJ.

CHAPTER 58

The newspaper headlines once again read, "Where is CJ?"

Some of CJ's supporters organized a memorial service in Griffith Park. Only a few hundred people attended, but the LAPD was there in full force. Many of the faithful gave testimonies of how CJ had changed their lives, while other enraged followers accused New York officials of stealing CJ's body for medical experiments and demanded that they be held accountable.

Seated near Dee, Teddy and Carla were Sammy and Cheyenne, along with Hawk, Shorty, Dusty, Reverend Thomas, Chad, Marquita and Clarence Prescott. Although keeping her distance from Dee and the others, Meka Maxwell was there as well. However, she had not come to report, but to mourn the man she had so relentlessly persecuted.

As Bishop Hanks delivered a heartfelt eulogy that brought the crowd to tears, Shorty whispered to Hawk, "You hear about Sebastian?"

"Heard they found him with his brains blowed out."

"Cops said it was murder."

"Hmph. Everybody know that nigga killed hisself. Who gon' kill somebody and leave all that money behind?"

Shorty looked up at Hawk, his face hard as ice, "Not me. But whoever capped him saved me the trouble."

Hawk's eyes met Shorty's and he nodded. There was no love lost for Sebastian. No grief. They grieved only for CJ, the beloved friend sent from God, the friend that had loved them so much that he willingly died on their behalf.

After Bishop Hanks concluded his remarks, Rev stepped up to the microphone. Ever the consummate actor, he stood in front of the crowd looking as distraught as the rest of them felt. "We've come here today to remember Reverend CJ." He took a deep breath before bravely continuing, "CJ was good man. A man of integrity and dedication. The good CJ did in his short life, will be remembered long after we have all returned to dust. But this is not a sad occasion. No." He said, smiling brightly. "CJ would not want us to mourn his death. He'd want us to celebrate his life," said the gifted orator in an attempt to whip up the crowd. "So we need to celebrate CJ's home going, this morning. Have mercy!"

Suddenly a stunned silence fell over the crowd. No one had seen CJ come onto the dais, but suddenly there he was. "Mama look!" Carla exclaimed. "He did it. He did it, Teddy. He did it!"

"I knew he would," he said, remembering CJ's words.

"I'll lay my life down willingly and I'll take it up again."

Some of the women fainted, while others fell to their knees. Inspired by what he assumed to be a reaction to his excellent performance, Rev continued with even more vigor. "We came here to sing the praises of our brother who has gone on to glory."

When Carla raced onto the stage and threw herself into CJ's arms, he simply said, "Carla." Never had there been a one-word utterance more charged with emotion.

402

At the sound of CJ's voice, Rev whipped around and came face to face with the man whose demise he had so ruthlessly orchestrated. Consumed by overwhelming fear, he began backing away, shaking his head in utter disbelief. No. No, you can't be here. You're dead," he muttered.

CJ glanced at him as he gently extricated himself from Carla's embrace. "You gotta let me go," he said softly, his eyes locking with hers. "I have to go to my Father."

"But . . . I thought we were going to be together."

"We will," he said. "In paradise."

Reluctantly, Carla accepted his words and stepped back. CJ moved toward Rev who was still backing away and shaking his head. "Get away from me. You're not real. You're dead. I saw you die." CJ kept advancing and Rev kept backing up until he accidentally stepped off the platform and fell onto his back.

As CJ slowly stepped down the three steps of the stage, Rev escaped into a world of total insanity, scooting backwards on his backside and sobbing hysterically. Fearing this must surely be Judgment Day, he confessed his sins in front of the transfixed crowd. "I did it. Okay? I did it," he blubbered. "I molested those boys. I stole from the church and did everything I could to make sure you got executed. I wanted you dead. I wanted you dead. God forgive me, I wanted you dead!"

God may have forgiven Rev, but the outraged mourners had no forgiveness in their hearts. Shouting angry curses and threats at the deranged preacher, they charged toward him with deadly intentions. CJ raised his hands and shouted, "Peace!" The rambunctious crowd stopped, growing eerily silent. "The law will take care of this man," CJ said. "He's not worth staining your hands with his blood."

CJ returned to the stage as the cops hauled off what was left of Rev. "I told you while I was still with you," he said, "that

403

everything written in the Bible about me must be fulfilled, '*He will suffer and rise from the dead and repentance and forgiveness of sins will be preached in his name,*'" CJ quoted.

"Today, you are witnesses to the fulfillment of that prophecy. And I want you to know that nothing can ever separate us from God's love. Neither life nor death. No power in the sky above or in the earth below. Not even the powers of hell can separate us from God's love. So know that I will be with you to the very end of time."

As he spoke, lightning flashed in the sky and an immense cloud appeared on the horizon, surrounded by a brilliant light– a ferocious whirlwind, sweeping toward them at an incredible rate of speed. As the terrified onlookers scurried out of its path, some falling to the ground, others hiding behind trees, CJ stood tall. Turning to Carla, he said, "I'll always love you." Before she could respond, the whirlwind whipped onto the stage, sucking CJ into the vortex and whisking him up toward heaven, beyond the clouds and out of the sight of the astonished onlookers.

An awesome silence reigned over the park. Finally, her soul erupting with incredible joy, Marquita rose from the ground and burst into song, "I'm going up yonder . . ." As she sang, the Holy Spirit came upon the crowd and everyone stood to their feet, emerged from their hiding places and joined her in song.

Surrounded by joyous singing and shouts of *Hallelujah* and *Praise the Lord,* Dee closed her eyes, tears sliding down her face. "Don't be sad, Ma," said Teddy, draping his arm around her shoulder. "He did what he said he would do. He came back."

"I know," she said, smiling through her tears. "I'm good. It just would've been so nice if he could have changed the hearts and minds of all the black folks like set out to do. Guess that'll never happen now." she said with a shrug.

"Don't be so sure," Carla said with an impish smile as she rubbed her hand over the emerging bump in her belly.

THE END

About the Author

Gwen Lester-Cunningham is an author, screenwriter and actress. She has appeared onstage in Chicago, Los Angeles and New York. Gwen also won the prestigious Walt Disney Screenplay Award for *A Voice in the Wilderness*, which was originally written as a screenplay.

The mother of two and the grandmother of five, Gwen lived many years in Los Angeles, California where she studied writing at UCLA. She presently resides in Chicago, Illinois with her husband Larry.